From the *New York Times* be
***Leaving the World* comes th**
a woman whose one choice,
comes back to ha

AMERICA IN THE 1960s WAS ... L upheaval—of civil rights protests and antiwar marches, of sexual liberation and hallucinogenic drugs. More tellingly, it was a time when you weren't supposed to trust anyone over the age of thirty; when, if you were young, you rebelled against your parents and their conservative values.

But not Hannah Buchan.

Hannah is a great disappointment to her famous radical father and painter mother. Instead of mounting the barricades and embracing this age of profound social change, she wants nothing more than to marry her doctor boyfriend and raise a family in a small town.

Hannah gets her wish. But once installed as the doctor's wife in a nowhere corner of Maine, boredom sets in . . . until an unforeseen moment of personal rebellion changes everything. Especially as Hannah is forced into breaking the law.

For decades, this one transgression in an otherwise faultless life remains buried. But then, in the charged atmosphere of America after 9/11, her secret comes out and her life goes into free fall.

ALSO BY DOUGLAS KENNEDY

FICTION

Leaving the World

The Woman in the Fifth

Temptation

A Special Relationship

The Pursuit of Happiness

The Job

The Big Picture

The Dead Heart

NONFICTION

Chasing Mammon

In God's Country

Beyond the Pyramids

STATE *of the* UNION

A Novel

DOUGLAS KENNEDY

ATRIA PAPERBACK
New York London Toronto Sydney

ATRIA PAPERBACK
A Division of Simon & Schuster, Inc.
1230 Avenue of the Americas
New York, NY 10020

This book is a work of fiction. Names, characters, places, and incidents either are products of the author's imagination or are used fictitiously. Any resemblance to actual events or locales or persons, living or dead, is entirely coincidental.

Originally published in Great Britain in 2007 by Hutchinson

First Atria Paperback edition February 2011

ATRIA PAPERBACK and colophon are trademarks of Simon & Schuster, Inc.

For information about special discounts for bulk purchases, please contact Simon & Schuster Special Sales at 1-866-506-1949 or business@simonandschuster.com.

The Simon & Schuster Speakers Bureau can bring authors to your live event. For more information or to book an event, contact the Simon & Schuster Speakers Bureau at 1-866-248-3049 or visit our website at www.simonspeakers.com.

Manufactured in the United States of America

10 9 8 7 6 5 4 3 2 1

Library of Congress Cataloging-in-Publication Data

Kennedy, Douglas.
State of the union / by Douglas Kennedy.
p. cm.
1. Self-realization in women—Fiction. 2. Women teachers—Fiction. 3. Family secrets—Fiction. 4. Maine—Fiction. I. Title.
PR6061.E5956S73 2011
823'.914—dc22 2010031160

ISBN 978-1-4516-0209-8
ISBN 978-1-4516-0212-8 (ebook)

For Max and Amelia.
But also for Joseph Strick.

Some rise by sin, and some by virtue fall.

—*Measure for Measure*, act 2, scene 1

PART One

1966–1973

ONE

AFTER HE WAS arrested, my father became famous.

It was 1966—and Dad (or John Winthrop Latham, as he was known to everyone except his only child) was the first professor at the University of Vermont to speak out against the war in Vietnam. That spring, he headed a campuswide protest that resulted in a sit-down demonstration outside the Administration Building. My dad led three hundred students as they peacefully blocked the entrance for thirty-six hours, bringing university executive business to a standstill. The police and National Guard were finally called. The protestors refused to move, and Dad was shown on national television being hauled off to jail.

It was big news at the time. Dad had instigated one of the first major exercises in student civil disobedience against the war, and the image of this lone, venerable Yankee in a tweed jacket and a button-down Oxford blue shirt being lifted off the ground by a couple of Vermont state troopers made it onto newscasts around the country.

"Your dad's so cool!" everybody told me at high school the morning after his arrest. Two years later, when I started my freshman year at the University of Vermont, even mentioning that I was Professor Latham's daughter provoked the same response.

"Your dad's so cool!" And I'd nod and smile tightly, and say, "Yeah, he's the best."

Don't get me wrong, I adore my father. Always have, always will. But when you're eighteen—as I was in '69—and you're desperately trying to establish just the smallest sort of identity for yourself, and your dad has turned into the Tom Paine of both your home town *and* your college, you can easily find yourself dwarfed by his lanky, virtuous shadow.

I could have escaped his high moral profile by transferring to another school. Instead, in the middle of my sophomore year, I did the next best thing: I fell in love.

Dan Buchan was nothing like my father. Whereas Dad had the heavy-duty Waspy credentials—Choate, Princeton, then Harvard for his doctorate—Dan was from a nowhere town in upstate New York called Glens Falls. His father was a maintenance man in the local school system, his late mother had run a little manicure shop in town, and Dan was the first member of his family to go to college at all, let alone medical school.

He was also one shy guy. He never dominated a conversation, never imposed himself on a situation. But he was a great listener—always far more interested in what you had to say. I liked this. And I found his gentle reticence to be curiously attractive. He was serious—and unlike everyone else I met at college back then, he knew exactly where he was going. On our second date he told me over a beer or two that he really didn't want to get into some big ambitious field like neurosurgery. And there was no way that he was going to "pull a major cop-out" and choose a big-bucks specialty like dermatology. No, he had his sights set on family medicine.

"I want to be a small country doctor, nothing more," he said.

First-year med students worked thirteen-hour days, and Dan studied nonstop. The contrast between us couldn't have been more marked. I was an English major, thinking about teaching school when I graduated. But it was the early seventies, and unless you were going through the grind of med or law school, the last thing anyone had on their mind was "the future."

Dan was twenty-four when I met him, but the five-year age gap wasn't huge. From the outset, I liked the fact that he seemed far more focused and adult than any of the guys I had been seeing before him.

Not that I knew that much about men. There had been a high school boyfriend named Jared—who was bookish and kind of arty and totally adored me, until he got into the University of Chicago, and it was clear that neither of us wanted to sustain a long-distance thing. Then, during my first semester at college, I had my one short flirtation with freakdom when I started seeing Charlie. Like Jared, he was very sweet, very well read, a good talker, and "creative" (which, for Charlie, meant writing a lot of what was, even to my impressionable eighteen-year-old eyes, really turgid poetry). He was heavily into dope—one of those guys who was usually smoking a joint with their breakfast coffee. For a while, this didn't bother me, even though I was never really into his scene. Still, in retrospect, I needed this brief descent into bacchanalia. It was '69—and bacchanalia was in. But after three weeks of putting up with the mattress on the floor of the crash pad where Charlie lived—and his increasingly obtuse, stoned monologues from deepest Spacey Outer—there was an evening when I came over to find him sitting around with three friends, passing around a humongous joint while blaring the Grateful Dead on the hi-fi.

"Hey . . ." he said to me, then lapsed into silence. When I asked him over the din of the music if he wanted to head out to a movie, he just said "Hey" again, though he kept nodding his head sagely, as if he had just revealed to me some great deep karmic secret about life's hidden mysteries.

I didn't hang around, but instead retreated back to campus and ended up nursing a beer by myself in the Union, while tearing into a pack of Viceroy cigarettes. Somewhere during the third cigarette, Margy showed up. She was my best friend—a thin, reedy Manhattan smart-ass with a big shock of black curly hair. She'd been raised on Central Park West and went to the right school (Nightingale-Bamford), and was super-smart. But, by her own admission, she had "fucked up so badly when it came to opening a book" that she ended up at a state university in Vermont. "And I'm not even into skiing."

"You looked pissed off," she said, sitting down, then tapping a Viceroy out of my pack and lighting it up with the book of matches on the table. "Fun night with Charlie?"

I shrugged.

"The usual freak show over at that commune of his?" she asked.

"Uh-huh."

"Well, I guess the fact he's cute makes up for—"

She stopped herself in midphrase, taking a deep pull off her cigarette.

"Go on," I said, "finish the sentence."

Another long, thoughtful drag on her cigarette.

"The guy is high every moment of the day. Which kind of doesn't do much good for his use of words with more than one syllable, does it?"

I found myself laughing, because in true New York style Margy had cut right through the crap. She was also ruthlessly straight about what she saw as her own limitations . . . and why, three months into our freshman year, she was still without a boyfriend.

"All the guys here are either ski bums—which, in my thesaurus, is a synonym for *blah*—or they're the sort of dopeheads who have turned their brains into Swiss cheese."

"Hey, it's not for life," I said defensively.

"I'm not talking about your Mr. Personality, hon. I'm just making a general observation."

"You think he'd be devastated if I dumped him?"

"Oh, *please.* I think he'd take three hits off that stupid bong of his, and get over it before he exhaled the second time."

It still took me another couple of weeks to break it off. I hate displeasing people and I always want to be liked. This is something that my mother, Dorothy, used to chide me about, because also being a New Yorker (and being my mom), she was similarly no-nonsense when it came to telling me what she thought.

"You know, you don't always have to be Little Miss Popularity," she once said when I was a junior in high school, and complained about not winning a place on the Student Council. "And not fitting in with the cheerleading crowd seems cool to me. Because it's really okay to be smart."

"A B-minus average isn't smart," I said. "It's mediocre."

"I had a B-minus average in high school," Mom said. "And I thought that was pretty good. And, like you, I only had a couple of friends, and didn't make the cheerleading squad."

"Mom, they didn't have cheerleaders at your school."

"All right, so I didn't make the chess team. My point is: the popular girls in high school are usually the least interesting ones . . . and they always end up marrying orthodontists. And it's not like either your father or I think you're inadequate. On the contrary, you're our star."

"I know that," I lied. Because I didn't feel like a star. My dad was a star—the great craggy radical hero—and my mom could tell stories about hanging out with de Kooning and Johns and Rauschenberg and

Pollock and all those other New York School bigwigs after the war. She'd exhibited in Paris, and still spoke French, and taught part-time in the university art department, and just seemed so damn accomplished and sure of herself. Whereas I really didn't have any talent, let alone the sort of passion that drove my parents through life.

"Will you give yourself a break?" my mother would say. "You haven't even begun to live, let alone find out what you're good at."

And then she'd hurry off for a meeting of Vermont Artists Against the War, of which she was, naturally, the spokesperson.

That was the thing about my mom—she was always busy. And she certainly wasn't the type to share casserole recipes and bake Girl Scout cookies and sew costumes for Christmas pageants. In fact, Mom was the worst cook of all time. She really couldn't care less if the spaghetti came out of the pot half stiff, or if the breakfast oatmeal was a mess of hardened lumps. And when it came to housework . . . well, put it this way: from the age of thirteen onward, I decided it was easier to do it myself. I changed the sheets on all the beds, did everyone's laundry, and ordered the weekly groceries. I didn't mind coordinating everything. It gave me a sense of responsibility. And anyway, I enjoyed being organized.

"You really like to play house, don't you?" Mom once said when I popped over from college to clean the kitchen.

"Hey, be grateful someone around here does."

Still, my parents never set curfews, never told me what I couldn't wear, never made me tidy my room. But perhaps they didn't have to. I never stayed out all that late, I never did the flower-child clothes thing (I preferred short skirts), and I was one hell of a lot tidier than they were.

Even when I started smoking cigarettes at seventeen, they didn't raise hell.

"I read an article in *The Atlantic* saying they might cause cancer," my mother said when she found me sneaking a butt on the back porch of our house. "But they're your lungs, kiddo."

My friends envied me such noncontrolling parents. They dug their radical politics and the fact that our New England red clapboard house was filled with my mom's weird abstract paintings. But the price I paid for such freedom was my mom's nonstop sarcasm.

"Prince Not So Bright," she said the day after my parents met Charlie.

"I'm sure it's just a passing thing," my dad said.

"I hope so."

"Everyone needs at least one goofball romance," he said, giving Mom an amused smile.

"De Kooning was no goofball."

"He was perpetually vague."

"It wasn't a romance. It was just a two-week thing . . ."

"Hey, you know I *am* in the room," I said, not amazed how they had somehow managed to blank me out, but just a little astonished to learn that Mom had once been Willem de Kooning's lover.

"We are aware of that, Hannah," my mom said calmly. "It's just that, for around a minute, the conversation turned away from you."

Ouch. That was classic Mom. My dad winked at me, as if to say, "You know she doesn't mean it." But the thing was, she really did. And being a Good Girl, I didn't storm out in adolescent rage. I just took it on the chin—per usual.

When it came to encouraging my independence, Mom urged me to attend college away from Burlington—and gave me a hard time for being a real little homebody when I decided to go to the University of Vermont. She insisted that I live in a dorm on campus. "It's about time you were ejected from the nest," she said.

One of the things Margy and I shared was a confused background—Waspy dads and difficult Jewish moms who seemed to always find us wanting.

"At least your mom gets off her *tokhes* and does the art thing," said Margy. "For my mom, getting a manicure is a major personal achievement."

"You ever worry you're not really good at anything?" I suddenly said.

"Like only all the time. I mean, my mom keeps reminding me how I was groomed for Vassar and ended up in Vermont. And I know that the thing I do best is bum cigarettes and dress like Janis Joplin . . . so I'm not exactly Little Miss Bursting With Confidence. But what has you soul searching?"

"Sometimes I think my parents look on me as some separate self-governing state . . . and a massive disappointment."

"They tell you this?"

"Not directly. But I know I'm not their idea of a success story."

"Hey, you're eighteen. You're supposed to be a fuckup . . . *not* that I'm calling you that."

"I've got to get focused."

Margy coughed out a lungful of smoke.

"Oh, *please,*" she said.

But I was determined to get my act together—to win my parents' interest and show them that I was a *serious person*. So, for starters, I began to get serious as a student. I stayed in the library most nights until ten, and did a lot of extra reading—especially for a course called Landmarks of Nineteenth-Century Fiction. We were reading Dickens and Thackeray and Hawthorne and Melville and even George Eliot. But of all the assigned books in that first-semester course, the one that really grabbed me was Flaubert's *Madame Bovary.*

"But it's so goddamn depressing," Margy said.

"Isn't that the point?" I said. "Anyway, the reason it's depressing is because it's so real."

"You call all that romantic stupidity she gets into *real*? I mean, she's kind of a *schnook,* isn't she? Marrying that dull-ass guy, moving to a dull-ass town, then throwing herself at that smarmy soldier, who just sees her as a mattress, nothing more."

"Sounds pretty real to me. Anyway, the whole point of the novel is how someone uses romance as a way of escaping from the boredom of her life."

"So what else is new?" she said.

My dad, on the other hand, seemed interested in my take on the book. We were having one of our very occasional lunches off-campus (as much as I adored him, I didn't want to be seen eating with my father at the Union), slurping clam chowder at a little diner near the university. I told him how much I loved the book, and how I thought Emma Bovary was "a real victim of society."

"In what way?" he asked.

"Well, the way she lets herself get trapped in a life she doesn't want, and how she thinks falling in love with someone else will solve her problems."

He smiled at me and said, "That's very good. Spot on."

"What I don't get is why she had to choose suicide as a way out; why she just didn't run away to Paris or something."

"But you're seeing Emma from the perspective of an American woman in the late 1960s, not as someone trapped by the conventions of her time. You've read *The Scarlet Letter,* right?"

I nodded.

"Well, nowadays we might wonder why Hester Prynne put up with walking around Boston with a big letter *A* on her chest, and lived with constant threats from the Puritan elders about taking her child away. We could ask: why didn't she just grab her daughter and flee elsewhere? But in her mind, the question would have been: *where can I go?* To her, there was no escape from her punishment—which she almost considered to be her destiny. It's the same thing with Emma. She knows if she flees to Paris, she'll end up, at best, working as a seamstress or in some other depressing petit bourgeois job—because nineteenth-century society was very unforgiving about a married woman who'd run away from her responsibilities."

"Does this lecture last long?" I asked, laughing. "Because I've got a class at two."

"I'm just getting to the point," Dad said with a smile. "And the point is: personal happiness didn't count for anything. Flaubert was the first great novelist to understand that we all have to grapple with the prison we create for ourselves."

"Even you, Dad?" I asked, surprised to hear him make this admission. He smiled another of his rueful smiles and stared down into his bowl of chowder.

"Everyone gets bored from time to time," he said. Then he changed the subject.

It wasn't the first time my father had implied that things weren't exactly perfect with my mom. I knew they fought. My mom *was* Brooklyn Loud, and tended to fly off the handle when something pissed her off. My dad, true to his Boston roots, hated public confrontation (unless it involved adoring crowds and the threat of arrest). So as soon as Mom was in one of her flipped-out moods, he tended to run for cover.

When I was younger, these fights disturbed me. But, as I got older, I began to understand that my parents fundamentally got along, that theirs was a weirdly volatile relationship that just somehow worked, perhaps because they were such fantastic polar opposites. And though I probably would have liked them around more as I was growing up, one thing I did learn from their sometimes stormy, independent-minded marriage was that two people didn't have to crowd each other to make a relationship work. But when Dad hinted at a certain level of domestic boredom, I realized something else: you never know what's going on with two people . . . you can only speculate.

Just as you can only speculate about why a woman like Emma Bovary so believed that love would be the answer to all her problems.

"Because the vast majority of women are idiots, that's why," my mother said when I made the mistake of asking her opinion about Flaubert's novel. "And do you know why they're idiots? Because they put their entire faith in a man. Wrong move. Got that? *Always.*"

"I'm not stupid, Mom," I said.

"We'll see about that."

TWO

I'LL NEVER GET married," I announced to my mother just before starting my freshman year at college. This proclamation came right after one of her particularly virulent rants against my dad, which only ended when he locked himself into his study at the top of the house and blared Mozart on his hi-fi to muffle her. After she quieted down—courtesy of a cigarette and a glass of J&B—she found me sitting glumly at the kitchen table.

"Welcome to marriage," she said.

"I'll never get married," I said.

"Yes, you will—and you'll fight with the guy. Because that's what happens. That's the deal."

"It won't be my deal."

"One hundred bucks says you'll go down the aisle before you're twenty-five," my mom said.

"You're on," I said. "Because there's no way that's going to happen."

"Famous last words," Mom said.

"How can you be so sure I'm going to get married young?"

"Maternal intuition."

"Well, you're definitely going to lose that bet."

Six months later, I met Dan. One night a few weeks later, when we were already an item, Margy turned to me and said, "Just do me a favor: don't marry him *now*."

"Come on, Margy. I'm still getting to know the guy."

"Yeah, but your mind is made up."

"How can you say that? I'm not *that* transparent."

"Wanna bet?"

Damn Margy, she knew me too well. I'd liked Dan from the start, but I'd never said I was planning to marry him. So how was it that Margy and my mom had it figured?

"You're a traditionalist," my mom told me.

"That's so *not* true," I said.

"It's nothing to be ashamed of," she said. "Some people have a rebellious streak, some are timid, some are just . . . conventional."

"I really don't know why I bother talking to you," I said.

Mom shrugged. "Then don't talk to me. I mean, you're the one who came by here today for lunch, and also to ask my advice about Doctor Dan . . ."

"You really can't stand him, can you?"

"Can't stand Dan? What an absurd idea. Doctor Dan is every mother's dream."

"He thought you were nice."

"I'm certain Dan thinks most people are nice."

In Mom's universe, nobody interesting was normal or decent. Those virtues were for the terminally boring. And from the moment she met him, I knew that she'd filed Dan away under Dull.

The thing was: I never found him dull. He was just . . . normal. Unlike Mom and Dad, he didn't overwhelm you with himself, nor did he try to dazzle with his intellect or his accomplishments. He laughed at my jokes, he valued my views, he encouraged me in whatever I was doing. And he liked me for simply being me. No wonder my mom didn't really take to him.

"She wants what she thinks is best for you," Dan said after meeting her.

"The ultimate Jewish Mother curse."

"You should see it for what it is: good intentions gone a little astray."

"Do you always try to find the decent side of people?"

Another of his diffident shrugs.

"Is that a terrible thing?" he asked.

"I think it's one of the reasons I love you."

Now how did that slip out? I'd only known the guy for ten weeks, but, in private, I'd already decided.

Unlike some of my college friends, who seemed to sleep with a new guy every weekend, I wasn't really into "free love" any more than I wanted an "open relationship" with Dan. From the outset, we had an unspoken agreement that we'd remain monogamous—because we both wanted it that way.

During the Easter weekend, we drove five hours to visit his father in Glens Falls. Though we'd now been together for several months, it was the first time I'd met his dad (his mom having died, at the age of forty, of an aneurysm during Dan's junior year in high school). The weekend went just fine. Joe Buchan was a first-generation American. His parents had come over from Poland in the early 1920s, and immediately ditched the name Buchevski for the all-American "Buchan." His dad had been an electrician, so Joe became an electrician. His dad had been a serious patriot, so Joe became a serious patriot, volunteering for the Marines after Pearl Harbor in 1941.

"Ended up in Okinawa with four of my friends from Glens Falls. You know about Okinawa, Hannah?"

I shook my head.

"Less you know about it, the better," he said.

"Dad was the only one of his friends who came back alive," Dan said.

"Yeah, well, I just was the lucky one," Joe said. "During a war, you can do your damnedest to avoid getting shot or blown up. But if a bullet has your name on it . . ."

He paused. He took a pull of his bottle of beer. "Was your dad in the war, Hannah?"

"Yes. He was based in Washington and for a short time in London—something in Intelligence."

"So he never saw action?" Joe asked.

"Dad . . ." Dan said.

"Hey, it's just a question," Joe said. "I'm just asking if Hannah's dad ever came under fire, that's all. I know he's some big peacenik . . ."

"Dad . . ." Dan said.

"Hey, I'm not saying anything against the guy," Joe said. "I mean, I don't know him—and as much as I hate his peacenik attitudes, I gotta tell you, Hannah, that I respect his guts in standing up for—"

"Dad, will you please get off the soapbox now?"

"Hey, I ain't trying to insult nobody."

"I'm not insulted," I said.

Joe squeezed my arm. It was like having a tourniquet applied to it.

"Thatta girl," he said, then turned to his son and added, "Y'see, we're just havin' an exchange of views here."

I felt right at home with their banter . . . even if the home in question was so damn different from my own. Joe Buchan didn't own many books, and had a wood-paneled rec room in the basement, where he spent a lot of time on his very own Barcalounger in front of the big Zenith color television while watching his beloved Buffalo Bills get the crap kicked out of them every weekend.

"I hope he doesn't think I'm some eastern snot," I asked Dan on the drive back to Vermont.

"He told me he's in love with you."

"Liar," I said, smiling.

"No, it's the truth. You totally won him over. And I hope you didn't mind all that stuff about your dad . . ."

"It really didn't bother me. In fact, I thought it was kind of cute—him going to all that trouble to find out about Dad . . ."

"Hey, he's an electrician. And if there's one thing I know about electricians, it's that they're obsessed with knowing everything there is to know about whatever they need to know about. Which is why he read up on your dad."

"He's so normal and down-to-earth," I said.

"No parent is completely normal."

"Tell me about it."

"But your folks are pretty stable."

"In their own wayward way."

"We'll never be wayward," he said with a laugh.

"I'll hold you to that."

We'll never be wayward. I knew that this was Dan's way of telling me that he wanted us to last. Which is exactly how I felt—in spite of the whispering voice that said, *Hold on. You're still only a sophomore . . . everything's in front of you . . . Don't box yourself in so soon.*

It took another six months for Dan to come out and say, "I love you." It was summer, and Dan had won a place in a program for medical students at Massachusetts General Hospital in Boston. When he found out that he'd been the one University of Vermont medical student chosen for this program, he said, "Feel like spending the summer with me in Boston?" It took me about two seconds to say yes. Within a week, I'd found us a cheap sublet at $85 a month in Cambridge. I also found out about a remedial reading program in Roxbury run by Quakers, but completely nondenominational, and in need of volunteer teachers. So I applied and was accepted—no salary, just $25 a week for carfare and lunch, and the chance to do a little good.

My dad was delighted when I told him how I'd be spending my vacation. My mom also expressed her approval—though, being Mom, it was tinged with reservations.

"Promise me you'll get out of Roxbury before dark. And promise me you'll try to get some nice local guy to walk you to the subway every night and put you on the train."

"By local guy, do you mean 'black'?" I asked.

"I am not being racist," she said. "But though your dad and I might think it's admirable that you're choosing to spend your summer this way, down in Roxbury you're going to be perceived as a white liberal interloper . . ."

"Thanks, Mom."

"I'm just telling the truth."

As it turned out, Roxbury wasn't as sinister as expected. Yes, it was a slum—and the signs of social deprivation were everywhere. But the Dudley Street Project was run by a mix of educational professionals and local community workers—and didn't wear its liberal credentials on its sleeve. They put me in charge of a half-dozen ten-year-olds—all of whom had limited reading skills, to the point where *The Cat in the Hat* was a big challenge to them all. I won't say I transformed them in the seven weeks I was there, but by the end of the summer, four of my gang were able to tackle *The Hardy Boys*—and I knew that I had found something I loved. Everyone talks about the "rewards" of teaching, of "giving something back" or "making a difference." The truth is, there's also a kick about being in charge, being the boss. And when one of my gang had a breakthrough, I felt a real buzz . . . even if the kid himself didn't recognize what he'd just achieved.

"You mean," Margy said on a long-distance call from New York, "it isn't all Sidney Poitier where the kids are thugs at the start, but, by the end, come up to you with tears in their eyes and say, 'Miz Hannah, you've changed my life'?"

"No, hon," I said. "All the kids hate being in this summer school—and they look upon me as their warden. But at least they're learning."

"It sounds more useful than what I'm doing."

Courtesy of her mother's connections, Margy had landed a summer internship at *Seventeen*.

"But I thought magazines were supposed to be glamorous."

"Not this one. And all the uppity interns from the Ivy League and the Seven Sisters look down on me because I go to Vermont."

"Bet you can drink more beer than they can."

"Bet I also don't end up married to someone named Todd, like all of them will. Speaking of which, how's *la vie domestique*?"

"Well, I hate to say it, but . . ."

"Yeah?"

"We're doing wonderfully."

"God, you're boring."

"Guilty as charged."

But it was the truth. Mom was right: I did like playing house. And Dan was just great when it came to dealing with the dull domestic stuff. Better yet, we didn't crowd each other, even though the best thing about the summer was the discovery that Dan was such good company. We always had something to talk about, and he took such an interest in the world around us. I was hopeless when it came to keeping track of everything that was going down in Vietnam, whereas Dan knew about every Army offensive, every Vietcong strike-back. And he got me to read Philip Roth—in order, as he said, to begin to understand "Jewish Mother fixations."

My mom had read *Portnoy's Complaint* when it was first published in 1969. When I mentioned to her that I'd finally gotten around to it this summer, her reaction took me by surprise.

"Don't you dare think that I'm like Mrs. Portnoy."

"Oh, please."

"I can just imagine what you tell Doctor Dan about me."

"Now who's being paranoid?"

"I am *not* being paranoid . . ."

Her tone was suddenly strange—almost as if she were a little unhinged about something.

"What's wrong, Mom?" I asked.

"How weird do I sound?"

"Weird enough to get me worried. Has something happened?"

"Nothing, nothing," she said. Then she quickly changed the subject, reminding me that my dad was coming down to Cambridge on Friday night to address a rally in Boston against the invasion of Cambodia.

"He'll call you when he gets to town," she said, and hung up.

On Friday morning, at the Dudley Street Project, I received a message from my dad, telling me to meet him after the rally at the Copley Plaza Hotel, where a news conference was going to be held. The rally was at five that afternoon, on the steps of the Boston Public Library.

I was late and Copley Square was so packed that I found myself standing halfway down Boylston Street, listening to my father's voice amplified along the city streets. There he was, a speck on a platform several hundred yards from where I stood. Yet the voice I was hearing wasn't a magnified version of the one that used to read me bedtime stories, or calmed me down after one of Mom's tirades. It was the voice of a Great Public Man: bold, stentorian, confident. But rather than feel a certain daughterly pride in his brilliant oratory and his popular acclaim, a certain sadness took hold of me, a sense that I didn't have him to myself anymore . . . if, that is, I ever did.

Trying to negotiate my way to the Copley Plaza Hotel afterward was a nightmare. Though it was less than a quarter of a mile from where I was standing, the crowd was so dense and so slow to disperse that it took me nearly an hour to reach its front door. When I got there, the cops had thrown a security cordon around the place, and weren't letting anyone in unless they had press ID. Fortunately, at that moment, a reporter from *The Burlington Eagle,* James Saunders, came up to the barricade, flashing his press badge to the cop. I'd met him when he'd interviewed Dad at home, and suddenly called out his name. To my relief, he remembered me immediately, vouched for me to the cop on duty, and whisked me inside.

The Copley Plaza was a dumpy-looking hotel with a large conference room on the second floor. It was packed with people, most of whom seemed to be less interested in the impromptu press conference going on at one end of the room than in all the free cold cuts and beer on the tables stacked in the opposite corner. There was a lot of smoke—cigarettes commingling with the sweet, unmistakable aroma of dope. There was a young guy onstage, going on about the need to maintain confrontation with "all the cogs in the military-industrial complex." Around three reporters were listening to him.

"Oh God, not him," James Saunders said.

I stopped scanning the room for my dad, and turned my attention to the stage. The speaker was in his early twenties, shoulder-length hair, a big walrus mustache, very slim, dressed in faded jeans and an unpressed blue button-down shirt that hinted at some preppy origins behind the hippie look. Margy would have said, "Now that's what I call a cute radical."

"Who's that?" I asked Saunders.

"Tobias Judson."

"I know that name from somewhere," I said.

"Probably the newspapers. He was a big cheese during the Columbia University takeover. Mark Rudd's left-hand man. I'm surprised they let him in, given his reputation for trouble. Very smart guy, but dangerous. Still, he doesn't have to worry about much—his dad owns the biggest jewelers in Cleveland . . ."

I spotted my father in a far corner of the room. He was speaking to a woman around thirty, with waist-length chestnut hair and aviator-style glasses, dressed in a short skirt. They were close together, talking intensely, and at first I thought she was interviewing him.

But then I noticed that, halfway through their very involved conversation, she reached down and took his hand in hers. My dad didn't pull his hand away. On the contrary, he squeezed hers and a little smile formed on his lips. Then he leaned over and whispered something in her ear. She smiled, let go of his hand, and walked away, mouthing something to him as she left. And though I'm not exactly a professional lip reader, I was pretty damn certain that she said, "Later . . ."

My father smiled at her, then glanced at his watch. Looking up again, he scanned the room, caught me in his sights, and waved. I waved back, hoping he didn't notice the shock I was registering right now. In the few seconds I had before he reached me, I resolved to act as if I had seen nothing.

"Hannah!"

He gave me a big hug.

"You made it," he said.

"You were great, Dad. As always."

Tobias Judson had finished his onstage speech and was walking toward us. He nodded toward Dad, then quickly looked me up and down.

"Nice speech, Prof," he said.

"You did well up there yourself," Dad said.

"Yeah, I'm sure we both added to our FBI files today," he said. Flashing me a smile, he asked, "Do I know you?"

"My daughter, Hannah," Dad said.

Judson did a small double take, but recovered fast and said, "Welcome to the revolution, Hannah."

Suddenly his hand shot up as he saw some woman across the room.

"Catch you whenever," he said to us, then headed toward her.

My father and I ended up in a little Italian restaurant near the hotel. Dad was still very charged up after the rally. He ordered a bottle of red wine and drank most of it, railing against Nixon's outrageous orders for "covert incursions into Cambodia," and praising Tobias Judson as a real star of the Left—the next I. F. Stone, only even more charismatic.

"The thing about Izzy Stone is that, for all his brilliance, you always get the feeling that he's shaking a finger in your face, whereas Toby has the same analytical sparkle, plus a genuine ability to seduce the listener. He's quite the ladykiller."

"One of the side effects of being a great public radical, I suppose."

He arched his eyebrows . . . then noticed that I was studying him directly.

"The world loves a young Tom Paine," he said.

"I'm sure the world loves a Tom Paine of any age," I said.

He refilled our wineglasses and said, "And like all such attractions, it's fleeting."

He looked up and met my gaze. And asked, "Are you anxious about something, Hannah?"

Who the hell was she?

"I'm kind of worried about Mom," I said.

I could see his shoulders relax.

"In what way?" he asked.

I explained about our phone call, how she seemed very preoccupied, if not downright weird. He nodded in agreement.

"Well, I'm afraid your mom had some bad news a few days ago—Milton Braudy decided not to take her new show."

Oh God, that *was* bad news. Milton Braudy ran the gallery in Manhattan where Mom exhibited her paintings. He'd been showing her work for almost twenty years.

"She would have handled it very differently in the past," Dad said. "Called Braudy an S.O.B., flown down to New York to confront him, and forced her way into another gallery. But now she just sits in her studio, refusing to do anything."

"How long has she been like this?"

"Around a month."

"I didn't really hear it in her voice until yesterday."

"It's been building up for a while."

"Are things all right between you guys?" I asked.

My father looked up at me—surprised, I think, by the directness of the question. I'd never before asked him anything about his marriage. There was a moment or two when I could see him wondering how to respond, how much truth I needed to know.

"Things are what they are," he finally said.

"That's a little enigmatic, Dad."

"No—*ambivalent.* Ambivalence isn't a bad thing."

"In marriage?"

"In everything. The French have an expression: *Tout le monde a un jardin secret.*"

Everyone has a secret garden.

"Do you see what I'm getting at?" he asked.

I met his cool blue eyes. And I saw, for the first time, that my father had many different compartments to his life.

"Yeah, Dad . . . I think I get it."

He drained his glass.

"Don't worry about your mom. She'll get through this . . . But do yourself a favor, don't let on that you know about this."

"Surely she should tell me herself."

"That's right. She should. And she won't."

And then he changed the subject, asking me all about my job, interested in the stories I told him about my students and working in Roxbury. When I said how much I liked teaching, he smiled and said, "It obviously runs in the family."

Then he glanced at his watch.

"Am I keeping you from something?" I asked, trying to make the question seem as innocent as possible.

"No. It's just, I did say I'd drop in on a meeting that Toby Judson and company are having at the hotel later on. This has been a good talk, Hannah."

He called for the check. He paid it. We stood up and walked out into the muggy Boston night. He was a little tipsy from the wine, and he put his arm around me and gave me a big paternal squeeze.

"Want to hear a fantastic quote that I heard today?"

"I'm all ears," I said.

"Toby Judson told it to me. It's from Nietzsche, and it goes: *There is no proof that the truth—when and if it is ever revealed—will be very interesting.*"

I laughed and said, "That's pretty damn—"

"*Ambivalent*?"

"You took the word right out of my mouth."

He leaned over and kissed me on the cheek.

"You're a great kid, Hannah."

"You're not too bad yourself."

I was only moments away from the T stop at Copley Square, but I suddenly felt like walking . . . especially as there was a lot to think about. It was after midnight when I reached our front door. The lights were on. Dan was home.

"You're back early," I said.

"They gave me time off for good behavior. How was dinner with your dad?"

"Interesting. In fact, so interesting that I walked all the way home from Back Bay, thinking about . . ."

I stopped myself.

"Yeah?" Dan asked.

"Being back at college in the fall, and . . ."

Another pause. Should I really say this?

"Go on . . ." Dan said.

"Whether we should get a place together when we get back to Vermont."

Dan let this sink in for a moment. Then he reached into the icebox and pulled out two beers. He handed one to me.

"Good idea," he said.

THREE

"WELL, I'M NOT exactly shocked," my mother said when I told her the news. "In fact, I had ten bucks riding with your dad on whether you'd move in with him as soon as you got back here."

"I hope you spend the money well," I said.

"Can I help it if you do predictable stuff? Anyway, even if I did object—on the grounds that you are cutting yourself off from the sort of 'personal experiences,' to be euphemistic about it, that you should be having at this stage of your life—would you listen to me?"

"No."

"My point entirely."

The only good thing about this maddening conversation was that it hinted that my mother was possibly emerging from the down period she had experienced after it all went wrong with her art dealer. Not, of course, that she would ever dream of telling me about this setback, or let on about what was eating her up. That would have meant confessing weakness—vulnerability!—in front of her daughter. Mom would have rather walked across a campfire than admit such things to me.

So she never mentioned her new work being rejected by Milton Braudy. Nor did she ever even intimate that the show wasn't happening. She simply carried on as if nothing had happened. But when I returned alone from Boston at the end of August to begin apartment hunting (while Dan finished his final week at Mass General), it was clear to me that, despite her usual swagger and cynicism, she was still in a bad place. Two dark rings had shown up beneath her eyes. Her nails were chewed up, and I could detect a very slight tremor in her hands whenever she lit up a cigarette.

Then there was the situation between herself and Dad. Fighting was always a part of their domestic repertoire. Now things had suddenly gone very quiet between them. During the ten days I was at home, they seemed to barely acknowledge each other. Then late one evening, I finally did hear my parents talking. Only this time, the conversation was conducted in shrill hisses. I'd gone to bed early, and was jolted awake when I heard them going at each other downstairs. The fact that they were squabbling in angry whispers was, in itself, unnerving (my mom always having to scream her way through an argument). Like a little child, I crept out of bed, opened my door as silently as possible, and tiptoed to the top of the stairs. Though I was now in closer proximity, their dialogue was still only barely discernible, as it came out in angry undertones.

"So is she meeting you in Philly this weekend—?"

"I don't know what you're talking about—"

"Bullshit. I know exactly what's—"

"I've had it with your accusations—"

"How old is she?"

"There is nobody—"

"Liar—"

"Don't talk to me about lies when I know all about—"

"That was ten years ago, and I haven't seen him since—"

"Yes, but you still rubbed my nose in it—"

"So is this your revenge now? Or does she just have some fucked-up Daddy complex—?"

I couldn't take any more of this, so I snuck back into my room, crawled into bed, and tried to vanish into sleep. This proved impossible—my mind was trying to come to terms with what I'd just heard and how I wished that I hadn't eavesdropped.

The next day I found an apartment. It was located around a quarter mile from campus, on a quiet, leafy street with lots of old Gothic frame houses. This one was a little run-down on the outside (its green clapboard needed repainting, its front porch had a couple of loose floorboards), but the apartment was huge. A big living room, a big bedroom, an eat-in kitchen, a bathroom with an old claw-foot tub. The asking rent was only $75 a month . . . whereas an apartment of this size in this neighborhood would usually have gone for around $135.

"But the reason it's so cheap," I told Dan on the phone that night, "is because it's in grim condition."

"I kind of figured that. Define grim?"

"Really awful peeling wallpaper, old carpets with cigarette burns and scuzzy stains. The bathroom looks like something out of *The Addams Family,* and the kitchen's pretty basic."

"You paint a pretty picture."

"Yeah, but the good news is that the place has got fantastic potential. There are proper floorboards under the carpets, the wallpaper could be easily stripped away and the walls repainted, and there's this amazing old bath . . ."

"Sounds great, but two days after I get back, I go straight into classes. And I'm just not going to have the time . . ."

"Leave it to me. Anyway, the *really* good news is that the landlord is so desperate to let the place, he'll give us two months free rent if we fix it up."

After signing the lease, I bought several gallons of cheap white paint, some brushes, and rented a sander. Then I spent the next eight days stripping wallpaper, replastering the many cracks in the walls, covering them with several coats of paint, and glossing all the woodwork. Then I pulled up the carpets and tackled the floorboards, finally staining them a natural color. It was satisfying work—and I loved the sense of accomplishment when I cleared away all the dustcloths and paint cans, and was able to look at the clean, airy apartment I had created.

"You told me it was a complete dump," Dan said when he first saw it.

"It was."

"Amazing . . ." he said, kissing me. "Thank you."

"Glad you're pleased."

"It's a home."

Those were exactly the words that Margy used when she came to see the place a few days later. She'd just returned from New York, and had settled into her dorm room before running over to check out my first apartment. Since finishing the work, I had managed to root around assorted thrift and charity shops for some very basic furniture, all of which I stripped and stained. There were the usual boards-on-cinder-block bookshelves, and a couple of Chianti bottle lamps, but also a fantastic brass double bed which I picked up for only $50. There was also an old-fashioned New England rocking chair which only set me back $10, and which I had painted a dark green.

"Good God, it's *Better Homes and Gardens* goes college," Margy said.

"So you don't approve?"

"*Don't approve?* I'm envious as hell. I'm living in this student box, whereas you have got yourself a home. And who did all the interior decorating?"

"My handiwork, I'm afraid."

"Dan must be thrilled."

"Yeah, he likes it. But you know Dan. He's not really into 'stuff.'"

"Honey, you can give me that antimaterialist crap, but, believe me, you've got style. Your mom check it out yet?"

"She's not in a great place right now."

"That sounds like the sort of discussion best accompanied by some cheap red wine."

And she pulled a bottle of Almaden Zinfandel out of her shoulder bag.

"Call it a housewarming gift."

We opened the wine. I found two glasses.

"So tell me . . ." she said.

The whole story came out in a rush, starting with my mom's strange interlude in July, the scene with my dad and that woman in Boston, and culminating with the revelations heard at the top of the stairs. When I finished, Margy threw back the rest of her wine and said, "You know what my answer is: *So what?* And yeah, I know that's easy for me to say, as he's not my dad. But so what if he's got a mistress tucked away somewhere? Just like you really shouldn't get worked up about your mom cheating on your dad."

"That bothered me less."

"Of course it did, because you're Daddy's Little Girl. And him cheating on Mom was really like him cheating on you."

"Where'd you learn that, Psych 101?"

"No, I learned all about this sort of shit when I was thirteen. I answered the phone one night in our apartment in New York. There was this drunk on the other end, asking me if he was speaking to my father's daughter. When I said yes, the guy told me—and these were his exact words: 'Well, I'd like you to know that your daddy is fucking my wife.'"

"Good God."

"The guy later called my mom and told her the same thing. Turns out it wasn't the first, second, or even third time Dad had done this. As my mom told me: 'Your stupid asshole father can never be discreet. He always chooses women who make a fuss. I could have just about handled the infidelity. It's having my nose rubbed in it that's making me call it quits.'"

"She left him after that?"

"Tossed his ass right out of the door . . . metaphorically speaking. The evening after that phone call, I came home from school and there was my dad, packing. I broke down in front of him, and begged him not to go, as I certainly didn't want him leaving me in Mom's clutches. He held me until I calmed down, and then said, in his best tough-guy accent: 'Sorry, kid, but I got caught with my pants down, and now I'm paying the price.'

"Half an hour later, he was out the door—and I never saw him again. Because he took off for a little postmarital breakup vacation in Palm Beach, and had a heart attack on the golf course a week later. So much for his Bogart cool. Mom throwing him out killed him."

I had known that Margy's dad had died young—until now I hadn't known the circumstances.

"My point," Margy said, "is that you've got to stop looking at your parents as *parents* and start seeing them as typically fucked-up adults . . . which is what we're going to become eventually."

"Speak for yourself."

"Now *that's* really naive." She stubbed out her cigarette and lit another. "Anyway, what does Dan think about all this?"

"I haven't told him yet."

"You're kidding me."

"I just . . . I don't know . . . I'm sort of embarrassed by the whole business."

There was certain family crap that I still felt nervous about sharing with Dan. And though I knew that Margy was right—that it was hypocritical *not* to let my guy in on the parental dirty linen—there was a part of me that was privately ashamed of all this bad behavior, and was worried that, somehow, it would make Dan think differently of me.

"For Christ's sakes," Margy said when I articulated this fear to her, "when will you grow up? You have *nothing* to be sorry about here. So why don't you just tell him about it, and you won't be feeling so guilty about nothing."

"Fine, I'll do it."

But every time I planned to discuss it with him, something stopped me—either Dan seemed too preoccupied, or he was just too tired, or I didn't think the moment was appropriate. When, a few weeks later, I admitted to Margy that I still hadn't told him, she rolled her eyes and said, "Well, at this point, I wouldn't say anything. I mean, it's not like you betrayed him or anything. You just didn't want to talk about this. So it's the first secret you've kept from him. It won't be the last."

"I still feel guilty about it."

"Guilt is for nuns."

Maybe Margy had a point. Maybe I did make far too big a deal about all this. Especially since Dan only seemed to have a passing interest in my family, and was very good at dedicating whatever free time he had to us. More tellingly, my parents seemed to find a way out of the bad place into which they'd tumbled. We cut each other quite a wide berth that autumn. My mom and dad came over once to see the new apartment (and Mom made a predictably catty comment about how I had "such good nesting instincts."). Dad and I managed only three lunches in the first few months of the fall term (during all of which he hardly mentioned Mom at all). But then, when I came over for Thanksgiving dinner alone (Dan was with his dad in Glens Falls), I immediately noticed a definite change of mood. They were both a little tight when I showed up, laughing at each other's jokes—and even giving each other the occasional come-on look. It was nice to see, but it left me wondering what had triggered the end of their Cold War. I found out after dinner, when we were finishing the second bottle of wine, and I too was now feeling pleasantly smashed.

"Dorothy had some good news this week," Dad said.

"Let me tell it," she said.

"I'm all ears," I said.

"I'm having a show at the Howard Wise Gallery in Manhattan."

"Which is one of the best modern art galleries in the city," my dad added.

"Congratulations," I said, "but isn't Milton Braudy annoyed?"

Mom's lips tightened and immediately I felt like kicking myself.

"Milton Braudy didn't like the new show, so he dropped me. Happy now?"

"Why would that make me happy?" I asked.

"Well, you evidently take such pleasure in my failure . . ."

"I didn't say that."

"You asked me if Milton Braudy rejected me . . ."

"It was an innocent question," my dad said.

"Bullshit . . . and while you're at it, stay out of this. This is between her and me."

"You're completely overreacting," I said. "Per usual."

"How dare you. I never—repeat, *never*—come down on you about your own little shortcomings . . ."

That last comment caught me like a left to the face. My voice was suddenly raised. I was saying things I'd never said before.

"You never *what*? All you do is criticize me . . . or make your stupid snide comments about how I never live up to what you . . ."

"You're just so fucking thin-skinned, Hannah, that you take my *occasional* caustic comment to be a personal attack . . ."

"That's because you're always attacking me . . ."

"No—I am simply trying to push you out of your rut . . ."

"Dorothy . . ." Dad said, pleadingly.

"A rut!" I yelled. "You're telling me I'm in a rut?"

"You want the truth, here it is: I cannot begin to fathom why, at the age of twenty, you have turned into some milk-and-cookies housewife type."

"I am not a damn housewife."

"You even refuse to curse properly. Why can't you say 'fucking housewife' like—"

"Like *what*? Like some displaced Greenwich Village artist—"

"That's right—get vicious—"

"That is *not* vicious. Calling me a housewife, on the other hand—"

"—is an appropriate observation. But hey, if you want to trap yourself in a nice little domestic cul-de-sac with the doctor of your dreams—"

"At least I haven't cheated on him—"

I stopped myself. Across the table, my father put his face in his hand. My mother simply glowered at me.

"Like *whom*?" she said, her voice suddenly quiet, but full of menace.

"Drop it, Dorothy," Dad said.

"Why? Because you told her?"

"Dad told me nothing," I said. "Voices carry—especially *your* voice."

"So go on, big mouth," Mom said. "Finish the question. Or do you want me to answer it for you, and tell you how many women your father's fucked over the years, or how many lovers I've—"

"Enough!" my father shouted. I stood up and bolted for the front door.

"That's right, run away from the tough stuff," my mom yelled after me.

"Haven't you said enough?" my dad shouted back at her.

I slammed the door behind me, and went charging off down the street, crying. I kept running. It was about thirty-five degrees outside and I had left my coat behind, but there was no way I was going back to get it. I wanted nothing to do with that woman again

By the time I reached home fifteen minutes later, I was shaking with cold and rage. But my rage was now mixed with a terrible sadness. Mom and I had fought often, but never with such brutality. And her cruelty—though always there, below the surface—had never before erupted with such fury. She'd wanted to wound me badly—and she'd succeeded.

I needed to call Dan in Glens Falls, but I didn't want to ruin his Thanksgiving by crying on the phone. I half expected a call from my dad. None came. So around eleven that night, I dialed Margy in Manhattan. Her mother answered, initially sounding half awake, then annoyed.

"Margy's out with friends," she said sharply.

"Could you please tell her Hannah called?"

"Could you please not phone again at such a ridiculous hour."

And she hung up.

I threw myself into bed after this. It was time to call it a day.

Margy never called me back—her mother probably didn't give her the message. But I did ring Dan the next morning.

"You don't sound good," he said.

"Pretty hideous evening with my parents."

"How hideous?"

"I'll tell you when I see you."

"That bad?"

"Just come home, Dan."

He didn't press me for details (that wasn't Dan's style). Nor did I want to give him any—because I was still trying to figure out how to explain the fight to him, without having to tell him that I kept assorted family problems from him this summer, and that he was a central part of my mother's rant against me. My dad, however, helped me work out a way of letting Dan know that a serious rift had developed between my mother and myself.

He showed up that morning around ten minutes after I finished talking to Dan. He looked tired—his eyes bloodshot, his manner uncharacteristically tense. He had my coat slung over one arm.

"You forgot this," he said, handing it to me at my front door. "It must have been a cold walk home."

"I didn't notice," I said.

"I'm truly sorry, Hannah."

"Why? You didn't say anything horrible to me."

He looked at me directly.

"You know why I'm sorry."

Pause. I asked, "Do you want to come in for coffee?"

He nodded.

We went upstairs to the apartment and sat in my kitchen. As the percolator percolated, Dad glanced around.

"This is really a splendid flat. It's to your credit."

I smiled an inward smile. My dad—a quiet Anglophile—was probably the only man in Vermont to call an apartment "a flat."

"I'm glad you approve," I said. "Mom didn't."

"Yes, she did. She told me how impressed she was. But, naturally, she would never tell you such a thing, because that's how she is, and we've talked about this before, and you know it isn't going to change, so—"

"Thank you for trying to defend me last night."

"Your mother went completely over the top. And it was my fault completely."

"No, I provoked it. If I'd only kept my big mouth shut . . ."

"You weren't at fault. Dorothy just took things the wrong way, and felt you were taking pleasure in her rejection by Milton Braudy."

"You know that's insane. I was simply asking her a question . . ."

"You're right. You're utterly right. But your mother is a very proud woman, and she's now convinced herself that you insulted her and were deliberately cruel. And I know—believe me, I *know*—that her interpretation of what happened is completely outrageous. And even though I have tried to explain this to her, she won't see sense."

This stopped me short.

"What do you mean by that?"

He drummed his fingers on the table, reluctant to speak.

"Come on, Dad . . ."

"I told her I didn't want to be the messenger . . . that if she was going to make this sort of threat, she should tell you herself—"

"What sort of threat?"

"—but she was adamant that, if I didn't deliver her message, she simply wouldn't explain . . ."

"Explain *what*?"

He put his hand over his face.

"That she refuses to talk to you until you apologize."

I stared at him, dumbfounded.

"She can't be serious."

"Right now, I think she's deadly serious. Then again, it's just the morning after. She hardly slept at all, and I want to believe that her overreaction is just an extreme response to a family quarrel that got out of hand. So give it a day or two . . ."

"Dad, I am not apologizing. Tell her from me: there is no way I am saying sorry."

"I don't want to be the messenger again."

"Well, you agreed to do it for her . . . you can now do it for me. That's the least you owe me."

Dad looked away. I immediately felt awful.

"I'm sorry," I said. "I really didn't mean that."

"I think you did—and I deserve it."

"Are you going to leave her?"

He shrugged.

"What's her name?" I asked.

"Who?"

"The woman I saw you with in Boston."

Now it was Dad's turn to look appalled.

"You saw me with—"

"A woman, around thirty, long brown hair, very slender, very attractive, talking with you in a very up close way at the hotel after the rally, and then suddenly squeezing your hand. It happened just when I came into the room where the press conference was being held. You didn't see me come in. Which meant that I happened upon this little scene, unobserved."

"Oh shit . . ." he said in a half whisper.

"So what's her name?"

"Molly . . . Molly Stephenson. She's a fellow at Harvard. She writes regularly for *The Nation*."

"Well, I didn't think you'd be cheating on Mom with a hairdresser. Is it serious?"

"It was . . . for a while."

"And now?"

"I ended it. Reluctantly."

"Were you in love?"

He met my gaze.

"It was a fling . . . yet one which developed into something more serious than either of us expected."

"But you stopped it . . . to stay with Mom?"

Another quiet nod.

"And what about her little adventures?" I asked.

"Inconsequential."

"Didn't they bother you?"

"It's hard to take a moral stance on these things when you yourself—"

He broke off.

"I'm truly sorry, Hannah."

"You've said that already."

"I don't blame you for being angry," he said.

"I'm not angry at you. I'm not pleased, but . . . I sort of understand. She's fucking impossible."

My father looked genuinely surprised. It was the first time I had ever used that word in front of him.

"I'm pretty impossible too," he said.

"Not from where I sit."

"I'm lucky in you."

"Yeah," I said, "you are."

He met my smile, then stood up.

"I'd better get going."

"The coffee's ready."

"I've got a stack of papers to grade before everyone gets back Monday. Lunch next week, per usual?"

"Per usual."

"And I will tell your mother what you said, even though . . ."

"What?"

"Well, to be honest with you, I think it might make things worse."

"So be it," I said.

He put on his coat.

"One last thing," I said. "What do you think I should tell Dan?"

"Whatever you think he needs to know," he said.

So when Dan came back the next evening, I gave him an edited version of Thanksgiving night. And I felt horrible about only revealing part of the story, and editing out all that adulterous stuff I didn't want him to hear. But once you set a half-truth in motion, how can you ever come clean without looking like an equivocator . . . someone who hid stuff from view for reasons that even she herself considers shaky? So I simply reduced the blowup to that passing comment about Mom's ex-art dealer, which in turn sparked off a fight, in which she accused me of being Little Miss Straight . . . a premature housewife.

"Does she think I'm to blame?"

"No, I think she blames me entirely."

"You don't have to soft-pedal things for my benefit. I know she doesn't approve of me."

"Mom doesn't approve of anyone."

"She thinks I'm a stiff."

"She's never said that," I said.

"Now you're just trying to protect my feelings . . . which really isn't necessary. Your mom is as transparent as Saran Wrap."

"I don't care what she thinks. And if she doesn't want to talk to me again, that's fine with me."

"She'll talk to you again."

"What makes you think that?"

"You're her only child. She'll see sense."

But a week went by and I heard nothing from her. Dad didn't mention her during our lunch the Wednesday after Thanksgiving—and I didn't bring her up. When I still hadn't heard from her after a second week, I mentioned her silence when I met Dad at the diner where we always ate on Wednesday afternoons.

"You didn't tell me last week if you gave Mom my response to her ultimatum."

"That's because you didn't ask," he said.

"Well, did you?"

"Of course I did."

"And what was her reply?"

"Tacit rage."

"Anything else?"

"Yes. She said, 'If that's the way she wants it, fine by me.'"

"How long do you think this will last?"

"I suppose that depends on whether or not you want to speak with her again."

"Dad, if I apologize to her, I'm essentially telling her it's all right for her to continue to dump on me."

"Then don't apologize. But do understand: she'll dig her heels in and not talk to you for a very long time."

"Have you been through this often with her?"

He smiled a sad smile. "What do you think?"

At that moment, I saw my father not as the dynamic, self-assured professor, or the hugely respected and charismatic public man. Instead, he became a sad middle-aged guy locked in a very complex and difficult marriage. And one thing was now very clear to me (something I never really wanted to admit to myself): my mother was something of a monster. An intelligent, talented, witty monster . . . yet a monster nonetheless.

With this realization came the thought . . . or maybe it was the fear: what if she doesn't speak to me again?

"I really better go," Dad said. "I have forty essays to get through. By the way, I won't be able to do lunch next Wednesday. I'm off to Boston for a few days."

I looked at him directly.

"Business?"

He met my gaze and smiled.

"No. Pleasure."

After he left, another thought struck me: my father had just confided in me. Not that he ever mentioned he was back seeing Molly Stephenson, although in the weeks leading up to Christmas he was in Boston three times. He never talked about what he got up to down there, and I didn't ask him either. Nor, to his credit, did he cancel any more of our lunches, as he seemed to work his class and travel schedule around our Wednesday date at the diner. Once, when I told him that he didn't have to meet me every Wednesday, he was delightfully outraged.

"Not meet you? It's the highlight of my damn week."

Intriguingly . . . *wonderfully* . . . our conversations after the Thanksgiving fiasco did not center around Mom and our ongoing domestic strife. Rather, Dad seemed to want to talk about anything but.

"Have you given any thought to a term abroad yet? You only have a few semesters left."

"Sure, I've thought about it . . ."

"Everyone should spend a little time in Paris."

In fact, there was a University of Vermont program in France that Margy and I had already looked into, but . . .

"I've got other things on my mind right now."

Dad pursed his lips and nodded. There it was—the elephant in the living room; the thing we both kept trying to avoid dealing with.

"I still haven't heard from her, Dad . . . and it's only two weeks until Christmas."

He looked distinctly uncomfortable.

"I'll talk to her again."

When I didn't hear from him for another week Dan advised me to call my mom and see if some sort of reconciliation (without apology) was possible.

"At least you can console yourself with the thought that you tried to make peace with her," Dan said.

He did have a point, and though I completely dreaded the thought of phoning, I bit the bullet and made the call the next morning.

"Hello?"

Her voice—loud, no-crap—jolted me. My voice, on the other hand, was shaky and low.

"Mom, it's Hannah."

"Yeah?"

That was it. A flat, indifferent monosyllable, drenched in contempt. The phone shook in my hand. I forced myself to speak.

"I was just wondering if we could talk?"

"No," she said. And the line went dead.

Half an hour later, I was in Margy's room, my eyes red from all the crying I had done en route from my apartment.

"Fuck her," Margy said.

"That's easy for you to say."

"You're right—it is easy for me to say. But I'll say it again: fuck her. She has absolutely no right treating you this way."

"Why are our parents so completely insane?" I asked.

"I think it has something to do with failed expectations," Margy said. "Plus the fact that, in America, we're all supposed to have these perfect families. Ozzie-and-fucking-Harriet: that's the role model . . . even though Lizzie Borden is closer to the truth. I tell you, there's no way I'm doing the kid thing . . ."

"You can't know that now."

"Oh yes I can. Just as I can also tell you that I truly hate my mother."

"Don't say that."

"Why not? It's true. And the reason I loathe her is because she's made it so clear over the years that she completely loathes me. Like don't you hate your mother for the stunt she's pulled?"

"Hate is a horrible word."

"That's the difference between you and me. You do this Emily Dickinson thing . . . always hiding your real feelings behind this veneer of New England gentility . . . whereas I am Manhattan Direct. And if I were you, I'd tell that witch where to get off, arrange to have Christmas Day with Dan, and let her stew by herself in her own venom on the day."

I actually took Margy's advice and went home with Dan to Glens Falls. Before we left, Dan counseled me to make one final pre-Christmas stab at fence mending . . . without uttering the two words she insisted on hearing from me.

"I know what's going to happen," I told him.

"Yeah, but there's an outside chance that the thought of you not being home for Christmas might just break down the wall she's put up between you two."

"Her vanity—her pride—is more important to her right now."

"You'll feel better for giving it another shot."

"You said that the last time, Dan."

"Then don't call."

I stood up and went to the phone and dialed home. Mom answered. "Yeah?"

"I just wanted to wish you Merry Christmas . . ." I said.

"That's two days from now."

"Yeah, but as I'm not welcome at the house right now . . ."

"That's your decision."

"No, that's *your* decision, Mom."

"And I've got nothing to say to you until you apologize. So when you're ready to apologize, call me."

"Why are you being so fucking unreasonable?" I yelled.

Her tone remained cool, almost amused. "Because I can be." And she hung up.

I threw down the phone, stormed into our bedroom, and fell down on the bed. Dan came in and put his arms around me.

"I'm sorry," he said. "I shouldn't have . . ."

"Don't apologize for her asshole behavior. You're not at fault here."

The day before we left for Glens Falls, Dad called and asked if he could stop by the apartment around noon. I told him Dan would be out, but I'd certainly be here. When he showed up, he had a couple of wrapped packages under one arm, as well as a bottle of something in a brown paper bag.

"Beware of professors bearing gifts," he said with a smile. I gave him a hug. We went upstairs.

"How about an eggnog?" I asked, moving to the fridge.

"I've got something a little more appropriate," he said and handed me the brown bag. I opened it. Inside was a cold bottle of champagne.

"Wow," I said, studying the label. "Moët et Chandon. It looks expensive."

Dad just smiled. He opened the bottle with great assurance. I watched him ease the cork out, thinking: *My dad is so elegant, so poised. No wonder this Molly Stephenson flipped over him.* He had such presence, such class. And though I had vowed to fight all negative thoughts so close to Christmas, I couldn't help but see my mom as an ogre who'd trapped him, and with whom he was only staying out of a deep sense of loyalty.

"Penny for them?" he asked.

"Nothing . . ." I said, trying to sound nonchalant.

"It's Dorothy, isn't it?"

"Are you surprised?"

"Hardly. But you know she's hurt herself too . . . to which I say: too damn bad. But as I really don't think talking about your mad mother is going to do either of us much good, my suggestion is: let's drink the champagne."

My first sip of champagne told me: this is one of life's true pleasures. My second sip convinced me: I really must go to Paris next year.

Dad must have read my thoughts, as he said, "Another reason to spend your junior year in France is that it will so enhance your palate when it comes to life's more epicurean pleasures"—Dad always got terribly loquacious when tipsy—"and you will discover why all smart Americans love Paris. In Paris, you can be a true *libertine* . . . and no one will criticize you for it. On the contrary, they'll approve."

"Why didn't you stay, Dad?" I asked.

"That's a question I've often asked myself. There was even a teaching post in American history opening up at the Université de Paris. But . . . I had a thesis to defend back at Harvard, and there was a big part of me that felt I really couldn't be a professional expat. If America was my subject, my argument, I really needed to be in the thick of it . . . especially during the darkest part of McCarthyism, when our essential liberties were—"

He broke off, refilled his glass, then downed the champagne in one long go.

"Will you listen to me, making excuses for myself. I came back to America because I lost my nerve. And I also felt I had to prove something to my father by finishing the Harvard doctorate. Imagine turning down a job at Princeton just to get back at your old man; just to show him that you didn't need his idea of respectability."

I had heard about him turning down Princeton before, but in the past the story had been told in a triumphant manner: Dad against the establishment; Dad the maverick who didn't need the Ivy League professorship. Now . . .

"But look at what you've achieved here in Vermont. I mean, you're famous . . ."

"As an ephemeral radical, maybe. But as soon as this war ends, my fifteen minutes of fame will evaporate with it . . . and no bad thing either."

"But how about the Jefferson book?"

"That was ten years ago, Hannah, and I haven't published a damn thing since then. Which is my own damn fault. Dispersion of energies—better known as spreading oneself too thin. And the truth is: I've started three other books since the Jefferson tome. Just couldn't sustain them. Another loss of nerve, I'm afraid."

"Dad, aren't you being a little hard on yourself?"

"Sorry for myself is more like it. Sorry for inflicting it on you."

"You're not inflicting anything on me. I'm really pleased we can talk."

He took my hand, squeezed it, then took a deep breath. We finished the champagne. Dad stood up and said, "I best get back home."

"I'll miss you on Christmas Day."

"Not as much as I'll miss you."

For the next six months I adjusted to Mom's absence from my life. Though I was baffled, hurt, and furious about her behavior, another part of me simply missed her. Why did she have to ruin everything on a point of pride? Why was she so determined to bend me to her will? I knew the answer to those questions. She'd given it to me already: *Because I can.*

And unless I said, "I'm sorry . . ."

Oh, to hell with it.

I maintained that point of view through winter and spring. I also kept myself busy, throwing myself into all my classes (I particularly loved Balzac—his novels were all about the destructiveness of families), and hanging out a great deal with Margy at the Union, smoking cigarette after cigarette. Since Christmas, my onetime occasional smoking habit had turned serious. When Dan first noticed I was now puffing away heavily, all he asked was, "How many a day?"

"Around twenty."

He just shrugged and said: "Your call."

Even though he mightn't have approved, he wasn't going to lecture me on the dangers of cigarettes . . . especially as half the students in med school smoked during class.

Margy, of course, was exultant about the fact that I was now a serious smoker.

"I knew they'd hook you eventually."

"Why's that?" I asked.

"You're so straight, you need one bad habit. And the best news is, when you get to Paris next year, you'll fit right into the café scene. The way I hear it, most French parents give their kids a pack of Gauloises when they're twelve and tell them to get on with it."

I stubbed out my cigarette and lit another.

"I don't think I'm going to Paris next year," I said.

Now it was Margy's turn to stub out her cigarette. Then she looked at me with a mixture of dismay and disapproval.

"You serious?" she said.

I avoided her accusatory gaze.

"I'm afraid so," I said.

"Dan didn't stop you, did he?"

On the contrary, Dan was fully supportive of my semester in France, telling me that he'd come over for Thanksgiving, and that living in Paris really was something I should do.

"You know he wouldn't pull something like that," I told Margy.

"So you stopped yourself."

It wasn't a question, it was a statement of fact . . . and wholly accurate. No one had pressured me, or dropped subtle hints, or made me feel as if I was endangering anything by going away. No, it was *me myself I* who talked myself out of my junior year abroad—and it largely centered on one deep-rooted fear: if I buzzed off to Paris, Dan would drop me. I knew this was an absurd fear, both self-punishing and stupid. But I couldn't stop it from taking hold of me. Fear is a curious thing. Once it has you in its grip, it is hard to shake off. Naturally, I should have talked to Dan directly about all my worries, but every time I was about to bring the subject up, another fearful thought crossed my mind: if you confess you're worried he'll leave you, then he *will* leave you.

So I waited until the application deadline for the Paris program had passed, then told Dan of my decision. He wasn't disappointed. A little surprised, perhaps, as I reeled off a prepared list of lame justifications, culminating with, "And, of course, I'd miss you." And I reached out to ruffle his hair.

"But you shouldn't let that keep you here. Like I said before, I would have come over for Thanksgiving. We'd only have been apart for around twelve weeks . . . which is really nothing."

Oh God, I knew he'd be so *reasonable.*

"Why don't we plan to do Europe the summer we both graduate?" I said.

"That's cool, but I don't want you to feel that you're staying here for my benefit, or out of some weird fear that I wouldn't be here when you got back. Because you know that just wouldn't happen . . ."

"I know that," I lied. "But really, my mind's made up . . . and it's for the best."

He studied me carefully. I could tell that he was bemused by my decision; that he just didn't buy it, and was wondering why the hell I'd made it. But, in true Dan style, he didn't push for a further explanation.

"Your call," he said.

Dad, however, went right to the heart of the matter. We were in our usual booth in the diner when I told him.

"This is because of her, isn't it?"

"Not entirely, Dad."

"I wish I could believe that," he said.

"Does it matter?"

"Actually, it does."

His tone was stern, peeved. My nervousness—already extreme—amplified.

"I just don't think it's the right moment to go to Paris."

"Oh that is such bullshit, Hannah."

I was stunned by the ferocity of his response.

"You're making a decision which is all about security at a time in your life when the last thing you should be thinking about is security."

"Don't you dare lecture me about security," I said, suddenly angry. "Especially after the games you've been playing . . ."

I stopped myself. "Sorry," I said quietly, pulling a cigarette out of my pack.

"I probably deserved it," he said.

"No, you didn't. But I certainly haven't deserved the crap that's been heaped on me for the last few months either. And if Mom was a little happier . . ."

"Your mother has never been happy. *Never.* So *please,* do not think that, if I were making her happy, she would never have turned on you like this. She turns on everyone eventually. You can't win with her. And that's why I'm leaving her."

That last sentence caught me unawares. I tensed.

"Do you really mean that?" I asked.

He nodded, keeping his gaze firmly level with mine.

"Does she know yet?"

"I'm going to tell her at the end of the semester. I know it's another six weeks, but I want the explosive repercussions to happen when there's nobody around."

"Is it the other woman?"

"I'm not leaving Dorothy because of her. I'm leaving because our marriage is no longer tenable . . . because she's impossible to be with."

"But will this other woman be coming up here to live with you?"

"Not immediately. There will need to be a certain cooling-down period—and, quite frankly, I don't want tongues to wag any more than they will once the news gets out. And I need to ask you something . . ."

"I know: don't tell anyone. As if I would . . ."

"You're right, you're right. It's just . . ."

"You don't have to explain, Dad. But I need to ask you a favor in return: don't drop the bombshell until after Dan and I have headed to Boston for the summer. I doubt she'd contact me, but I just don't want to be around when things turn ugly."

"You have my word about that. And I won't bring up Paris again . . ."

"Even though you think I'm making a huge mistake."

He smiled.

"That's right. Even though I think you're making a huge mistake."

Dad didn't make any further mention of his plans in the weeks leading up to final exams and summer vacation. When my grades came in—two A-, one B+, one B—he took me out for a final lunch a few days before I left town.

He knew that I had found work at a private school in Brookline that gave summer remedial courses, and that I'd be making a whopping $80 a week, which struck me as a small fortune. And he knew that we'd managed to rent the same sublet apartment we'd had last year.

"Can you give me the number again?" he asked quietly. "I may be calling you in a couple of days."

A week later, the phone rang at around three in the morning. It was Dad, his voice terse, frightened, almost otherworldly.

"Your mother tried to commit suicide," he said. "She's in intensive care here at the Fletcher Allen Hospital, and they don't expect her to make it."

We were dressed and in Dan's car within fifteen minutes. Driving north, we said nothing. Dan sensed that the last thing I wanted to do right now was talk. And to his infinite, amazing credit, he left me alone with my thoughts. I chain-smoked on the three-hour drive north, staring blankly out the window, trying to fathom what had happened—and how I could have stopped it.

We drove straight to the hospital. Dad was in the waiting room adjoining Intensive Care. He was slumped in a chair, staring down at the linoleum, a lit cigarette in a corner of his mouth. He didn't embrace me, or burst into tears, or even take my hand. He just looked up at me and quietly said, "I should never have told her."

I put my arm around him. Dan caught my eye, nodded toward the door, and left the room.

"What exactly happened?" I asked.

"A few days ago, I finally got up the nerve to say I'd be moving out—that I didn't want to be married to her anymore. Her reaction threw me. I was expecting screaming and shouting. Instead, I got silence. She didn't want to know any details, any reasons, or whether Molly was waiting in the wings. All she said was, 'Fine. I'll expect you to be packed up and gone by Friday.'

"The next forty-eight hours, I hardly saw her. She left me notes—*Will be sleeping in the spare room . . . Don't take anything that isn't yours with you . . . My lawyer will be calling yours next week*—but assiduously avoided me. Then, around six last night, I came home and found her slumped in the car in the garage. At first I couldn't see her—because the car was full of smoke. She'd also managed to tape the gap in the window shut—so she was obviously very serious about doing the job properly. If I had shown up fifteen minutes later . . .

"Anyway, I managed to get her out of the car, then called 911, and kept doing mouth to mouth until the ambulance showed up. They took over and . . ."

He put his face in his hands, then looked directly at me.

"The doctors said she'd swallowed around twenty-five tranquilizers before turning on the engine. She's still unconscious, still on life support . . ."

He stared back down at the floor.

"They don't know if there's brain damage, or whether she'll even be able to breathe without a respirator. The next seventy-two hours are critical."

He went silent. I held him tighter, wanting to say something that would make things better; that would assuage our shared guilt. But I was in shock—and knew that nothing I said would change anything.

"Can I go see her?" I asked.

Dan came with me into Intensive Care, a steadying arm on mine. The nurse leading us through the unit said nothing until we reached her bedside. I blanched with shock. She didn't look like my mother—more like some strange medical sculpture, enveloped in tubes and wires, surrounded by lumpy machinery, with a grim plastic mouthpiece fastened between her lips. I could hear the steady *whoosh* of the nearby ventilator, forcing air in and out of her lungs. Dan turned to the nurse, pointed to the chart hanging on the end of the bed, and asked, "May I . . . ?" She nodded assent, pulled it off, then handed it to him. He scanned it briefly, his face impassive . . . though he did chew on his lower lip as he read (a sure sign that he was tense). I kept looking down at Mom. Part of me wanted to feel anger at her for doing this, for being so selfish and vengeful. But all I could feel was shame and liability. And one thought kept haunting my brain: *why didn't I apologize?*

As we left the ICU, Dan had a few quiet words with the nurse, then turned to me and said, "All the vital signs are stable, and though they won't know anything definitive until she's conscious, there are no clinical indications that she's suffered brain damage."

"But they can't be sure, can they?" I asked.

"No, they can't."

Dan stayed with us for the next twenty-four hours—and, once again, he displayed an amazing restraint and sensitivity when it came to *not* asking all the obvious, difficult questions. Only once when we were out of Dad's earshot did he inquire, "Did your father say if she'd been threatening this for a while?"

"No, but, as you know, she's been unstable for months . . ."

I was about to blurt out the truth, but a little voice whispered in my ear: *Careful here.*

"I gather there's been some bad stuff going on between them for a long time."

"Someone else?"

"I think so, yeah."

I tensed, waiting for him to ask, "How long have you known about this?" but he said nothing. Once again, I was astonished by his thoughtfulness, how he always put my feelings in front of his own; how he maybe accepted that I didn't have to tell him everything . . . even though I felt lingering guilt about the things that I did keep from him.

We'd sublet our apartment to some friends for the summer, so we spent the first night at my parents' house. It was strange to be back there after all these months, strange to be sharing the narrow single bed in my old room with Dan. Not that I slept. Even though I had been up the entire night before, I couldn't surrender to unconsciousness, and instead found myself wide awake an hour after getting into bed. I wandered downstairs and found Dad sitting up, smoking. I bummed a cigarette off him and we sat there saying nothing for a very long time. Finally he broke the silence.

"If she lives, I won't leave her . . . even though I'll regret that decision for the rest of my life."

Dan had to go back to Boston that morning—the hospital was insistent he return to work.

"I can be back here in three hours if . . ."

He stopped himself. *If* . . .

I called the school. The acting summer headmistress was both understanding and annoyed. I said nothing about my mother's suicide attempt, only that her condition was touch and go.

"Well, you obviously must be with her . . . and we obviously must work around this problem."

It's not a problem, I felt like screaming. *It's life or death.*

For the next three days there was no change in her condition; no sense of what the outcome would be. Dad was constantly at the hospital. I could only handle two short visits a day and instead busied myself by playing housekeeper. In the days since Mom was rushed to the hospital, the house had turned into a garbage dump—so I set myself the task of imposing order on chaos. Not only did I thorough-clean the house, I also threw out tons of old magazines and newspapers that Dad had been keeping, and even (with his permission) realphabetized the several thousand books that were scattered around the house. Anything to keep busy, to be distracted.

We said very little to each other—our conversations continued to be light, superficial, avoiding the big question that hung over us. But every time the phone rang, we jumped.

A week went by and I received a call from the school, saying that, under the circumstances, they would have to replace me for the rest of the summer. The very next morning, the phone rang at five-thirty.

Dad answered it. I was already out of bed, heading downstairs, when he yelled up to me, "She's opened her eyes."

We were at the hospital half an hour later. The attending doctor informed us that though Mom had regained consciousness, she was still on the respirator. More tellingly, in the few hours since her eyes had opened, she hadn't attempted to speak, nor had she shown much muscle activity.

"This could be significant . . . or it simply could be that the cocktail of tranquilizers and carbon monoxide which she ingested has yet to completely leave her system, which means that it is still holding her in a narcotic thrall. Only time will tell, I'm afraid."

We were brought into the ward. Mom was still swathed in wires, tubes, and machinery, but she was awake and stared at us blankly, her eyelids occasionally blinking. I took her hand and squeezed it. She didn't return the squeeze—so her hand lay limply in mine.

"It's good to have you back, Dorothy," Dad said, his voice calm, reasonable.

No response.

"You had us worried," I said lamely.

No response.

"Can you hear us, Dorothy?" Dad asked.

There was the slightest nod of the head, then she closed her eyes.

I sat with her for the next few hours. I went home, took a nap, and was back by six to sit with her again. Dad came in around eight. He insisted on taking me home, saying there was no point in me staying by her side all night. I didn't want to leave, but two nights without sleep convinced me he was right. Back home I collapsed into bed, but was up at seven the next morning and at the hospital an hour later. This time, she seemed a little clearer. When I asked her a few questions—*"Do you know where you are? Could you try to squeeze my hand?"*—she responded with a nod. When I felt her fingers wrap around mine, I started to sob. I put my head against her shoulder and let go, the shock of the last two days (and all the anguish of the past months) suddenly pouring out.

"I'm sorry, I'm sorry, I'm so sorry," I whispered.

She squeezed my hand harder and nodded in acknowledgment.

The next day, Mom came off the respirator. During the afternoon, she sat up and began to talk. That night, Dad went in to see her by himself. They spoke for over an hour. When he came out of the room, he said, "She'd like to see you now."

I went inside. She was sitting up in bed, still looking weak, small. But much of the medical paraphernalia had been taken away—and her eyes, though tired, had regained some of their sharpness. With a little nod of the head she motioned me over to the chair by the bed. I sat down. I took her hand. She didn't take mine. Instead, she leaned over to me and whispered: "I knew you'd apologize eventually."

FOUR

THE DOCTORS WERE amazed by Mom's rapid recovery.

"Considering the number of pills she took and the fact that she was on the verge of asphyxiation," one of them told me, "it is remarkable that she pulled through—and with no permanent damage. She must have a ferocious will to live . . . despite doing what she did."

I wasn't surprised at Mom's fierce need to pull through. In my darker moments, I couldn't help but wonder if she had set up the whole attempted suicide as a grand attempt to reestablish her dominion over her wayward husband and her insolent daughter.

"Makes sense to me," Margy said when I called her in Manhattan a few days after Mom came back to life. "And I think you're right about her wanting to punish you both. If your father hadn't found her, she would have, at the very least, made you both feel guilty for the rest of your lives—so that would have been a victory of sorts. My advice to you is: get the hell out of there before she really gets her claws into you."

I was sorry about lots of things in the wake of Mom's recovery. Sorry that I had been so fiendishly manipulated. Sorry that I had lost my summer teaching job (and the $80-a-week salary that came with it). Sorry I would be stuck in Vermont next semester. Sorry that my father had suffered emotional blackmail. But, most of all, I was sorry that I'd said "I'm sorry."

She'd really done a number on me—denying me her love in order to extract the apology that her pride demanded. And I'd caved under the most extreme duress imaginable. *Never again,* I told myself. I'd never apologize for some "wrongdoing" that I felt wasn't wrong. I would never be blackmailed into the sort of crippling guilt that I had suffered for the past few months. Margy was right. I needed to get the hell out of town.

For Dad's sake, I waited a few days until Mom was formally discharged from the hospital before hightailing it back to Boston. I made certain the house was immaculate for her arrival, something she did comment upon—"My God, Hannah, you really are a housewife." I ensured that the icebox was full, and that there were a couple of casseroles ready for defrosting in the freezer.

"We're going to put this entire episode behind us," Mom said to me on the day she got back home. "We're going to forget that all this has happened, and carry on as normal."

I went pale with shock. The nerve—the *chutzpah*—of the woman. But rather than tangle with her, I just nodded quietly—and, later that day, walked over to the bus station in town and bought myself a one-way ticket to Boston the next afternoon.

Dad had gone into withdrawn mode ever since she'd come out of her coma. He never did tell me what was said between them during their first post-suicide-attempt chat. Nor did he seem willing or eager to discuss how he was feeling right now and how things between them would progress from here. Instead, he seemed to realize that he was now trapped.

The morning I left, I brought Mom her breakfast. I'd overslept slightly, so when I got to her room, it was almost nine-thirty. She was already sitting up in bed, reading that week's edition of *The New Yorker*. Near the phone by the bed was a notepad. I glanced at it, and noticed that Mom had scribbled down a phone number with a Boston area code. I was suddenly nervous.

"Sorry I'm late," I said, putting the tray down on the bed. "Tea and toast as usual. Is that enough for you?"

"So you're starting to teach school again tomorrow?" she asked, completely ignoring my question.

"That's right," I said.

"The Douglas School in Brookline, isn't it?"

"I don't remember mentioning it to you."

"Your father told me when I asked him last night. And I just called the Douglas School this morning—and do you know what they said?"

I met her cold gaze. And said, "They told you that they had to let me go last week because my mother was at death's door."

"You told them I tried to kill myself?" she asked, her voice perfectly reasonable.

"No, I didn't think that was any of their business."

"But you just lied to me about having to return to Boston to start work. You're out of work, aren't you?"

"Yes, thanks to you, I'm out of work."

A thin smile appeared on my mother's lips.

"You didn't have to rush back here to join the deathwatch, but you did. However, now that I am back in the land of the living, you are rushing back to Boston, even though there's no job to go back to. So would you mind explaining *why* you're running off so fast?"

"Because I don't want to be around you."

The thin smile grew tighter.

"Yes, I did think that was your reason. And to be blunt about it, Hannah *dear,* I don't care. I really don't. I received the apology I deserved from you. So now, if you want to see me again, fine. If you don't, that's fine too. The choice is entirely yours."

That night, as I sat seething in our kitchen, telling Dan what she had said to me, I vowed to keep her as far outside my life as possible. Dan certainly concurred with this.

"Do yourself a favor," he said. "Cut her off."

As hard as that was to accept, I followed his advice—not by completely ending any contact between us, but by simply maintaining the most minimal of communications with her. During the few weeks I had left in Boston, I made a point of phoning her every Sunday morning for a polite, controlled, unemotional conversation about her well-being. If she asked me any questions about myself, I'd respond. But only if she asked.

When we got back to Vermont at the end of August, filling the time productively became an obsession. I threw myself into classes, but dropped French in favor of a History of Education course, because speaking French in Vermont only served to remind me that I'd stopped myself from living in Paris the next year.

I kept such thoughts at bay, except when Margy sent the occasional postcard from Paris—regaling me, in one hundred words or less, with some tart observation about French stand-up toilets, or why Gitanes tasted like an exhaust pipe, or how she would never again sleep with a Romanian émigré saxophonist with dentures.

Did I feel envy for Margy's adventures in France? Absolutely (though I could have definitely lived without sex with the toothless Romanian émigré). But I kept busy and I plowed ahead through junior year.

Two weeks after we started the winter term, Dan came back from med school holding a letter and looking pleased. He'd just got news that he'd been accepted for an internship in Providence.

"I know it's not the most glamorous of places," he said, "but this is a great break for us—and Rhode Island Hospital is such a great facility. Hell, half the people in my class are having to make do with internships in Nebraska or Iowa City. At least we're still staying in the Northeast. Anyway, the good news is that they don't want me to start until mid-July, which means we could definitely go to Paris for our honeymoon."

That made me pause for thought.

"Is that a proposal?" I asked.

"Yes, it is."

I moved over to the window and looked out at the snow.

"You know," I said, "when I was seventeen, I vowed I would never get married. But I hadn't counted on meeting you . . ."

"Well, I am very glad you did."

"I'm glad too," I said, turning back to him.

"So does that mean you accept?"

I nodded.

So there it was: I was going to marry Dan. My future was tethered to his and, as such, it was secure.

Around three days after this conversation, Dan received some annoying news. Two interns at Rhode Island Hospital had just left, and as they were now short-staffed, they needed him to start work right after graduation.

"Can't you negotiate?" I asked.

"They're really adamant I begin on June 8. If I say no, the next guy on the list will get the internship. And the fact that it's Rhode Island Hospital, where most of the interns came out of Ivy League medical schools . . ."

"So we're not going to be able to have that month in Paris after all?"

"Things change. I'm sorry."

I swallowed my disappointment. Ten days later—on one of those rare perfect late-summer New England days, where the sky was a great big dome of blue and the August mugginess was mitigated by a tangy wind—I married Dan in the First Unitarian Church in Burlington. The service—short, unsanctimonious, and to the point—went off without a hitch. So too did the lunch in the Old Town Hall. Dan made a very nice speech about how I was the best thing that ever happened to him. Dad, of course, was in erudite form—saying how, in a world of constant political uncertainty and ongoing generational conflict, it was a "rare and wonderful thing" to have a daughter who was also such a great friend and such a great support against "life's usual vicissitudes," and that, in his modest parental opinion, Dan was a most lucky fellow. In my little speech, I gave effusive thanks to my dad for teaching me that curiosity is one of the most essential components of life, and for always treating me as an equal (a near-truth); to Dan for showing me that good guys aren't an endangered species; and to Mom for "endlessly challenging me" (a comment which, as intended, was wide open to interpretation), and for throwing such a good bash.

Two days later, we moved to Providence. We found another run-down apartment in another clapboard house, which I knew I would spend much of the summer fixing up. And I did manage to find a full-time teaching job in a private day school in town, teaching English and American history to sixth-graders. And Dan's father gave us a great wedding gift. It was a four-year-old Volvo station wagon—Electric Orange with cracked brown leather seats—which we both thought was the height of cool.

Margy, meanwhile, had put her Paris plans on hold. Her mother had fallen down a flight of stairs while smashed, and had been confined to a wheelchair with a broken hip.

"It looks like I have to play dutiful daughter and stay with her for the summer," she said during a phone call. "As you can imagine, I am not pleased being forced into this Florence Nightingale role—and often wonder, in my darker moments, if she deliberately tumbled down those stairs to keep me from returning to Paris."

"You'll get back to Paris."

"Damn right I will," she said. "As soon as madame is able to stand up and lean against a bar again, I'm on the next flight across the Atlantic. Meanwhile, I've been looking for magazine work, but everything is filled up. So I've found a dumb job at the Museum of Modern Art."

"That doesn't exactly sound like a bad place to work."

"Hey, I'm not a curator. It's a job in the gift shop. But it is a job. And it will pass the time until Mommy Dearest has healed and I can flee the country."

Later that night, over dinner in the apartment, I told Dan about Margy's change of plans, and how she was almost certain that her mother staged the accident to keep her from leaving.

"Well, Margy would say something as neurotic as that," he said.

"Hey, I thought the same thing when my mom tried to kill herself."

"There is a considerable difference between an actual suicide attempt and Margy thinking that her crazy mother deliberately threw herself down a flight of stairs to keep her at home. Then again, having never had direct experience with New York neurotics, I'm not an expert on their brand of craziness."

"That's because you're so ultrarational . . ."

He looked at me with surprise.

"You think I'm *ultrarational*?"

"Just a little too controlled sometimes, that's all."

"Well, thanks for telling me . . ."

"Hang on, I'm not trying to start a fight here."

"No, you're just making comments about my rigidity."

"I called you rational, not rigid . . ."

"*Ultra*rational . . . which is just about the same as rigid. And, hey, I'm really *sorry* if I strike you as a stiff . . ."

"What the hell has gotten into you?" I said.

"Do I attack your personality? Do I make little asides about your little flaws?"

"Such as?" I said, suddenly furious.

"Such as your *own* damn rigidity . . . the way you always keep yourself so tightly in check, always terrified of maybe putting a foot wrong, or displeasing me, or, God forbid, doing something adventurous."

I couldn't believe what I'd just heard.

"*What?*" I yelled. "Everything—*everything*—I have done ever since I've known you has been geared toward *you . . . your* studies, *your* career . . ."

"That's what I'm saying, Hannah. *I* have never, *ever* stopped you from doing anything. You're the one who's stopped yourself—who refused to go to Paris, who followed me around during the summers . . ."

"You felt I was *following* you, like some goddamn puppy dog?"

"You're not hearing me. I'm always happy that you are with me. But I know deep down you feel just a little thwarted by being so hemmed in . . ."

"I have never said I was feeling *thwarted . . .*"

"Well, you sure as hell have *shown* it."

"Well, thank you for speaking 'the truth.' And while you're at it, give yourself an A for perceptiveness, and an A-plus for having the most monumental ego."

"Ego? Me?"

"You don't think I see the ruthlessness behind the Mr. Nice Guy façade?"

As soon as that was out of my mouth, I regretted it. But that's the thing about a fight, especially a fight with the person to whom you are the closest, and with whom you *never* fight: when it gets going—when, out of nowhere, everything suddenly implodes—all sorts of horrible stuff comes tumbling out. And you suddenly find yourself unable to stop yourself from saying . . .

"You don't think I see how you always put you and your work first, always?"

"Shut up," he said, then grabbed his jacket and charged toward the door.

"That's right—run off, don't face up to—"

He turned back and looked at me with pure rage.

"You're the one with shit to face up to."

And he slammed the door behind him.

I don't think I moved for around three minutes after he stormed out. I was in shock, wondering: *where did all that come from?* I couldn't believe what he had said. I couldn't believe what *I* had said. And what shook me the most was the realization that everything said was, in some desperate way, true.

It's your own damn fault, said a voice in my head.

Yeah, but he started it.

An hour went by, then two, then three. It was now well after midnight, and I was starting to get freaked, because, outside of night shifts at the hospital, Dan never stayed out late.

I waited up until one a.m., then called the hospital.

"I'm sorry," the receptionist told me, "but Dr. Buchan isn't on duty tonight . . . no, he's not been in."

There was nothing I could do until he got back here, so I simply crawled into bed, pulled the sheet over my head, and tried to ignore our neighbor playing Grand Funk Railroad at an excessive volume.

Somehow I finally gave in to sleep—a very light sleep, as I jolted awake as soon as I heard our front door close. I glanced at the alarm clock. Four-thirty a.m. I got out of bed. Dan was in the kitchen, making himself a cup of coffee.

He looked tired and strained.

"Where've you been?" I asked.

"Driving," he said.

"For seven hours?"

He shrugged.

"Where did you go?"

"New Haven."

"That's . . . a hundred and fifty miles from here?"

"One hundred and seventy-two miles, if you want to get technical about it."

"Why New Haven?"

"I got on I-95, turned south, and started driving."

"What made you stop?"

"Work. You."

"Even though I've followed you around like a puppy dog?"

"I never said that."

"You implied it."

"Look, why don't we just accept the fact that it was a fight . . . our only bad fight ever . . . and that a lot of stupid stuff—"

"Do I disappoint you that much?" I asked.

"Hardly. And do you think I'm really Mr. Ruthless?"

"No."

He looked up at me and smiled.

"Then let's just . . ."

He reached for me and pulled me toward him. I didn't resist. He kissed me deeply, his hands suddenly moving all over me. I opened my legs and pressed my groin against his, my tongue now deep down his throat, my left hand gripping the back of his head. We stumbled out of the kitchen and into the bedroom, still locked in an embrace. We pulled off our clothes and he was inside me within seconds. His ardor surprised me. His usual gentleness—and reserve—had suddenly vanished. He was drilling into me with abandon. And though part of me was shocked by the roughness of his onslaught, another part of me liked it—and I responded in kind, digging my nails into his neck, arching my back so he could thrust deeper. I came before he did, the ferocity of my orgasm blocking out all sense of time, place. For a moment or two, I was nowhere—and it was a wonderful place to be. A few moments later, Dan slumped against me, burying his face deep into my shoulder. We said nothing for a very long time. Then he looked up at me and smiled.

"We should fight like that more often."

Dan had to get up around ten minutes later—to shower and shave before starting his six a.m. morning shift. Before leaving, he brought me a cup of coffee in bed, kissing me on the head.

"Better go," he said quietly.

After he left, I sat up in bed with my mug of coffee and tried to keep my growing anxiety at bay: we'd made love right in the middle of my cycle. And I hadn't been wearing my diaphragm.

For the next few weeks, I focused my energies on renovating the apartment. My period never arrived. When it was four weeks late, I forced myself to call our local doctor and arrange for a pregnancy test. The next day, I drove down to his office and was handed a glass beaker and directed to the bathroom. When I returned with the urine sample, the doctor said, "Call my nurse tomorrow and she'll give you the result."

After the test, I took myself out for lunch, followed by a movie at a cheap fleapit theater downtown. I arrived home around five. Dan had gotten back before me. He was sitting at the kitchen table, drinking a bottle of beer, looking unhappy.

"You're back early," I said.

"You're pregnant," he replied.

I felt myself tense.

"The nurse from Dr. Regan's office just rang with the test result," Dan said. "She said they'd gotten the results early, and figured you wanted the news straightaway."

"I see . . ." I said, avoiding his gaze.

"Congratulations," he said, "and thanks for letting the father in on the news."

"I was going to tell you," I said.

"Well, glad to hear it . . . since I was somewhat involved. How long have you known?"

"I just found out."

"You know what I mean. When did you suspect?"

"About two weeks ago."

"And you kept this from me all this time?"

"I didn't want to say anything if it wasn't true."

"Why? Because you were planning to do something about it without me knowing?"

"You know I'd never do that," I said. "Of course I'm keeping it."

"Well, that's something. I'm still pretty damn shocked that you didn't say anything."

"I didn't want to get your hopes up, just in case . . ."

That was a complete lie. I didn't say anything because I was too scared to say anything. Even though I knew I'd have the baby—even though I was certain Dan wouldn't flip out—something in me stopped myself from letting him in on the early news. And the problem was that I really didn't understand what stopped me from telling him. All I knew was: I couldn't. Still, he seemed to buy my fraudulent explanation, saying, "You still should have let me know. Like we're in this together, right?"

"Of course," I said quietly.

"And as long as we're both happy . . ."

"It's great news," I said, trying not to sound too somber.

"It's the best news," he said, taking me in his arms. I accepted his embrace. I played along, trying to be cheerful at a moment that I knew was momentous, but which (to me anyway) seemed clouded with ambiguity. I didn't know what to feel.

Later on, as Dan drank a third celebratory beer and I sipped tea, he made all the appropriate noises about how the baby's arrival wouldn't change my work as a teacher, as he was sure we could find someone around here to look after the kid while I was off teaching.

"I'm going to have to tell the school before I start," I said.

"I'm sure they'll be cool about it."

"But one thing," I said. "I don't want this news mentioned to anyone in either family for a couple of months—just in case I miscarry before the first trimester."

"Whatever you say."

But of course I broke my own demand for secrecy by telling my one great confidante. Margy called me one evening while Dan was on a night shift, to let me know that, as her mother had finally hired a part-time nurse to attend to her many needs, she'd flown the coop and had found a small apartment across town.

"So why haven't you rushed back to Paris?"

"Because they've made me assistant manager of the museum gift shop—and I know that's a really lame excuse, but hey, it's just a temporary job and I've signed a year's lease on the studio, and I know I'm hemming myself in, and blah, blah, blah, blah . . . which is another way of saying that I'm not going to talk about this anymore. What's up with you?"

And after swearing her to total secrecy, I let her in on the news of my pregnancy.

"You're shitting me," she said.

"If only . . ."

"You going to keep it?"

"Of course."

A silence. I could tell that Margy was fighting the urge to give me advice.

"Hey, if you're happy, I'm happy."

"By which you mean you think I'm out of my mind."

"You want the truth? Yeah, the idea of being a mother at twenty-two would freak the crap out of me. Because it just isn't me. Still, I am not you, and I'm sure you'll be brilliant at it."

"But now I'm trapped."

"Hon, everybody's trapped."

True, and most of us set the trap that snares us. Or we walk straight into a situation that we know will cause us problems—and do nothing to stop it. I could so easily have dashed into the bathroom for a moment to put in my diaphragm. I could have told Dan to come outside me. But I said nothing, did nothing. And now my destiny was sealed.

Later that day, I called the headmaster of the school where I was to start teaching in September and explained that I would be having a baby around mid-April of next year. I could actually hear his sharp intake of breath as I broke this news.

"Well, I certainly thank you for giving me advance warning," he said. "I presume you just found out."

"Yes—and believe me, it was totally unplanned," I said, sounding stupidly guilty, as if it was his business whether or not it was intended.

"These things often are," he said, sounding like he wanted to get off this subject, then adding that he'd have to talk to the head of the Middle School about the implications, and he'd get back to me as soon as possible.

"Oh . . . my congratulations, of course," he added drily.

Thanks a lot. And thanks even more for the letter which came a few days later explaining in a measured, reasoned way why the school would no longer be able to offer me a job this autumn—as the very fact that I would be having a baby in the spring would rule me out of that trimester, and considering that I'd be a first-year homeroom teacher—never an easy escapade, in his experienced opinion—I'd be balancing such hefty new responsibilities with the equally hefty burden of pregnancy blah, blah, blah . . .

I balled up the letter, tossed it in the trash basket, and thought: *That's me screwed.*

"Can't you take them to court or something?" Margy asked when I called up to scream about losing my job.

"Dan's already looked into that. The fact that they're letting me go before I even start gives me little comeback. More to the point, there's nothing on the statute books protecting a woman from unfair dismissal on the grounds that she's pregnant."

"You shouldn't have told the school."

"Lying's not my style."

"You're just too straight."

"Yeah, it's a real character flaw."

"So what now?"

"Well, there's a teacher's course at the University of Rhode Island, just twenty minutes out of town in Kingston. And as the baby's due in mid-April, they told me I could take my finals next autumn. The other good thing is that they might be able to find me a little substitute teaching—which is kind of crucial, as we're really going to need some extra money."

"You still haven't told your parents?"

"It's top secret until I'm ready to tell them."

"Your mother being your mother, I bet she picks up on you being knocked up before you get around to letting her in on the secret."

Per usual, Margy was clairvoyant. I had to drive up to Vermont the next day—to pick up a few final bits and pieces from our old apartment, still in storage in my parents' barn. I hadn't seen Mom in around six weeks, and as soon as I stepped through the front door, she took one look at me and said, "Don't tell me you're pregnant."

I tried not to react. I failed.

"No way."

"Then why did you turn chalky when I asked you that question?"

I dodged an answer—as I suddenly felt a bout of nausea coming on. I dashed down the hallway to the little toilet under the stairs. I made it just in time. God, how I despised being sick like this. And I knew Mom was going to give me the third degree as soon as I stopped hugging the toilet.

In fact she didn't wait that long. Instead, she knocked on the door and asked, "You all right in there?"

"Must have been something I ate," I said between retches.

"Bullshit," she replied, and thankfully dropped the subject for the remainder of my visit.

Back in Providence, I killed time by signing up for a swimming course at a local pool, and dedicated an hour every morning to my French books, trying to crack the subjunctive tense and expand my vocabulary. I also volunteered at the local McGovern headquarters and spent ten days sticking leaflets into mailboxes and stuffing envelopes at the Rhode Island campaign headquarters in Providence.

"You know you're working for a lost cause," some big beefy postman told me one day when I followed him to a mailbox on some suburban road.

"But it's the right cause," I countered.

"A loser's a loser," he said. "And I only vote for winners."

"Even if they're crooks?"

"Everyone's a crook," he said, and continued his rounds.

That's just not true, I felt like shouting after him. *There's a lot of integrity out there.* But I knew it sounded lame—even though I so wanted to believe it was true.

"What else do we have except our integrity?" I found myself asking Margy when I related this story to her on the phone that night.

"Our bank accounts?"

"Very funny."

"Hey, can I help it if I am a remorseless cynic?"

"Cynicism is always cheap."

"But at least it's amusing."

"Don't talk to me about amusing. I live in Rhode Island."

"Why don't you jump the train down here for a couple of days?"

"I'm only married a couple of months."

"Big deal. Anyway, Dan's working all the time, isn't he?"

"It's not the right moment."

"When *is* the right moment, Hannah?"

"Let's not play this old tune again, please."

"Hey, it's your life, sweetheart. And no one's putting a gun to some cocker spaniel's head and saying: *If you don't spend a weekend in Manhattan with Margy, we'll shoot this dog.*"

Then grad school finally started. The University of Rhode Island wasn't a particularly high-powered place, and everyone there seemed to grasp the fact that, as universities go, this was very minor-league . . . and not the Harvard Graduate School of Education, just an hour up the road. Still, the teacher's course covered all the basics, two of the professors were enthusiastic, and within six weeks of starting the course, the placement office found me a weekend job in a remedial school in town, which brought in $50 a week—and filled the time.

And time passed quickly. Suddenly, it was November, and Nixon won every state in the union except Massachusetts. (The fact that McGovern lost Vermont was something of a personal blow to Dad, who'd made his campaign in that state something of his own personal crusade.) Around the same time, Mom decided to pay me a visit, during which I finally gave her the official news that I was pregnant. Her reply was predictable.

"Hell, I knew that months ago. Any reason why you waited so long to tell me?"

"Because I knew you'd give me a hard time about having a baby so soon."

Mom smiled a dangerous smile. And said, "Well, Hannah, at this point you are a very big girl—and if you want to limit your life at such a young age, why should I stop you? In any case, you never listen to a word I say."

The day after Mom headed back to Vermont, Dan and I went out to dinner at a little Italian place near our apartment. After we ordered, he asked, "How'd you like to leave Providence at the end of June?"

"I'd like that very much," I said. "But aren't we stuck here for your residency next year?"

"Something interesting just came down the pike today," he said, then explained how the chief resident in pediatrics at the hospital—a certain Dr. Potholm, who had become something of a mentor to Dan, since he was now considering becoming a pediatrician—had told him of a job opening in Maine.

"Potholm has a friend at Maine Medical—that's the big hospital in Portland—who called him the other day, asking if he knew of any bright young internist who wanted to spend a year as a GP in a place called Pelham . . ."

"Never heard of it."

"Nor had I. Looked it up on a map this afternoon. It's a small town of around three thousand, around an hour due west of Portland, located in lake country, somewhere near Bridgton . . ."

"Which I've also never heard of."

"Anyway, it seems their GP—a guy named Bland—has decided to do a year overseas with the Peace Corps, so it's a twelve-month gig."

"After which we'd return to Providence?"

He looked at me with amusement.

"Which is your idea of hell?" he asked.

"Put it this way: it's a big country."

He laughed and said, "Tell you what. Why don't we drive up to Pelham this weekend, check the place out, and then decide what our next move will be."

Which is what we did—and around half an hour after we arrived in Pelham, I found myself thinking: *this is promising.* Dan had similar thoughts—and three days after we got back home, he phoned the officer from the Maine Regional Health Authority who'd interviewed him, and told him that, if they were interested in him, he was certainly interested in spending twelve months as the doctor for Pelham, Maine.

Within a week, they called back to tell him he had the job. A few days later, I made the call I was dreading to my mother. When I told her the news, she said, "I always knew you'd end up in a really small town. It's just your style."

FIVE

MY SON, JEFFREY John Buchan, was born on April 8, 1973. It was, according to the obstetrician, a "straightforward delivery"—even though fourteen hours of labor, ameliorated by gas during the final big push, didn't strike me as exactly straightforward. But I didn't care. Jeffrey was beautiful—and when the nurse first handed him to me and he snuggled his head against mine, I was smitten. Then, after Dan pulled out his Instamatic and took the first snapshots of mother and child, the nurse relieved me of my son, telling me I needed to rest. And I collapsed into the sleep I so craved.

That was the last decent sleep I had for the next three months. Name any and every postnatal complaint a baby can suffer—colic, cradle cap, lactose intolerance—Jeffrey experienced them all. Dan was sympathetic . . . but only up to a point. My dad was also sympathetic—reminding me, on the phone, that I too had had colic during the first eight weeks of my life. Then he changed the subject to the one thing he wanted to discuss constantly: the emerging Watergate scandal. Dad's past appearance on the Nixon Enemies List had just led to a whole new round of press interviews and speaking engagements for him, but he did find time to drop down to Providence for a day with Mom to meet their first grandchild. Afterward Mom sent us a beautiful old-fashioned baby carriage, and she did call me every other day to find out how I was doing, though anytime I mentioned just how damn tired I was and wondered out loud whether I'd ever see the end of Jeffrey's assorted ailments, she wasn't exactly wildly sympathetic.

"Welcome to motherhood—which, in my experience, is one long kvetch. But the good news is that after you've spent twenty-one years raising Jeffrey, he'll simply resent you."

When I recounted this statement to Margy, she said:

"Hey, just accept the fact that your mom is probably a manic-depressive and you'll stop getting so damn distressed about everything she says to you."

Margy was standing in my living room with a tumbler full of Smirnoff in one hand. She'd come up to Providence a couple of weeks after the baby was born. I was just home with Jeffrey, suffering broken nights.

"Well, he's really cute . . ." Margy said, trying to sound convincing.

"For someone who screams all the time."

"Well, you know me. It's the screamers who always win me over. Did the doctors give you any idea how long this might go on?"

"Until he goes to college."

During the two days that Margy was up visiting me, Dan didn't make an appearance, though he did call to explain that all hell was breaking loose at the hospital. There had been a teenage pileup on the interstate, he had just dealt with a severely dehydrated nine-month-old girl whose Christian Scientist parents had spent the last seven days treating her chronic diarrhea with prayer, and then there was the big-deal city counselor who had a coronary on the golf course and . . .

"Right, I've got the picture," I said.

"Don't be angry, sweetie."

"I'm not angry . . . I'm just weary. And I hate when you call me sweetie."

"How's Margy getting on?" he asked, changing the subject.

"Desperate to have a child."

"Really?"

"No."

"Oh . . . that's a joke, right?"

"Yes, Dan, it's a joke. How much sleep did you get last night?"

"Maybe three hours."

"Isn't that dangerous . . . for your patients, that is?"

"Haven't killed anyone yet. Listen, I will try to get home tomorrow . . ."

"Margy will be gone by then."

"Sorry."

When I put down the phone, Margy (who was sitting opposite me in the kitchen during this entire conversation) fired up another cigarette and said, "Well, that sounded warm and cuddly."

I just shrugged and filled the percolator with more coffee.

"Things a little difficult between you guys right now?" she asked.

"No, everything's real warm and cuddly . . ."

"Hey, I didn't mean to pry."

"And I didn't mean to sound like a bitch. Sorry . . ."

"Jeffrey's asleep right now, so why don't you try to catch a nap . . ."

"But if he wakes up?"

"You got some bottles of formula in the icebox?"

I nodded.

"Then I'll heat one up on the stove."

"Make sure it's not too hot, not too cold . . ."

"Roger Wilco, Goldilocks."

"And if he's colicky, the best thing is to rub his back until . . ."

"I know—the kid burps. Now get into that bed . . ."

I surrendered to sleep the moment I pulled the blankets over me. The next thing I knew, Margy was shaking me. I glanced at the clock. I had been asleep less than thirty minutes, and was so out of it I couldn't comprehend her first few sentences. But I snapped awake when she said, "He just vomited down my back."

I was up in seconds. Sure enough, Jeffrey was hysterical. Margy, in her panic, had put him back in his crib, still covered in puke. He had somehow managed to end up on his belly and was understandably terrified and panicked. I picked him up. I put him across my shoulder and started stroking his head. Almost instantly he threw up all over me, then began to wail like someone who had decided that life was completely hopeless. At this moment in time, it certainly seemed that way to me too.

Half an hour later, with Jeffrey back napping in his crib, Margy and I sat at the kitchen table, smoking.

"If I ever start getting broody," she said, "remind me about this morning."

"Will do," I said. "And if I'm ever deranged enough to do this again . . ."

"I'll vomit on you, okay?"

When Margy left for Manhattan early the next morning, she looked beyond tired—having walked the floors with me and Jeffrey all that night.

"Don't worry, I'll sleep on the train," she said. "And, unlike you, I will actually be able to crash out for eight hours tonight. Any chance you could hire in a nurse for a couple of nights so you can get some decent sleep?"

"Can't afford it. But I am going to have to find some sort of child care to look after him while I'm packing us up for the move to Maine."

"Should be nice, living in a small town. Real . . . uh . . . quaint."

I laughed. "You are the worst liar I've ever met."

"Hey, it's got to be better than Providence."

A couple of weeks later, we closed up our apartment and headed north—our entire worldly possessions packed into a U-Haul van that Dan drove. I followed in the Volvo, with Jeffrey in the backseat. Miracle of miracles, he slept for most of the six-hour journey—no mean feat, considering New England was in the middle of a heat wave and our venerable Volvo wasn't exactly air-conditioned.

But as soon as we reached our new home in Maine, Jeffrey started to wail again. So did I. In the week or so since Dr. Bland had headed off, a pipe had burst in the kitchen, flooding the entire downstairs of the house. We walked in to discover water everywhere. I blinked with shock. Jeffrey, currently across my shoulder, must have sensed my distress, as he flipped into howling mode. Dan waded into the kitchen, let out a loud "Oh shit," and returned with his pants drenched. I immediately headed for the front door, sat down on the front steps, and tried to calm myself and Jeffrey down.

Dan came out, looking deeply displeased.

"I don't believe it," I said.

He nodded and glanced at his watch. It was nearly six. Darkness would arrive within the hour.

"First things first: let's find us somewhere to spend the night."

The choice of accommodations in Pelham, Maine, wasn't exactly enormous. There was just one option—a small motel on the edge of town. It was a real mom-and-pop place: little cabinlike units, with the sort of cheap wood-paneled walls that I'd seen in dozens of rec rooms, and a flowery carpet with assorted cigarette burns and coffee stains.

"Don't worry," Dan said. "I'll get us out of here by tomorrow."

Actually, it took us two weeks to finally exit that joyless motel. This was not due to Dan's lack of action. On the contrary, he was on the phone five minutes after we checked in, talking with plumbers, the resident nurse, and Pelham's only cop, who, as it turned out, knew Dr. Bland's sister. Not only that, he even had her phone number in Lewiston, and he promised to give her a call straightaway.

"How did he have her number?" I asked.

"His brother went out with her in high school—and Farrell's wife happens to be her oldest friend."

"This *is* a small town," I said.

Ten minutes later, the phone rang. I answered it and found myself speaking to Delores Bland. Without asking me my name, she said, "You the new doc's wife?" and then launched into a monologue, telling me that Joe Farrell had just called her, and she was furious on our behalf because that pipe had leaked last winter and she had told her brother to get it repaired, but he was so cheap that he tried to repair it himself, and now he was in Africa, and she was going to have to get the insurers on the phone tomorrow, and the plumber had just called and he was en route to the house right now, and wasn't the motel horrible, but she would only expect that from the guy who managed it—Chad Clark—who really was a creepy momma's boy who never brushed his teeth when she knew him in high school, and maybe we could take the little apartment over the doctor's office, which is where Nurse London lived until she got pregnant by Tony Bass, who ran the local service station and had to get married, and *jeez, wasn't that a mistake and a half,* and she wanted to drive right over to Pelham tonight, but she was a tenth-grade homeroom teacher at Franklin Pierce High School in Auburn, and tonight the school was presenting the musical *Li'l Abner,* which she simply had to attend, but she would be on the phone first thing tomorrow to Nurse London-now-Bass, and if we wanted somewhere to eat tonight, we'd best drive over to Bridgton, which was only fifteen minutes by Route 117, and when we got to Bridgton there was this "real nice" restaurant called Goodwin's which had great hamburgers and the best milkshakes in Maine called Awful Awfuls *'cause they were Awful Big and Awful Good,* but be sure to ask for one with extra malt in it, 'cause that only cost a nickel extra and . . .

Halfway through this monologue I had to pull the phone away from my head. But I did thank Delores for her help and we did take her advice and drove over to Bridgton. It wasn't hard to find Goodwin's, as it was the only restaurant in town. I couldn't face up to a triple-patty hamburger or a forty-eight-ounce Awful Awful. However, it was a long time until breakfast, so I forced down a grilled cheese sandwich and tried to interest Jeff in a few spoonfuls of ice cream. But he was building up to one of his extended wails—which, as I well knew, always started with a series of whines before quickly transforming into a lamentation that could go on for hours. Sure enough, ten minutes after we sat down, Jeff went ballistic.

"Great," Dan said under his breath.

"At least you won't be up all night with him," I said, hating the strident tone that had entered my voice.

"We'll both be up with him tonight," he said.

"Well, that'll be a change," I snapped back.

"I've only been putting in sixteen-hour days . . ."

"And I've only been putting in twenty-two-hour days . . ."

We said nothing on the drive back to Pelham. We said nothing when we got back to the motel. I put Jeffrey into the bed next to me. Dan sat in one of the armchairs and stared at the old black-and-white television, which looked like it dated back to the Eisenhower years. Our son must have sensed the tension between us, because he refused to settle down. I walked him around every corner of the room at least a dozen times. I let him suck my breasts dry. Dan dozed in the armchair. I finally got back into bed with Jeff, pleading with him to cut us some slack and give us the most nominal of breaks by simply conking out for a couple of hours. He refused to cooperate—until around five-thirty that morning, when he finally closed his eyes and nodded off. Within moments, I passed out as well—waking with a start when he started his prewail rumble again. I was still fully clothed—my body clammy and stiff with tiredness. I glanced at my watch: 7:45 a.m. We'd been asleep for just over two hours. Dan was not in the room, but there was a note beside me on the bed: *Gone out. Meet me at Miss Pelham's for breakfast.*

Miss Pelham's was the one restaurant in town—more of a diner, with a couple of booths and a lunch counter. Dan was seated in one of the booths, a pad of paper in front of him. As I sat down, I noticed that he was finishing a to-do list. He got up and relieved me of Jeffrey, cradling him on his lap.

"You get some sleep?" he asked.

"Yeah. And you?"

"I've crashed in better armchairs."

The waitress came by. She was a short, stubby woman in her fifties, a pencil protruding from her bun of blond-gray hair, a coffeepot in her left hand.

"Morning, hon. Bet you could use some of this after the little surprise you got yesterday. And can I heat up a bottle for junior there? It's Jeffrey, isn't it?"

"That's right," I said.

"Well, he's a total cutie," she said, pouring me a mug of coffee. "Got the bottle, hon?"

I dug it out of my shoulder bag.

"Thanks," I said.

"Happy to oblige. Name's Chrissy, by the way. And you're Hannah, right?"

"Nice to meet you," I said, trying to smile through my tiredness. As soon as she headed off with the bottle, I turned to Dan and said, "She seems friendly."

Chrissy returned with the bottle.

"There you go, Doc," she said, handing Dan the bottle. "Nice to see a fella doing some mommy work for a change. You're a lucky woman there, Hannah. And hey, since I guess you're going to have to move into the apartment above the doctor's office, you're going to really need it painted—like fast. 'Cause Nurse Bass kind of kept it poorly. Then again, between ourselves, Betty Bass is a great nurse, but real sloppy when it comes to, uh, *everything else*. But I guess you probably heard all about that by now."

"Not really," I said, trying to dodge local controversy.

"Well, you will. Anyway, Billy's the local decorator around here—and I was speaking to him last night after I heard about the flood at Doc Bland's house. And since we figured you'd be coming here for breakfast this morning, he wanted you to know that he could start work this afternoon . . . and he'll meet you at the apartment at nine this morning. Which means you've got time to try our Miss Pelham's Special: three eggs sunny-side up, corned beef hash, four sausages, hash browns, and if you're real hungry, we can add a pancake or two."

I had no appetite and stuck with toast. Ditto Dan, who looked absolutely exhausted after his night in the chair. We said little during breakfast—our conversation restricted to the checklist that Dan made up of things we'd have to do immediately to get ourselves out of that damn motel.

Still, the Pelham bush telegraph was seriously up and running, because by the time we reached the doctor's office, a mere three-minute walk from Miss Pelham's, a small welcoming party was already in place. I knew Nurse Bass from our previous visit—a very tall, very thin woman in her late thirties with permanently exhausted eyes and heavily chewed fingernails. But the other two were strangers. Nurse Bass was all business, telling Dan how she had heard Dr. Bland complain about leaky pipes at home in the past, how she was willing to look after Jeffrey during the day over the coming weekend so we could get ourselves sorted out, and when he had a minute to spare this morning, there was a ten-year-old boy in a nearby parish who was complaining of bad stomach pains, which could be appendicitis, and if he wouldn't mind doing a house call . . .

"Looks like you're going to have to bunk upstairs for a while," the nurse said, turning her attention to me. "It's not much—and I'll admit it, I kind of didn't look after the place when I was living there. But still, it wasn't much before I moved in. And Billy here . . ."

Billy was a chunky guy in his early thirties with a wild mop of carrot-colored hair, a cliff of big buckteeth, and a goofy grin on his face. He was dressed in paint-splattered overalls and a Red Sox cap.

"Sure still isn't much up there," he said, interrupting her. "Sure needs some money spent on it."

"Money's something we don't have much of," I said. I felt a light but telling kick on the leg from Dan, who jumped in and said, "What Hannah means is . . ."

"No need to explain," said the short woman, "'cause I know what it's like, just out of med school, on an intern's salary, with a baby, trying to make a start somewhere. Heck, that was my brother's situation when he came back to Pelham to start his practice here."

She pumped my hand vigorously, then did the same to Dan.

"Delores Bland, by the way. Bet you folks slept real bad last night, 'cause no one sleeps well at that motel. But hey, into every life a little rain must fall, and the good news is I've got our insurance man on the job right now at the house, and I've just sent a telegram to Ben in Africa, telling him what happened, and I know that if you have to spend some money fixing up the apartment, the practice will reimburse you, 'cause that apartment's gonna be a good rental investment once it gets yanked into the 1970s, and hey, if you're looking for some entertainment tonight, well the production I saw of *Li'l Abner* at my school . . . just as good as Broadway, I tell you. Not that I've ever seen a Broadway show, but still . . ."

Nurse Bass rolled her eyes and said, "Sorry to interrupt your life story, Delores, but I've got kids to get back to. So if you wouldn't mind . . ."

The doctor's office was located in a plain two-story clapboard house. There was an old-style open staircase at the back of the building. We all trooped up it to a door that was just about hanging on to its hinges and a torn mosquito screen. When we walked inside, my first reaction was, "Oh God . . ."

The apartment was very, *very* small: one cramped bedroom, a living room that was around twelve feet square, an alcove kitchen with vintage appliances (including a twenty-year-old fridge with the cooling element on its roof), and a bathroom with rusty drains. The wallpaper was peeling in places, all the furniture was sagging, all the ceilings were low, and there was a general aroma of dampness emanating from the threadbare carpet.

"This isn't great," Dan said.

"Well, can't say I disagree with you," Delores Bland said. "The problem is, you've got to live in town. That's the deal . . ."

"I know," Dan said quietly. An agreement had been made between the municipal authority of Pelham and their resident doctor that he would live within the town limits, so as to be permanently on call and within a five-minute drive of most residents.

"Let's go back to the house," I said, "and see if there's any possibility that the damage might not be as bad as . . ."

Delores Bland shook her head. "Architect told me this morning there's no way this place'll be habitable for months."

"Well, surely there's somewhere else in town that's rentable," I said.

"Nope," Nurse Bass said.

"Are you absolutely positive?" I asked.

"Small place, Pelham," she said. "Everyone knows when anything's up for rent. And there's nothing right now."

"Would it be okay to talk to the architect directly?" I asked.

"If it makes you feel better, Mrs. Buchan," Delores Bland said.

So we walked over to Dr. Bland's waterlogged house. The architect was there. He was named Sims; a rail-thin man in his late forties, with horn-rimmed glasses, a tattersall shirt, a clip-on tie.

"Came by here months ago to do a survey for a new back porch that the doctor's wife wanted," he said, "and told her then and there that the place needed new plumbing. Wish they'd listened to me."

"Are you absolutely certain, Mr. Sims, that the house is out of bounds for us?"

"The water damage is extensive. And coupled with the dry rot that I've found everywhere . . . well, put it this way: I hope Dr. and Mrs. Bland have a very comprehensive insurance policy. They are certainly going to need every available penny to put things right. I'd say the work will take three months. Maybe more."

As we all walked back to the apartment, my eyes scanned the six or so shops and offices that lined Main Street. There wasn't a real estate agent in Pelham.

"What happens when someone wants to sell or rent a place around here?" I asked Nurse Bass.

"They put up a sign."

Back inside the apartment, I felt my despair accelerate. But I reined it in by trying to stay focused on the task at hand. So I asked Billy if he could completely repaint the place, take up the carpets, sand and stain the floorboards, and install a new kitchen with new appliances. By the time I had finished the list of must-dos he was grinning from ear to ear.

"No problem, ma'am," he said. "The more work the better."

Delores Bland spoke directly to Dan.

"You do realize, Doctor, that the practice won't be able to pay for any of this until the insurance claim is settled. But once Billy gives us a written estimate, and I've written to my brother and gotten his agreement . . ."

"Okay," he said to Delores Bland. "We'll pay for the initial work and the practice can reimburse us."

"Dan, that could take weeks . . ." I said.

Dan clasped one of my wrists and asked Billy, "How long do you think it will take to get the work done?"

"'Bout a week."

"Fine. And my wife will want to discuss things like colors and kitchen fittings and the like. Isn't that right, Hannah?"

I nodded.

"You'd best be making that house call now, Doctor," the nurse said.

Dan turned to me and said, "This shouldn't take long. I'll meet you back at the motel."

He headed off, as did Delores Bland, promising to get back to me as soon as she heard from her brother. Billy turned to me and said, "There's a carpenter in Bridgton I know, and we can also get all the appliances at the Sears there."

"Might you be able to call the carpenter and see if he's free this afternoon?"

"Sure can."

"Then as soon as you hear from the guy, please come by the motel and we'll head off to see him. I want to get all this started straightaway."

"Fine by me," Billy said, flashing me another of his goofy grins.

I brought Jeff back to the motel—and waited for Dan to return. I waited to hear back from Billy. And I kept looking at the confines of this motel room and thinking: *I want to run away now.*

Jeffrey, thankfully, remained asleep. I paced the room, wondering what I could do next, but I knew that things were temporarily out of my hands. Billy finally called after two hours and said that the carpenter was in, and he'd be by to pick me up in thirty minutes.

"I'm going to have to bring my son along," I explained.

"Fine by me," Billy said. "I like babies."

But Dan showed up a few minutes later, looking drawn and tired.

"Sorry that took so long," he said, "but the boy did have acute appendicitis, and I accompanied him to the hospital in Bridgton, where they're probably operating on him right about now."

Dan said that he'd be willing to bring Jeff over to the office for the afternoon if I wanted to get some sleep. I explained that I was heading off momentarily with Billy.

"You're working fast," he said.

"What choice do we have here?"

"That wasn't meant to sound like an accusation."

"I know. I just need to jump down your throat today."

Dan laughed.

"I don't blame you," he said.

There was a knock on the door. Billy was standing outside.

"Hope I'm not interrupting anything," he asked.

Billy drove a beat-up Plymouth station wagon that dated back to the mid-sixties and looked a bit like a moving garbage dump. The two front seats had been splattered with paint and assorted other liquids. The rear seats and the trunk were piled high with decorating apparatus: old paint cans, dirty brushes, bottles of turpentine, filthy drop cloths, a ladder, assorted tools, an ashtray overflowing with compacted butts, and around five empty giant-sized Awful Awful containers scattered on the floor.

"You seem to like Awful Awfuls," I said, attempting to make conversation.

"They're real good," he said, then fell silent.

"What's your favorite flavor?"

"Caramel . . . with an extra scoop of malt."

Silence.

"Maybe we can go there after we get done with the carpenter and Sears," I said.

"Sounds good."

Silence.

As I came to discover, Billy was unable to initiate chat. He'd respond to questions, then he'd lapse into his own head again, that harmlessly eccentric grin as permanently fixed to his face as the ever-present L&M cigarette clamped between his stained teeth. Through persistent questioning, I did learn that he'd been brought up in Pelham, that he was an only child and his dad had left his mom when he was very young. He'd been sent away to a school "for kids like me" when he was around eight, and with the exception of vacations, he had spent the next ten years in assorted special schools around the state.

"When I was eighteen, my uncle Roy gave me a job in Lewiston. Roy runs a decorating company there. Does plumbing too. Worked with him for three years. Taught me lots."

"Why'd you come back to Pelham?" I asked.

"Mom got sick, needed me here. And Lewiston's a city . . . well, sort of a big town, I guess. But too big for me."

His mother died around a year after he returned home, and in the five years since then, he'd set himself up as the one and only decorator/plumber in Pelham.

"Not a lot of work around town, but when a place needs sprucing up or a pipe bursts, they call me."

"Did you ever fix the pipes over at the Bland place?"

"Never asked. Doc Bland kind of did all that stuff himself. Real jack of all trades, the doc."

"And obviously not much of a plumber."

Billy laughed—a loud, barking laugh.

"Ain't gonna answer that question, ma'am."

"You must call me Hannah."

"Okay, Hannah, ma'am . . ."

Billy might not have been much of a conversationalist, but he certainly knew his stuff when it came to dealing with the carpenter. And he insisted—pleasantly—that we be given a "professional discount" on the white sink and toilet and tiles I'd chosen at Sears. After he'd won that argument and I'd paid for everything, we made a quick stop at Goodwin's. Billy ordered two extra-large Awful Awfuls, drinking one there and downing the other on the way back to Pelham, chain-smoking between sips. Back at the motel, I found no one in the room, so I walked over to the doctor's office—and was surprised to discover Dan alone.

"Where's Jeff?" I asked.

"Nurse Bass said she'd take him for the afternoon, give me a chance to catch up on some paperwork."

I sank down into the chair opposite Dan's desk—the patient facing the doctor—feeling more tired than I had felt in . . . well, the truth was, I couldn't now remember a moment since Jeffrey was born that I didn't feel completely drained. But at this juncture in time, all I wanted my husband to do was to get up from behind his desk, walk around to where I was sitting, take me in his arms, and tell me everything was going to be all right.

But instead, he just sat there, tapping his pencil against a stack of files on his desk, waiting for me to leave him in peace.

"Have we made a huge mistake here?" I suddenly heard myself blurting out.

Dan stopped tapping the pencil.

"What do you mean by that?"

What I mean is: me . . . you . . . him . . . everything . . .

"I'm just talking nonsense."

"You sure?"

I stood up.

"Maybe everything will look better after a night's sleep," I said.

"How did you get on with . . . what's his name again?"

I brought him up to date on the situation with Billy.

"In his own strange way he seems to know what he's doing. He's promised to give me an estimate for his work tonight, but with the kitchen and the bathroom, we're talking at least a thousand dollars, which is just about all the spare cash we have right now."

"You heard what Delores Bland said: they'll pay."

"And if they renege on that, then what?"

"They won't."

"How can you be so certain?"

"Because I'm the doctor here, and Pelham doesn't want to lose its doctor."

His voice was perfectly calm and controlled, but the hint of steel was unmistakable; a quiet diagnostic authority that he now turned on me, saying, "Give me a half hour to get through this paperwork and we'll take everything from there. And Nurse Bass is expecting you to pick up Jeff. Her house is second on the left down Longfellow Street."

I left his office, hating the fact that he'd treated me like a patient.

Longfellow Street was a little side alleyway off Pelham's main drag. Nurse Bass's house was a small ranch-style structure. As I walked up the front steps, I heard a television blaring inside—the loud animated voices of Rocky and Bullwinkle. I knocked on the door. Betty Bass answered it. She had a cigarette in her mouth and Jeffrey in one arm, sucking away on a pacifier that I didn't recognize as one of his own.

"Oh, hi," she said.

"Thanks for looking after him."

She just shrugged, then added, "My mom looks after my Tommy while I'm at work. You want to leave your kid with her, no problem."

"That's really nice of you," I said.

"Did Billy get everything sorted out for you with the carpenter?"

"He certainly did."

"He'll get the job done well," she said.

"We're certainly counting on him."

"He's real okay, Billy, especially considering his . . . uh . . . problem, and everything else he's been through."

And she explained that Billy had been born with the umbilical cord around his neck, suffering brain damage as a result.

"'Course his mother really didn't know how to cope with him. She was a total lush who kept having run-ins with the wrong kind of man . . . one of whom got real drunk one night when Billy was around eight and beat him so bad they had to rush him to Maine Medical in Portland. Poor boy was on life support for a week—and when he came out of his coma, the state took him away from his useless mother and put him in special schools for the next ten years of his life. The only good thing that ever came of the whole damn business was what happened to the guy who landed Billy in the hospital. Three nights after the cops picked him up, he was found dead in his cell."

"Did he kill himself?"

"That was the official story. Still, nobody asked any questions. As far as everyone in Pelham was concerned, it was the right ending to the story. And the amazing thing is, once Billy finished school and learned the decorating trade in Lewiston, he still wanted to come home to his mom. Mind you, by that point she was in a bad state—cirrhosis of the liver and all that. Still, she was delighted to have him back, and when she died two years later, Billy was pretty cut up . . . or as cut up as Billy ever shows. That's the thing about that boy—doesn't have a mean bone in his body, doesn't think badly of anyone . . . which kind of makes him unique round here."

"I'm sure that's not true," I said.

Nurse Bass just smiled a dry smile at me.

The next morning, I showed up at Miller's Grocery Store with Jeffrey. Miller's was the only place to buy food in town—a real old-style general store. In addition to the usual tins and boxes of stuff, it also served as Pelham's butcher, tobacconist, and newspaper shop. When I walked in, the woman behind the counter—in her early fifties, with a heavily lined face, wearing a smocklike apron, her hair in curlers, a cigarette in her mouth—nodded at me and said, "You're Dr. Buchan's missus."

"Uh . . . that's right," I said.

I must have seemed genuinely surprised, as the woman said, "Don't sound amazed. It's a small town. Hear you're not happy at the motel."

"My name's Hannah," I said, changing the subject and proffering my hand.

"Yeah, I knew that," she said, reluctantly shaking my hand.

"And this is my son, Jeffrey."

"Cute baby," she said laconically.

I remained all smiles. "And you are . . . ?"

"Jesse Miller."

"Very nice to meet you, ma'am."

By the time I left the shop twenty minutes later, Jesse Miller was acting civilized toward me. No, we hadn't become best friends, nor was she suddenly behaving in a gregarious, approachable manner (my powers of persuasion weren't that good!). But she was, at least, being courteous and pleasant—and that pleased me.

Over the next few days I kept up the charm offensive. I made certain I was friendly and open with everyone I met. Just as I also reacted with good grace if there was a setback—like the carpenter being delayed several days on finishing the kitchen cabinets.

"Hope you won't be too cross with me about that," Billy said when he broke the news.

"Why would I be cross with you?" I asked. "It's not your fault."

"Jesse Miller really bawled me out when the carpenter was late building new cabincts for her shop."

"I'm not Jesse Miller."

This provoked a big laugh from Billy.

"Can't say I disagree with you there."

Nor did he disagree with me about the flintiness of Nurse Bass, or the fact that everyone I met seemed to be so wary of outsiders.

"Well, I guess it's kind of the way things work here: until they get to know you, they're a little bit suspicious."

"And when they finally get to know you?"

"They're *really* suspicious."

Whenever Billy made a funny comment, not only would his strange laugh become explosive, but he'd also turn his back on you—as if he couldn't bear the scrutiny of anyone else seeing him so convulsed. Then again, Billy had trouble making eye contact with others. Whenever we talked he always turned away, staring down at his shoes, focusing his attention on the nearest wall . . . anything to avoid looking at you. But he wasn't at all slow on the uptake. In fact, he was much more in tune with everything going on around him than most people. For all his outward diffidence, it was clear that he had an empathy for other people's problems—and even wanted to help put things right.

One night, around a week into the renovations on the apartment, I couldn't surrender to sleep, so I got up around midnight and, having checked that Jeff was totally conked out, I left a note on the pillow next to Dan, telling him I'd gone out for a walk. I wandered out of the motel and walked up Main Street. A full moon was out. As I passed by Miller's Grocery, and the municipal library, and the one-room schoolhouse, and the Pelham Baptist Church, and the Pelham Episcopal Church, and the Pelham Third Church of Christ, Scientist, I couldn't help thinking about that day six months earlier when Dan and I had driven up here to meet Ben Bland and look around town. Dr. Bland was a very laid-back guy, and though he had shoulder-length hair and a big mustache, he seemed to be an accepted member of the community. And he painted such a great visual picture of life in Pelham—a small, tightly knit but accepting community; the sort of place where everyone left their doors open, where everyone went to church (but nobody made a big deal about it); where it was only a fifteen-minute drive to Sebago Lake—one of the most beautiful inland waterways in New England—and less than a half hour to the ski slopes of Mount Bridgton. I remember sitting in Miss Pelham's, thinking: *This is so rustic, so unadorned, the real America . . .*

Now all I could think was, *I could have been in Paris.*

My anxious reverie was interrupted by the sight of a light in the near distance . . . specifically, a light in the window of the apartment over the doctor's office. Approaching it, I saw the outline of Billy up on a ladder, a paint roller in one hand, a cigarette between his teeth. I glanced at my watch: twelve-thirteen a.m. I suddenly felt a massive stab of guilt as I realized he was working so late for us . . . *for me.*

I walked over to the back staircase behind the office and climbed up it, tapping quietly on the door. I could hear a radio playing in the background—what sounded like a play-by-play commentary of a baseball game. I opened the door. Billy was still up on the ladder, his back to me. I was terrified of surprising him, so I simply called his name softly. He seemed befuddled for a moment, turned around, and smiled when he saw it was me.

"Hey, Mrs. Buchan . . ."

"Billy, do you know what time it is?"

"No. Do you?"

"It's after midnight."

"So the Red Sox must be playing the Angels."

"What?"

"The Red Sox are out in California tonight—that's why the game is on so late. You a Red Sox fan? I'm a real Red Sox fan. My dad was supposed to be a real Red Sox fan too."

"You never knew him?"

"I showed up, he disappeared."

Another shy smile.

"Smoke?" he asked, fishing out his crumpled pack of L&Ms from his paint-splattered overalls.

"Thanks," I said, taking one. He took out a book of matches and lit one. After touching the tip of my cigarette, he lit his own, and started wolfing it down. After three deep drags, nearly half the cigarette was gone.

"Do you really like working this late?" I asked.

"I'm not much of a sleeper. And a job . . . it's something to do, right? And you need to get out of that motel fast, ma'am . . ."

"Billy, as I've told you before, my name isn't *Mrs. Buchan* or *ma'am* . . . it's Hannah, okay?"

As I said this, I reached out to touch his arm—in what I thought was a simple act of reassurance. But as soon as my fingers made contact with his wrist, Billy flinched and pulled away.

I was thrown by this.

"Sorry if I . . ."

He shook his hand, signaling me to say no more, then walked around the room in a little circle, puffing heavily on his cigarette, trying to calm himself down. I wanted to say something but sensed it was better to remain silent. After a few moments, he tossed the now-dead cigarette on the floor, lit another, and said, "I've got to get back to work now."

"Billy, I didn't mean to . . ."

Another frantic wave of his right hand.

"I've got to get back to work now," he said.

"Fine, fine," I said, even though everything wasn't fine, and I didn't know what to do to make things fine, except leave. So that's what I did.

"See you tomorrow, Billy."

He looked away and said nothing.

The next morning, I wheeled Jeffrey back down to the apartment. It was around eleven, and Billy was already working. When I walked in, Billy nodded shyly, climbed down off the ladder, fished out his cigarettes, and offered me one.

"You haven't been here all night, have you?" I asked as he lit my cigarette.

"Oh, heck, no," he said. "Got home around . . . I dunno . . . sun was just coming up."

"But that was probably around six-thirty. Surely you need more than four hours' sleep."

"No, four hours just about does it. Anyway, you need to get out of that motel, and all going well, you might just be able to move in here next weekend."

"That would be great, but not if you're going to lose more sleep—"

"You really should talk to Estelle Verne," he said, cutting me off.

"Who?" I asked.

"Estelle Verne. She's the town librarian, and she needs an assistant."

"Oh . . . right," I said, just a little confused by the change in the conversation's direction.

"I told her about you, and how you want a job."

"Did I ever say that to you?"

"Uh, I dunno . . . but you do want a job, right?"

"I don't know . . . I'm still taking care of Jeffrey during the day . . ."

"But Betty Bass's mom will look after him while you're at the library . . ."

God, everyone in Pelham really did know everything about everyone else.

". . . and you really don't have to worry about Mrs. Bass's mom. I know she don't keep the neatest house, but she's real good with kids . . ."

"I'll talk to Nurse Bass's mom today, okay?"

"And you'll talk with Estelle Verne too?"

"Billy, you're really organizing my life," I said.

"Just want you to be happy here, ma'am."

"But I am happy here."

"No, you're not," he said, stubbing out his cigarette on the floor.

Then he turned away from me, picked up his roller, and went back to work, letting me know our conversation was now over.

I went downstairs, feeling numb and confused. I walked into the doctor's office. Nurse Bass was behind the reception desk. She gave me a nod, then turned back to some papers she was filing and said, "Doctor's busy right now."

"Fine," I said. "Tell him I stopped by—and that it's nothing important."

I turned the baby carriage around. As I started to leave, Nurse Bass asked, "You going to take the job at the library?"

I forced myself to smile.

"We'll see," I said.

SIX

EVERY SO OFTEN, you run into someone with whom you instantly click, who, from the outset, becomes your friend. This was the case with Estelle Verne. From the moment I walked into Pelham Public Library, she put me at my ease.

"So you're my new assistant," she said, as I approached her desk.

I was thrown by this. "Am I coming to work here?" I asked.

"Looks that way to me."

"But don't you want to interview me first?"

"No need—even before you walked in here I knew you'd be just fine."

"How?"

"Pelham's a small town, and everyone kept telling me that you were an independent-minded cookie, which immediately made me think: that's my new assistant."

Estelle Verne was around fifty. She was a slight woman—she couldn't have stood more than five feet two—with sharp features and a short mane of salt-and-pepper hair. But it was her eyes that told me she wasn't merely a flinty, small-town New England type. They radiated mischief, intelligence, and a fiercely independent point of view.

She was a real Maine girl. Raised in Farmington, where her father had taught at the local teacher training college, Estelle had gone to the University of Maine in Orono, where she majored in English and library science. Then she'd found a job at the Carnegie Library in Portland, where she met a man in his mid-thirties who came in one day and asked her if the library had a copy of Sinclair Lewis's *Babbitt.*

"I thought that showed good taste—and the fellow was pretty reasonable-looking: well dressed, polite, seemed to be curious about things, because he started asking me for recommendations of other books to read. That's when I met George Verne. Turned out he was a banker in a town I'd never heard of called Pelham, where his dad had been the banker before him. He came to Portland once a week on business, and he wasn't married, and he asked me if I was doing anything for lunch.

"He took me to a little luncheonette near the library, and though I found him a little dry, I did like his intelligence and his curiosity about books and current affairs and ideas. He was full of stories about the three years he served in the Army during the war, helping liberate Italy, actually serving under General Patton.

"The next week, he came back into the library, returned the Sinclair Lewis, asked me for James Jones's *From Here to Eternity,* and invited me out again to the same luncheonette. That was the beginning of things between us. And I was pleased—because I was thirty, still living in a rooming house, and had pretty much given up on the idea of marriage or having kids. All the other men I'd met in Maine seemed to be put off by my waspish tongue, but George Verne never seemed to be bothered by that. On the contrary, I think, back then, he thought my sarcasm was worldly. Which, to a boy from Pelham, it probably was."

Those weekly lunches turned into weekly dinners. After three months, he invited Estelle to Pelham for the weekend—to the big red clapboard house off Main Street in which Pelham's only banker resided with his widowed mother. Mrs. Verne was very frail at the time, but still ran her son's life.

"I think she liked me, because I could think for myself, and also because she knew she wasn't long for this world—she had a very fast-acting bone cancer—and there would be another woman to step in to organize her son. Or, at least, that's how I'm sure she saw it.

"Now, believe me, if you think Pelham's a nowhere place now, you should have seen it in 1953. But Mrs. Verne was a shrewd old operator—she could tell I thought Pelham was about as appealing as a life sentence. But on the afternoon before George was going to drive me back to Portland, she told her son to take a powder for an hour, then sat me down in what she called 'the parlor'—she was that kind of nineteenth-century New England lady—and cut me a deal. If I'd marry George and move to Pelham and have his babies and keep the Verne name alive, she'd give me a library. That's right—my very own library. Up until then, Pelham had just three stacks of books in the basement of the Episcopalian church. What she proposed was renovating the building you're in right now, which used to be a feed store, and giving me $10,000 to stock the place with books. There was a bit of family money that she had to spend or see it end up in the IRS man's pocket—so the library was one big tax write-off. And she also got to marry off her aging son at the same time. And I guess I was thinking: *He's not the worst. I get to have kids. And I also end up with a library I can do anything I want with. And I'm going to make George buy me a secondhand car as a wedding gift, so I can drive off to Portland whenever I need to make an escape.*

As it turned out, Estelle discovered that day-to-day life with George was something of a bore. He was tight with money and turned out to be one of those secret drinkers who put away a bottle of booze during the course of the day. The kids she wanted never arrived ("I often wondered if all that rye whiskey he drank caused the problem"). They quickly drifted apart, and when Old Mrs. Verne died two years after their marriage, they started leading completely separate lives.

"Still, it really didn't bother me. Because Mrs. Verne had been true to her word when it came to the library. She even used her influence with the local district council to get ongoing funding for its upkeep and its staff. And this year, when the Democrats finally won the council elections for Bridgton and environs—and that's what they consider us, *environs*—I was finally able to convince the cheap bastards to pay for an assistant. And you're it."

Estelle quizzed me about a wide range of subjects—beginning with my taste in books. She approved of my love of Flaubert and Edith Wharton, and surprised me by saying that my dad's book on Jefferson was one that she always recommended to anyone who ever asked for "something about the Founding Fathers." She wanted me to know that, when she first moved to Pelham, she too had found it hard to fit in. "I was an interloper who was corrupting young minds in Pelham—not that there are too many of those—by stocking Norman Mailer's *The Naked and the Dead* in the library. It probably took me the better part of two years before anyone here began to consider me part of the woodwork."

"Well, that means I might as well accept my outsider status until we leave next summer."

"Now I don't want to sound unduly pessimistic about things, but that does strike me as a prudent way forward. Because everyone in Pelham is suspicious of anyone who's not from Pelham until they've lived there long enough to be finally considered *from Pelham* . . . if you follow my logic here. But at least you've got one ally here now."

The job suited me perfectly—nine-thirty until two, five days a week, for which I'd receive a whopping $60. I didn't care. A job was a reason to get up in the morning, a source of focus beyond the all-encompassing business of minding a baby. I knew now that I wasn't cut out to be the stay-at-home little wife-and-mother—and, without work, I felt adrift, housebound, resentful. Oh, how my mother would have laughed.

"Of course, you're going to need someone to look after the baby while you're at the library," Estelle said. "And though I know she's not the warmest person on the face of the planet . . ."

I laughed.

"How could you say such a thing?" I asked.

Later that morning, I stopped by the doctor's office with Jeffrey. Nurse Bass was behind the reception desk. Per usual, she was chilly.

"I've taken the job at the library," I said.

"Uh-huh," she said, all enthusiasm.

"And I'd like to talk to your mom now about looking after Jeffrey."

"Come by tonight," she said.

Barbara London liked to be called Babs. Unlike her daughter, she was a gregarious, friendly woman with an easy laugh. She was around sixty: tall, hefty, and (as I came to discover) always dressed in a housecoat that was dappled with baby food and cigarette ash. Though I was now smoking almost a pack a day, my intake struck me as downright moderate compared to Barbara London's habit. She seemed to have three Tareytons on the go at any one time.

Still, from the outset, she won me over with her no-crap charm.

"Now that's what I call one *gorgeous* baby," she said, reaching down to pick Jeffrey up. Surprisingly, my son didn't seem to mind these alien hands clutching him.

"We're gonna get along real fine, you and me," she said to Jeff. "And you're gonna have fun here."

"Here" was the living room of the house that Babs shared with her daughter, her grandson, and her son-in-law, Tony. He ran the local garage and, like his wife, he was the strong, sullen type. As I was chatting with Babs, he came into the room—wearing overalls and a T-shirt, carrying a can of Schlitz. Though he was thin—with a wispy mustache and hangdog eyes—his biceps were noticeably bulky. So too was the Marine Corps tattoo on his left arm, the words *Semper Fidelis* dyed red.

"Hey," he said quietly.

"This here's the doc's wife," Babs said. "And that's her little boy, Jeffy."

"Drive a Volvo, don't you?" he asked.

"That's right," I said.

"Gotta go," he said, and started leaving the house. Before he reached the door, his wife emerged from the kitchen, her baby, Tom, over one shoulder.

"Where you going?" she asked Tony.

"Out," he said, and was gone.

"He say where he was going?" she asked her mother.

"Yeah. Out," Babs said, then turned to me and asked, "Get you a beer, hon?"

I accepted a can of Schlitz and a Tareyton cigarette. Betty had put her boy into his playpen. Babs picked up Jeffrey and placed him alongside Tom. The playpen was filled with assorted wooden toys and looked like it needed a good cleaning—but I tried not to stare at it for too long.

"Now, hon," Babs said, "as I am lookin' after Tom here while Betty is out, I would be delighted to add Jeffy to our happy home."

She gave Betty a big toothless smile. Her daughter glowered back at her.

"That would be wonderful," I said, then explained the hours I'd be working and asked her how much she wanted a week to look after Jeffrey.

"Don't want nothin'," she said. "'Cause, like I said, I'm already babysittin' my grandson here . . ."

"You've got to accept something from me," I said.

"Okay, five bucks."

"A day?"

"With you on sixty bucks a week? Hell no. Five bucks a week will do me fine. Keep me in smokes."

Later that night, when Dan walked in after work, his appearance threw me. He'd had a haircut. Not a minor trim, but a radical crop that reduced his shoulder-length hair to short back and sides.

"Let me guess," I said. "You've enlisted."

My attempt at wit did not play well, as Dan looked tired and strained.

"So you don't like it?" he asked, sounding testy.

I didn't take the hint and change the subject. Instead I said, "No, I don't like it. It makes you look like a drill sergeant."

"I only got it cut because . . ."

"I know, I know. It's easier to fit in here this way."

"Something like that, yes. And you think that's a *conformist* thing to do, don't you?"

"Dan—"

"It offends your *counterculture* sensibilities, right?"

"Why the hell are you so angry?"

"I'm just wrecked, that's all," he said, kicking off his shoes and flopping down on the bed. "And it's been a particularly bad day."

"So that gives you the right to take it out on me?"

"I wasn't taking anything out on you."

"Yes, you were."

"You're not happy here, are you?"

"I'm not happy in this damn motel."

"That's not what I'm talking about."

"Hey," I said, trying to steer us off this subject, "I took the job in the library."

"Yeah, I heard," he said.

"Aren't you pleased?"

"Of course I'm pleased. And Nurse Bass told me that you agreed to let her mom look after Jeff. Politically, it's the right call."

"I liked Babs, although . . ."

"Yeah?"

"It's a little grubby in there."

"But not so grubby that . . ."

"I wouldn't dream of leaving Jeff anywhere that wasn't safe."

"I know that."

"Glad to hear it," I said.

"Are you trying to start a fight?" he asked.

"No," I said, "you were the one who started it."

We moved out of the motel the next day after settling a bill for almost $200 for the two weeks we spent there. Considering that Dan was only being paid $600 a month and that we had been offered free accommodations at Bland's house as part of the deal, it was just a little galling to have to pay for the pleasure of camping out at that "charming" motel.

"Don't worry—we'll get it back," Dan said.

"You know, I've also just written out a check for six hundred dollars to Billy for all the repairs . . . which essentially wipes out any savings we have."

"I'll get on to Delores tomorrow."

"No, *I'll* get on to her. You worry about your patients, let me take care of the move-in."

Actually, it was Billy who did the move-in. We'd been storing what little furniture we had in a local barn that he'd found for us. Now he hauled everything out, lugged it up the narrow back stairs, and reassembled it in the freshly painted apartment. Because of its relatively cramped size, we just had room for our double bed, a chest of drawers, a sofa, a large easy chair, and a simple pine table and chairs. Billy had done fantastic work. Considering the grim state of the place when we'd arrived, the transformation was astonishing. Freshly painted white walls, stripped and sealed floorboards, a renovated kitchen, and a toilet that no longer looked like a public health violation. I tried to forget the tiny size of the space. It was simply good to be somewhere clean and relatively airy, with our own simple furniture. And thanks to Billy's amazing energy (he started moving our furniture at seven in the morning), we had the entire apartment unpacked and set up by the time Dan came home that evening.

"Coming home" for him meant mounting the back stairs from his office. When he showed up that evening, he had Nurse Bass with him. She blinked in shock when she saw the renovations, but quickly recovered and said, "Just wanted to see what you'd done here."

"It's Billy who did the work," I said, nodding in his direction. He smiled shyly and continued adjusting a kitchen shelf. "Feel like a beer?"

"Got stuff to do at home," she said.

"It's fantastic, isn't it?" Dan said, looking around.

"Makes a change," she said, then turned and left.

"Well, I think it's great," Dan said and kissed me. "Thank you."

Later that night, he made love to me. Try as much as I did to engage in the act, I still felt curiously detached. This was not the first time I'd been indifferent during sex—especially as we'd hardly made love since Jeffrey was born.

"You okay?" he asked afterward.

"Yeah, fine."

"It didn't sound like . . ."

"I didn't want to wake Jeff," I said.

"Right," he said, but he didn't sound convinced.

"Can I go to sleep now?" I asked.

Happily, Dan didn't push this point—or demand why exactly this part of our marriage had hit a bad patch. I couldn't explain it myself. I realized this was crappy behavior. And I knew that I wasn't treating Dan fairly. But right now, all I could see was an endless, empty horizon of broken nights and dirty diapers. And every time I turned on the television and saw news coverage of an antiwar demonstration, or watched footage of the Allman Brothers concert at Watkins Glen, or read in *Time* about Vonnegut's new novel—I felt as if I had been physically removed from everything interesting in 1973. I woke up every morning with this terrible sinking feeling that I had landed myself in Permanent Dullsville and there was nothing I could do except tough things out. I was trapped. And I hated it, especially the fact that I myself had constructed the dead end in which I now found myself.

But when my mother showed up a week later she knew immediately that things weren't exactly stable between us.

"So when did you stop having sex?" she asked me.

"I'm still having sex with Dan," I said.

"You mean you're duty-fucking him."

"That's a little blunt, Mom."

"But accurate. And who can blame you, living in this dump?"

I didn't know if she was referring to the apartment or Pelham—and didn't push to find out. Instead I said, "Don't all new marriages go through their teething pains?"

"Stop smoothing over the cracks, Hannah. You're not getting on—and it shows."

"Everything's fine."

"Liar."

Much to my surprise, Mom didn't press me further about the state of my marriage. Nor did she make many scathing comments about Pelham, except to say that she liked Estelle and thought Nurse Bass (whom she met outside Dan's office) was "a quintessential example of Grumpy White Trash." Maybe her lack of nonstop acerbity had something to do with the fact that her flying visit was just a quick layover en route to a talk she was giving at Bowdoin College about her work. A few days before she arrived, she called to explain that she was passing through Maine, and didn't have a lot of time, but wanted to drop by and see me and her grandson.

"How much time is 'a little time'?" I asked.

"About six hours."

True to her word, she arrived in Pelham at eleven, and left at five. I showed her around the library and introduced her to Estelle. Then Dan took us all out to lunch at the local diner. He was preoccupied throughout, dashing off after forty-five minutes when Nurse Bass called to tell him that some pregnant farmer's wife had just burst her waters. That's when she asked me when I stopped having sex with Dan. And though she'd been briefed about the disaster that was our apartment, her only comment when she saw it was, "Where do you run to after you and Dan have had a fight?"

"We don't have fights," I said, wondering if my nose was about to enlarge, Pinocchio-style. My mom just rolled her eyes and changed the subject, asking me what I did for fun around here.

"Well, there's Sebago Lake and some great hikes . . ."

"So where have you hiked?"

"Nowhere."

"And how many times have you been to the lake?"

"We're planning to go next weekend. Anyway, with all the problems we've been having with somewhere to live . . ."

"So I guess you watch a lot of TV."

"Well, that old black-and-white set of ours only pulls in two channels. Anyway, I'm not much of a television type. And between my job in the library and looking after Jeff . . ."

"I know: a rich and fulfilling life."

Long pause—during which I fought back tears and the desire to scream, rage, and tell my mother exactly what I thought of her. She saw this—and reacted out of character, coming over to me and squeezing my arm and saying, "If this gets too much, if you really feel like you're heading for the edge, you can always come home."

I looked at her, stupefied.

"You mean that?" I asked.

"Of course I do. And I mean you *and* Jeff."

"You wouldn't want us."

She gave me a tough, no-bullshit look.

"How do you know what I want?"

Again she changed the subject, mentioning that Dad had just written an "extended jeremiad" for *Harper's* about appearing on the White House "enemies list," and pushing for a congressional judicial inquiry, especially in the wake of the firing of the special prosecutor, Archibald Cox.

"You did hear about the Saturday Night Massacre, didn't you?" Mom asked, mentioning the recent evening when Nixon dismissed the entire judicial team that was investigating the Watergate break-in.

"I read about it in *Time.*"

"*Time* is the American *Pravda.*"

"Don't you think that's a little extreme, Mom?"

"Sure it is . . . and so what? Anyway, you should subscribe to *Harper's* because then you can read your father coming across all Jeffersonian and pretending that he has some influence on affairs of state . . . whereas the truth of the matter is that he is just some minor-league academic at some minor-league—"

I didn't want to hear this, so I cut her off, asking, "And where is Dad right now?"

"Off at an American Historical Conference in Seattle, then heading across the border to Vancouver Island, allegedly to hole up in some hotel for ten days and work on his new book. But what he doesn't know is that *I* know he's traveling with his new girlfriend, who—"

"Mom, I'd rather not know."

"*What* would you rather not know? The identity of your father's newest twenty-four-year-old conquest, or the fact that, yet again, your father is fucking around?"

"Both."

"But why? It's all just part of life's rich cavalcade. And like the dumb schmuck that I am, I've accepted that we now have an 'open' marriage, and all I have to do is turn the other cheek, pretend that nothing is going on . . ."

Her face tightened—and for a moment or two, I thought she was going to cry. But when I tried to put my arm around her to console her, she took a step back from me.

"I'm fine," she said, regaining control of her voice. "Just fine."

We spent what remained of the afternoon visiting the work site that was the Bland house ("You shouldn't simply screw them for the renovations on the apartment," Mom said, "but for all the marital crap they caused you"), then we drove over to Sebago Lake. This was Mom's idea. She'd spent several summers there at summer camp and hadn't been back for years.

"It's about time you looked at your neighboring natural wonder," she said. "It's only fifteen minutes away."

Mom was right about the wondrousness of Sebago Lake—a vast expanse of becalmed water, set amid dense woodlands and minor hills. As it was a weekday, the lake was all but empty—one sole canoeist rippling its mirrored surface. We went down to the water. Jeffrey was asleep in his stroller, so we left him on the bank while we walked the few yards to the edge of the lake. Mom kicked her shoes off and tucked her toes into the mud, shivering as the chill of the water hit.

"I'd forgotten how damn cold it was," she said.

"Well, count me out," I said.

"Coward."

We fell silent, staring out at all that water. Out of nowhere, my mom reached out, took my hand, and held it. I looked over at her. She didn't make eye contact. She just kept staring out in the direction of that soft autumn sun, which was just beginning to recede and bathe the lake in a bourbon glow. For a moment or two, she seemed to be smiling. For a moment or two, she seemed to be content—something I could never remember her being before. I wanted to say . . . *what*? That I so loved and feared her? That I always so wanted her approval and never seemed able to earn it? That I knew her own life was full of deceptions and disappointments, but that, *shit*, we were here together now and had the chance to . . . ?

I didn't complete that thought, because almost as if she were reading my mind, Mom disengaged her hand from mine and clutched her arms around her.

"Cold . . ." she said.

"Yeah," I said quietly. The moment had come and gone.

"Thirty-four years," she said.

"What?"

"I was at this lake thirty-four years ago. Summer camp. Christ, how I hated the great outdoors, especially since, just to really torture me, my mother had chosen this camp full of shiksas from Westchester County. I was the only Jewish girl there, which meant that all those vicious little Waspy bitches thought I put the *id* in *Yid* . . . not that anyone had any idea what an id was back in 1940. Still, I did do one big id thing that summer: I lost my virginity on the far side of the lake. And since one of the camp counselors found me and the guy in mid-act . . ."

"Do I really want to know this, Mom?"

"Sure you do. And you know, the guy in question, Morris Pinsker—can you imagine losing your cherry to someone named Morris?—is now a very respected orthodontist in New Jersey."

"How do you know that?"

"Saw a wedding announcement for his daughter, Essie, in *The New York Times* around six months ago. Morris, Essie, and his wife's named Mildred. You'd never guess they were Jews."

"I thought you said you went to a Waspy camp?"

"There was a neighboring camp of circumcised boys—and occasionally, we had a social or a dance . . . although I know some of the Waspy mothers objected to all their Greenwich, Connecticut, daughters mixing with the Hasidim . . ."

"And that's how you met the future orthodontist and ended up with him in the woods?"

"Yeah, it was as prosaic as that. And the thing was, it just . . . *happened.* I met the guy at this campfire dance, he asked if I wanted to take a walk by the lake, the next thing I knew we were doing it under a tree."

"But you hardly knew . . . what was his name again?"

"Morris. That's right. I'd only known him for around ten minutes before I let him get into my pants."

"Why do you feel it necessary to tell me this?"

"Because it's another example of just how idiotic life really is. And because it's the first time I've been back here since."

"So that's why you really wanted to visit me?"

"You got it," she said, giving me a sardonic smile. "A romantic déjà vu by the lake."

"That incident was romantic?"

"You've got to be kidding. Especially since Morris had spots all over his ass."

I couldn't help but laugh.

"And when the counselor found you with Mr. Spotty Ass . . . ?"

"I was expelled from the camp, sent back to Brooklyn in disgrace. Your grandfather refused to talk to me for two months, and my mom kept telling me I was a whore."

"That must have been fun."

"Hey, it's always complicated between parents and kids . . . as you'll find out."

"I'm sure I will."

We fell silent for a moment. Then, "How can thirty-four years go so fast?" she asked.

"A year still seems pretty long to me."

"Wait until you're fifty—and time just seems to evaporate around you. Blink once it's Christmas, blink again it's summer. And you realize you've got—what?—twenty, twenty-five of these blinks left, and you start to wonder what the sum total of everything really is, and you make dumb, stupid pilgrimages to some backwoods lake where you humped some guy with pimples on his *tokhes.*"

Jeffrey began to stir. Mom said, "I guess that's my cue to shut the fuck up."

She drove us back to Pelham, dropping us off in front of the apartment. She turned down my offer of a cup of tea, telling me she'd better start heading off to Brunswick and her talk at Bowdoin. But she did get out of the car to kiss Jeffrey good-bye.

"Don't give your mother too hard a time," she told him. He just gurgled in response. Then she leaned over and did something highly unusual—she hugged me. Not a big, all-enveloping, let-me-comfort-you-with-maternal-warmth hug—but nonetheless *a hug*. It was something Mom rarely dispensed.

"You know where to find me if you need me," she said, then drove off.

The next day, at the library, Estelle said, "I really liked your mom. A complete original."

"That she certainly is," I said. "But sadly, not the happiest camper who ever walked the face of the planet."

"Hey, it comes with the territory."

"What territory?"

"Being an original . . . which is a little easier in a place like New York. But in small-town Vermont? It's like being a cyclone trapped in a well. Lots of combustion."

"That's a polite way of putting it," I said.

Certainly I wasn't going to turn into a trapped cyclone in Pelham. I was working very hard to maintain a bright perspective on everything. The job in the library wasn't exactly taxing—stacking books, checking out books, ordering books, dealing with the few members of the public who crossed our doors. If we had eight to ten visitors a day, it was an event—though once a week, all twelve kids from the local primary school came in and caused pleasant mayhem for around an hour. Otherwise, there wasn't much in the way of work to fill up my five-hour day.

"Are you sure you need an assistant?" I asked Estelle after my third week there.

"Of course I don't," she said. "But I do want the company . . ."

Estelle was really good news—funny, bright, and incessantly curious. Bar my father, she was about the best-read person I'd ever met ("Well, what else am I supposed to do around here?"). She made a point of spending one weekend a month in Boston, to visit the Museum of Fine Arts, make a concert pilgrimage to Symphony Hall, haunt the used bookshops around Harvard Square, and eat cherrystones and halibut at some place on the harbor.

"Didn't you ever think of getting a job down there?" I asked.

"Sure, I thought about it when I was working in Portland. And after George died, I did think, *Now's your chance.*"

"What stopped you?"

"Myself, I guess," she said, lighting up a cigarette. "Like there's no reason for me to stay here—except the library, which is my baby, but which is never going to be more than what it is right now. But . . . I don't know . . . something has always kept me from making the leap. Fear, maybe . . . even though I know that sounds kind of lame."

"No," I said, "it doesn't."

She looked at me and smiled, and said, "Someone once said that the biggest roadblocks you encounter in life are the ones you construct for yourself."

"Tell me about it."

She offered me a cigarette from her pack.

"You're still young."

"True, but I often feel as if I've really shortchanged myself."

"Welcome to adult life. Anyway, you can still do something about it."

"Like what? Leave Dan?"

A long pause.

"I have thought about it," I said.

"Are things that bad between you?"

"Not really. Just a little . . . static, I guess would be the right word."

"Static isn't an uncommon thing in most marriages. Anyway, you've had a couple of big changes over the past few months, not to mention . . ."

"I know, I know—getting shut out of Bland's house. And yeah, I know I should be patient, and yeah, I know I should also take into account all the upheavals, and yeah, I know I'm probably being very hard on him . . ."

I stubbed out my cigarette, and reached for another.

"How long have you been together now?" she asked.

"Since my freshman year at college."

"And there's been no one else?"

I shook my head.

"Well, that's admirable," she said.

"And a little boring too?"

"I didn't say that."

"No, I did."

I lit my cigarette.

"You never heard any of this from me," I said.

"Don't worry—I am the only person in Pelham who believes in keeping a confidence. But if I may impart a small piece of advice, it's this: hang in there. Dan strikes me as a pretty good guy, and as you may know, he's made a very good impression in town. People do like him. And though it might be difficult now, a certain equilibrium usually returns to a marriage if all the basics are right . . . and if he's not doing anything drastic like cheating repeatedly on you or beating you up all the time."

"Cheating *repeatedly*?" I asked.

"All men cheat."

"Did your husband?"

"No, George was too boring for that."

"You sound disappointed."

"A little drama wouldn't have hurt things. But George didn't do drama. The fact is, George didn't do anything out of the norm."

"Nor has Dan."

"How can you be so sure?"

"I know the guy. And even if he wanted to cheat, he hasn't."

"Why's that?"

"Because, like most med students, he's been too damn busy over the last four years."

Though I knew I had a confidante in Estelle, I made a decision not to bore her further with my personal stuff. I didn't want to be defined by my problems, and there was a deeply ingrained New England side of me that considered it inappropriate to speak about personal mess. Anyway, the mess wasn't that appalling. Though the apartment was cramped, we were both so relieved to be out of that damn motel that we didn't complain about the constrained space in which we were operating. On the contrary, every time I saw Billy around town, I would always tell him how pleased we were with the great job he had done for us. And he was so committed to seeing things right for us that he often showed up at the apartment, toolkit in hand, wondering if there was anything that needed repairing.

"I think that guy has a crush on you," Dan said to me one evening.

"Oh, please," I said.

"You should see the way he looks at you."

"Well, there's nothing wrong with that . . . unless, of course, you're jealous."

"That is a joke, right?"

"Yes, Dan. That is *definitely* a joke."

I quickly changed the subject, because as part of my new domestic strategy I was trying to avoid all conflict between us. Ten months, three days—that was the length of our sentence in Pelham. The time would pass, I told myself.

"There's only one way to live here," Estelle said one morning. "Leave as often as you can."

But as we had still "just arrived" in Pelham, I wouldn't be venturing far beyond its boundaries. So the day's routine became the routine of my days. I'd get up with Jeff at six and make breakfast. Dan would leave for work at seven-thirty. I'd do household stuff until it was time to drop Jeff off at Babs's house. After that, I'd grab a muffin and a coffee at Miss Pelham's and head to the library. At two, my working day was done. I'd pick up Jeff at Babs's house, and then load him in the car and drive over to Bridgton, where there was a Stop-n-Shop supermarket that had all the stuff you couldn't buy at Miller's—though I made certain I did purchase at least $5 of essentials at Miller's every week, otherwise my lack of custom (bar the morning paper and cigarettes) would be noted. On the days when I didn't have to go to the supermarket—and if it wasn't raining—I'd drive Jeff and myself over to Sebago Lake and wheel him for half a mile along the path that had been cut by the water's edge, always marveling at just how damn beautiful it was, how limitless it seemed.

Then it was home to get Jeff fed. After that, I would get dinner ready and finish up any other domestic or child-care chores. Dan would arrive back around six—though it could be later if he had to make an early-evening house call, or had to visit a patient at Bridgton Hospital. Dan loved spaghetti and lasagne, so I did my best to oblige—though three days a week we did eat lamb chops or an omelet or meat loaf.

We always tried to have wine with dinner, although Dan would restrict himself to a glass or two. Most of his evenings were now spent studying big, weighty textbooks on orthopedics because my husband had now decided to become a "bone man" and to pursue a residency in orthopedics at the end of our year in Pelham.

I only discovered that Dan had made this decision when, one morning, Tom Killian, the local postman, dropped by the library to ask if we had any new Hornblower novels in stock, and to mention in passing that Dan must be into some very serious reading right now, as he'd just delivered two big boxes of books to his office. When I got home that afternoon, the books were already stacked up by the easy chair in the living room where Dan usually sat in the evening. That night, over dinner, I said, "That's a lot of books . . ."

"Yeah, decided to bone up on orthopedics," he said.

"Pun intended?"

"Yeah—pun intended."

"You've decided to become an orthopedist?"

"Certainly thinking about it."

"Well, you're obviously more than thinking about it if you've just ordered all those textbooks. They must have cost a fortune."

"Two hundred and twelve dollars—postage included. You have a problem with that?"

"Of course not. What happened to pediatrics?"

"I'm not ruling out pediatrics . . ."

"But as you've just spent a small fortune on orthopedic textbooks . . ."

"Okay, I should have talked this over with you. Sorry. It's just . . . I kind of thought you'd be disappointed that I wasn't following pediatrics."

"I'm surprised, that's all. I mean, orthopedics is pretty nuts-and-bolts stuff, isn't it?"

"I kind of like that aspect of it—and the surgical dimension. There are all these new breakthroughs that might come about in the next ten, fifteen years—hip replacements, plastic joints . . ."

"Sounds totally nuts-and-bolts to me."

"It's interesting . . . and it will probably be very lucrative."

"*Lucrative?*" I said, repeating the word with considerable surprise. "Since when did you get interested in *lucrative*?"

"Is this how you want to live for the rest of your life?" he asked, pointing to the apartment.

"This is not how we're going to live forever. This is a stopgap solution . . ."

"I know what it is, and I know that once we're in the Bland place, we'll be much happier. But I still don't want to be thirty-five and trying to support a family on eight grand a year."

"You could still be a very successful—and very good—pediatrician . . ."

"And deal with chicken pox and diaper rash and tonsillitis until I'm sixty-five? Where's the challenge in that?"

"I just wish you'd have told me you were thinking this way."

"Okay, Hannah. Point taken. It won't happen again."

What else could I say but "Fine"—and wonder why Dan always had to be so damn secretive, why he kept such big considerations to himself and refused to involve me in the decision-making process. But not wanting to travel down that road, I decided to accept his apology and let him get on with his nighttime studying of all things orthopedic.

So after dinner five nights a week, Dan would curl up in his armchair and plunge into his textbooks, making copious notes on yellow legal pads. The apartment was so small that it was impossible for me to do anything but read while he studied—though I did negotiate an hour every week when he put down his books and we watched reruns of *Rowan & Martin's Laugh-In* together. Otherwise, I read novels and was in bed most nights by ten-thirty.

Day in, day out, my routine hardly varied. Dan often worked Saturday mornings, but we always tried to take a long walk somewhere on Sundays. We were never invited around to anyone's house—largely because the only other young couples with children in Pelham were people like Nurse Bass and her husband, who looked upon us as college types with whom they had nothing in common. Even Estelle, for all her friendliness at work, didn't want to socialize after hours (she hinted to me on several occasions that she treated home as a refuge and didn't see the need to have friends around, especially as she escaped often to Portland or Boston). So we really had no one to hang with except each other—and given that Dan was filling every possible hour with study . . .

Meanwhile, Dad was back in the news, having just been interviewed on ABC bitterly condemning the decision to award Henry Kissinger the Nobel Peace Prize with Le Duc Tho for negotiating a cease-fire in Vietnam. It was a "cease-fire"—as Dad pointed out in his best outraged patrician tones—that had yet to come into effect.

I called Dad a few days later. He was, per usual, affectionate and harried. He didn't have long to talk, as he was rushing to a lecture, but he was glad that I saw him on national television, and now he was certain that he was at the top of the Nixon Enemies List, and did I read his article in *Harper's* with the very clever title "Dynamite Money" about the machinations that went on to award Kissinger the Nobel? And how were things in Pelham? And was his grandson doing well? And got to go now, will call in a couple of days, hope you are keeping busy up there.

Well, by my estimation, I was reading five books a week, which did keep my nights busy. Meanwhile, the job was steady. Bar the usual daily banter with Estelle, it was free of all surprises. Jeff slept progressively better. Dan and I continued to make love twice a week, and though I tried to show some interest, I continued to feel detached throughout, occasionally faking orgasm just to let him think I was engaged in the event. We continued to act as if all was well between us.

"There are times when I feel as if I am simply some cardboard cutout, being moved from place to place, day in, day out," I told Margy during one of our weekly phone calls. "And I don't know how to break out of this, except by doing something dramatic, which would mean creating havoc. And as there is no way I am going to create havoc, I have no choice but to continue acting out this damn role I'm in. Come June we will be gone from Pelham, and we'll either be back in Providence or in some third-rate city like Milwaukee or Pittsburgh for Dan's residency in fucking orthopedics, because Dan really prefers third-rate cities, and I'm too damn lame and tame—hey, that rhymes!—to do anything about it, and I'll probably get pregnant again, and I might as well write off my entire life, and I think I'm really beginning to sound like a self-obsessed bore, and maybe I'll get off this subject and ask you what's going on in your life?"

Margy laughed. "Well, at least you haven't completely lost your sense of humor."

"Yeah, that surprises me too. But come on, make me jealous and tell me everything that's going on in the big bad city."

"Well, on the guy front, it's the usual Bum of the Month club—the last loser being a would-be playwright named Mark who had a production of his latest magnum opus in some warehouse way downtown. Anyway, the play was all about the persecution of St. Sebastian for his boy love predilections—and the subject matter should have told me something, because two days after the opening, Mark broke down and confessed that he was, in fact, a switch-hitter. As in: bisexual. As in: 'Oh shit, do I know how to pick 'em.'

"Anyway, the somewhat better news is that it looks like my days in gift shop sales are numbered, because I have a new job."

"That's fabulous, Margy."

"No, it's public relations, which isn't fabulous, it's about selling the fabulousness of others. Still, it's one of New York's biggest PR firms, a friend of a friend of my mother got me the introduction, I did the interview and seemed to make a reasonable impression, because they've offered me what's called a junior account executive."

"So why aren't you sounding thrilled?"

"Oh, listen, I'm not depressed about it. It's just that schmuck Mark rang up yesterday to ask me if I could return his original Broadway cast album of *Company,* and when I said I had just landed this job, do you know what he said to me? 'Can you think of anyone who said, when they were ten years old, "When I grow up I want to be a public relations executive"?'"

"I hope you didn't listen to him."

"Of course I did—and of course I think he has a point, and I feel like I'm totally selling out, because didn't Haldeman and Ehrlichman and all those other Nixon henchmen start out in public relations?"

"Yeah—and Hitler was a housepainter . . . but that doesn't mean all housepainters are fascists."

"Bad analogy, Hannah."

"You know what I'm saying. . . . Look, if you don't want the job," I said, "don't take it. Vanish off somewhere."

"You mean, maybe I could do something really worthy, like teach in Indonesia with the Peace Corps and then come back to New York in two years and discover that I'm qualified for nothing, and that everyone chasing all the junior account executive positions is now three years younger than I am, and I'm back at square one again. No, this is a start at *something* . . . and at least you get to drink a lot in public relations, so that's one compensation. Listen, why don't you negotiate some time off for good behavior and get down here for the weekend?"

That night, I broached the subject with Dan—now that Jeff was no longer dependent on my breast for food and was sleeping through the night.

"I think you should do it," he said, cutting me off.

"You sure?"

"Babs can look after Junior all day, I can deal with the nights, and anyway, you could use a break from all this, I'm sure."

To say that I was pleased was the understatement of the year. I was completely amazed and thrilled that Dan was so understanding, so willing to give me the time-out that I desperately needed. More than that, for the first time in some months I found myself thinking: *He's actually my ally.*

The next afternoon, after picking Jeffrey up from Babs's house, I drove over to Bridgton to the only travel agent in the area, and reserved a place on a flight in ten days' time from Portland to LaGuardia on Eastern Airlines. The cost of the flight shocked me—nearly $100 round trip. But then I did my sums and worked out that, thanks to the little I'd saved from my $60 per week paycheck, I could afford to splurge, figuring that I might spend, at most, another hundred dollars during the four days and three nights I was there.

Four whole days in New York. It seemed like a complete fantasy. Margy was arranging everything, from tickets to Sondheim's new show, *A Little Night Music,* to a night on the town with a bunch of her friends.

But staring at myself in our bedroom mirror, I saw a small-town Earth Mother looking back at me. All those pasta suppers and the lack of exercise had added about seven pounds to my frame. I vowed that I'd lose five pounds before I left for New York next week.

"What's with the Bugs Bunny diet?" Dan asked me when I served him lasagne at dinner that night while I stuck to shredded carrots on cottage cheese.

"I'm just trying to drop a few pounds, that's all."

"You look fine."

"Well, thank you—but I still could lose a little weight."

"So Margy and her friends don't think you're some chubby country girl? Believe me, no one in New York is going to care how fat you are . . . even if you're not really fat."

Not really fat? Thanks a lot, Doc.

Still, I didn't care whether Dan thought I was being a little excessive on the dieting front. I continued on the Bugs Bunny regime while also making all the arrangements for my time away—from getting Babs to agree to take Jeff all day ("I don't want any extra money," she told me, "just one of those paperweights with the Empire State Building inside, which snow when you shake them"), to negotiating time off with Estelle, to calling the local cab company in Bridgton and arranging an early-morning taxi to the airport in Portland.

Everything was in place, everything was ready—including my little weekend bag, which I had packed three days before my departure. Margy had arranged to take two days off work and told me she'd even meet me as I came off the Eastern flight at LaGuardia.

Two days before my departure, I was at work in the library, stacking books as fast as possible so I could get back to reading E. B. White's *Here Is New York,* when Dan walked in. I glanced at the clock on the wall. It was 11:05 a.m.—and from the time of day and the look on my husband's face, it was clear that something was terribly wrong.

"What's happened?"

"My dad's had a heart attack."

I shut my eyes—and, as selfish as it is to admit it, my first despairing thought was: *I'm going nowhere this weekend.*

"How bad?" I asked.

"Massive. He was at work when it hit. Until the ambulance guys arrived, everyone thought he was dead. They managed to get his heart going again, but . . ."

He bit his lip, trying to stay in control. I put my arms around him. He buried his head in my shoulder, stifling a sob.

"Just spoke to the hospital in Glens Falls. They say if he lasts a week, it will be a miracle."

"Can you go there now?"

"I've got appointments until three, but Nurse Bass has called the Regional Health Authority in Lewiston and they're finding a doctor to cover for me until I get back. I really can't be gone more than a week, because then the town won't have full-time coverage . . ."

I put my finger to his lips.

"The important thing right now is that you get to your father's bedside. Is there a flight?"

"It would mean going to New York and waiting four hours for a little puddle jumper to Syracuse, then it's a two-hour bus ride to Glens Falls. Also, Nurse Bass found out it's over two hundred bucks one way. So I'm going to take the bus. There's a Trailways from Lewiston at four this afternoon. Goes kind of a convoluted route—across to Burlington, then into New York State . . ."

"Why don't you take the car?"

"Because you'll need it this week. Anyway, once I'm there I can use Dad's car."

"Dan, it's crazy spending twelve, thirteen hours on a bus."

"I don't want to drive. I can't drive right now. I'm too . . ."

He released himself from my embrace, wiped his eyes, glanced at his watch, and said, "I've got patients . . ."

"Dan, I'm so sorry."

He just shrugged and left.

Later that afternoon, I drove my husband to Lewiston. En route he said very little, except, "I feel bad about New York."

"It's kind of beyond your control."

"As soon as this is all done, you can get down there."

"New York's not exactly going anywhere."

I dropped him off at the bus depot in Lewiston. He gave me a fast peck on the cheek and said, "I'll call tomorrow, tell you what's going on."

Then he grabbed my cigarettes off the dash, picked up his bag, and disappeared into the gray linoleum interior of the Trailways station. He didn't turn back once to look at me.

On the way back to Pelham, I tried to keep my disappointment at bay. Margy was as let down as I was.

"This is rotten luck—for both of us. I was really looking forward to a wild weekend with you."

"Well, as soon as things are settled . . ."

"You mean, as soon as Old Man Buchan kicks it . . ."

"Yeah, as soon as we've got him in the ground, you'll see me in Manhattan."

"How's Dan handling it?"

"In a very Dan way."

Margy understood. "He's in shock," Margy said.

"He almost cried—then thought better of it."

"Cut the guy some slack. Losing your dad is a very big thing."

"I know, and he's dealing with it as best he can. But, once again, he's left me feeling all isolated and outside of his life."

"You're just feeling disappointed about canceling the trip to New York."

"It's not just that, Margy."

"It'll pass, hon. Really it will. And you'll be down here visiting me in no time. But for the moment . . ."

I know, I know. Keep your chin up. Look for the silver lining. Be the loving, supportive spouse.

When he rang me the next afternoon, Dan did sound absolutely exhausted. The bus trip had taken fourteen hours. He'd only arrived in Glens Falls at six that morning, and had gone straight to the hospital, where his father was in the intensive care unit.

"Clinically, he's all but dead," Dan said in a quiet, matter-of-fact voice. "There's been extensive, irreparable neurological damage, coupled with cardiovascular trauma. The thing is, despite the fact that the myocardium is totally compromised—and there seems to be no cerebral activity—his heart is still beating strong. His will to live is ferocious. It could be weeks, months before he goes . . . How has your day been?"

I did feel immensely sorry for Dan—and told him so.

"If I could, I'd jump back on that bus right now and come straight home," he said. "This is just going to be one long deathwatch."

Later that day, around six, there was a knock on the door. It was Billy. He smiled shyly at me, then looked down at his shoes.

"I heard about Doc Buchan's dad. I'm real sorry."

"I'll make certain he knows that."

"Okay," he said, nodding his head. Then he fell silent.

"Anything else, Billy?"

"Just wondered if you needed some work done around the place."

"Everything's just fine—thanks to you."

He flashed another of his goofy smiles, but kept avoiding my gaze.

"Just was over working on the Bland house today. Mr. Sims lost his new plumber, so he had to call me, ha, ha."

"No problems over there?" I asked, trying to sound polite, yet desperately wanting to end this conversation as soon as possible.

"Should have it all ready for you in another five, six weeks."

"Well, that's great."

Another awkward pause. Then, bless his intervening heart, Jeff started to bawl.

"Listen, I'd better be going," I said.

"Oh . . . right," Billy said.

"Thanks for coming by."

"You sure you don't need anything repaired or fixed?"

"If anything goes wrong, you'll be the first to know."

I closed the door and went over to the playpen where Jeff was crying his eyes out. I picked him up, smelled his diaper, and wrinkled my nose. Then as I lay him down on the floor to change him, the phone rang. I reached for it while unfastening one of the diaper pins, half expecting Billy to be on the line and making me wonder how I should continue treating his strange friendliness. But instead I heard a male voice ask, "Hannah Latham?"

"It's Hannah Buchan, actually."

A little laugh. "Oh, right, forgot you got married."

"Who is this?"

"Toby Judson."

"Who?"

"You don't remember meeting me? Tobias Judson?"

The penny dropped.

"Hang on, are you the Tobias Judson of Columbia sit-in fame?"

"The very one. And I met you briefly with your dad a couple of summers ago in Boston. Remember?"

Of course I remembered. It was the evening when I saw Dad with *that woman.*

"How did you get my number, Toby?"

"Your dad gave it to me."

"I see," I said.

"And he said if I happened to be passing through Maine, I should look you up."

"You're in Maine now?" I asked.

"Ever heard of a restaurant called Goodwin's—home of the Awful Awful?"

"You're in Bridgton?"

"You got it—and I was wondering: you wouldn't have a floor I could crash on tonight?"

SEVEN

MY TWO-MINUTE CONVERSATION with Toby Judson made me nervous. Not that he said anything weird or unsettling. If anything, the guy was charm itself. He explained with a little laugh that he was "on the run" from his doctoral thesis at the University of Chicago (which was now a year overdue) and had been hitching around the country. He said he fully understood that I would have to check with my husband before deciding if I could put him up for the night, and gave me the phone number at Goodwin's so I could call him back and let him know if he should start thumbing a ride in the direction of Pelham. There was nothing sinister in his repartee—and hey, calling up friends of friends out of nowhere, introducing yourself, and asking for a spare floor to crash on was simply the done thing. This also wasn't just a friend of a friend . . . this was a friend of my dad's, and a guy who had made news across the country for helping turn Columbia University into an ideological battleground during the big sit-down strike there. Toby Judson was something of a campus radical legend, so I certainly knew who he was.

No, what bothered me was—how can I put it?—his know-it-all tone, the air of easy familiarity, the little sarcastic laugh that entered his voice when I used my married name (no doubt, that had made him immediately write me off as totally bourgeois). But maybe my unease came from the fact that I, in turn, hated myself for being so hesitant, so cautious, so *bourgeois*. Still, I *was* a married woman living in a very small town, so . . . I took down his number at Goodwin's, hung up, and called my dad in Vermont.

Much to my surprise, he was at home when I rang. Better yet, he was not his usual preoccupied self. He seemed genuinely concerned about Dan's father and he also wanted to know everything that Jeffrey was up to—all his little developmental milestones.

"I know I owe you a visit," he said. "Life has just been a little too full."

"Speaking of visitors," I said, then mentioned my phone call from Toby Judson.

"Typical of Toby to hit the road like that," he said. "He might be the brightest kid I've run across in thirty years, but he can never apply himself when it comes to the long haul. One of the best public speakers I've ever heard—articulate, funny, ferociously well-read, and a really good writer to boot. You should have seen the stuff he published in *Ramparts* and *The Nation.* Great style—and a brilliant analytical mind."

"Sounds like a smart guy," I said, interrupting Dad's rave review.

"Can you put him up for a couple of nights?" Dad asked.

"Well, as you know, Dan's not here right now."

"And the neighbors might talk?"

"Something like that."

"Tell Dan—and also tell the neighbors before they can start gossiping. That's the time-honored New England way of defusing rumors. And don't worry, he won't talk politics at you all the time. That's not Toby's style."

After hanging up, I called Dan in Glens Falls but got no answer. I glanced at my watch. It was nearly seven-thirty p.m.—and I couldn't keep the guy waiting in Goodwin's for the rest of the night. I also thought Dan would be cool about it, so I called back Goodwin's. Toby must have been standing by the phone, since he answered immediately.

I said, "My dad sends you a big hello."

"Did he also tell you that I don't wear fangs and don't sleep in a coffin?"

"Oh, you come highly recommended."

Another of his sardonic laughs.

"Glad to hear it," he said. "And your absent husband doesn't mind?"

"He's got other things on his mind right now. His dad is dying."

"That's a drag."

Nice turn of phrase you've got there, mister.

I went silent. "Sorry," he said. "I don't do sympathy very well."

"Listen, I can only put you up for a night or two."

"And that's all I'm planning to stay."

I told him where to find us in Pelham.

"Shouldn't be too difficult," he said. "Be there as soon as I can hitch a lift."

I hung up, whipped around the house, washed up the dishes in the sink, put away a couple of diapers that had been drying by the stove, cleaned the toilet and the bathroom sink, and thought to myself: *You really* are *bourgeois.* I even changed out of the baby-food-splattered overalls that I had been wearing all day, exchanging them for a pair of jeans and a Mexican blouse that I had bought a few years ago at some groovy little shop in Boston, and which still looked reasonably, well, *groovy,* I guess.

Then I picked up the phone and tried Dan again. No answer, so I dialed a local number. Nurse Bass picked up on the second ring. It was hard to hear her, as the television was, per usual, blasting away in the background.

"Will ya turn it down, for Christ's sakes," she yelled, before coming back to me and asking, "You calling to tell me the doc's dad's dead?"

"Not exactly. I've been trying to get through to him this evening, but I'm getting no answer at his dad's house . . ."

"Well, he's probably at the hospital."

"Yeah, that's what I figured too. But I know he checks in with you to find out about his patients—and just in case he calls late tonight and might worry about ringing me afterward in case I've gone to bed, would you mind telling him that a friend of ours has come to stay for a few days and we'll probably be up until about midnight?"

I know this all sounded a little contrived but I didn't care. Because if Nurse Bass had seen a strange man emerging from our front door tomorrow morning, I wouldn't have heard the end of it. So, as Margy might have put it, I was covering my ass. Nurse Bass took the bait.

"Who's the friend?" she asked.

"Someone from college," I said, then wished her a good night and hung up.

As it turned out, Dan called thirty minutes later. He sounded strained.

"Dad's heart arrested twice this afternoon but they brought him back."

"Was that a good idea?"

"Of course not. But doctors are legally bound to try to keep the patient alive—even if he's completely brain-dead, like Dad is now."

"You sound wrecked."

"I *am* wrecked—and I want out of here. Fast. If Dad arrests again, I think that's it."

"Well, we want you back. Have you spoken with Betty Bass tonight?"

"Not yet."

So I explained how I left a message for him, just in case he called late, about our surprise visitor. When I filled him in, Dan said, "As long as he's off our floor by the time I get back, it's fine by me."

"I'm only doing it as a favor to Dad. They were 'comrades in arms' on the barricades."

"Well, if he gets in your way, kick him out. Oh . . . it was smart to tell Betty about him showing up. Good thinking, Batman."

"Get some sleep, hon."

"I miss you."

After we hung up, the thought struck me: *That was about the most affectionate conversation we've had in weeks, maybe even months.*

An hour went by . . . and still no sign of the famous Tobias Judson. Then another hour. I was just about to leave a key under the mat and a note on top of it, telling him I'd gone to bed, when there was a knock on the door.

I opened it. It had been around three years since I'd met him, and there was so much going on that night that I hadn't really registered much about him. But the first thing that came into my head when I found Toby Judson on my doorstep was: *He's kind of cute . . . if you like the bearded intellectual type.*

Actually, his beard wasn't really a *beard,* more like a heavy stubble that softened his very angular face. He was tall and thin, with bushy black hair and little round John Lennon glasses. He wore a frayed blue button-down shirt, a crew neck navy blue sweater with a couple of holes in the sleeves, gray bell-bottom corduroys, and hiking boots. Though he looked scruffy, the good breeding immediately shone through. So did the perfect teeth—the result, no doubt, of hundreds of hours spent in the orthodontist's chair.

I saw the perfect teeth when he gave me the perfect smile as I opened the door.

"Sorry about the delay," he said, "but there are no cars between Bridgton and Pelham after sunset."

"Oh God, I should have said something."

"Why? Have you ever tried hitching from Bridgton to Pelham after sunset?"

"No. Not even before sunset."

"So why are you apologizing? Mind if I come in?"

"Oh, sorry, sure."

He lifted the backpack on the floor beside him, its camouflage cloth dappled with mud, while the rolled sleeping bag fastened to the top needed a good wash.

"Looks like you've been on the road for a while," I said.

"Three straight days from Chicago—something I don't recommend doing."

"Didn't you stop off anywhere to sleep?"

"No, but I did catch around six hours the night before last in the back of a truck that was hauling refrigerators from Pittsburgh to Albany."

He dropped his backpack on the floor by the sofa and looked around.

"Cozy," he said.

"You mean small."

"Is this what they offer the doctor around here in the way of living quarters?"

"Not exactly," I said, and explained about the flood at Chez Bland.

"Ah yes, the pitfalls of Do It Yourself . . . a largely middle-class obsession which allows the bourgeoisie to think they can do without skilled laborers from the proletariat classes."

"I kind of thought of DIY as more of a weekend hobby, not to mention a way of saving money."

"My point entirely: eliminate the proletariat by having their work seized by an educated elite who consider, say, rewiring a house to be a *hobby* that any college graduate can master. Didn't you know that Marx had a whole chapter on Plumbing and the Redistribution of Wealth in *Das Kapital*?"

"You're joking."

He put on a Groucho Marx voice and flicked an imaginary cigar.

"Lady, if you believe that, you'll believe anything."

"Well, I didn't believe it."

"Just like your dad, who once told me that the key to being a proper historian is having a first-rate bullshit detector."

"Didn't my father borrow that line from Hemingway?"

"'Immature poets imitate, mature poets steal.'"

"T. S. Eliot?" I asked.

"I am impressed," he said.

"Oh, reading is something I get to do a lot of around here. Why don't you sit down, make yourself at home."

"Thanks," he said, plopping down on the floor.

"You can use the sofa, you know."

"Yeah, but my jeans are so damn scuzzy after three days on the road that they might dirty up your furniture."

"So you are a member of the bourgeoisie?" I said lightly.

"Touché. But, to be completely classist about it, I am a member of *la grande bourgeoisie*—Shaker Heights, Cleveland, division, where every Jewish-American girl is a princess."

"And where every Jewish-American boy . . . ?"

". . . is a tax-lawyer-in-waiting."

"Where did you go wrong, then?"

"I got addicted to politics—and to disturbing the peace."

"Feel like a beer?"

"That would be splendid."

I went to the icebox, pulled out two cans, and handed him one.

"Schaefer," he said, studying the label. "A good, honest American beer."

"No, it's not good—it's just cheap."

"I'm surprised a doctor and his wife have to do cheap."

"Dan is still an intern and this is Nowhere, Maine—where the pay, even for a doctor, isn't that great."

"Well, as Uncle Joe Stalin used to say, a year in Siberia is good for the soul."

"Stalin never said that."

"You do have a first-rate bullshit detector."

"Yeah, I know crap when I hear it."

Jeffrey started to cry in the bedroom.

"Didn't know you had a kid."

"Well, now you do," I said.

I went inside and picked him up out of his crib, kissing him on the head. Then I lifted him up and smelled his very dirty diaper. I brought him back into the living room.

"This is Jeffrey Buchan," I said. "Say hello to Toby, Jeffrey."

I lay Jeffrey down on the changing mat I kept near the television, unfastened the safety pins, and removed the dirty diaper. Toby glanced over in our direction.

"Better you than me," he said.

"Hey, it's just shit. And shit, as your Mr. Marx once put it, is the essence of life."

"Marx never said that."

"I know, but it still sounded good. And speaking of shitty smells, your three days on the road have left you a little ripe."

"Sorry about that," he said. "Any chance I could use your bath? I need a long soak."

"Not only can you use the bath, I *insist* you use the bath. And while you're at it, give me all your dirty clothes and I'll throw them into the wash."

"Hey, you don't have to be my maid."

"Yeah, but I have this thing about body odor. So the quicker you and your clothes are washed, the faster this apartment is going to smell better."

As I finished changing Jeffrey, Toby started to open his backpack. I went into the bedroom, found a dirty pillowcase in our laundry basket, returned to the sitting room, and handed it to him.

"Here, put everything into that."

He did as ordered, then went into the bathroom, closed the door, and half opened it a few moments later, his bare arm appearing with a handful of his clothes.

He closed the door again and I could hear the water running. I returned to Jeffrey who had amazingly drifted off back to sleep. I put him back in his crib, picked up the bag of clothes, and went downstairs to the laundry room behind the doctor's office. After I loaded Toby's smelly clothes into the machine, I stepped out into the street. A voice called behind me.

"Hey there, Mrs. Buchan."

Damn.

"Hello, Billy. What has you out late?"

"Often take a walk around now. Everything working okay in the laundry room?"

I stiffened. "How did you know I was in the laundry room, Billy?"

"Why else would you been down here around eleven p.m.?"

Good point.

"See you've got a visitor," he said.

"How did you see that, Billy?"

"Saw him walk into town earlier, and come to your door."

"I thought you only went out for a walk a few minutes ago."

He avoided my questioning gaze.

"Been out a lot tonight."

Evidently. "He's an old college friend of ours."

"Ain't any of my business, ma'am. Just making an observation, that's all. Hope I didn't trouble you or nothing."

Well, frankly, Billy, you did. Because I'm wondering if—and why—you're watching my front door all the time.

"Not to worry, Billy. Good night."

"And a real good night to you, ma'am."

As I went back upstairs I made a mental note to ask Estelle tomorrow if Billy ever had a history of stalking people . . . or if I was the first person to be honored with his excessive interest.

Once inside the apartment I checked on Jeffrey, who was still sleeping soundly. The bathroom door remained closed. A half hour went by, during which I continued trying to work my way through Pynchon's *Gravity's Rainbow* and wondering was it me or Pynchon that was making it such hard going. Then I walked over to the bathroom door and tried to listen for sounds of life within. When none came, I knocked on the door. No response. I knocked again. Still no response. I called out Toby's name—twice. Now I was nervous. One final loud knock on the door and I flung it open.

"Toby!"

He was lying naked in the bath, fast asleep, his head well above the top of the water. I glanced in his direction, then turned my eyes away and left the room shouting his name again. This time he came to, looking thoroughly disoriented, evidently wondering where the hell he was right now, and who was this woman trying to wake him up.

"Jesus fuck . . ." he said, squinting madly.

"And a very good morning to you."

"It's morning?"

"Hardly. But you have been asleep in there for over half an hour and I was worried you might have drowned."

"Sorry, sorry . . ."

"Hey, just glad you're still with us. Feel like eating now?"

"That would be great."

"How does an omelet sound?"

"Very edible."

He emerged around ten minutes later, clean-shaven, wearing a fresh T-shirt and a pair of jeans.

"Thanks for rescuing me from the watery depths," he said. "It would have been a stupid way to go."

"Well, six hours of sleep in three days is kind of a recipe for disaster."

He sat down at the kitchen table. I offered him another beer and heated up the frying pan.

"Why are you hitchhiking?" I asked. "Wouldn't it be easier to buy a Greyhound pass?"

"Sure. But the whole point is to have an *On the Road* experience. You know, coast to coast by thumb—and maybe get a couple of magazine articles or a book out of it."

"And what made you decide to start in Maine?"

"The first truck that picked me up got me to Akron, Ohio. The second lift to Pittsburgh, then Albany, then Plattsburgh, where I spent half the night in a twenty-four-hour diner, then a retired Marine Corps captain got me as far as Manchester, New Hampshire—which might just be the most fascist town in America . . ."

"Did you tell the Marine Corps captain that?"

"Hell no. I didn't discuss politics with him—I wanted to keep the lift. Anyway, after Manchester I hooked up with a trucker heading north to Bangor. He had some truck stop girl he was seeing in Lewiston, so he detoured off the highway and he dropped me in Bridgton because—"

"My dad told you, 'If you ever need a bed for the night in Maine, call Hannah'?"

A shrug.

"He did mention you were up here when I told him I was hitting the road and gave me your number. I've phone numbers of friends and friends of friends around the States. Anyway, if you're doing a trans-American hitchhike, Maine is a good geographic starting point. Top of the country and all that."

"No doubt, your doctoral adviser isn't exactly pleased that you've decided to vanish for a year."

"So speaks a prof's daughter. Nah, he was pretty cool about it—and he knows that if I get a book out of this trip, it will raise my profile quite a bit, which will help get me the right tenure-track job when the time comes, blah, blah, blah, blah, blah . . . and yeah, I have these hidden careerist facets to my character."

"Or maybe not so hidden. What was the doctoral thesis on?"

"'Do It Yourself Plumbing and Marxist Redistribution of Communal Wealth.'"

"Very funny."

"It's not far off. The real subject is the sort of DIY Marxism that Allende tried to practice in Chile."

"You've spent time in Chile?"

"You mean, you never read my *stunning* collection of dispatches from Santiago in *The Nation*?"

"No, I only read *Playboy,*" I said, "for the interviews."

He laughed. "I deserved that."

"Yes, you did."

He looked at me. "I really like your style."

I fought back a small blush.

"So," I said, "having failed to save America from Vietnam, and Chile from the CIA, you decided to run back into the protective arms of the Ivory Tower."

"Man, you're brutal—and right on the money."

I served up the omelet, grabbed two more cans of beer from the icebox, and listened to Toby's stories about his time in Chile and how he got a little too friendly with an older revolutionary named Lucia, who turned out to be working as a paid informant for "our spooks in Washington" and who was appointed to a big job in the Pinochet regime after the coup.

"Assistant undersecretary for Chilean-American affairs—of which she already had considerable experience, courtesy of yours truly."

"You're lucky she didn't have you hanged, drawn, and quartered."

"Ah, but as soon as Allende was 'suicided,' a sympathetic guy in our embassy got a message to me in Santiago that I had around twelve hours to get out of Dodge, as I was on a death squad list. So I took his advice, hightailed it to the airport, and just managed to talk my way onto the last flight of the night, which happened to be bound for Miami. Pinochet's goons broke into my room around an hour after I was in the air."

"Now I see why you wanted to do something nice and quiet afterward, like a PhD."

"Yeah, you can't stay on the barricades forever . . . though your dad might be the exception to that rule."

Toby went into a glowing testimonial about my dad—how he had "the most acute historical mind" he had ever encountered; how he had a real interest in his comrades and never tried to "pull that Jimmy Stewart paternal shit" on anyone younger than him; and how, unlike so many people he'd met in the antiwar movement, he was less interested in his public image than he was in "sticking it to the man."

"I don't think my father minds the public attention."

"Didn't Lenin say that all revolutionary leaders need ego and the id?"

"Sounds more like Freud to me."

"Probably is—since I just made it up. Good omelet, by the way."

"Well, that's what us housewives are good at—cooking and having babies."

"I can't imagine that you're just a housewife."

"No, I also work in the local library. And if you say, 'That's interesting,' I won't talk to you again."

"That's interesting."

Long silence, during which he stared directly at me, challenging me to blink, laugh, whatever. After one very long minute, I cracked, giggling. He laughed too.

"You're a piece of work, did you know that?" I asked.

"That's what my father always told me: 'Toby, vy you bein' such a schmuck and tryin' to be Emma Goldman? The FBI, they come to my door, they say: "Your son, he vants to tear up the Constitution of the United States and set up a Marxist state." I tell 'em: "Nah, he just thinks the revolutionary stuff vill get him laid."'"

"Does your father really talk like that?"

"Just about. He came over from Wrocław in 1930—just before it completely hit the fan there for Polish Jews."

"And did he really say that to the feds?"

"So he told me."

"And did you become the big revolutionary to get laid a lot?"

"Well, radical ideas are an aphrodisiac."

"Who said that? Sonny Liston?"

He laughed, then asked, "Are you happy being a librarian?"

"No—I want to teach. But opportunities aren't exactly thick on the ground in Pelham, and just having had the baby . . ."

"Excuses, excuses."

I tensed and said nothing.

"Did I touch a sore spot?" he asked.

"Yes, you did."

"I could say sorry, but I wouldn't mean it."

"Well, at least that's honest."

"Or as honest as I ever get."

"Which is more honest, I suppose. Another beer?"

"Actually, what I'd like to do now, if you don't mind, is crash."

"Fine by me—it's late. And I'm a working mom, so I'm up early. What are you planning to do tomorrow?"

"Well, I could hit the road if I'm in the way here."

"You're not in the way. And don't you want to rest up for a couple of days after your marathon trip?"

"That would be cool."

"Dan won't be back for at least three days—that is, unless his dad dies before then, in which case I'll have to head off with Jeffrey to Glens Falls. But really, you're welcome to stay for a couple more nights if you like."

He reached over and touched my arm.

"Thank you," he said.

I could feel my cheeks redden, and hoped they weren't noticeable, and I wondered why the hell I had reacted that way to his touch.

I helped him arrange the cushions from the couch on the floor to create a makeshift bed. He rolled out his sleeping bag, which looked even dirtier when fully unfurled.

"Give that to me tomorrow and I'll wash it for you," I said.

"You really don't have to wait on me like this."

"I'm not waiting on you. I'm just offering to put your sleeping bag in a washing machine and turn it on . . . which isn't exactly a big deal, now is it? But let me guess: you grew up in a house full of servants and you always feel a lingering class guilt about having help around the house."

A pause as he continued making up his bed.

"We didn't have servants," he finally said. "Just a maid named Geneva—which sounds very Aunt Jemima, I know—but, hey, it was Shaker Heights . . ."

"And it certainly gave you something to rebel against."

In the bedroom, Jeffrey started to stir—a tentative cry that I knew would build up into a massive yelp if I didn't get to him in the next minute.

"I'd better go sort out Monsieur," I said.

"This has been fun," he said.

He looked at me with those bedroom eyes of his—and I found myself wanting to get into my own bedroom fast.

"Get some sleep," I said.

I managed to settle Jeff down in a couple of minutes. Then I got undressed, slipped into bed, and tried to concentrate on my book. But I kept replaying our conversation in my mind, and found myself thinking: *He got me to sound like Dorothy Parker, or some real New York smartypants. He made me feel smart. More than that, he took me seriously . . .*

I turned off the light. I tried to sleep. I couldn't. I kept replaying that moment when I found him asleep in the bath . . .

I turned the light back on. I read for two hours, forcing myself to navigate Pynchon's vision of America the Deranged. Once or twice I heard Toby stir in the next room—and listened intently for signs that he might be up and about. But eventually such restive noises were superseded by the metronomic sound of him snoring. I cursed myself for acting like a love-struck teenager, turned off the light, and finally surrendered to sleep.

When Jeff woke me around six hours later, I snuck into the kitchen to heat up a bottle for him, and saw that Toby was still passed out on the floor, his head and naked shoulders protruding from the top of his sleeping bag. When I returned an hour later to use the bathroom, he was still fast asleep. I got dressed, fed Jeff some gooey oatmeal, then scribbled a note to Toby, telling him where to find breakfast stuff and asking him to stop by the library sometime before noon "after you've explored all the wonders of Pelham."

I did my usual morning routine, dropping Jeff off at Babs's house, stopping by Miller's for my cigarettes.

"Heard you got company staying with you," Jesse Miller said.

Her tone was completely mild and unthreatening—she was just making a passing comment—so I replied in a similar vein.

"That's right—an old college friend of ours has dropped by for a couple of days."

"And how's the doc's dad?"

"Still alive, but only just."

"Tell him how sorry I am the next time you're speaking to him."

"I will," I said.

When I reached the library, Estelle said, "So I hear you're entertaining lone men on your own."

"Oh for God's sakes . . ."

"Hon," she said, "welcome to Pelham."

Over our morning coffee I answered her assorted questions about my houseguest—sticking to the line that he was an old college friend—then tried to keep myself busy with work. An hour or so later, as I was restacking books, I heard the door open and Toby ask Estelle if I was around.

"Ah," she said, "so you're the tall, dark stranger who wandered into town last night."

Toby laughed, and I hurried out from the stacks, wiping book dust off my hands en route.

"Don't listen to my boss," I said, "she's an agent provocateur."

"I have a soft spot for agents provocateurs," he said, extending his hand to Estelle. I could see Estelle looking him over, and trying (without success) to suppress a smile.

"So you were at UVM with Hannah and Dan?" she asked him. I could see Toby do a double take—and for one horrible moment I thought he might say, "Who told you that?"

But to his immense credit, he understood what was going on and said, "That's right. Hannah's dad was my adviser."

Estelle seemed to buy this, but another unsettling thought clouded my head. *Say she works out who Toby is? Surely she must have read about all the sit-downs at Columbia and how this Toby Judson was the chief provocateur. Then she's going to think: Why did Hannah lie to me?*

And she'd be right to think that, because there was no reason why I couldn't have told her the truth. That's the problem with lies—they always push you into a corner, from which there is little chance of escape without looking like a duplicitous fool.

"How'd you sleep?" I asked him.

"Like the dead," he said. "I even feel vaguely human today. And I've just spent the last half hour exploring the delights of Pelham. Quite a friendly place. As soon as I walked into the luncheonette . . . what's it called again?"

"Miss Pelham's," I said.

"Yeah, well, as soon as I walked in there and sat down, the waitress said, 'You wouldn't happen to be the college friend who's staying with Doc Buchan and his wife?'"

He winked at me, and I was sure Estelle caught the hint of conspiracy between us.

"We like to live in each other's back pockets in Pelham," Estelle said. "Which means we have a kind of communal intelligence service that would make the CIA envious. And we hate when anyone does anything out of the norm—like having an old male friend stay when her husband's away."

"Well," Toby said, "wasn't it Conrad who said: 'It's only those who do nothing that make no mistakes'?"

"*Heart of Darkness*?" Estelle asked.

"*An Outcast of the Islands*," Toby said.

"So what are you planning to do today?" I asked Toby, trying to change the subject.

"Not really sure. Any ideas?"

"If you like the Great Outdoors," Estelle said, "we've got plenty of it around here."

"Yeah, you could go over to Sebago Lake, maybe rent a canoe if you know how to navigate one."

"Oh, I was sent to summer camp like every Shaker Heights kid."

"You grew up in Shaker Heights, Ohio?" Estelle asked.

"I'm afraid so."

"Well, one of my maternal aunts married someone from Shaker Heights. Name of Alisberg. Ever heard of them?"

"Nope," Toby said.

"She's still alive, my aunt . . . well, just about. And I talk to her once a month—and she knows everybody in Shaker Heights—so I must mention you to her the next time we speak. What did you say your last name was?"

"I didn't, but it's Mailman. However, I doubt your aunt would remember my folks, because they moved to Florida around fifteen years ago."

"Oh, Ruthie's the sort who remembers everyone she's ever met. What did your dad do?"

"A lawyer."

"Listen," I said, interrupting, "if you want to go to Sebago Lake now, I can lend you the car."

"That would be cool," Toby said.

"Do you know how to drive a gear shift?"

"No problem," he said, motioning that I should follow him out to the street. "Nice meeting you," he said to Estelle.

"You too," she said.

I grabbed my cigarettes off the reception desk (Christ, did I need a smoke now) and told Estelle I'd be back in a minute.

Outside on the street, I offered Toby a cigarette. He shook his head. I lit one up. As I sucked in a deep lungful of smoke, Toby arched his eyebrows and said, "Now would you mind explaining why you did something so dumb like tell everyone I was an old college friend?"

"Because I thought the idea that you were Dan's friend wouldn't—"

"Yeah, yeah," he said, cutting me off. "That's what I figured when that waitress mentioned it. God forbid it should be some guy who *doesn't* know the good doctor, staying all alone with his wife while he stands vigil by the hospital bed of his dying father."

"All right, I was a coward," I said.

"No, you were just being prudent—and I understand that. And I know that, if I had used my real name, your librarian friend would have worked out who I was, and how we weren't all great pals at UVM . . . as if I'd have gone there in the first place."

"Hey, there's no need to get all Ivy League about it."

"All right, I'm a snob. But listen, don't worry if she does eventually work out who I am. You can always say something like, 'Because of his radical credentials, he prefers to travel under an assumed name' . . . and yeah, I do know that sounds pretentious as hell. But she strikes me as a pretty cool woman for a small-town librarian, so I think she'll work out why I don't exactly announce who I am and what I've done over the years."

"My, what a big head you have."

"All the better to impress you with, my dear."

"You'd make a shitty Big Bad Wolf."

"I'll take that as a compliment. You sure you don't mind me taking the car?"

"As long as you don't wreck it. It's the orange Volvo parked behind the doctor's office. And Sebago Lake's just about fifteen minutes from here . . ."

"Why don't we do Sebago Lake this afternoon?"

"We?"

"Yeah—you and me and Jeffrey. I can take the car now and drive over to Bridgton to get the necessary supplies for the dinner I'm going to cook for you tonight."

"There's no need for you to cook dinner."

"I know. I'd like to cook for you. And before that I'd like to take you and Jeffrey out for a canoe ride on the lake . . . especially as it is such a spectacular fall day."

He held out his hand for the keys.

"So does that sound like a good plan?" he asked.

I dropped the keys in his hand.

"Sure," I said.

He asked me what time I got off work. I told him. He said, "That should give us a good two hours on the lake. By the way, I didn't lock the apartment door on the way out. Was that cool?"

"There's no such thing as theft in Pelham. Only nosiness. See you at two-thirty."

Back in the library, Estelle gave me a very knowing smile.

"Well, he is seriously dreamy."

"Yeah, and I'm seriously married."

"Hey, I'm just making an aesthetic judgment . . . though if I was all alone with him in that small apartment of yours . . ."

"I'm not all alone with him. I do have my son there."

"No need to get all serious on me, Hannah. I'm just kidding around."

"You know what it's like here, Estelle."

"Everyone knows he's Dan's friend too. So you're covered if, in the privacy of your own home, you want to undress him with your teeth."

"Ha."

"Two of those and you'd be laughing. And speaking of laughs, what the hell was a boy from Shaker Heights doing at the University of Vermont? No one outside of the Northeast ever goes there."

"He was a ski bum."

"That makes sense . . . though I've never met a ski bum who quoted Joseph Conrad."

"Well, now you have."

When I got back to the apartment with Jeff after work, Toby was already there, unpacking a vast array of Italian produce in the kitchen. I blinked in amazement as real olive oil and cloves of garlic and actual Italian sausage and a big wedge of Parmesan cheese and a bottle of Chianti appeared out of the paper bag.

"Where did you get all that?" I asked.

"Didn't you know you had an Italian deli in Pelham?"

"Come on, tell me how you found this stuff."

"I asked around, that's all."

"Asked where?"

"At the supermarket in Bridgton—which, outside of Chef Boyardee tomato sauce, has absolutely nothing in the way of Italian stuff. But someone at the shop told me about this little place off Congress Street in Portland, which apparently is the only Italian deli in the entire state of Maine. So I drove over there, and *hey, presto:* the makings of a great *rigatoni con salsiccia.*"

"You drove all the way over to Portland?"

"It's only an hour each way—and your Volvo seems to be able to handle all those bumpy back roads. Not the prettiest of towns, Portland. Still, the deli was quite a find. The owner's named Paolo, his dad came from Genoa, worked as a fisherman on the Maine coast, then set up this little operation which the son now runs . . . I got the whole story, not to mention a cup of very good espresso."

"I don't believe this."

"Ask and you shall find out. And don't look so startled. I was just in the mood for cooking Italian."

"I'm impressed, that's all."

I was also a little ashamed that it had taken an out-of-stater to suss out that there was an Italian deli within an hour of here. Not that I ever got any farther than Lewiston these days. *Ask and you shall find out.* That was the problem—I never asked about anything.

Toby finished putting the last of his Italian shopping away, then turned to me and said, "So, shall we head to Sebago Lake while we still have a couple of hours of light?"

Toby insisted on driving us over to the lake—"I never get the chance to drive in Chicago"—only he went by a new route, bringing us to a picnic area on the far side of the lake where there was also a place to rent canoes.

"How'd you find out about this place?"

"Asked at a gas station in Bridgton where I could rent a canoe at the lake."

"Ask and ye shall find out."

"As Jesus once said to Karl Marx."

"Amen."

It was a short walk from the parking lot, past the picnic tables, to a little cabin at the lakefront manned by a lone guy in his fifties, renting canoes and rowboats.

"You're my only customers today," he said. "Come October, there's hardly anyone on the lake anymore."

I looked at the canoes and kept thinking how easy they were to capsize.

"Mightn't it be safer in a rowboat?" I asked the lake guy.

"Oh come on," Toby said, "for the authentic Maine experience, you've got to cross Sebago Lake by canoe. Anyway, it's a perfectly calm day. Better than calm. No wind whatsoever."

"Your husband's right," the lake guy said. "It's glass out there today—and you've just as much chance of capsizing in a rowboat as you do in a canoe. Anyway, we'll fit you all out with life jackets."

Toby, however, chose not to wear his. "I like to live dangerously."

"Well, excuse me, *husband,* if I'm Little Miss Prudent," I said, "but Jeff and I are going to wear ours."

"Well, *wife,* not everyone has to be as vain as me," he said.

At least Toby was right about the stillness of the lake. It was one of those rare, peerless fall days when the sun was at full wattage, the air was suffused with a tang of impending winter, and the wind was nowhere to be felt. I sat in the bow of the canoe with my son clutched against me as Toby, in the stern, paddled us out into the middle of that becalmed inland sea. I looked north, south, east, west—all possible horizons, all defined by water and woodlands, its foliage alight with reds and yellows from the fiery end of the color spectrum. I leaned back, pulling Jeffrey even closer to me, and stared up at the sky—a hard blue dome, empty of all hints of impending gloom. I breathed deeply—the air so pure, so crisp, that I actually felt light-headed. And for a brief time, I lost all sense of the world beyond here. Everything that worried me, all my misgivings about my life, all the emotional baggage that I dragged with me, day in, day out . . . for a couple of precious minutes, it all fell right off me. There was no past, no future, no personal complexities, no sense of inadequacy or regret, and no guilt. There was only the moment: the lake, the trees, the limitless heavens, my son asleep against my chest, the dimming sun still incandescent on my face. And I found myself thinking: *So this is what bliss is . . . fleeting, short-lived, ephemeral . . . and gone. In a moment.*

At the other end of the canoe, Toby had also fallen silent. He stopped paddling and sat back, staring up at that great blue void.

"Are you religious?" he finally asked, breaking the moment.

"Not really, though I wish I was."

"Why?"

"Oh, the sense of certainty, I suppose. The idea that you are not totally responsible for everything that happens to you. And, of course, the belief that there is something beyond all this."

"That would be a pretty damn amusing discovery," Toby said. "Life after death . . . though, personally speaking, from everything I've read about it, I think I'd find heaven pretty damn boring. Nothing to do but contemplate paradise. What would I do all day? There'd be nothing to change."

"How can you be so sure that you'll end up in heaven?"

"Good point, especially if God also happens to be a Columbia University graduate."

"You really caused some chaos down there."

"They deserved it."

"Who's *they*?"

"The university administration and the board of trustees. Letting the CIA operate covertly out of the think tanks they had set up at Columbia. Accepting large donations from companies that make napalm. Allowing the science labs to be used for research by the military-industrial complex."

"But did you manage to change anything in the end?"

"We did get Columbia to renounce the napalm money from the big corporations, and the chemistry department did agree to stop working on several Pentagon projects."

"That's something, I guess."

"You don't sound impressed."

"Am I supposed to be impressed?" I asked.

"Revolutionary change doesn't happen overnight—especially in such an ingrained capitalist system like the United States. The problem here, unlike pre-Bolshevik Russia, is that the proletariat lives under the illusion that they can push their way into the bourgeoisie through hard work and obedience to the secular state. You don't have the same sort of downtrodden serf class as existed in czarist Russia. Instead, the exploitation is hidden under the guise of consumerism—making the working classes feel they need that new car, that new washing machine, that new remote control color television . . . all the totemic goodies of a rabidly acquisitive . . . am I boring you?"

"No, I'm listening," I said.

"But you're also sitting with your head back against the stern, staring up at the sky."

"Can you blame me? Look at where we are."

"Point taken."

"I'm not trying to make a point, Toby."

"No, but I stand guilty of shooting off my big mouth, as usual."

"You talk a good game."

"Really?"

"Oh come on, you *do* know that. And it is interesting."

"But not in the middle of a lake on a day like today."

"You're learning," I said.

Long pause.

"Why did you ask me if I was religious?" I asked.

"Because I get the sense that—how can I say this without sounding totally asinine?—you're searching for some sort of meaning."

"Isn't everyone? But religion's too easy. 'God is watching you . . . God will help you overcome your problems . . . and if you play by the rules on earth, you'll get life ever after.' I don't believe it for a moment."

"But you do want to believe *something,* don't you?"

"You mean, the way you *believe* in revolutionary politics, or the way my dad believes in nonviolent political change?"

"Perhaps."

"Actually, what I really want to believe in is myself—and my ability to do something well."

"What do you mean by that?"

I was reluctant to delve into the things that were nagging me about my life—not just because I was certain that they seemed so banal and housewifey compared to the "forces of revolutionary change" that Toby was dealing with, but also because it seemed strange (not to mention a little shabby) to be talking about how trapped I felt while holding my son in my arms.

But I still said, "What I mean is that I know it's 'bourgeois conventions' that are keeping me in my place and stopping me from doing anything special. But I'm helplessly tied to those conventions. Because the idea of doing something really radical—like walking out on my husband and son—is simply impossible."

"Hey, not everyone can play Trotsky," he said. "And breaking social convention, especially when there is a kid involved, isn't easy. But you can make little acts of protest against all the day-to-day stuff you have to put up with."

"Like what?"

He smiled at me. "Like anything that goes against the marital contract, or what is expected of you, or how you're supposed to behave."

A long silence.

"I don't think I could do that."

"Do what?"

"Do what you are suggesting."

"I'm suggesting nothing. I'm just saying that your husband probably doesn't realize what a lucky guy he is . . . and what a remarkable person you are."

"That's flattery."

"Maybe, but it's also accurate."

"What makes me remarkable?"

"The way you see things . . . and the fact that you're beautiful."

"Now you really are talking shit."

"Have you always suffered from such a poor self-image?"

"Yeah—and I haven't blushed like this since . . ."

"Last night."

I said nothing. I just felt myself blushing some more.

"Let's get off this subject," I said.

"Good timing, since we've also got to get off this lake."

He picked up the paddle, sat up straight in the stern, and began the half-hour paddle back toward the shoreline—the sun just beginning its slow descent toward dusk. We said little on the way back, though the thought did strike me that no one had ever called me remarkable before. I kept mulling over what he said to me about marriage:

Breaking social convention, especially when there is a kid involved, isn't easy. But you can make little acts of protest against all the day-to-day stuff you have to put up with . . .

But the one *little* act of protest that I could make struck me as an enormous step—and a frontier I could not cross without suffering calamitous guilt.

We reached the shore, we returned the canoe, we loaded ourselves back into the car. Toby drove again—as Jeffrey had woken up and was demanding nourishment. So I sat in the back with him, feeding him from the bottle I had brought along.

"Doesn't he mind that it's cold?" Toby asked.

"When you're hungry, you're hungry. Anyway, how do you—the great *I'll never have children* guy—know all about cold bottles of formula?"

"I used to feed my two nieces when they were babies."

"Ever change a diaper?"

"I don't do diapers—as my sister well knew."

"Is she your only sister?"

"She was my only sibling."

"*Was?*"

"She died a few years ago."

"Oh God, that's terrible."

"Yes," he said quietly, "it was."

"Had she been ill or something?"

"Something," he said in a way that hinted he didn't want to talk about this anymore.

Darkness was falling when we reached Pelham. Toby parked the car outside of the doctor's office. Inside, I could see Nurse Bass doing some paperwork at the reception desk. She looked out as the car pulled up—and I watched her watching us, taking in the detail that Toby was behind the wheel, that he was helping me bring in Jeff, and that we had evidently been somewhere together for the afternoon. I waved to her and flashed her a big false smile. She immediately looked away, glancing down at the pile of papers on her desk.

Upstairs, I changed and fed Jeffrey, then put him in his playpen. Toby rolled up his sleeves and began to chop garlic.

"Anything I can do to help?" I asked.

"Yeah, get lost for a while and let me get on with the cooking."

"You sure about that?"

"Like totally sure."

"Mind if I take a bath, then?"

"Why would I mind? And if Junior here starts acting up, I'll just give him a glass of Chianti to keep him quiet. Okay?"

I couldn't remember the last time somebody cooked for me, or when I had the luxury of soaking in a very hot tub for over an hour. Even at night, when Dan was home and Jeff was asleep, the idea of a really long bath always seemed an overindulgence—and Dan was always good at reminding me (mildly, of course) of all the domestic stuff that still needed to be done. But now I was determined to lie there without interruption until Jeff needed me or Toby told me dinner was ready . . . though I did keep the door ajar, just in case my houseguest could not handle my son's occasional obstreperousness.

But, from what I could hear through the door, Toby and Jeff got on just fine—and around an hour into my lengthy soak, the chef announced that dinner would be ready in about twenty minutes. So I hauled myself out of the bath, toweled myself down, put on a robe, and dashed into the bedroom. I went into the closet and chose a long flowery skirt and a white gauze shirt that I had always liked but rarely wore.

"You look beautiful," Toby said as I came into the living room.

"Oh please . . ." I said.

"Why do you blush when I say that?"

"Because (a) I'm not used to it, and (b) you're not my husband."

"But (c) it's just a comment . . . and (d) it should be taken as such. Cool?"

"Cool."

"Glass of wine?"

"Sure, but let me call Dan first."

I sat down on the sofa, picked up the phone, and dialed Glens Falls. Dan answered on the third ring. He sounded close to despair.

"I got a phone call around seven this morning, saying they thought he was going . . . so I rushed down there. But by the time I got to his bedside, he'd rallied again. The doctor told me he's never seen anyone like Dad—he's exactly like a prizefighter who's about to be called out and always seems to rally on the ninth count. He just doesn't want to let go—and who can blame him? Though, if I stay here much longer, it's me they'll be carrying out feetfirst."

"Then come home," I said tersely, even though it was the last thing I wanted right now.

"That's exactly what I'm planning to do in two or three days. How's things?"

I gave him a pretty anodyne synopsis of the day's events, leaving out the canoe ride on Sebago Lake, but mentioning that our "houseguest" was still here.

"Is he okay?" Dan asked, sounding not terribly interested.

"Yeah, fine."

"Sorry if I sound a little out of it. I am. Got to go. Kiss Jeff for me. Tell him his daddy misses him."

And with a fast good night, he was off the phone. I hung up the receiver, reached for my cigarettes, lit one up. I felt suddenly edgy.

"Everything okay?" Toby asked, handing me a glass of wine.

"Yeah, fine . . ." I said, taking a big gulp of wine and another drag off my cigarette. "Well, no, actually, things are not fine."

"Is it all to do with his dad?"

"And other stuff. But to tell the truth, that dinner smells too damn good to spoil it with *other stuff.*"

He topped up my glass. "Then let's eat," he said.

I brought Jeff back to his crib, but he resisted all my efforts to settle him down and began to cry when I walked back into the living room.

"Great," I said. "Just great."

"He obviously doesn't want to leave you alone with me."

"Or maybe he wants another glass of wine."

"Bring him in—and I promise you that our conversation will so bore him, he'll be asleep in fifteen minutes."

I did as ordered, lifting Jeff out of his crib and balancing him on my knee as we ate. The food was sensational. *Rigatoni con salsiccia*—a round pasta baked with Italian sausage, a homemade tomato sauce, and a thin crust of Parmesan cheese—was the best Italian dish I'd ever eaten. The garlic bread was perfect—Toby didn't just use fresh garlic and oregano, but had also managed to obtain proper Italian bread. And halfway through the meal, Jeff did tire of all this grown-up chat and passed out.

"Where did you learn to cook like this?" I asked as Toby opened the second bottle of wine.

"Prison."

"Yeah, right."

"Well, I was in jail twice."

"For how long?"

"Around two nights in both instances—and I was let off without charges. The feds really don't like wasting their time prosecuting civil disobedience. But the truth is: I learned how to cook Italian courtesy of a woman named Francesca, whom I met at Columbia."

"Was she Italian-American or Italian-Italian?"

"Italian-Italian. A Milanese—and her parents were good Gucci Communists, which meant that their daughter had read her Marcuse and her Che Guevara, but also knew how to dress and how to make a great *rigatoni con salsiccia.*"

"So we're eating her recipe?"

"Indeed we are."

"And this Italian Communist was, no doubt, beautiful and very worldly?"

A smile. "Yes, on both counts. And you're jealous."

"Because I wish I was beautiful and worldly."

"What did I say at the lake?"

"You were just making me feel good."

"I was telling the truth."

"I wish I could believe that."

"Your husband has done a real number on you, hasn't he?"

"Not totally."

"Your mom as well?"

"She's a rather critical woman."

"A ballbuster . . . something your father confided to me several times. And I'm sure it wasn't easy growing up with a dad who was so much in the public eye and so sought after."

"Especially by available women."

"And what's such a big deal about that?"

"No big deal."

"You don't really believe that. You hate the fact that your dad slept around. Although you'd never have the courage to cheat on your husband."

"How do you know that?"

"Because it's written all over you," he said, smiling.

Silence. I reached for my cigarettes, lit one up, and asked, "Can I have another glass of wine, please?"

He refilled my glass.

"Did I speak a little too bluntly?" he said. "Did I *tell it like it is*?"

"You don't really care if you did, do you?"

"Who likes hearing the truth?"

"I don't need to hear what I already know."

"Whatever you say."

"You really *do* think I'm a hick."

"No, *you* think you're a hick. I think . . . well, you remind me a lot of my sister, Ellen."

"What happened to her?"

"Ellen was a very decent woman. Perhaps too decent. Always trying to please everyone, always putting others first, always downplaying her own needs and ambitions. An incredibly bright woman—magna cum laude from Oberlin—who got trapped in a dead-end marriage with an accountant. Within four years, she'd had three kids and felt totally hemmed in—her husband, Mel, turned into one of those schmucks who think a woman's place is at the stove. But instead of doing the difficult, dangerous thing and breaking free, she felt duty-bound to tough out the marriage. Little by little, she slid into a major depression. Mel—a real Mr. Understanding—kept taunting her about 'being such a downer.' He actually threatened to have her institutionalized if she didn't snap out of it. She told me this three days before her car went off the road in a remote spot up the Lake Erie coast. She'd plowed right into a tree. And as she wasn't wearing a seat belt—"

He broke off for a moment, staring into his glass of wine.

"The cops found a note in her very neat handwriting on the dashboard: *Sorry I had to do this—but my head just hurts all the time, and it's hard living with a hurt head.*"

Another pause. Then, "A month after Ellen's suicide, I got arrested for tossing back a police tear gas grenade during the Chicago convention riots. Two months after that, I was back at Columbia, spearheading the siege of the administration building. And yeah, my sister's death and those other events are completely interrelated. What happened to her completely radicalized me—made me want to lash out at every conformist asshole in this country. That's the thing about America—if we don't knuckle down and accept our roles, society crushes us. That's what people like me and your dad are really fighting against. Ellen tried to break free. Ellen was destroyed. And that's your fate if you don't . . ."

His hand slid across the table and his fingers laced through mine. "If I don't what?" I asked, my voice a whisper.

He tightened his grip on my fingers.

"If you don't break free," he said.

"I don't know how to break free."

"It's easy," he said. "You just . . ."

That's when he kissed me, his mouth covering mine. I didn't resist. On the contrary, I'd been so desperate to kiss him for the past day that I was all over him in a moment. We slid off our chairs and onto the nearby couch. He was now on top of me. I opened my legs and pushed myself up against him, his penis hard within his jeans. He began to pull my skirt up. I dug my nails into his back, my tongue down his throat. And then . . .

Then . . . Jeffrey started to cry.

At first I tried to ignore his whimpers. But as they escalated into a full-scale roar, I froze.

"Oh, great," Toby said, rolling off me.

"Sorry," I said, then jumped up, pulled down my skirt, and raced into the bedroom. Jeff calmed down once I picked him up. I cuddled him against me and slipped the pacifier back into his mouth. I sat down on our bed, rocking my son, my head spinning, an ever-creeping guilt seizing me. As I pulled Jeffrey closer against me, I felt something close to horror.

"You okay in there?" Toby called from the next room.

"Yeah, fine," I said. "Just give me a moment."

Once I was certain Jeff was on the verge of nodding off again, I gently put him back in his crib, covered him with his little blanket, and stared down at him, gripping the side of his crib for support.

I can't do this . . . I just can't do this.

The door opened. Toby came in, a glass of wine in each hand.

"Thought you could use this," he whispered, handing me one.

"Thanks," I said, accepting it. He leaned over and kissed me. I sort of responded, but he could immediately sense my reserve.

"You okay?" he asked.

"Yeah, fine."

"Good," he said, kissing my neck. But I hunched my shoulders against him and said, "Not here."

We went back out into the living room. As soon as he closed the bedroom door behind us, his hands were all over me again. This time, though, I gently pushed him away.

"What's wrong?" he asked.

"I just can't."

"The kid?"

"That and—"

I broke off, walking to the other end of the room, looking out the window.

"Bourgeois guilt?" he asked.

"Thanks for that," I said, not turning around.

"Hey," he said, coming over and putting his arms around me, "can't you take a seriously bad joke?"

I turned and faced him. "I want to, but—"

He kissed me.

"It's not a big deal," he said.

"I—"

Another kiss.

"No one will know," he said.

"I'll know."

Another kiss.

"So?"

"I'll have to live with—"

Another kiss.

"Guilt is for nuns," he said.

I laughed. And kissed him. And said, "Then I'm a Mother Superior."

He laughed. And kissed me. And said, "You are beautiful."

"Stop."

"You are beautiful."

Another kiss.

"Not now," I said.

Another kiss.

"Then when?" he asked. "When?"

When? The question that had been plaguing me all my life. *Paris when? New York when? Career when? Independence when?* And, as always, I had a ready-made, play-it-safe answer: *not now.* He was right. *When? When? When would I ever take a chance?*

Another kiss.

You are beautiful.

When had Dan last said that to me?

Another kiss—and I felt his hand reaching down, pulling up the back of my skirt again.

"Not here," I whispered, suddenly remembering that we were kissing by a window.

"Don't worry," he said, reaching over to pull down the blind. "It's night. The place is deserted."

I glanced out the window as the blind came down and thought I saw someone standing in the shadows looking up at us.

"Who's that?" I hissed.

Toby stopped lowering the blind and peered out the window.

"You're seeing ghosts," he said.

"You sure?"

The blind closed behind him. He gathered me up in his arms.

"There is nothing to worry about," he said.

Another kiss. And another kiss. And another kiss.

I took him by the hand. I led him to the bedroom. Jeff was fast asleep. I turned toward Toby and pulled us both down onto the bed. Telling myself, *Nothing to worry about. Nothing at all.*

EIGHT

WE MADE LOVE twice that night. By the time Toby fell asleep, it was nearly three in the morning. I was still wide awake—spent, depleted, expended, played out, but *wired.* Because my son was sleeping just three feet away from the bed where such unbridled ardor had taken place . . . the bed I had only ever shared with Dan until tonight.

Once Toby had dropped off to sleep, I extricated myself from his pleasurable grip (he had his arms bound tightly around me) and checked again on Jeff. Still conked out, oblivious to everything. During our love-making, I'd had the occasional dreadful thought that I'd find Jeff sitting up in his cot, staring at all this wild physical activity being acted out in front of him. And though I would rationalize to myself that his six-month-old brain certainly wouldn't register what was going on before him, even the thought that I had considered sleeping with another man in front of my son . . .

I backed off from the crib, returned to bed, and actually clasped the pillow over my ears to block out that angry, reproving voice that was telling me, in no uncertain terms, just what an immoral monster I'd been. Just as the rational, Bad-Girl side of my brain was shouting back, *Drop the guilt trip. Toby's right: guilt is for Carmelites. Anyway, why beat yourself up over the fuck of your life?*

That's what still had me reeling—the sheer amazing out-of-body experience that making love with Toby had been. The way he was able to unlock . . .

I got up and walked into the living room. I grabbed my cigarettes and lit one, then stormed over to a kitchen cabinet where I kept the one bottle of liquor we had in the house—a fifth of Jim Beam bourbon. I found a glass. I poured a slug. I threw it down. It numbed the back of my throat but did nothing to dampen down my anxiety. So I resorted to diversionary tactics—and washed all our dinner dishes, all the pots and pans Toby had used. Then I noticed that the kitchen floor was pretty damn dirty, so I got out a bucket and mop and scrubbed the linoleum. After that, I found a sponge and a bottle of Mr. Clean, and I tackled all the kitchen surfaces, not to mention the bathroom. While negotiating a particularly bad ring of gunk in the bathtub, I thought, *So this is how you celebrate the best sex you've ever had . . . Are you pathetic or what?*

Guilty. Guilty as charged.

After finishing the bathroom, a wave of exhaustion hit me. I put away the cleaning supplies, flopped on the sofa, lit up yet another cigarette, and wished to God I could calm down. But the guilt was all-pervasive and uncontrollable, like a fever that kept spiking and wouldn't respond to any medicine.

He has to go in the morning. He has to pack up his backpack and hit the road before sunrise. Then I have to wash the sheets—twice, at least—and thorough-clean the bedroom to make certain that any evidence of his whereabouts has been scrubbed and vacuumed away. Then I will try to forget all this has happened. I will file it away in that box marked "Off Limits" and wipe it from my memory . . .

Like fuck you will.

I slammed my fist down on the coffee table, trying to end this inane debate. I glanced at my watch. Five-fifteen. Tomorrow was nearly here—and the day would be one long exercise in self-reproach. One more cigarette and I would try to get an hour or so of sleep . . . before Jeff sprang into action.

But as I was lighting my fourth cigarette of this guilt-ridden all-nighter, the bedroom door opened. Toby staggered out, completely naked, looking scarcely awake. He squinted at me, as if it was hard to discern me in his half-asleep state.

"Don't tell me you're feeling guilty," he said, walking over to where the bottle of bourbon had been left on a countertop.

"What makes you think that?"

"Oh please," he said, pouring some bourbon into a glass. "Rattling around here like Banquo's ghost, doing dishes, *cleaning house* . . . it was all pretty damn audible in the bedroom. And it also woke me up."

He brought the glass of bourbon over and sat next to me on the sofa.

"Sorry," I said.

"Don't be sorry about anything," he said, stroking my face. "Especially about the sex. Because sex is *just* sex—and fucking is good for the psyche. A way to shake your fist against convention, entrapment, death."

"Yeah, you're right," I said.

"You sound deeply unconvinced."

"No, I'm fine."

"Then why can't you sleep right now?"

"Because . . . this is all new territory for me."

"Don't tell me you're worried about 'betraying' your husband and all that conventional stuff."

"I'm trying not to be."

"It's a little late for that now, isn't it? If you didn't want to fuck me, you shouldn't have fucked me."

"That's not the point," I said quietly.

"Then what is the point? Let's follow the Socratic argument here. You wanted to fuck me, even though you were also worried about feeling guilty. But you decided that the fuck was worth the guilt, even though you knew you'd be feeling guilty afterward. In other words, you engaged in a pleasurable activity, knowing full well that you'd hate yourself for doing it—which is kind of skewed, masochistic logic, isn't it?"

I hung my head. He said, "Oh, for Christ's sake, don't act like a schoolgirl who's been chastised . . ."

"Well, aren't you chastising me?"

"No, what I'm doing is trying to snap you out of this guilt jag. It's pointless and it's self-defeating."

"It's easy for you to say that—you're not married."

"It all comes down to perception: how you want to interpret an event, the way you want to color it, to turn it into a commentary on yourself . . . or simply see it for nothing more than what it is."

"Maybe you're one of those lucky types who don't have a guilty conscience."

"And maybe you're the sort of person who always has to beat herself up, and can't just live in the moment."

I hung my head again. Nobody likes hearing the truth about themselves.

"'The mind is its own place, and in itself can make a Heaven of Hell, a Hell of Heaven.' Know it?"

"Yeah."

He touched my chin with his finger, gently raising my head up again.

"Milton had a point, didn't he?" he asked.

I nodded.

"Well, stop making a hell of things, eh?"

I said nothing. He kissed me lightly on the lips, then asked, "Is that your idea of hell?"

I said nothing. He kissed me again.

"Still feeling hellish?"

"Stop it," I said quietly, but I still accepted his next kiss.

"Look, if you want me to go . . ." he said and he kissed me again, "just say the word and I'm gone."

Another kiss. This time I reached up and pulled him toward me.

"Don't go yet," I said.

We made love on the sofa—slowly, gently, with no rush to finish, no sense of time beyond this time, this place, this precise extraordinary moment. When we finished I held him tight—not wanting to let him go. I felt myself choke back a sob—and worked hard to control it. But he heard it.

"Not more guilt?" he asked.

No—the sad, terrible realization that I was falling hard for this guy . . . and that I would have to let him go.

"Please stay a few more days," I said.

"I'd like that," he said. "I'd like that a lot."

"Good."

Eventually dawn's early light found the gaps in the blinds and sent eerie autumnal rays across the room. In the bedroom I could hear Jeff stirring. Toby went off to have a bath. I dealt with my son's assorted needs—and after changing and feeding him, placed him in his playpen as I made coffee. Toby emerged from the bathroom. We sat at the table and said nothing, possibly because we were both so damn tired after a night without sleep, but also because we really didn't need to say anything right now.

I finished my coffee. I showered and got dressed. When I came back into the living room, Toby was crouched down by the playpen, making funny faces for my son's benefit. Jeff giggled wildly—and all I could think was: *Why isn't this man my husband?* With that thought came a split-second reverie of a life with Toby . . . the fantastic conversations, the fantastic sex, the mutual respect, the sense of shared destiny . . .

Now you really are acting like a lovesick teenager. The guy is the original free spirit. Here Today, Gone Tomorrow. You're a fuck to him, another notch in the belt, and nothing more.

But then he lifted Jeff up and buried his head in his stomach and made all sorts of funny noises, causing my son to howl with laughter—and I immediately wanted to have a kid with him.

Oh, lady, are you some idiot.

He put Jeff back in the playpen, then came over and kissed me gently on the lips.

"You look lovely," he said.

"No, I look wrecked."

"You really do love giving yourself a bad time."

I kissed him back and said, "Stick around and maybe I'll lose the habit."

He returned the kiss.

"Invitation accepted."

"So what are you going to do today?" I asked.

"First order of business is to go back to bed."

"Lucky you."

"When you get back from work, you can grab a nap."

I cupped his backside in one of my hands and pulled him toward me.

"Only if you'll grab it with me."

"You're on," he said.

There was one final long kiss before I glanced at my watch and said, "I really have to go."

"Then go," he said. "And don't spend the day thinking that everyone knows you've got some big guilty secret."

That fear had been one of a stream of paranoid thoughts that had run through my head all night: as soon as I showed my face around

Pelham this morning, everyone would know. It would be written all over me.

Just act as if nothing has happened—because, as far as everyone is concerned, nothing has happened . . . unless you indicate otherwise.

So when I brought Jeff over to Babs's house, I just smiled my regular smile and tried to act nonchalant when she said, "Looks like you haven't slept all night, hon."

"Jeff had bad colic . . ."

"Real curse, that one. When Betty was six months old, she kept me awake for two straight weeks with her damn colic. Felt like I was about to go gaga by the end of it all."

"Well, that's just about how I feel now—and I've only had a day of it."

"He keep your visitor up last night?"

"Uh, no . . ."

"Must be a pretty sound sleeper, then."

Was she giving me a telling look—or, worse yet, was I blushing or acting suspicious?

"Never heard him stir."

"Guy must sleep like the dead. You gonna want him at the same time today?"

"Want who?" I asked, sounding jumpy.

"Your baby boy, of course. Who'd you think I was talking about?"

"Sorry, sorry. Sleep deprivation kind of makes me scatty."

"Listen, you want a nap this afternoon, I can keep him on till four or five."

I liked the sound of that. It would give me a couple of hours alone with Toby.

"You sure it wouldn't be an inconvenience?"

"Your little boy is never an inconvenience. And you really look like you could use some time alone in bed."

By which you mean . . . ?

"Well, thanks, Babs," I said. "I'm really grateful."

"You take as long as you like in bed, okay?" And she gave me a little wink.

As I walked over to Miss Pelham's, I kept trying to analyze that damn wink, wondering what the hell it meant, had she read me like an open book, or put two and two together to make four . . . or whether she was just pulling my chain, seeing if she could get some sort of rise out of me. But why would Babs do that, unless she had definite suspicions . . .

I stopped into Miller's Grocery for my *Boston Globe* and cigarettes.

"You're looking tired today," Jesse Miller said to me.

"Bad night with the baby."

"Uh-huh," she said, handing me my paper and smokes. "When's the doctor back?"

"Any day now, I hope."

Uh-huh. Was that just one of Jesse's usual uncommunicative grunts . . . or was that a who-you-trying-to-kid uh-huh? And why did she ask about Dan's return in the same damn breath?

When I reached the library an hour later, Estelle said, "Well, everyone's speculating whether you're up to anything."

"Jesus-fucking-Christ . . ." I said, hoping I sounded sufficiently outraged.

"Hey, it's just the usual malicious small-town speculation. Everyone privately realizes that nothing's going on. You'd have to be insane to do something like that in a place as all-knowing and miserable as Pelham. People just want something to talk about—and the fact that you've got a good-looking college friend staying with you while the Doc is out of town, well, it gives everyone a chance to think about something other than their petty problems for an hour or so."

I didn't mention Estelle's observation to Toby when I got home. Maybe that had something to do with the fact that, as soon as I was in the door—and he saw that I was baby-less—he pulled me straight into bed. I didn't put up a struggle, but I was just a little conscious that we were making love directly above Dan's office. Knowing that the bed creaked loudly, I insisted that we pull the mattress onto the floor. Toby didn't like this interruption, especially as we were half undressed and all over each other when self-preservation and common sense took over. Then again, if I really had any common sense and self-preservation, I wouldn't be trying to pull a mattress to the floor while my lover cupped his hands over my breasts and kissed the nape of my neck.

"Give me a hand here," I giggled.

"This is more fun," he said.

"And more work for me."

"You're being paranoid about the bed."

"You heard it creak last night."

"No . . . I was otherwise engaged."

"Very funny."

He buried his face against the side of my neck.

"C'mon, just one big tug," I said, feeling myself get wetter.

"All right, all right," he said—and grabbed hold of the side of the mattress, hoisting it down with one ferocious pull. I fell on top of it. He followed—and I pulled him straight inside me, desperate to hold on to him, terrified that we'd make too much noise, trying to lose sight of everything beyond this room, wondering if we could be heard downstairs, not caring a damn whether we could be heard downstairs, wanting him to get up and leave town as soon as we were finished, wanting to keep him here for as long as possible, wondering if this was what love was, telling myself I was playing an insane game, never wanting this moment to end.

Afterward, we clung to each other and said nothing for a very long time. He ran his finger slowly down my face, and finally broke the silence.

"It's shitty luck, isn't it?" he said.

"What is?"

"You being married."

I put my finger on his lips. And said, "Let's not talk about that. This is too nice, too—"

But he cut me off.

"And when your husband comes back tomorrow or the next day, how are you going to file this little affair away? *Une petite aventure,* as the French tend to call it; *un rêve* that will seem even more like a dream with the passage of time?"

"Toby, please don't spoil . . ."

"Spoil what? The illusion that this is something more than it is?"

I suddenly felt very worried about the direction this conversation was taking.

"This can only be what it is," I said.

"'And I have always relied on the kindness of strangers,'" he said, putting on a Southern accent. I felt as if I had been slapped across the face.

"That was a nasty thing to say."

"Sorry."

"No, you're not."

"You're right, I'm not sorry. I'm angry. Angry that you're trapping yourself in such a dead-end marriage, in such a dead-end town. Angry that you can't run off with me . . ."

"You want me to run off with you?"

"Damn right I do."

"Oh, Toby . . ." I said, putting my arms around him again.

"Don't 'Oh, Toby' me. The fact is, you're not going to run off with me because you couldn't turn your back on—"

"What can't I turn my back on?" I said. "My 'bourgeois comfort'? My 'domestic subservience'? My 'need to uphold traditional American values'? I'd walk out of this town, this *marriage,* for you right now . . . if it wasn't for my son."

"He shouldn't be an excuse."

"Jeffrey is not an excuse. You know nothing about parenthood. No matter how tied down your kids make you feel, you'd still scratch out the eyes of anyone who would dare try to take them away from you. I never understood this until I became a mom . . ."

"A mom," he said, the sarcasm showing. "Is that how you see yourself—*Mommy?*"

"You're being cruel."

"Only because I want to snap you out of your complacency . . ."

"I am not fucking complacent."

"If you stay here, you will be. Whereas I can offer you . . ."

"I know what you can offer me. Romance, passion, adventure—all that big, heady stuff. Don't you think I want that? Don't you think I want to escape all this? But to do that, I would have to leave my son. And I cannot—*will not*—ever do that."

"Then you will always be caught up in this bullshit scene. The doctor's little wife."

I stiffened. "You don't know that."

"People don't change that much," he said.

"Are you always such a fucking absolutist?"

"Hey, why so testy? Don't tell me I struck a nerve."

I stood up and started reaching for my clothes.

"Are you always such an asshole?"

"Are you always so damn touchy when confronted with the truth?"

"You don't speak the truth; you speak crap and act as if it's the truth."

"Individual perception is everything."

"Yeah, you're right," I said, pulling on my jeans. "And do you know what I *perceive* right now? The fact that I've made a terrible mistake."

"It certainly didn't sound that way when we were fucking."

I turned and looked at him straight on. "That's exactly what this was for you: a fuck."

"Well, what was it for you? Love?"

He said that last word with such disdain that it landed like a slap across the face. I said nothing. I just continued to get dressed—avoiding his smirking gaze. Then when I was ready to leave, I said, "I have to go over and pick up Jeff now."

"And . . . ?"

"I'm happy to drive you over to Lewiston tonight. There's a Greyhound bus station."

"You're throwing me out?"

"I'm asking you to leave."

"All because I asked you to run away with me."

"That's not it . . ."

"Okay, because I had the audacity to challenge your image of yourself . . . to consider you special enough to want to try to make a life with you. And what do you do? You go ballistic—and tell me I'm an asshole and ask me to leave. And maybe I deserve that, because my style is just a tad confrontational. But if there's one thing I know about getting someone to embrace revolutionary change—whether political or personal—it's this: sometimes you have to hit them hard to shake them up."

"I don't need shaking up."

"I think you do. But listen, I think I'm just telling you stuff you've told yourself dozens of times, which is why you're screaming at the messenger. And before you bawl me out again, you don't have to drive me to Lewiston. I'll just get my stuff together and hit the road. I'll be gone by the time you get back."

"Fine," I said, and headed to the door. Then, when I got there, I suddenly turned back to him.

"Stay till morning," I said.

"Why?"

"So I can think this over."

As I walked downstairs, I deliberately passed in front of the doctor's office to gauge Nurse Bass's reaction to me. She was, per usual, seated behind the reception desk. She looked up as I walked by, gave me one of her usual curt nods, then returned her gaze to the *Reader's Digest.* Nothing in her face hinted that she had heard anything while Toby and I were upstairs. I walked on over to her house, trying to stay calm, trying to sort through the jumble of thoughts and fears that were racing around my head. I had been a fool to become so furious at Toby—because what he said had been fundamentally true. I did feel trapped. I did feel thwarted. I did feel unloved—and I knew how much I was to blame for being in a place I didn't want to be in. Just as I was flattered, *dazzled,* by the fact that Tobias Judson—star radical extraordinaire, a pinup among women lefties—actually wanted to run away with me. And he seemed genuine enough that he was willing to fight with me about it. How right he was about the way I had embraced the complacent option. And how I wanted to get back into bed with him at the earliest possible moment . . . preferably as soon as Jeff was down for the night.

But. But. But. The voice of reason—of boring play-it-safe conformity—kept whispering in my ear. Let's say you run off with the guy. You do the unthinkable—you abandon your son, leaving him behind with his father—and hit the road with the amazing Mr. Judson. He brings you everywhere. You meet all his famous friends. You go to Washington and have lunch with Senator McGovern. You go to Chicago and talk politics with Abbie Hoffman. You go to New York and visit Columbia, where he's treated like a radical deity—the John Reed of our times. You stay in hotels, motels, and friends' spare beds. You make love every night and the sex is never less than three-orgasm good. You sit in on meetings where he pitches an article to the editor of *Ramparts* or Carey McWilliams at *The Nation.* You attend the lunch where he talks over his book idea with an editor at Grove Press. Your parents approve of your choice of guy—and have few qualms about your walking out on your spouse and child ("It's about time you did something extreme," your mother tells you. "And frankly, I should have walked out on you and the Professor when you were five and I knew you were going to fuck up my life."). You are the envy of all those women you see at Toby's talks (besides everything else, he's also on a lecture circuit). You try to bask in his glory, but secretly feel like nothing more than an appendage. And no matter how good the sex is . . . no matter how interesting the people you meet are . . . you are haunted by one simple, terrible thought: You haven't simply left your son, you've also betrayed him—and in a way that would affect his life forever. You have failed him.

And then, in the midst of all this terrible longing for Jeff, this ongoing private grief, Lover Boy announces one day that he feels a little trapped by having a full-time woman in his life; that the moment has come when "we should both experiment with other alternatives" (or some such shit). You're devastated. You're terrified of being abandoned. You plead with him not to turn you out, to give you another chance. Your entreaties fall on deaf ears. "Hey, everything's ephemeral," he says. So you grab a Greyhound heading north and end up back in Pelham, where everyone looks at you as if you are the Fallen Woman, and where Dan slams the door in your face after telling you that it's too late for apologies or second chances. There will be no reconciliation—Dan has met a very nice, very available nurse at Bridgton Hospital who is now helping him raise Jeff and whom your little boy will consider his own mother . . . for his father will tell him (as soon as he's able to understand such things) that his real mother abandoned him for her own selfish, venal needs.

By the time I reached Babs's house, I was thoroughly spooked. I knocked on the door. It opened. Babs was holding Jeff in her arms. He gave me a big smile—and, per usual, my heart melted.

"I can't thank you enough for giving me the extra couple of hours today," I said.

"Well, he was no trouble whatsoever," she said. "You manage to get some sleep?"

"A little."

"You sure look like you've just gotten out of bed," she said. "And if I was you, I'd try to get a big long sleep tonight. If you don't mind me saying so, you could use it."

"Well, thank God it's the weekend."

"I hear ya. Have a good one, hon."

As I walked back into the apartment, the smell of frying garlic and tomatoes filled my nostrils. Toby was in the kitchen, adding ground beef to a hot, olive-oily skillet.

"You didn't have to do that," I said.

"Why not?" he said. "I mean, I like to cook, we have to eat, and anyway, I thought it would be a nice peace offering."

I put Jeff into his playpen, walked over, and put my arms around Toby.

"Peace offering accepted," I said, kissing him deeply. "And I'm sorry for—"

He put his finger to my lips and said, "You don't have to explain anything."

Another long, heady kiss. Then, "There's still a bottle of Chianti left," he said. "Why don't you get it opened?"

I did as commanded—and as I worked the corkscrew, I glanced into the bedroom and noticed that not only had he pulled the mattress back onto the bed, but he had also remade it perfectly . . . right down to the hospital corners.

"My, you were raised well," I said, nodding toward the bedroom.

"Well, my mom threatened to take back my bar mitzvah money if I didn't make the bed every . . ."

The phone rang. I picked it up, fully expecting to hear Dan's voice. Instead, I found myself talking to a stranger.

"Hi, can I speak with Jack Daniels?" he asked, his voice low and edgy.

"Who?" I asked. Immediately Toby stopped stirring the sauce and looked over at me.

"Jack Daniels," the voice said, sounding impatient.

"There's nobody with that name here," I said.

"He told me he'd be there."

"Look, you must have the wrong number."

"No, this is the right number."

"And I'm telling you there is no Jack Daniels here."

"Yes, there is," Toby said, hurrying out of the kitchen and relieving me of the phone.

"Hi, it's me," he said into the mouthpiece, his voice barely more than a whisper.

"Toby, what's going on?" I demanded. But he silenced me with a wave of the hand and then showed me his back. I stared at him, wide-eyed, wondering why someone had called Toby here, and why the sinister-sounding guy on the line referred to Toby by an alias. I couldn't read Toby's face because every time I tried to look at him straight on, he turned away. Nor was he giving anything away on the phone, as his end of the conversation was monosyllabic: "*Yeah . . . right . . . I see . . . When? . . . You sure? . . . How long? . . . You saw what? . . . And that's it? . . . Okay, okay . . . Got it . . . Yeah . . . Right now . . . Yeah, tonight . . . Done.*"

After he hung up, he avoided my gaze. But I could see that he was looking blanched and nervous.

"Oh fuck, the sauce," he said, dashing over to the frying pan and stirring the congealed contents. From the way he was attacking the garlic, tomatoes, and meat it was evident that he was nervous.

"What was that all about?" I asked.

Silence. He kept stirring the pan.

"Who was that on the phone?" I asked.

Silence. He kept stirring the pan.

I walked directly over to him, turned the heat off the pan, and pulled the spoon out of his hand.

"Tell me what is going on," I said.

He walked over to the table upon which I had left the Chianti bottle, poured himself a glass, and drained it in one go. Then he said, "You have to drive me to Canada tonight."

NINE

IT TOOK A moment to sink in.

"What did you just say?" I asked quietly.

He met my gaze. "You have to drive me to Canada tonight."

It was the use of the imperative that got me. No *Could you please . . .* Instead *You have to . . .* as if I had no choice.

I studied him carefully and immediately his eyes betrayed his fear.

"I don't *have* to do anything, Toby," I said, my voice as composed as his own.

"Yes, you do. Otherwise the feds could show up here at any moment . . ."

The feds. As in: Federal Bureau of Investigation. I felt a stab of terrible panic—but tried not to show it.

"And why would the feds be showing up here?" I asked, reasonableness itself.

"Because they're looking for me."

"And *why* are they looking for you?"

"Because . . ."

He paused.

"Because *what,* Mr. Jack Daniels? Is that your *code* name or some such shit?"

"We never use real names on the phone, just in case someone's listening to the call."

"And why would somebody be interested in listening to your calls?"

"Because of who I am, what I do."

"Yeah, but what you do is rabble-rouse, and occupy university administration buildings, and write the occasional *j'accuse* article in small-circulation lefty magazines."

"True, but I've also had an affiliation with a certain group . . ."

"*What* certain group?"

He poured himself another glass of wine and drained it in one go.

"The Weather Underground."

Oh shit, oh shit, oh shit. The Weather Underground was the violent, radical wing of the student protest movement—a collection of shadowy "revolutionaries" who thought nothing of using dynamite to achieve their so-called political aims.

"You're a Weatherman?" I asked.

"Not exactly. As I said before, I have an affiliation with them . . ."

"An *affiliation*? What does that mean—you're a *subcontractor*?"

"When I was the head of Students for a Democratic Society at Columbia, I was in contact with an entire range of radical groups—from the Panthers to the Weathermen. And since most of the Weathermen came out of the SDS, we were particularly close to them. So close that, when I moved to Chicago, some of the group out there got in touch with me. I've never openly endorsed their use of confrontational violence—even though I do believe that, for revolutionary change . . ."

"Why are the feds chasing you?"

A pause. He started reaching for the wine bottle again.

"You don't need another drink to tell me," I said.

He moved his hand away and instead reached for my pack of cigarettes. He lit one, took two deep drags, and said, "Did you read about a bombing in Chicago a couple of weeks ago?"

"A government office or something?"

"The regional office of the Defense Department, to be exact about it."

"You bombed that office?"

"Hell no. Like I said, I would never do anything violent."

"You'd just support the people who were doing it."

"Political transformation demands theorists, activists, and anarchists. And yeah, it was the Weathermen who blew up the building. The thing was . . . they set the charge to go off in the middle of the night, thinking there was nobody there. But they didn't realize that the Defense Department had decided to start using a firm of private security guards to keep an eye on things at night. There were two guards in the building at the time. They were both killed."

"Hey, it was just a couple of working stiffs. In your book, it was a small price to pay for political transformation."

"That's not how I think."

"Bullshit—but that's beside the point. Did the security guys have wives and children?"

He took another drag on his cigarette.

"I think so," he said.

"You *think*?"

"Both married, five kids between them."

"You must have been very proud of your Weathermen friends."

"They weren't my friends," he said, sounding angry.

"Comrades, then?"

"Does it matter?"

"So if you didn't plant the bomb," I said, ignoring his question, "then why are you on the run?"

"Because after the bombing went wrong, the two operatives stayed with me for a couple of days."

"In other words, you harbored two murderers."

"I let them chill at my place, that's all."

"But isn't it a criminal offense to let murderers chill out *chez vous*?"

"They are not murderers."

"In my book, if they killed two men, they are murderers . . . and don't you go telling me that, because it was a political act, it's not murder."

"Think what you want," he said. "The fact is: once the heat died down, the two guys staying with me slipped out of town—to points unknown . . . at which point it was suggested to me by some people in the organization that I get out of Dodge for a while too, just in case the feds or the police put two and two together and worked out that I had been hiding the operatives. Which is exactly what happened."

"How did they work that out?"

"I didn't get all the details on the phone, but it seems there was an informer in the organization, because the feds raided my apartment last night. And according to the guy who called me, they found the number of Eastern Airlines on a notepad by the phone. And from there they were able to . . ."

"Hang on," I said. "You told me that you hitched out here."

He stubbed out his cigarette and reached for another. After lighting it up, he said, "That was a lie. I flew from O'Hare to LaGuardia, then changed planes to Portland."

"Why Portland?"

"You don't want to know this."

"Yes, I do."

"Because when word got out that we'd been infiltrated . . . and I was told it was best to vanish for a while . . . in my panic I called your dad."

"You *what*?"

"Look, your dad's always been a great friend and I've always turned to him for advice."

I couldn't believe what I was hearing.

"And he advised you to use my place in Maine as a hideout?"

Now he did avoid my furious gaze.

"Not exactly. But he did say that, if I did happen to be in Maine . . ."

"Oh, bullshit!" I yelled. "You were told to get lost, you called John Winthrop Latham for advice, and he said . . ."

I stopped myself because I remembered exactly my conversation with Dad that evening—how I mentioned that Toby said he was just bumming around the country, having "fled" his doctoral thesis at the University of Chicago. And what was my father's reply?

"Typical of Toby to hit the road like that. He might be the brightest kid I've run across in thirty years, but he can never apply himself when it comes to the long haul. One of the best public speakers I've ever heard—articulate, funny, ferociously well-read, and a really good writer to boot. You should have seen the stuff he published in Ramparts *and* The Nation. *Great style—and a brilliant analytical mind . . ."*

And then, *"Can you put him up for a couple of nights?"*

Dad knew all along what Toby had done, what he was actually fleeing. Dad set me up.

". . . and he said, 'My daughter has a place in Maine. Quiet little town, just a couple of hours from the Canadian border. And best of all, her husband's away right now . . .'"

"That's not exactly how he put it."

"Let me ask you something," I said. "If your face has been all over the papers as a wanted man . . ."

"According to the guy on the phone, the feds haven't gone public on this yet. They raided my apartment, they want to talk to me, but I'm not on the Ten Most Wanted list. They know who planted the bomb and have established that I simply 'aided and abetted.'"

"Still, why didn't you just make a run for it to the border?"

"The thought did cross my mind—and I discussed it with my comrades. But there was a genuine worry that, if the feds were already onto me, they'd be watching the border. Anyway, even if they weren't onto me just then, the problem for someone with a big FBI file for allegedly subversive activities is that once you cross into Canada, you can't get back into the States without, at the very least, getting the third degree from the American authorities."

"So you decided—with my father's blessing—to use this shitty apartment as a hideout, in the hope that you wouldn't have to do the Maple Leaf Rag to the High North?"

"Yeah, something like that."

"And while you were indulging in the hospitality of the Great Radical Professor's daughter, why not fuck her at the same time?"

"I think that was a pretty mutual decision."

"Yeah, but if you hadn't come on to me, I would have never dared make the first move. And I wouldn't now be in such a goddamn mess."

I clenched my fists and tried to think clearly. After a moment, I said, "As far as I'm concerned, if you have to flee to Canada, you can pack your bag and hit the road straightaway. But knowing what I now know, there's no damn way I am driving you to the end of Pelham Main Street, let alone the border."

"You have no choice."

"Oh, cut the melodrama. We both know that, even if the feds have already tracked your movements to Maine, they're not going to figure out—"

"What? That I'm not here? Christ, you are naive. Don't you know that, having worked out I'm in Maine, they'll try to figure out all my known contacts here? And I promise you that, knowing my connections with your dad, they'll open up his file, see that he has a daughter in Maine . . ."

"How the hell are they going to know that?"

"Hannah, as far as the feds are concerned, your dad is a big-deal troublemaker—not to mention, in their book, an Eastern establishment class traitor. And if there's one thing that Hoover hates more than the Eastern establishment, it's a radical from their ranks. I promise you, they've got such a comprehensive file on John Winthrop Latham, they don't just know the name of each of his mistresses, but the time, place, and position of every fuck he's had since . . ."

"Shut up," I said.

"And just to be on the ultrasafe side they'll have run countless background checks on you and your husband. So, believe me, the feds know that you live in Pelham—and with me now in Maine, it's not going to take them very long . . ."

"All right, all right," I said, the fear now evident in my voice. But even though I had been completely persuaded, I still wasn't going to aid and abet his run to the border.

"Look," I said, trying to sound calm and rational. "If the feds do show up here and you're gone, I'm still going to be in trouble for putting you up, right? Whereas if I help you flee, I will be guilty of criminal activity."

He reached for the wine bottle, splashed some more Chianti in his glass, threw it back, then regarded me with contempt.

"I knew you'd try to get out of it. But you're not getting out of it—and here's why. If you don't drive me to Canada and the feds *do* nab me before the border, I will tell them you harbored me for all that time they were looking for me, and I'll even drop in the fact that we were lovers, just to really stick it to you. And even if I do make it into Canada undetected, once I'm there the Weather Underground will release a statement to the press, saying I've fled and that, thanks to the 'fraternal courage of certain comrades in Maine,' I was able to get out of the country. I promise you, once the feds read that, they'll do another cross-reference with your dad's file and you'll have a dozen agents swarming around Pelham with photographs of me. And when they discover that I was here under an assumed name, and that you knew my true identity . . ."

"You son of a bitch," I said.

"You can call me any name you want," he said. "The fact is: this is a war. And in a war, you sometimes have to bend the rules to achieve your aims. And I don't care what you think of me or my methods. All I know is, as soon as night falls, you are driving me to Canada. And if you refuse—if you force me to go it alone—"

He reached over and scooped up the car keys that I'd left earlier on the kitchen table.

". . . I'll take your car and drive it myself across the border. If you call the cops to have me arrested, I'll talk . . ."

"All right, I'll fucking drive you," I said.

He favored me with a nasty little smile.

"Good," he said. "And I promise you, if you do exactly what I say, follow everything I tell you, you'll be back in Pelham by early morning tomorrow, and no one will have even noticed you were gone."

Then he asked me if I had a road map of Maine. I said there was one downstairs in the car. He asked me to get it. I left the apartment and went outside to the Volvo. Once there, I leaned against the passenger door and fought the urge to get sick. *Don't think, don't think. Just do what he asks. Get it over with. Get back here, and hope to hell that when the feds arrive, you can play naive and dumb.*

I opened the car door and took the map out of the glove compartment. Then I went back upstairs.

Toby was crouching down by the playpen, goo-gooing with Jeffrey.

"He got a little upset when he realized you'd stepped out. So I was keeping him happy."

I pushed by Toby, reached into the playpen, and picked up my son.

"I don't want you even looking at him again," I said.

Toby let out an amused laugh.

"Hey, suit yourself," he said. "But you do know he's coming with us to Canada."

"Did you actually think I'd leave him behind?"

"No, but I thought you might try to deposit him with that babysitter you use—just to keep him out of this."

"And raise more suspicion?"

"My point exactly. Glad to see we're on the same wavelength. Can I see the map?"

I handed it to him.

"Why don't you get that sauce heated up while I'm plotting our route. And could you get some spaghetti going too?"

"I'm not hungry."

"Well, you're going to be driving all night—and you're not going to be able to stop anywhere to grab a bite, so you'd better eat now."

I walked over to the kitchen and turned the heat on under the sauce. Then I dug out the big pot I used for pasta, filled it with water, put it on the stove, and turned on the gas flame. While I waited for the water to boil, I plucked Jeffrey out of his playpen, put him in his high chair, and fed him a jar of applesauce. Toby reached for another of my cigarettes—then motioned me over to the table.

"It's a pretty direct shot from here," he said. "We drive to Lewiston, take the interstate to Waterville, switch for Route 201, and drive straight north to Jackman and the border. Keeping well within the speed limit, it's five hours tops each way. If we leave in an hour—around seven-thirty—and considering the time you'll have to spend in Canada to cross back over another checkpoint, you should be back here tomorrow by seven a.m. And since it's a Saturday, you'll be able to sleep for most of the day."

I said nothing. I simply nodded.

"I'll get the rest of dinner together," he said, standing up. "Why don't you sort out what you need for the drive—and then you can call your husband."

I went into the bathroom, stripped off all my clothes, and took a very fast, very hot shower—washing away any lingering reminder of Toby Judson from my body. Twice during the shower, I felt myself about to start sobbing, but I fought the temptation to start feeling sorry for myself. *Get through this . . . get through this.* So I finished the shower, dried off, wrapped a towel around myself, and went into the bedroom. I dressed in jeans, a T-shirt, and a sweater. Then I stripped the stained sheets off the bed, dug out the spare set from the closet, and remade the bed. I found a small travel bag and stuffed it with a couple of clean diapers, a spare set of pins, baby clothes, and an extra canister of baby powder.

"Dinner's ready," Toby shouted from the other room. I emerged with the bundle of dirty sheets, and said, "Back in a moment."

"Hey, do you really need to do laundry right now?"

I turned back to him and said, "Yes, I do. Because I need to remove every trace of you from this house."

I went downstairs. I shoved the sheets in the washing machine, dumped in some powder, turned it on. Back upstairs, I accepted a plate of pasta from Toby, turned away from him, and ate standing up. Toby laughed another of his shitty little laughs.

"If you want to be that way . . ." he said.

I slammed my plate down on the counter. And said, "Let's get something straight here, mister. I will follow your orders. I will do exactly what you say in order to get you to Canada and out of my life. But beyond that, I want nothing to do with you anymore. And I especially don't want to talk with you—except about the simple logistics of driving you across the border. Are we clear about that?"

"Have it your way," he said.

I finished the spaghetti, then filled the percolator with coffee and put it on the stove. As I waited, I prepared a couple of bottles of formula to bring with me, and threw two jars of baby food into the bag. Once the percolator dome started turning brown, I found a thermos and filled it with coffee, then went over to the little pantry where I kept a spare carton of cigarettes and dropped two packs into the bag. I knew I would be smoking heavily tonight.

"One small, crucial detail," Toby said. "Do you have a passport?"

As a matter of fact, I did have one—having gotten one three years earlier when I thought I might be traveling to Paris for my junior year abroad. I nodded.

"Good—and while you're at it, why don't you find your son's birth certificate. You don't need this stuff for entering Canada—most of the time they just wave you through—but just in case we encounter an asshole official at the border . . ."

"Fine," I said tersely. I returned to the bedroom, went into the closet, opened the file box where I kept all important documents, and dug out the passport and birth certificate. Then I went back into the living room and picked up the phone.

"You calling your husband?" Toby asked.

I nodded.

"Tell him that . . ."

"Leave it to me," I said sharply. I finished dialing the number. There was no answer for three, four, five, six rings. He must be out. And if he's out now, he'll ring later. And we will have to wait for his call, because if he rings around ten and I'm not here, he'll get worried and call Nurse Bass and ask her to check up on me. And she'll find the apartment empty and the car gone. And then . . .

Or if we do wait around until ten and then leave, I won't be back until at least ten the next morning. And people will notice that the car isn't there when they get up in the morning (people in Pelham *always* notice these things). And then . . .

Seven rings, eight rings, nine rings . . .

"No one there?" Toby asked.

I nodded.

"Well, hang up and we'll hold on until . . ."

Suddenly, someone picked up the phone. It was Dan, sounding out of breath and tired.

"You okay?" I asked.

"Just dashed in from the hospital. Why are you calling?"

"Why am I calling? I just wondered how your dad was doing."

"Sorry, sorry," he said. "I'm just usually the one who calls."

"So?"

"He's still holding his own. Still comatose, but his heart is stronger than ever. And I've decided I'm out of here tomorrow."

Oh great.

"That's terrific," I said, trying to sound genuinely enthused. "Will you be taking the bus?"

"No, the plane."

Worse and worse.

"Isn't that a fortune?"

"An old high school classmate, Marv English, is running the local travel agency here—and he managed to get me a flight to Portland via Syracuse and Boston for fifty bucks one way."

"That's . . . great. What time do you get in?"

"It's an early start. The flight from Syracuse is at seven-fifteen, but there's a two-hour stopover in Boston . . ."

Well, thank God for that.

"Still, I should be landing at Portland at ten-thirty . . . which is a hell of a lot easier than fourteen hours on the damn bus. So can you pick me up?"

"Uh . . . sure."

"And what about our houseguest?"

"As it turns out, he has to be out of here tomorrow too."

"Good timing, then."

"Yeah."

"You okay?"

"What do you mean?"

"You sound a little tense, that's all."

"Just a bad night with Junior," I said. "He doesn't seem able to settle right now."

"Well, that will pass. Can't wait to get the hell out of here," he said.

"It will be great to have you back," I lied.

As soon as I put down the phone, I turned to Toby and said, "We have to go now."

"So I gather."

I walked over to the window and glanced out at the street. Night had arrived. I checked my watch. Six thirty-five. All the shops on Main Street had closed. The place was deserted.

"Coast clear?" he asked.

"Yes."

"Let's do it."

Toby went down to the car first, bringing his backpack and my overnight bag. Upstairs, I changed Jeff's diaper, put him in a new onesie, and remembered to bring two pacifiers and a couple of rubber toys to keep him occupied. Then, leaving a light on in the living room (just in case anyone was out walking and happened to glance upstairs at our place), I picked up my son and brought him downstairs. En route, he started to cry—evidently not pleased about being exposed to a midautumn frost and a very dark early evening. I closed the driver's door beside me and held out my hand for the car keys.

"No funny stuff now," said Toby. "You drive us to a police station, I promise you I'll—"

"Shut the fuck up and give me the keys."

He actually laughed—and dropped the keys into my outstretched palm. I turned on the ignition, put the car into gear, and pulled out onto Main Street. Jeff was still crying.

"Is he going to keep this up all the way to the border?" Toby asked.

"If he does, too damn bad."

I turned into Main Street. It still looked completely empty. Until . . .

"Oh shit," I said.

"Just keep driving."

"It's Billy," I said, recognizing his sloping gait and the way he hung his head while walking. But as he heard our car approaching he looked up.

"Wave to him," Toby said.

"Don't tell me what to do," I said. But as we drove by, I did nod in Billy's direction. He smiled shyly—and I could see him taking in the fact that Toby and I were in the car with Jeffrey.

"If he mentions anything, just tell him you were driving me to the Greyhound station in Lewiston."

"I'd worked that one out already."

"Well, bravo for you. Right turn here."

"I do know the way to Lewiston."

We fell silent—and stayed that way for most of the next five hours. I had tossed a pack of cigarettes on the dashboard before setting off. We slowly worked our way through them during the drive north. The narrow back road to Lewiston was free of traffic. When we reached the interstate, I stuck to the speed limit, resisting the temptation to pick up a little extra time by traveling five miles an hour faster than allowed. I kept glancing at the clock on the dash. By the time we'd reached Waterville—and the turnoff to Route 201—Jeff had fallen asleep. I switched on the radio and listened to the music being spun by Jose, the nighttime DJ who always sounded like he'd had two joints too many and favored Pink Floyd, Iron Butterfly, and other trippy bands. Next to me, Toby seemed lost in some sort of deep personal reverie—chain-smoking, staring out the window, taking my refusal to speak with him at face value, looking pensive and drawn and more than a little anxious. And me? One hundred different things were swirling around my head—most of them centering on my father, my husband, the shit sitting next to me in the front seat, how Dad had betrayed me, how I had betrayed Dan, how this horrible little man had used all of us for his own aims, and how I was guilty of the worst judgment imaginable over the past forty-eight hours. I so wanted to talk to Margy right now and tell her everything, but I couldn't help thinking that the phone might be tapped, that the feds would be waiting for me when I returned (or, worse, were standing by at the border, ready to nab us), and wondering if my marriage would survive all this, and if Dan would try to take Jeff away from me, especially if I was found guilty of a criminal offense, and how I'd never really be able to look at my father again after what he did, and how I was more scared now than I had ever been in my life, and . . .

"Let's stop here for a moment," Toby said, pointing to a gas station at the intersection of the interstate and Route 201. "We need to fill up and I need to take a leak."

We pulled over and drove up in front of a pump. As I turned off the ignition, Toby reached over and pulled out the keys, pocketing them.

"I'll hold on to these," he said.

I was going to call him names, but felt too tired, too tense, to do so. So I just said, "Fine," and got out of the car to check on Jeff. He was completely zonked out. I glanced at my watch. Nine-eighteen. Three hours to the border, all going well. So far, we were on schedule.

The gas station attendant—an elderly man with a match in the side of his mouth—came out and filled the car and squirted some water on the windshield and wiped it off with a squeegee. Toby returned with three more packs of cigarettes.

"Figure we might need these."

"Yeah, we will. The keys, please. Now it's my turn for a pit stop."

"You actually think I'd drive off with your son in the backseat?"

No, I didn't, but I wanted to make the point that I completely distrusted him. So I just stuck out my hand and snapped my fingers. Another of his smirks and he dropped the keys in my hand.

I went into the grubby toilet and held my breath against the stench of blocked drains as I had a fast pee. Then I splashed some water on my face and avoided gazing at the cracked mirror over the sink. The last thing I wanted to do right now was look at myself too closely, if at all.

When I got back to the car, Toby was paying off the attendant. As I climbed into the driver's seat, he turned to Toby and said, "Letting the little woman drive? That's brave."

"Hey, I get to sleep," he said, nudging him.

He climbed in next to me and shut the door.

"Well, he was a total sexist asshole," he said.

"Just like you."

That was the last exchange we had for the next 130 miles. The road north was long, wooded, quiet, and slow. The trees formed a canopy that often blocked out all moonlight and made me crane my neck to peer over the headlights as the route gradually turned into a steep climb toward Canada. We passed through a couple of obscure, blink-once-it's-gone towns—but these were the only outposts on an otherwise empty stretch of track. And it reminded me (as if a reminder were needed) just how empty and lonely Maine could be. I was preoccupied with the thought that if we did break down out here, there would be no way we could get any help until morning. By which time . . .

I reached for another cigarette—and checked the clock. Ten twenty-three. Had an hour vanished just like that?

"Feel like some coffee?" Toby asked.

"Yeah," I said. He reached down for the thermos, unscrewed the top, and poured me a cup. I balanced it against the wheel as I drove, managing to sip it slowly. Once I'd finished, I handed the cup back to Toby without saying a word. Then I reached for another cigarette, lit up, and took a deep drag.

The FM station I'd been listening to faded away into static. I flipped the dial, and heard a rapid-fire disc jockey talking in French. Quebec was near. I pressed down further on the accelerator and passed a sign saying: *Border: 15 miles.*

A quarter of an hour later, we rolled into the town of Jackman. The clock on the dash said twelve-ten. Toby told me to pull over. I stopped in front of the local courthouse.

"I'm going to drive us across," he said. "It'll look better that way. And I want you to sit in the backseat and pretend you're asleep next to our baby. If the Canadian border guy wants to ask you a few questions, he'll wake you up. But my guess is, he'll just wave us through—and with you asleep in the back, he won't be able to get a good look at your face . . . which is kind of what you want, right?"

"Yes, that's what I want."

"Oh, and leave the passport and birth certificate with me, just in case he wants to inspect them."

I dug out the documents. I put them on the dashboard. I opened the door, got out, then slid into the backseat. Jeff stirred slightly, making a few grumbly noises. But then I noticed that he'd spit his pacifier out. I scrambled around the darkened floor until I found it, then popped it quickly into my mouth to crudely sterilize it before plugging it back between his toothless gums. I stretched out on the seat, my head just next to the baby chair.

"You ready?" Toby asked.

"Yes," I said, and closed my eyes.

It was around a five-minute drive to the border. I could feel the car slowing down. Toby turned the radio off. There was a minute when we weren't moving, then the car crept forward a little bit more, then it came to a stop. I could hear a window being rolled down, and someone saying, in a Quebec accent, "Welcome to Canada. May I see some identification, please?"

There was a rustle of papers, a pause, then, "And what brings you to Canada, Mr. Walker?"

Mr. Walker?

"We're visiting friends for the weekend in Quebec City."

The beam of a flashlight hit my face. I blinked and decided it was best to act as if he had woken me up. So I began to stir, looking up at the border guy with bemusement.

"*Désolé* . . . sorry," he muttered.

"You go back to sleep, hon," Toby said.

I lay down again, covering my face with my hands.

"You're traveling late," the official said.

"Just got off work at six—and we can only drive long distances with Junior here at night, when he's fast asleep."

"Don't remind me," the official said. "My two girls cried if they were more than thirty minutes in the car. Anything to declare?"

"Nothing."

"No cigarettes, alcohol, foodstuffs?"

"Nope."

"And you'll be returning to the U.S. on . . . ?"

"Sunday evening."

"Have a nice weekend in Quebec," he said.

"Thanks," Toby said, putting the car in gear and inching us forward. Around a minute later, as we were gathering speed again, he said, "Don't sit up yet . . . just in case."

"I won't."

"Well, that was easy. Not that I expected it to be particularly hard. Family men always get waved right through."

So that's another reason why he wanted me to drive him across. Because when the Canadian officials saw him with his alleged wife and child, they'd ask no questions and simply presume that he was simply dropping into the country for a social visit.

"All right," he said when we were a few miles further down the road. "You can sit up now."

"Aren't you getting out here?" I asked as we passed a sign thanking us for visiting the town of Armstrong.

"No," he said.

"Then where?"

"Around forty miles north of here. A large town called Saint-Georges."

"Forty miles? That's going to put another ninety minutes on my journey."

"Can't be helped. That's where my rendezvous has been arranged."

"Your *rendezvous*?" I said, sounding outraged.

"You didn't think I'd just drift into Canada like some draft-dodging goof, did you? When the heat is on, we have people up here to look after us."

"So you knew we were heading to Saint-Georges from the moment you got that phone call?"

"Does that matter right now? Forty more miles and I'm out of your life. And yeah, this might mean you won't get back to Pelham until nine—but big deal. If hubby has to wait a little while at the airport . . ."

Jeff stirred awake and started to cry. Immediately I unstrapped him from his seat and lifted him onto my lap.

"It's okay, it's okay," I said, pulling him close and reaching into the bag for a bottle. But he pushed the bottle to one side and raised his cries by a few decibels.

"You're going to have to pull over," I said. "He needs to be changed."

"And my rendezvous is scheduled for twelve-thirty—and I'm running late, so sorry."

"Pull the car over," I said.

"No," he said, and sped up.

Somehow I managed to change Jeff on the backseat—though twice we hit potholes on the road and he nearly went flying. I left the dirty diaper on the floor and had to fight the temptation to dump it on Toby Judson's head. But this was no time for grandstand gestures. The faster we were in Saint-Georges, the better.

At ten after one, we saw the lights of a large-ish town in the distance. A few minutes later, we were on its outskirts. There was a small mill just off the side of the road. As we approached it, Toby flashed the Volvo's lights. Out of nowhere, some lights flashed back. Toby turned off toward the mill, killing the headlights. Suddenly, we were encased in another blast of light—as the brights of an approaching car blinded us. Toby stopped the car and turned off the engine.

"What the hell is going on?" I hissed.

"They just want to make sure it's us—and not someone pretending to be us . . . like the cops."

I heard a door open and footsteps approach. A shadowy figure approached the car. I now understood why they'd blinded us with bright lights. It ensured that I didn't see the identity of the person drawing near us. Instead, all I could discern was a form peering through the driver's-side window, tapping twice on the glass and receiving a clenched-fist salute from Toby. Then the figure retreated, and a few seconds later, the brights were cut and we were plunged into darkness, my eyes aching from this abrupt blackout. Jeff started howling, but I plugged a bottle into his mouth and it immediately soothed him.

"All right," Toby said. "Here's where I get off. A couple of very basic, very simple things. I am going to get out of the car, get my bag out of the trunk, then walk toward the other car. You are to stay put in the backseat until the other car has pulled away—and wait here until a good five minutes have passed. If you don't, there will be trouble."

"Anything else?"

He reached into his pocket, fished out a wad of money, and put a bill on the passenger seat next to him.

"Here's twenty Canadian dollars, which will buy you gas before the Coburn Gore border crossing."

"I don't want your money," I said, simultaneously thinking, *The bastard arrived in Pelham with a wad of Canadian dollars on his person, just in case . . .*

"When you leave here," he said, ignoring me, "take Route 204 heading to Lac-Mégantic. After that, you hook up with the 161 going to Woburn. *La frontière americaine* is only a few miles from there. All going well you should be crossing back into the Land of the Free around three a.m. The American border guy is going to be deeply curious about why you're traveling with a baby in the middle of the night. Tell him you've been visiting friends in Montreal—and you got a call late last night from your husband, saying that his dad was dying and you're rushing back blah, blah, blah. If he's suspicious, he might search the car—but since it's clean, he can't hold you for feeding him a story he finds fishy, so he'll have to wave you through. Then, because you've already traveled a ways south, it's a straight back-road shot to Lewiston and Pelham."

"And when the feds raid my apartment in the next day or two, what should I say then?"

He laughed.

"They're not going to raid you," he said.

"If they found out that you flew from Chicago to Maine . . ."

"I didn't fly from Chicago to Portland. I hitched—because it seemed safer to hitch, just in case they were watching the bus stations, the airports . . ."

"Hang on, you told me they found an Eastern Airlines number on a pad in your apartment and then worked out . . ."

"I lied . . . to make sure you were scared enough to drive me here. And yeah, that was yet another shitty thing I pulled on you—but on behalf of the Revolution, I thank you for making your small but vital contribution to—"

"Get out," I said.

"Your wish is my command. One final thing: as much as you may now hate me, I am a man of my word. Now that you have gotten me here in one piece and without hassle, I will keep my promise that, if and when I am ever asked if anyone helped me across the border, I will never mention your name. And my advice to you now is: forget any of this ever happened."

"Believe me, that's exactly what I'm planning to do. Now beat it."

"Do yourself a favor, Hannah—stop trying to be good all the time."

"I said: beat it."

A final smarmy little smile. Why did guys like this always think they were so superior? *Stop trying to be good all the time.* But if the last two days had shown anything, they'd shown that I wasn't good. On the contrary, I had compromised everything important in my life for the sake of . . .

Behind the wheel, Toby flipped the brights twice. This was answered with a Morse code reply with headlights.

"Okay," he said. "Remember to stay still for five minutes after the car goes. Have a good life . . . if that's possible."

The headlights suddenly burst into life, enveloping us in a dazzling white glow. Toby got out of the car and slammed the door. A moment later, I heard the trunk open and close, then his footsteps on the gravelly ground. A moment or two later I heard a car start up and the headlights suddenly pulled away from us, beamed themselves in another direction, and disappeared.

I did exactly as instructed. I sat in the backseat, hugging Jeff close to me, trying to remain calm, trying not to let everything I had been holding in check suddenly burst out. I knew that if I started crying now, I wouldn't be able to stop—and the one thing I had to do now was get myself and my son back home.

So when the five minutes were up, I strapped Jeff back in his seat (he hated this and wailed loudly to let me know), climbed back into the front, lit up the cigarette I had been craving for the past twenty minutes, tossed back a fast, semisteadying cup of coffee, put the car in gear, and hit the road.

It was now just after two. I followed Toby's directions—driving slowly through the sleeping center of Saint-Georges, then picking up the 204 for Lac-Mégantic. I resisted the temptation to crank up my speed—this two-lane blacktop was narrow and full of unexpected twists—and I was relieved to get to Lac-Mégantic and the turnoff marked *Route 161: Woburn et la frontière americaine.* This road turned out to be even narrower than the previous one—and very dark. As I pushed closer to the frontier, I kept telling myself: *Just be cool with the guy at the border . . . act like a normal person . . . and he'll buy your story and wave you through. Show any fear and you'll end up in a small room, answering a lot of questions you really don't want to be asked.*

Every five kilometers there was a road sign, informing me I was that much closer to the border. With every passing sign, my fear cranked up a notch or two, and even though I tried to convince myself that the fear was overblown, I was so edgy and tired that I had lost all perspective. Anyway, the fact of the fucking matter was I had helped a wanted criminal escape across an international boundary . . . and though my help may have been coerced, I nonetheless aided and abetted . . . because I was terrified that he might expose the affair we'd had. And I could just hear some flinty old judge, looking down sternly at me and informing me that, on account of letting my own venal fear of exposure for the sin of adultery cloud my notion of right and wrong, he had no choice but to sentence me to . . .

La frontière americaine: 3 kilometres.

A quick stop for gas and I'd be there in less than ten minutes. *Keep calm, keep calm.*

As I edged closer and closer, I suddenly wished that I wasn't such a complete nonbeliever in God, the Almighty, Jahweh, the Alpha and the Omega, whatever. Because if there ever was a time in my life for prayer, it was now. But I had been guilty of enough hypocrisy over the past few days. I wasn't going to augment it by pleading for help to some Supreme Being whom I knew didn't exist.

So instead, I decided to bargain with myself—to take a vow that, if I got through this whole experience unscathed, if I made it across the border without incident, if the feds didn't show up, if that creep Toby Judson didn't reveal anything about who got him to Canada, if Dan didn't become suspicious of me for some reason—I would atone for all my transgressions by being as good as I could be. I'd accept my destiny as Dan's wife. I'd go where his career took us. I'd support him completely, and would damp down all dreams of escape. I'd do everything I could for Jeff and any other children we might have. Their needs—and those of my husband—would always come before mine. And I'd accept all the compromises and limitations of my life with grace, knowing that, if my selfish, venal behavior had been uncovered, I would have lost everything. You can't escape your actions, any more than you can escape yourself. There's a price to be paid for everything. And if in the future I mourned the freedom I'd given up, the small scope I'd imposed on my life, I'd always remind myself that this was the price extracted for my transgressions—and that, maybe, I'd gotten off lightly.

La frontière americaine: 1 kilometre.

There was a gas station up ahead. I filled the car. I dumped the dirty diaper. I cleaned out the ashtray that was brimming with butts. I freed Jeff for a few moments from his car seat and rocked him in the night air. I went into the shop and paid the $11 for the full tank of gas (God, it was expensive up here). I blew the change on five packs of cigarettes, a couple of candy bars, and a large cup of coffee. I loaded Jeff back into his car seat and handed him a rubber rattle that he seemed to favor, in the hope that it would keep him occupied while we crossed over to the States. I positioned myself behind the wheel, took a steadying breath, turned on the ignition, and drove.

There were no formalities leaving Canada—just a sign thanking you for visiting the country and wishing you a *Bon Retour*. There were around five hundred yards of no-man's-land before I arrived at a shed with the Stars and Stripes on a flagpole and a large sign saying: *Welcome to the United States.*

I was the only traveler at this hour of the night. The border official walked slowly out of the shed. He was a chunky man in his thirties, wearing a green customs uniform and a large wide-brim Forest Ranger–style hat. He ambled over to the car, nodded at me, then studied the license plate and walked once around the vehicle before stopping in front of the now rolled-down passenger window.

"Evening, ma'am," he said.

"Hi there," I said, forcing a smile.

"You're traveling awful late . . . or maybe awful early."

"It's not by choice, sir." And I explained how I'd been up visiting friends in Quebec and got a call from my husband only a few hours ago, saying that his father was dying.

"I could have stayed till morning, but I knew I wouldn't forgive myself if I didn't get back . . ."

"Yes, I can certainly understand that. So how long have you been out of the States?"

"Just two days."

"And do you have any identification for yourself and your baby?"

I handed over the passport and the birth certificate.

"That certainly works as ID," he said with a smile. He scrutinized the documents, then handed them back to me, and asked if I was bringing anything back from Canada.

"Just a couple of packs of cigarettes."

"Well, you're free to go. Drive friendly."

And he waved me through.

I waved back as I drove on. *First hurdle crossed.* I glanced at the dashboard clock. Three-ten. If I kept up a steady speed, I should make Pelham by eight-thirty—enough time to wash the dishes, give the apartment a fast going-over, have a quick shower, and make a beeline for Portland Airport.

Jeff complained much of the way south. I stopped twice to change/feed/cuddle him but he wouldn't settle down. Still, I had no choice but to keep driving, keep awake, keep telling myself that I just had to pull myself through a very long day ahead.

The sun broke around seven-fifteen. Fifty minutes later, I rolled into Pelham. As soon as I brought Jeff into the house and put him in his playpen, he conked right out. I envied him. Having hardly slept the previous night (when guilt and sexual craziness kept me awake) I had now been awake for nearly forty-eight hours.

However, I didn't have time to consider my exhausted state. I simply needed to get the house in order and get out of here. So I washed up all the dinner dishes and pans from the previous night, did a fast scrub of the bathroom, vacuumed around the bedroom, and made certain that nothing telltale (like a strange cigarette butt or discarded male underwear) had been left by the bed. Then I made another pot of coffee, and threw myself into the shower, blasting the water in an attempt to keep myself awake. I ran downstairs with a handful of laundry, and noticed to my shock that the stained sheets I had put in the machine the night before had been hung up to dry. And just as I was wondering if I had lost my reason and had forgotten I'd hung them up, I heard a voice behind me, "Hope you didn't mind me helping you out with the laundry."

I spun around. It was Billy, standing near me, a bucket in one hand, a long extension ladder under the other arm.

"You hung up the sheets to dry?"

"Yeah," he said, all smiles. "Saw you put 'em in last night before you left with that fella . . ."

"You saw me put in the sheets?"

"Well, I happened to be around here when . . ."

"Billy," I said in a calm, reasonable tone, "the laundry room is in the back here . . . which means that the only way you could be watching is if you made a deliberate effort to put yourself somewhere where you could . . ."

"I wasn't spying or anything," he said, suddenly very defensive. "I was just *watching*, that's all."

"Hey, I'm not angry at you," I said, deciding this was not the right moment to get into a discussion about the difference between spying and watching.

"You sure?"

"I'm sure."

"Good, 'cause I was planning to wash your windows this morning."

"You don't have to do that."

"Told the doctor I would around a week ago—before he left town."

"Well then, by all means wash our windows."

"You *really* sure you're not angry at me?"

"We're friends, Billy."

That brought a smile to his face.

"We sure are," he said, "and I'd never say anything about you leaving town last night with that fella."

Oh God . . .

"Well, I was just bringing him to the bus station in Lewiston."

"But you were gone all night."

"How do you know that?"

"Your car wasn't here until this morning."

"I had a flat, had to stay in a motel all night."

"With the fella?" he said, giving me another of his skewed smiles.

"Hardly," I said. "Anyway, he was gone on the bus before I had the flat."

"You kiss him good-bye?"

"What?"

"Saw you kiss him once."

"Where did you see this?"

"Saw it in your window."

"When?"

"A night or two ago."

"Around what time?"

"Oh, it was real late. I was out walking, saw the light on, looked up, there you were, kissing the guy."

"Was anyone else with you?"

"Heck no. Main Street was deserted. I was the only person out."

"And did you tell anyone that you saw me?"

"Heck no again. You're my friend. I wouldn't do that."

I was about to touch his arm, but thought better of it, remembering what happened the one time before this when I made that mistake.

"Well, I truly appreciate that, Billy. Secrets are very important between friends—and I am very, very grateful to you for keeping this one."

"You going to leave the doctor for this fella?" he asked, his tone as nonchalant and nonthreatening as before.

"Of course not. It was just a kiss good night, that's all."

"A real *long* kiss good night, the way I saw it," he said, laughing his goofy laugh. Was he indirectly threatening me . . . or was this just his way of reporting events?

"It was just a kiss, that's all. But if you mention anything to anyone about that kiss—or about me not getting home last night—it could cause me a lot of problems."

"Would you stop being my friend?"

"Well, put it this way: if you asked me to keep a secret and then I told somebody about your secret, what would you do?"

"I'd stop being your friend."

"And you'd be right to," I said. "Because friends keep secrets, right?"

"You bet they do."

"So I can trust you with my secret, Billy?"

"You bet you can."

"Thank you."

He gave me a shy smile, and said, "Can I wash your windows now?"

All the way to Portland Airport, I fought the temptation to throw up. I was now sick with worry that Billy might somehow spill the beans and bring my entire life down around me. I ripped open another pack of cigarettes and smoked three during the hour-long drive, my lungs raw from nonstop chain-smoking for the last eighteen hours.

When Dan got off the plane, he waved at us, then gave me a tired hug and kiss before fetching Jeff up in his arms to say "Hi, big fella" and handing him back to me.

When we got into the car, he sniffed all the accumulated cigarette smoke and said, "God almighty, have you turned into a chimney?"

I said nothing, but I was grateful to let him drive us home. I settled down into my seat and listened to his angry monologue brimming over with resentments about the way the second-rate hospital in Glens Falls had treated his father, and the indifference of some long-standing neighbors . . .

"Am I boring you?" he asked.

I realized I had nodded off.

"Sorry. I had a terrible night with our boy. If I caught two hours of sleep, it was something."

"I didn't mean to sound like such a cantankerous old shit," he said. "It's just been one godawful week."

I reached over and stroked his face. "Well, it's good to have you back."

"Your visitor leave?"

"Last night."

"Was he in the way?"

"A little bit—one of those boring lefty types who talks revolution all the time."

"Well, I'm sure your dad was pleased you put up with him."

"Yeah, I'm sure he was."

We stopped in Bridgton on the way home for food. When we reached Pelham, I had visions of Billy waiting out in front of the doctor's office, saying, "Still told nobody about you kissing that fella!" But Billy was nowhere to be seen. Dan took in the apartment with a cursory look and said something about getting in touch with "that awful Sims guy" about when we could move into the Bland house. I made lunch. Afterward, when Jeff nodded off for his afternoon nap, Dan put his hand on my thigh and motioned toward the bedroom. Though I could have screamed with tiredness, I followed him, took off my clothes, and spread my legs and tried to appear passionate.

I drifted off to sleep, and awoke sometime later to the sound of a ringing telephone. As I stirred, I saw that it was dark outside. I glanced at the clock by the bed. Five forty-two p.m. I had been asleep for around three hours. Dan opened the bedroom door.

"You feeling better?"

"A little, yeah. Thanks for letting me have the nap."

"No sweat. Listen, your dad's on the phone."

"Tell him I'll call back."

But I didn't call him back that night. The next morning, the phone rang about eight-thirty. But it wasn't my father—it was Nurse Bass, wanting to speak to Dan. As he hung up, he reached for his coat and medical bag and said, "Looks like Josie Adams's son has gotten an advanced case of tonsillitis. I'll be back in an hour tops."

Five minutes later, the phone rang again.

"Hannah, it's Dad."

I said nothing.

"Hannah?"

"What?"

"You okay?"

I said nothing.

"Hannah?"

"What?"

"You upset about something?"

"Now why would I be upset about something?"

"Look, whatever's going on, I just wanted to say that I've heard from our mutual friend, and he told me how you helped him out. I'm so pleased that you . . ."

I hung up—and found myself gripping the side of our armchair for a few minutes in an attempt to calm down. *You upset about something?* Didn't he have any idea about anyone else's feelings? Was he that self-absorbed? But he must have understood that, by sending that shit to me, he'd put me under suspicion with the federal authorities. Why else would he have talked in such coded language about "our mutual friend"?

The phone rang again. "We seemed to have been cut off," he said.

"No, I hung up."

"Hannah, I didn't mean to place you in harm's way."

"But you did, you did, you . . ."

I started to sob. Everything I had kept under control for the past few days suddenly came out in a torrent of anguish. I hung up. The phone started to ring again. I raced out of the living room and into the bathroom. I filled the sink with cold water and then found myself hanging on to its edge. The phone kept ringing. It took me a good quarter of an hour to get myself under control again. I splashed some water on my face, then caught sight of my reddened eyes in the mirror—underscored by deep black rings—and couldn't help but think that I was suddenly looking older and a lot less wise.

I dried my face. I walked into the kitchen and put the percolator on for coffee. I poured myself a small shot of bourbon and downed it in one go. I treated myself to a refill, and felt considerably better as its anesthetic warmth did its work. I lit a cigarette. I poured myself a cup of coffee. I took a deep breath. The phone rang again. I picked it up.

"Hannah . . ."

"I don't want to speak to you," I said.

"Please hear me out."

"No."

"I'm sorry."

"Good. You should be."

I hung up. The phone rang and rang. I didn't answer it.

My dad didn't call after that. But three days later, just after Dan had headed downstairs to his office, a letter arrived Special Delivery, postmarked Burlington, Vermont. I recognized my father's neat, taut handwriting on the front of the envelope—and though I signed for the letter, I immediately tore it up and threw it away. Then I loaded Jeff into his baby carriage, deposited him at Babs's house, and moved on to Miller's for my paper and cigarettes. When I got to the library I made coffee, then opened my newspaper. As I browsed through the *Globe,* my eye caught a small UPI item on page 7, under the headline "National News in Brief."

WEATHERMAN ESCAPES TO CANADA

Tobias Judson, 27, the onetime co-leader of the Students for a Democratic Society who helped shut down Columbia University during the student protests of 1968, has fled to Canada following his alleged involvement with the bombing of the Department of Defense office in Chicago on October 26. In a statement issued by Revolutionary Press International—an international underground news agency—Judson stated that, though he was not a member of the Weather Underground group that claimed responsibility for the Chicago bombing, he had aided his "fraternal comrades in the struggle"—and was forced to flee to Canada in order to avoid "persecution" by federal authorities. According to the Federal Bureau of Investigation, Judson has had a long-standing affiliation with the Weather Underground and harbored the two alleged Chicago bombers—James Joseph McNamee and Mustafa Idiong—after the explosion at the Federal building which killed two security guards. The FBI said they are working with the Royal Canadian Mounted Police to apprehend Judson, who was recently spotted in Montreal.

I read the article twice, vastly relieved that there was no photograph of Toby, and that they hadn't listed his assorted aliases—one of which might have been the Tobias Mailman he had used here. I knew that Estelle read the *Globe* every morning but couldn't see how, without a photograph, she would be able to connect the Weatherman now on the run with the guy she drooled over while he was in Pelham. In fact, she'd made little mention of Toby since Dan had come back—bar one comment, "Back to the marital grind, I suppose," on the Monday after Dan had returned.

I scoured all the Maine papers at the library that day, to see if they made any mention of Judson—or had dug up a photo of him. *The Portland Press Herald* had run the same UPI item as the *Globe*—reduced to around three lines and buried in a corner of a page. I made a point of watching network news that night at home. Nothing on any of the three networks, nothing on the All News/All The Time AM radio station from Boston that my little transistor radio was just about able to pull in.

Days passed—and I woke every morning with a terrible dread that today would be the day when the feds would arrive, or Judson would issue another asshole statement from the High North implicating me, or Billy would tell Nurse Bass about seeing me in deep embrace with Mr. Revolutionary, or my father would show up and confront me about the manner in which I had cut him off, and the entire desperate truth would come oozing out and drown me.

But . . . nothing happened. I woke up. I got my husband and son ready for the day. I did my early-morning routine. I went to work. I picked up Jeff. I went home. Dan came home. We ate. We talked a bit. We watched TV or read. We made indifferent love twice a week. The weekends came and went. The working week started again. And in the midst of all that . . .

Nothing happened.

Oh, things happened. My dad wrote me another letter—which I also threw away. I got a phone call from my mom, who said she just wanted to say hello and asked all sorts of roundabout questions about how things were going, and talked a little about a new exhibition she was working on, and then, as a matter-of-fact aside, asked me, "Anything wrong between you and your dad?"

"No," I said calmly. "Why?"

"Anytime I've mentioned him recently, you've gone all quiet, even a little sad. And when I've asked him if you've had a falling out or something, he's clammed up. So go on, Hannah—spill it. Why the rift?"

I surprised myself by remaining completely composed and cool in the face of the third degree.

"There's no rift," I said.

"Then what's the problem?"

"There's no problem."

"You are such a hopeless liar."

"Listen, I've got to go now . . ."

"Hannah, don't play games . . ."

"I don't play games—and you know it."

"I want some answers."

"And I have none to give. Good-bye."

She called three more times that afternoon. But I held my ground, refusing to give anything away. Because I had also reached the conclusion that, as I could never win my mother's approval, it was useless trying to pursue it. And the very fact that I was no longer chasing her love rendered her powerless over me.

"You *will* tell me what's going on," she finally yelled into the phone.

"There's nothing to tell, there's nothing to say."

I hung up again and didn't answer the phone when it rang and rang for the next hour.

Of course, there was everything to tell, everything to say—and like anybody with a terrible secret, I was desperate to talk about it, to share it with someone. And so, when Margy called the next afternoon and immediately shot off into one of her wonderful motormouth monologues—"Just sitting behind my dumbass desk at this dumbass office still doing this dumbass PR job, and wondering how my best friend, who I haven't spoken to in about a month, is doing right now"—I said, "Listen I can't talk right now . . ."

"What's up?"

"It's just not the right moment. But are you around tomorrow—say at four p.m.?"

"Sure . . ."

"Be at your desk at four and I'll call you then."

I hung up and picked up the phone and dialed Babs and asked if she would mind looking after Jeff until six-thirty tomorrow, as I was heading into Portland on a little shopping expedition. That night over dinner, I told Dan that I'd heard about this great Italian deli in Portland, and thought I'd borrow the car tomorrow afternoon and drive over there.

"Can you get real Parmesan?" he asked.

"That's what the *Press Herald* said."

"Well, that sounds worth the trip to me."

I left work an hour early the next day and got to Portland just after two. I found the little Italian joint and dropped nearly thirty dollars on wine, cheese, pasta, authentic Neapolitan canned tomatoes, garlic, bread, amaretto cookies, real espresso, and even a small two-cup espresso maker that you put on the stove. It was the cost of our weekly grocery bill, but I didn't care. The owner insisted on fixing me one of his "famous" provolone hero sandwiches, washed down with two glasses of Chianti "on the house." I was still feeling a little light-headed when I reached the telephone exchange at Central Portland Post Office and told the operator on duty that I wanted to place a station-to-station call to New York City.

"Booth Four," she told me.

I entered the booth. I sat down on the hard wooden chair adjacent to the little table on which an elderly phone sat. After a moment it rang. "Your call's being put through," the operator said. Then I heard a ringing tone and a decisive click as the operator left the line. Margy answered after two rings.

"Hannah?" she asked immediately.

"How did you know it was me?"

"It's four o'clock—and I've been worried sick for the last twenty-four hours about what the hell is wrong with you."

"Lots," I said.

"As in . . . ?"

"As in: I am making this call from the Portland, Maine, Post Office because I am worried that Big Brother might be listening in on my phone line."

It took around twenty minutes to get through it all—and I must have told it pretty damn well because Margy, one of the world's great interrupters, said nothing for the length of the story.

When I finally finished, there was a long silence.

"You still there?" I asked.

"Oh, I'm here, all right," Margy said.

"Sorry if I chewed your ear off with that."

"No. It was . . . riveting."

"So what do I do now?"

A long pause. Then she said, "Nothing."

"Nothing?"

"There's nothing to do. He's gone. The feds aren't on your tail. Your husband doesn't know—and I doubt that sad kid Billy will ever risk losing you as a friend by saying something, and your dad will definitely keep his lips sealed . . . and, by the way, you are going to have to forgive him, but you know that already . . . so . . ."

Another pause.

"You've gotten away with it," Margy said.

"Have I?" I asked, sounding surprised.

"You know you have."

"But what about the repercussions?"

"If you've gotten away with something, there are *no* repercussions—except those you bring down on your own head."

"That's what I'm talking about. How do I live with it?"

"It's simple: you just do."

"I don't know if that's possible."

"You mean, you don't know if you can forgive yourself?"

"I *can't* forgive myself," I said.

"You have to forgive yourself."

"Why?"

"Because you didn't commit a crime . . ."

"Yes, I did."

"A misdemeanor, Hannah. But not a crime. Come on, sweetheart. Your body pulled you one way for a few crazy days, and then that bastard gave you no choice but to do what he said. In my book, the only crime you're really guilty of is being human and weak like the rest of us."

"I wish I could see it that way."

"You will."

"How can you be so sure?"

"Because it's what happens. You have a secret. It might seem like a terrible secret at the moment. But in time, it will just be a little room that only you know about, and that only you can enter. I promise you, after a while you won't want to enter it at all. Because it won't seem that important to you anymore. And because, bar you and me, nobody will ever know that this secret exists.

"And now, hon, I am being called into a dumbass conference. So . . ."

We ended the call, promising to speak again the following week. I hung up. I stood up and paid the telephone operator. I went outside. I got into my car and drove back to Pelham thinking, *No one really gets away with anything. Or should that be, no one with a conscience really gets away with anything.*

I took my time getting home, delaying my arrival as late as I could. When I finally rolled into town around seven, Dan was already at the apartment with Jeff. My son looked up as I entered, then returned to tossing his wooden blocks around the crib. My husband gave me a light peck on the top of my head, then looked into my bags of Italian goodies and said, "That all looks pretty nice. Get the Parmesan?"

I nodded and began to unpack the bag. The bill came out with a box of pasta. Dan picked it up and whistled loudly when he saw the price.

"Gosh, that was expensive."

"Don't you think we deserve to treat ourselves now and then?" I said.

Though I said it without much in the way of attitude, something in my tone made Dan change his.

"You're right," he said. "Treating ourselves is a good thing. What's for dinner, by the way?"

I said that I would be making an authentic Italian lasagne.

"Neat," he said. "Think we should open a bottle of that Chianti you bought?"

I nodded my approval. As Dan rumbled around for a corkscrew, I turned and stared at my very beautiful son—and thought about the pact I had made with myself and knew that, if Jeffrey wasn't here, I wouldn't be here either.

Dan turned around—and must have caught my pensiveness, as he asked, "You okay?"

There is a price to everything.

I smiled. I kissed my husband. I said, "Everything is just fine."

PART TWO

2003

TEN

THE SNOW WAS starting to fall heavily as I climbed into my car. Only in Maine would you get a near blizzard in early April. Being a hardened New England native, I've always liked our ferocious New England winters. Recently, however, all the strange climate change stuff meant that there was one year when we didn't see a single flake of snow. This winter, on the other hand, the mercury plunged to 15 below in early January—and with Easter now almost upon us, it still refuses to budge above freezing. And the snow keeps coming down.

The engine on my Jeep started on the first go, as usual, and the heating kicked in by the time I had pulled out of the parking lot. The Jeep had been my fiftieth birthday present. Just recently, Dan said maybe it was time we traded it in for the most recent model—or some other kind of SUV. I flatly refused. It's bad enough that I knock around Portland in such a large vehicle (although it's great on snowy nights like tonight). But the idea of dumping another ten grand into a new Jeep Cherokee when my current model is still running so well strikes me as unnecessary. Dan, on the other hand, thinks nothing about trading in his Lexus every two years.

"We can afford it," he gently reminds me whenever I raise a qualm or two.

I turned the radio on to NPR. There was a live relay of a Boston Symphony Orchestra concert—Levine conducting the Second Symphony of Sibelius: perfect music for a dark, wintry evening.

I negotiated my way out of downtown Portland, passing an entire area of old 1930s office buildings that had been left abandoned for years—and were, at one time, scheduled for demolition. But that was before the big boom in the mid-nineties, during which southern Maine benefited from an influx of enervated young professionals, fleeing big-league metropolitan areas. And every time there was some *Town & Country* article about Portland being one of the most livable small cities in America, the property values seemed to jump by another ten percent. Which is why those abandoned office buildings downtown had all been turned into fashionable lofts, which could now run you up to $500,000 for 1,600 square feet . . . whereas our own house in Falmouth . . .

No, I'm not getting into that topic again. Nowadays in Portland, anytime you're over at somebody's house for dinner, real estate becomes a central conversational point. In this sense, I suppose we've just managed to catch up with everywhere else. But it also makes me think: Why do we always seem to spend so much time these days talking about stuff we own and stuff we want to own?

It's only a five-minute shot up the coastal interstate from downtown Portland to the town of Falmouth Foreside, where we live. Maine Medical Center—the state's best hospital and the place where Dan operates—hovers on a hillside halfway between the city and our home. Dan doesn't have far to travel—and he likes it that way.

As I signaled for the Falmouth Foreside exit, my cell phone rang. "Hannah, it's Sheila Platt here."

"Hi there," I said, trying to sound enthusiastic. Sheila was a longstanding member of the reading group to which I belonged. Initially, we'd been just a book group. Just a few months ago, I suggested we start alternating a play with a book—because a play gave us the chance to read it aloud, acting out the various parts. What's more, Portland was full of book groups, and I convinced the six other women in our "congregation" that it would be interesting to try something beyond *Pride and Prejudice*. Just this evening, we'd read our way through the first two acts of *Measure for Measure*—and, per usual, our discussions of the play afterward had turned into one long catfight between Sheila Platt and her bête noire in the group, Alice Armstrong.

Alice was an art instructor at a local junior college; divorced and amusingly bitter about it. Her husband, another art teacher, had left her for a very successful corporate lawyer, who helped him screw Alice in the divorce settlement ("I was so angry at the bastard, I stupidly agreed to his shitty terms, as a way of showing him I didn't need him anymore. I tell you, pride always costs you dearly"). She was very smart and very thwarted—a talented illustrator who couldn't find any outlet for her work in Maine, and had to plug away at the teaching job to support her two kids. She was also politically savvy, with a strong streak of mischief—which is why I should have known better than to let her choose one of Shakespeare's foremost problem plays as our next "group read." Not only is *Measure for Measure* predicated on its ethical complexity, but it also raises all sorts of questions about the interrelationship between political and sexual power, as well as exploring the narrow frontier between religious piety and hypocrisy. Given Sheila's evangelical Christianity and her pronounced admiration for our current commander in chief—and Alice's equally pronounced "radical secularism" (as Sheila contemptuously dubbed it) and her vocal pro-choice feminism—it only figured that the play would get them rubbing each other the wrong way . . . which, I sensed, was Alice's exact intention.

"The whole play is about hypocrisy," I said at the start of our post-read-through discussion. "Puritanical hypocrisy."

"Now when you say 'hypocrisy,'" Alice asked, "are you talking about sanctimoniousness or deceit?"

"Both, I guess. Angelo is a man whose moral rigidity is undercut by that most human need for sex."

"But the sex thing is really a cry for love," Sheila Platt said.

"No, it's a total sex thing," I said. "It's about power."

"But Hannah, he *does* tell her that he loves her," Sheila said.

"As far as I'm concerned," Alice said, "Angelo is a typical power-mad male politician who plays the devout-Christian card, moralizing like hell about the weaknesses of others, while simultaneously using his authority to try to force a nun to sleep with him. And what makes the play so damn relevant is that Shakespeare understood that sanctimonious, finger-pointing types are usually the most morally compromised people going. Look at that hypocrite Newt Gingrich, calling Clinton the greatest sinner imaginable after his dumb thing with Lewinsky, while simultaneously carrying on an affair himself . . ."

"The difference is," Sheila said, "that Mr. Gingrich wasn't the president . . ."

"Yeah, he was only Speaker of the House," Alice said.

". . . and he didn't lie under oath," Sheila said.

"No, he just lied to his wife, while trying to bring on the downfall of a political opponent whose sexual transgression wasn't as serious as his own."

"Oh, please," Sheila said, sounding angry. "You don't think taking advantage of an intern . . ."

"She was over twenty-one, which makes her a consenting adult. And no, I don't think a blow job is the same thing as leaving your wife . . ."

Sheila and a few of the other women in the room let out an audible gasp.

"Do we really have to put up with such vile talk?" Sheila asked.

"Now, getting back to the text . . ." I said.

I hated sounding like "the teacher." But though I always ended up playing moderator during these punch-ups—steering a decidedly neutral course between warring factions—I privately enjoyed the fact that Alice had no interest in keeping her opinions to herself. On the contrary, she insisted on confronting Sheila—because (as Alice privately admitted to me) Sheila represented everything she detested in George W. Bush's America. Just as Sheila once told me that, to her, Alice was "just an old hippie."

Tonight, however, there had been a certain "to the death" quality to their verbal sparring; a hope that some particularly vindictive comment would have the desired effect, leaving the victim so punch-drunk and embarrassed that she'd have no option but to leave the group.

"Is this a good time to talk?" Sheila asked.

Frankly, it was never a good time to talk to Sheila Platt. She constantly irritated me. I didn't like her sobby little voice, or the sanctimonious way she always went on about "finding the good in everyone" even though she was the sort of ultraconservative who had campaigned for the return of the death penalty in Maine and for banning gay marriages. She was also known around town as a malignant gossip who dished the dirt on others while maintaining a benign, saintly smile on her face.

I really couldn't stand her—but took care that she never knew how much I truly disliked her. After thirty years in Maine, I had learned how to keep my opinions to myself.

"Is this a good time to talk?"

"I suppose so," I said.

"I wanted to have a word after we finished tonight, but I saw you were deep in conversation with *Ms.* Armstrong."

She came down heavy with the invective on the *Ms.* I was going to say something about how we were not *deep* in conversation, but decided to let it ride.

"So what did you want to talk about, Sheila?"

"I just wanted to let you know that I will be taking a ballot among the other members to see if everyone else feels the same way I do about Alice Armstrong."

"And if they do, what then?"

"We'll be asking her to leave."

"You can't do that," I said.

"Oh yes we can. She's a disruptive influence . . ."

"Sheila, there are many members of the group who consider you a disruptive influence . . ."

"I haven't heard that."

"Well, *I* have. And though you might not like Alice's politics, they *are* Alice's politics—and we must respect them as such. Just as we have to respect yours."

"Even if you don't agree with them."

"To the best of my knowledge, I've never had a political discussion with you. Or, at least, I've never said anything while you've aired your views."

"Well, it's pretty darn clear you're not a Republican—and everyone knows you're a great friend of Alice Armstrong. And she's somewhat to the left of . . ."

"My friendship with Alice is not predicated on a shared political perspective. But even if it was, this has nothing to do with the reading group. And I am quite frankly appalled by your implication that I would side with Alice because we might be fellow liberals . . ."

"There!" she said triumphantly. "You admitted it."

"I've admitted nothing. You're twisting my words—and, quite frankly, I'm beginning to lose track of what this conversation is actually about."

"The fact that I will be asking for a vote to expel Alice Armstrong from the reading group next week."

"If you do that, I will call for a vote to expel you—and, trust me, it will pass."

A little pause. I could tell she didn't like that one bit. Because she had to know just how much people disliked her.

"Maybe I'll go off and form my own book group," she said.

"That's your prerogative, Sheila," I said. "Good night."

And I hit the button that disconnected the call.

There are very few individuals who make me want to lose faith with the human race. But Sheila Platt qualifies because, as with so many people these days, there can be no room for differences of opinions, or lively, contrary debate. Her point of view is the *only* point of view. Just like those rabid conservatives you see on talk shows, shouting down anyone who disagrees with their hyperpatriotism.

Just like my son, Jeff.

Jeff would have loved our reading group because it would have allowed him to lock horns with Alice Armstrong—locking horns with a liberal being one of my son's favorite pastimes. I discovered this the hard way over Thanksgiving, when Jeff and his wife, Shannon, came up from Hartford for the weekend with their baby daughter, Erin. Alice happened to drop by for a glass of wine. I introduced her to my lawyer son, and somehow the conversation turned to Bush's born-again political agenda. Forgetting that I had told her that Jeff worked as a corporate counsel to Standard Life in Connecticut, was very active in the Connecticut Republican Party, and had become (to my considerable shock) a "committed Christian," Alice went into one of her witty rants about how it didn't surprise her that his beloved party was now in the hands of the religious Right, since "most of the corporate creeps who run the party have also become Bible thumpers—to appeal to the God Squad in Dixie."

To his credit, Jeff didn't go ballistic when Alice made that comment—"going ballistic" being something my thirty-year-old son can do when he becomes displeased. He used to throw these wild tantrums as a two-year-old. When he was an adolescent, he was always considered a model student and a real team player—but one who could fall into a brief but terrifying rage when a letdown or a small personal failure clouded his path. When he was a senior in college, he came home for Easter with his right hand heavily bandaged. After some prodding from Dan, he admitted that he punched out a window in his dorm when he received a rejection letter from Harvard Law School (he did get into, and eventually graduated from, U. Penn Law, which wasn't exactly a second-tier school). Shannon seemed to be able to handle these out-of-body mood swings. Then again, she had cast herself in the role of the perfect stay-at-home wife—always going on about how delighted she was about changing little Erin's diapers, and supporting Jeff in his career, and really getting sniffy about those harridan Women Who Work—knowing full well that, after we left Pelham and Dan started his residency in Milwaukee, I found a job as a teacher and, bar a break when Lizzie was born, haven't stopped working since then. Too bad I hadn't invited Sheila Platt around on that Thanksgiving night. She wouldn't have just loved my son's Republican politics, but also his wife's pro-life obsessions—as Shannon's occasionally bragged to me about picketing abortion clinics in the Hartford slums. I had to wonder if she'd march on a similar clinic in the white-bread West Hartford suburb where she lives—or would that cause the wrong type of talk among all her fellow upscale housewives, who probably vote Republican but still understandably don't like someone threatening their reproductive rights . . . like my self-righteous daughter-in-law.

Of course I would never, *never* express such opinions in front of Jeff or Shannon. That's not my style. Nor is it Dan's style. Then again, Dan rarely expresses an extreme opinion about anything that doesn't have to do with orthopedic surgery or the American Medical Association or his beloved Lexus or the tennis that he plays and watches with ferocious avidity. Even when I pointed out—after her first visit to us as Jeff's "steady"—that Shannon would embrace the "little woman" role with a vengeance, Dan just shrugged and said, "They seem well suited."

"The thing I can't get over," I said, "is just how damn conservative she is."

"Jeff isn't exactly a flaming radical himself."

"My point exactly. He's going to get himself hitched to that girl and tie himself into the most old-fashioned marriage imaginable."

"But it's what he wants," Dan said, reaching for the sports section of *The Boston Globe* and coverage of the previous day's action at Wimbledon.

"I know it's what he wants. That's what worries me: our son has turned into an Eisenhower Republican."

"I think Eisenhower was a little more liberal than Jeff," Dan said. I smiled. My husband may not be the most naturally humorous man, but he has a quiet wit that still catches me off guard, and reminds me that there is a subtle subversive streak to this otherwise very conventional (and successful) doctor.

I pulled off the highway and drove the mile or so down the narrow two-lane road that led home to Chamberlain Drive. When Dan first landed the job as orthopedic resident at Maine Medical back in 1981, we bought a little three-bedroom Cape Codder on a half acre of land in Freeport . . . back when Freeport was just a small town that happened to have L.L. Bean on its doorstep and wasn't the big shopping destination that it has become today. We were on a road in the woods. The house—though small, with low-ish ceilings—was totally cozy. Anyway, after that nasty little apartment in Pelham all those years ago, anything larger than three shoe boxes struck me as palatial. And I loved the fact that, though we were only half a mile from the main road, there were no other houses within sight of our own. It seemed like we were in the middle of nowhere . . . especially on one of those sublime January mornings when you'd wake to hard sunshine and a freshly fallen shroud of snow, and the view from the kitchen was of fantastic frosted woodlands, cut off from all hints of modern life.

Back then, it wasn't hard to find a teaching job—and I landed a full-time one in Freeport High School within four months of moving there. Looking back on it now, it was a relatively uncomplicated time. Jeff and Lizzie were still both under ten, Dan was busy (but not fanatically so). We weren't rolling in money, but we certainly had enough to live well, and I approached my thirties with a certain . . . no, I really don't want to use the word *equanimity* here, even though it's apt. Put it this way: whatever desperate dissatisfaction I felt during those early years of our marriage—that sense of having shortchanged myself—had been replaced by a calm acceptance that, in the great scheme of things, mine was hardly a bad life. I liked my job. I liked being a mom. Most of all, I liked my kids and got such pleasure watching their personalities and worldviews taking shape. From the outset, Jeff was self-directed, very focused—and something of a perfectionist ("He's a real achiever," his fifth-grade teacher told me, "but boy, does he beat himself up when he gets something wrong"). Lizzie, on the other hand, had a true creative streak (she designed her very own puppet theater when she was five and informed me that she was writing a novel when she was eight). But she also seemed intensely vulnerable whenever a girl at school was mean to her, or if she wasn't chosen for a school play. God, the memories that brought back. I did my best to reassure her that these disappointments weren't a reflection on her; that you couldn't always be chosen for everything; that, frequently, life was simply unfair. "You're my pal," Lizzie told me after one such conversation. It was about the nicest thing she could have said to me—and I took pride in the fact that my kids looked upon me both as their mother and a friend.

Those first three years in Freeport were happy, low-key ones. But then, Dan's boss at the hospital retired, my husband was named head of orthopedics, and life suddenly began to accelerate. Not only was Dan back to working fifteen-hour days, he was also flying everywhere to attend assorted surgical conferences, pressing the flesh, making contacts, gaining expertise. Because Dan was a man with a plan: he had decided to turn the Orthopedic Unit at Maine Medical into the best in New England. Within six years he had achieved his aim. We hardly saw him for much of that time. Fifteen-hour days became seventeen-hour days. A two-day business trip turned into a series of two-week trawls around the country. Weekends with his kids became once-a-month events—and even then, they were frequently interrupted by emergency surgery at the hospital or the arrival of out-of-town medical bigwigs, all of whom (Dan assured me) would advance his cause.

Somehow I put up with all this frantic activity. When Dan started raking in the big bucks—and hinted that the head of orthopedics at Maine Medical and his family should be living in a grander house than our modest Cape Codder—I found a really delightful modern place. It was a five-bed A-frame, with cathedral ceilings, hardwood floors, and lots of natural light—just three minutes down a back road in Freeport, with views of Casco Bay. But Dan felt that a Very Important Doctor needed to live in a Very Important House in The Best Suburb of Portland. Which is how we ended up in the Very Big Colonial House on a Very Big Three-Acre Lot in the Very Exclusive District of Falmouth Foreside.

Ours isn't a big house—maybe 4,000 square feet, including the floor-through basement. But it makes a statement for Portland: The People Who Live Here Have Money. Or perhaps: The People Who Live Here Have Money But In True Maine Fashion They're Not Flashy About It. So the house is a straightforward white clapboard structure—well maintained, large, but unostentatious. There's no swimming pool or tennis court, no ornamental ponds or statues on the front lawn. And inside, well, I've never hired an interior decorator, but since the kids moved out, I have had the place redone in a style that is pretty much Shaker, but with an emphasis on comfort. Dan has remodeled the basement as his study-cum-playground—complete with a billiard table, a large array of computer equipment, and a massive stereo system that is so high-tech and refined that I think you could probably hear the left ventricle of Pavarotti's heart through it. There's also one of those big plasma televisions that I refuse to have upstairs . . . as (a) I think they're ugly, and (b) if I watch five hours of TV a week, it's an event. I also have an office on the first floor, but it's a little simpler: a nice Shaker-style desk, a comfortable chair, a small radio/CD player, a laptop computer, crammed bookshelves, a small sofa with a reading light, and little else. There have been days when I have sat at my desk, grading yet another eleventh-grade essay on *The Scarlet Letter* or *Franny and Zooey,* and have asked myself: Is this the sum total of a working life? But those are just the bad days—when I find myself fighting to remain interested in what I do. Thankfully, they are infrequent ones. I still like teaching. I like the challenge of standing up in front of a group of complex adolescents, many of whom have little interest in anything that isn't material or instantly visceral, and trying to get them animated about Hawthorne's take on Puritan America or Hemingway's reinvention of narrative prose, in the hope that it might hold their attention or even interest them. That's about all a teacher can ever wish for—the idea that something you talk about might just sink in, and get a student to rethink the way he sees things . . . for a moment or two, anyway.

I turned into our driveway, parked the Jeep, got out, and spent a good minute staring up into the swirling snow, willing myself to calm down. Then, when I had collected myself again, I went inside.

The house was dark, but I could hear television sounds from the basement. I went downstairs. Dan was sitting with his feet up, his evening glass of red wine on the side table, watching the Discovery Channel, which has become his latest fixation over the past few months. I came over and kissed him on the forehead.

"You're early," he said.

"Wasn't in the mood for a drink with Alice this evening," I said, walking over to the little bar in the corner of the room. I reached for a wineglass and the open bottle of Washington State pinot noir. "But I sure as hell feel like a drink now."

"Something happen?" he said, looking away momentarily from the nasty predators on the television.

"Yeah, Sheila Platt opened her mouth."

"You really have a problem with that woman."

"This is true. Maybe it has something to do with me having a low tolerance for idiots who mouth off and think they're intelligent."

"If you really had a low tolerance for idiots who mouth off, you'd never teach high school. How was the reading group? What are you doing again?"

I told him, then took a sip of wine.

"That certainly works," I said.

"It's a new winery on the British Columbia border. Raban Estates. Absolutely first-class stuff, and a rave review for this 2002 pinot in *Wine Gourmet* this month."

"With a price to match?"

"Thirty-five a bottle."

I took another sip.

"At that price, I've decided it's wonderful. Busy day?"

"Two hip replacements, one cartilage restructuring, and some high school hockey player whose tibia and pelvis were virtually crushed when he was driving himself to school in his Mazda Miata."

"What parent gives his high school kid a Mazda Miata?"

"A rich parent."

"How did you know what kind of car it was?"

"I asked the kid before the anesthetist put him under."

"The personal touch. I like it."

Dan smiled.

"If you're drinking," I said, "you're obviously not operating tomorrow."

"No, it's just back-to-back appointments from seven-thirty onward. What time are you heading to Burlington?"

"Around nine. But I have to grade papers tonight, so I'll leave you with the marauding . . . what are those nasty-looking animals?" I asked, pointing to the screen.

"Cougars. It's a documentary about the Canadian Rockies."

"Looks magnificent," I said.

"Yeah, we should think again about a vacation up around Banff."

"And get eaten by a cougar? Forget it."

"The chances of that are about as high as being hit by a meteorite. Anyway, we've been talking about doing Banff for a while."

"No, *you've* been talking about doing Banff for a while. Just like you've been talking about the Leeward Islands, the Great Barrier Reef, Belize, and everywhere else you've recently seen on the Discovery Channel. And, as usual, we'll end up doing a week in Bermuda, because (a) it's close, and (b) you can't afford any more time off."

"Am I that predictable?"

"Yes," I said, standing up and giving him another kiss on the head. "And now, I'm going to recharge my glass and deal with two dozen badly written term papers on Longfellow's *Evangeline*."

"That sounds like a task worthy of a drink."

"I shouldn't be too late."

"Well, I'll be turning in as soon as the cougars attack the herd of deer. Oh, there was a message for you from Lizzie on the answering machine. Nothing urgent, but she didn't sound her best again. Ongoing boyfriend trouble?"

"I won't know until I speak with her. But it could be."

"She should do the smart thing and marry herself a nice doctor."

I did a double take, then noticed that my husband was favoring me with a very mischievous smile.

"Yeah, I'll pass on your advice straightaway," I said with a laugh.

As I mounted the stairs to my office, I felt my anxiety level beginning to rise. Ever since this most recent breakup—her third in about two years—Lizzie had been sounding dejected, but with a slightly manic edge that I was beginning to find worrying. *She should do the smart thing and marry herself a nice doctor.* Dan was just being his usual dry self, but what he didn't know was that he had spoken the truth. Up until a week ago, Lizzie had been dating a doctor—a dermatologist, of all things (well, I guess it's better than a proctologist). She had kept this six-month relationship from Dan because the doctor in question was married—and a minor television celebrity. And though I assured Lizzie that her father wouldn't be prudish about her relationship with a married guy, she was adamant that I guard her secret.

It wasn't the first time that my daughter had confided in me. Nor was it the first time that she seemed reluctant to share details of her private life with her father. It's not as if Lizzie had a bad relationship with him, or that he had ever been a stern, dogmatic, do-what-I-say-not-what-I-do dad. On the contrary, Dan had been fairly relaxed with the kids—that is, when he happened to be around. In private, I've often wondered if Lizzie's endless search for a guy and Jeff's fervent embrace of Family Values Conservatism are somehow directly linked to Dan's absences during their childhood and adolescence. Then again, another part of me thinks: hell, the kids were both raised in a stable household, they had plenty of attention, they were always loved unconditionally, and they wanted for nothing. And if twenty-five years of teaching have taught me anything, it's that most children arrive in the world with a certain amount of their own baggage, which no amount of good or bad rearing is going to change. Having said that, I still worry constantly about them—especially Lizzie, who seems so terribly vulnerable and dissatisfied with things.

If you looked at her life you'd think: *She has nothing to complain about.* Her résumé seems enviable: A BA cum laude from Dartmouth. A junior year abroad in Aix-en-Provence (how I envied her that time in France). A constant boyfriend throughout those years (they broke up when he went to Stanford Law and she decided not to follow him because, as she later confided in me, she didn't want to repeat the parental pattern of marrying the person she met her freshman year in college). A year as a teacher in the Peace Corps in Indonesia (during which I fretted all the time that she'd be kidnapped by some mad militants). Then, when she returned to the U.S., she surprised me and all her friends by not entering teaching—as she always swore she would do—but instead enrolling for a one-year MBA back at Dartmouth.

"I don't want to be dependent on some guy to give me a good life," she explained at the time. "And nowadays, teachers just end up struggling—which, though noble, strikes me as a ticket to despair. So I might as well get the Big Money Degree, start earning the Big Bucks, build up a nice block of equity, and then have the freedom to pick and choose my next move in my mid-thirties."

It sounded like a straightforward objective—and though I did warn her that life never, *ever,* went according to plan, she was very focused on her goal. And as Dartmouth has one of the best business schools in the country, she was snapped up immediately on graduation by a big mutual fund company in Boston. Her starting salary was a jaw-dropping $150,000 per year—though she assured me this was "chump change" in the world of mutual funds. With her Christmas bonus the first year, she made a down payment on a loft apartment in the Leather District of Boston and sparingly outfitted it with designer furniture. Last year, she bought herself one of those spiffy new MINI Coopers, and the few weeks off she had each year (two was the most she was allowed) were spent in expensive resorts in Nevis or in Baja California.

On paper, it seemed like a pretty nifty existence. There was only one rub: Lizzie hated her work. She found it boring and one-dimensional to be managing other people's money, but whenever I gently reminded her that she didn't have to stay in the job if she didn't want to, she made the point that she had dug herself into something of a financial hole with the loft and the high-flying lifestyle, and that she just needed six or seven more years of bonuses to get her loft paid off, after which "I'll do whatever I damn well please."

My fear, however, was that she would have a very hard professional time over the next six or seven years, as every phone call (and we talked at least three times a week) brought with it a tale of some slight she had suffered at the office, some dispute with an obnoxious colleague, or the admission that she hadn't been sleeping well over the past few weeks.

And then there was her romantic life. First a jazz saxophonist and music teacher named Dennis with whom she fell madly in love, even though (as she admitted to me later) he did warn her from the outset that he wasn't the settling-down type and always fought shy of commitment. When she got clingy, he dropped her—and she went into a tailspin for a while, calling him up late at night, begging for another chance, phoning me at all hours in tears, telling me she'd never meet another man like Dennis, that she'd totally blown it, and if only he'd take her back . . .

After a week of these calls, I jumped into my car after school one afternoon, drove straight down to Boston, and (my luck was with me) made it to her office just as Lizzie was getting out of work. She looked drained, depleted, running on empty—and didn't even seem particularly surprised to see me. Her office was in the Prudential Center, and I suggested we walk over to the Ritz and treat ourselves to a medicinal martini. Just before we reached its front door—right in front of that lovely old Unitarian church near Arlington Street—she reached for me, put her head against my shoulder, and began to bawl her eyes out. I put my arms around her and, with passersby looking on with shock at such a public outburst of emotion, negotiated her across the street and onto a park bench in the Public Garden. I held her for a good ten minutes, thinking, *This is way out of proportion for a six-month romance gone wrong.* When she finally calmed down, I got her into the Ritz for that martini. I didn't have a hard time convincing her to down a second, and then tried to suggest that we all sometimes had excessive reactions to disappointments and rejections—and that they usually hinted at other underlying worries and pressures. But—and this was a really big *but*—it was important to remember that life was painfully short, that everything was fleeting, and that the heart was a most resilient muscle.

By the end of the evening she seemed to be gaining a little perspective. During the following months, she was in high gear—totally focused on her job and working out two hours a day at the gym. She'd bought herself a mountain bike and joined a club which did hundred-mile cycles every weekend. Then the doctor came into her life. Dr. Mark McQueen—a Brookline dermatologist. Forty-five. Married, two kids, and, according to Lizzie, wildly successful: "A big pioneer in the field of acne scarring." The very fact that Lizzie, with her splendidly sarcastic take on things, said this without irony made me feel that she was really smitten with this one. He also had his own program on a local cable station—*Face It*—a "how to improve your skin" show that was clearly aimed at the housewife population. The program had become something of a regional success story, and had been picked up by a variety of other cable channels around the country ("He's just signed a contract for his first *Face It* book," Lizzie said, all excited for him).

Anyway, McQueen had come along with a pal on one of those weekend bicycle trips. And that's how he met Lizzie. It was a complete *coup de foudre*—and within two months of meeting him, she told me that she knew "he was the one."

I counseled caution—telling her that an affair with a married man never had a happy ending. But she'd fallen hard, and (she assured me) so had the good doctor. I met him once—on a weekend visit to see Lizzie. He brought us to a very wonderful, very expensive restaurant—the Rialto at the Charles Hotel in Cambridge. He was unnecessarily unctuous in his attentions to Lizzie, and was far too fulsome about my teaching work, and his desire to meet Dan.

"When I heard that Lizzie's dad was a fellow doctor, well, I just knew that there was something preordained about us."

Oh, give me a break.

Then I learned that he drove a 7 Series BMW, that he "summered" on the Vineyard, and was planning to take Lizzie to Venice for a week next month ("Staying at the Cipriani, of course"). He dropped the name of his big-deal New York publisher, and told me that, since *Face It* was syndicated in California, he'd had offers pouring in from assorted Hollywood actors to be their "personal epidermal consultant." After I'd been told that he'd made varsity tennis at Cornell and was now being coached at the Brookline Lawn Tennis Club by Brooks Barker (who reached the quarterfinals of the 1980 U.S. Open), my heart really started to sink. When Lizzie excused herself to go to the bathroom, he leaned over toward me and said, "You know that your daughter is the best thing that ever happened to me."

"How nice for you," I said carefully.

"And though my domestic situation is a little complicated right now . . ."

"Lizzie said you were still living at home."

"That will change soon."

"Does your wife know about Lizzie?"

"Not yet. But I will be telling her . . ."

"Does she suspect?"

He pulled back, looking uncomfortable. "I don't think so," he finally said.

"You must cover your tracks very well, Doctor."

"I don't want to hurt anybody."

"But you will. If you leave your wife and children . . . they're nine and eleven, Lizzie told me . . ."

He nodded in agreement.

"Well, if you walk out on your family, they will be damaged. And if you decide to break it off with my daughter . . ."

"I won't be doing that. She's the love of my life. I have this total certainty about us . . . the same sort of certainty you must have had when you first met your husband . . ."

I was about to say something rather cutting—along the lines of "When my husband and I met, neither of us was married to someone else . . . and, by the way, I hate anyone who talks about certainty"—but I saw Lizzie heading back toward us. So I simply leaned over to him and whispered, "As I think you know, she's a fragile woman when it comes to love, and if you mess her up, you will fucking pay."

He actually blanched. He certainly didn't expect the bad language—or the Mafia-style threat—from a genteel schoolteacher like me.

And, of course, six weeks afterward he broke it off with Lizzie.

"Please don't tell Dad," she said when she called to give me the news.

"Honey, I've never said a word about this to your father—and I won't. Because you asked me to keep a confidence. But I don't think you should be afraid of your dad—because you know he's not the condemning type."

"But he'd still think me a screwup for doing this again."

I then got the entire saga: how Mark had finally broken down and told his wife; how she went berserk and threatened suicide; how he went to Lizzie and told her that he had to "do the right thing," even though he still loved her; and how he wouldn't entertain any of her pleas to keep seeing her clandestinely.

I found all this out a week ago. Since then, we'd spoken daily. What was troubling me now was the fact that Lizzie seemed so unnaturally calm. Over the past few days, she had insisted that everything was under control; she was *maintaining perspective* and had *a very Zen take on this.* But her voice was hushed, abnormally subdued—and I was beginning to doubt her constant assurances that she was just fine.

So I settled down at my desk, picked up the phone, dialed the phone numbers that linked us to our phone mail service, and played her message:

"Hi, Mom, hi, Dad . . . it's just me. Mom, can you call me when you have a moment? Don't worry if it's late. I'll be up."

Once again, she sounded a little otherworldly—making me wonder if she was suffering from insomnia or was on antidepressants. I checked my watch. Nine thirty-five p.m. Early for Lizzie. I took a large swig of wine and called her number. She answered on the first ring. "Mom?" she asked.

"You okay, hon?" I asked.

"Oh yeah, I'm fine."

"You sure about that?"

"Why? Don't I sound fine?"

Her voice was flat, lifeless.

"Just a little tired."

"Not sleeping. But I'm often not sleeping. So—"

She broke off. Silence.

"Work okay?" I asked, trying to fill the gap.

"I keep making the clients money, so yeah, sure, everything's fine."

Another silence. I asked, "And this sleeplessness . . . is it every night?"

"Has been. But now, when I can't sleep, you know what I do? I get up, get into my car, and drive over to Brookline."

"What's in Brookline, hon?"

"Mark's house."

Oh God . . .

"You drive over to Mark's house in the middle of the night?"

"Hey, don't sound shocked. I don't go in or anything. I don't ring the bell. I just wait outside."

"For what?"

"For Mark."

"But if it's the middle of the night, isn't Mark asleep?"

"Yeah, but he gets up really early to go jogging . . . even though I told him so many times that he's going to kill his knees that way."

"Has he seen you outside his door?"

"Oh yes."

"Has he said anything?"

"No, he just looks at me, turns, and jogs off."

"Have you approached him or his house?"

"Not yet."

"By which you mean?"

"If he doesn't talk to me soon, I'll have no choice. I'll ring the bell and have a chat with his wife."

Once again, it was her calm that unnerved me.

"Have you been trying to make contact with him anywhere else?"

"Oh, I've called him."

"And has he taken your calls?"

"Not yet. He's always been busy. But he will. Eventually."

"Where have you been calling him? At home?"

"Not yet. But I will start calling him there if he doesn't talk to me soon."

"So you've been calling him at his office, yes?"

"Yeah, and on his cell phone."

"And have you been calling often?"

"Every hour on the hour."

I opened a desk drawer and reached for the pack of Marlboro Lights that I kept there. I had long since curtailed my serious cigarette habit, but I still smoke three a day. It's a mild indulgence and a lot less toxic than the thirty-a-day addiction I once had. God knows, I needed a cigarette right now. I fished one out, lit it up, took a deep drag, exhaled, and said, "Now, you know, hon, that what you are doing could be construed, by some people, as harassment."

Her voice remained flat.

"But I'm not approaching him or anything," she said. "And if he just returned my call and agreed to talk with me . . ."

"What do you expect to get from him?"

"Well . . ." A pause. "I don't know . . ." Another pause. "Maybe if he hears what I have to say, he'll change his mind."

"But Lizzie, the very fact that he hasn't taken your calls, hasn't approached your car . . ."

"He has to talk to me!"

This sentence came out in a sudden shriek. As soon as it was uttered, she fell silent again. My stomach did cartwheels, while my brain went spinning into overdrive, wondering whether I should jump into the car right now and get down to Boston. But I had to be in Burlington tomorrow. Anyway, I doubted if my arrival would have any sort of stabilizing effect on her. Suddenly a thought crossed my mind.

"Lizzie, hon, I want you to do a big favor for yourself. I want you to go run a hot bath and have a nice long soak, and make yourself a cup of some sort of herbal tea, and get into bed, and make this a night that you will try to sleep straight through until morning. And if you wake up in the middle of the night, I want you to promise me you will not leave the apartment . . ."

"But he might talk to me this time."

"All I'm asking," I said, "is that you stay put tonight. Because if you don't get a decent night's sleep . . ."

"I work just fine on three hours."

"Do you have anything to help you sleep?"

"I've got some Sominex."

"Are you taking anything else right now?"

"My doctor suggested Prozac . . . but I know that once Mark talks to me . . ."

"Maybe you should speak to your doctor again about Prozac."

"Mom, all I need to do is talk to Mark. Okay?"

The tone was shrieky again.

"Okay," I said quietly. "But you will stay home all night tonight?"

"Mom . . ."

"Please."

Silence.

"If it makes you happy . . ."

"It would make me very happy," I said.

"Okay. But if he doesn't talk to me by this time tomorrow, I'm going back to his house. And this time I'm ringing his doorbell."

When we ended the call a few minutes later, I'd also extracted a promise from Lizzie that she'd phone in the middle of the night if she needed to talk. As soon as I hung up, I reached for my address book and found the card that McQueen had given me during that dreadful dinner with him in Cambridge. On the back, he'd scribbled his home number and his cell phone, telling me that "now that we're family" I should feel free to call him whenever.

"Whenever" had just arrived. So I dialed his cell phone—and when I received a recorded voice mail message, I tried his home number. A woman answered on the fourth ring. When I asked to speak to Dr. McQueen, she got very irritated, demanding to know who I was.

"Please tell him it's Hannah Buchan," I said. "I'm a patient."

"Don't you know how late it is?" she said.

Oh, give me a break. I'm a doctor's wife myself—and nine forty-five isn't exactly the middle of the night.

"Tell him it's urgent," I said. She put down the phone. When he picked it up a few moments later, his tone was nervous and he sounded like he was playacting for an audience.

"Ah yes, Mrs. Buchan," he said. "Hannah, isn't it? And how are you getting on with the new prescription?"

"It is important I talk with you now," I said in a very low voice.

"Now, I can understand your worry," he said in a bright, medical-man voice, "but it's not an unusual reaction. Might we be able to talk about this at length tomorrow?"

"Don't hang up on me, or I'll call right back."

"It's that bad, eh? Listen, I'd better take this in my study. I'll be putting down the phone for a moment, but will pick it up again in just an instant. Don't go away."

No chance of that, chum.

Around a minute later, he picked up again, sounding strained and talking in a near whisper.

"Are you crazy, calling me at home?" he hissed.

"It is a genuine emergency."

"You're as mad as your daughter."

I stiffened and suddenly felt real rage.

"Now, you listen to me, *Doctor,*" I said, the anger showing. "Lizzie is in a terrible place right now . . ."

"Tell me about it. She calls me morning, noon, and night. She lies in wait for me outside my house—"

". . . and she's doing this because you dumped her."

"I had no choice. My wife and my kids . . ."

"I warned you at that dinner . . ."

"I didn't think she would go so crazy."

"You can never predict someone else's feelings, especially when you've led them to believe that the game you were playing was for keeps."

"I wasn't playing a game . . ."

"You're a married man," I said. "Of course you were playing a game."

"I genuinely loved . . ."

"*Loved?* Since when did you stop loving the woman you told me was your destiny or some such—"

"Since she started stalking me, that's when."

"You have put her in this place . . ."

"Oh, please. She knew I was married when this whole thing started . . ."

"Don't you dare. You made it crystal clear to her that she was the love of your life."

"If she shows up here again, I'll call the police."

"And I'll call the AMA and make a formal complaint against you."

"For what? Sleeping with a lunatic?"

"Sleeping with a patient."

"She was never my patient. She saw me once as her dermatologist—a ten-minute appointment, during which I referred her to another specialist . . ."

"Once is enough, as far as the AMA is concerned."

"You're playing dirty."

"That's right. I am—and do you know why I am? Because Lizzie is my daughter."

"The complaint would be thrown out."

"Perhaps, but think of all the great publicity you'll receive along the way. How do you think a complaint against you would affect your emerging career as a television celebrity?"

Another long silence.

"So what do you want?" he finally asked.

"I want you to call her as soon as we're finished, and agree to meet her."

"It won't change my mind."

"If you don't call her, I promise you she'll be ringing your doorbell at home tomorrow night—because she told me that was her next step."

"What am I supposed to say to her?"

"That's up to you."

"I'm not going back to her."

"Then tell her that—in as clear and as kindly a way as possible."

"And if that doesn't work . . . if she keeps harassing me?"

"Then we'll get her some professional help. But before that, you must call her and tell her you'll see her tomorrow."

"I'm booked solid with appointments . . ."

"Find the time," I said.

"All right," he said quietly.

"And you'll call her at home now? She is definitely there, because I just got off the phone with her."

"Yes, I'll call her now."

And he hung up.

I put down the phone, and put my head in my hands. More than anything, I felt fear and guilt right now. Fear because Lizzie was in such a dark wood . . . and guilt because I wondered what we might have done during her childhood to nourish such desperate neediness, such fear of abandonment. She'd always been a great kid (and one with whom I had always had a close and relatively bump-free relationship), but that offered no comfort right now. I was about to light another cigarette, but instead I stood up and headed downstairs to the basement. I knew that, in the current situation, I could no longer keep Lizzie's secret. I had to talk to Dan about it, and get his counsel about what to do next.

But when I reached the basement, I found all the lights were off. So I returned upstairs to our bedroom. The lights were out in our room too, except for a small night-light that we always kept on in a corner of the room. Dan was already in bed, the duvet pulled up around him, fast asleep, dead to the world. Though I wanted to wake him up and tell him what was going on, I knew that it simply wouldn't be fair to rouse him now. It would have to wait until morning . . . no, damn it, I would be heading off to Burlington first thing . . . all right, I could leave him a note, telling him to call me on my cell phone and then I'd bring him up to date. I wouldn't soft-pedal the fact that I had kept this story from him at Lizzie's request. I'd come clean—and take the consequences.

I walked back to the basement, retrieved the bottle of wine from the bar, and brought it back to my office. I refilled my glass, fished out another cigarette, and resisted the temptation to call Margy in Manhattan. God, how I wanted to speak with her right now. After all these years, she still remained my closest friend, but Margy was in the middle of her own very dark wood—and although I know she would have looked upon the Lizzie crisis as a welcome respite from her own worries ("I love other people's emergencies," she once said), it was hard to know whether she'd be awake or asleep at this hour, given her general condition right now. So I lit up the cigarette (I was definitely going to break the three-a-day rule tonight), drank some more pinot noir, and tried to concentrate on the thirty term papers to be graded before morning. I had just finished with the second when the phone rang. I grabbed it immediately.

"Mom, great news," Lizzie said straightaway. "He called."

Stay neutral, I told myself.

"Well, that is good news," I said.

"And he wants to see me and talk things through."

"I'm very pleased."

"And I'm sure that, after he's heard what I have to say, he'll come right back to me. I know it. It's a certainty."

"Now it might be best not to get your hopes too high," I said.

"Mom, I can handle it. Okay?"

"Okay. You going to get some sleep tonight?"

"Oh yes."

"Will you call me tomorrow in Burlington to let me know how it all went?"

"Sure, Mom."

She sounded exactly like the fifteen-year-old she once was, getting all sulky about being asked to be home by eleven p.m. I wanted to take this as a sign that she was in a better place than she was half an hour ago, but I knew this was just wishful thinking. As soon as my flying Burlington visit was over, I'd be down to Boston.

"You know you can call me day or night, hon," I said.

"You've told me that already, Mom. Anyway, everything's going to work out fine."

No, it won't. But I couldn't say that. All I could hope was that, between now and tomorrow, McQueen would figure out some self-preservation strategy that would allow him to disentangle himself from Lizzie while simultaneously restoring her fragile equilibrium. Personally, I didn't know how the hell he'd pull it off. Because he wasn't in any position to give her what she so desperately wanted. That was the rub. My greatest worry right now was that she had so convinced herself she could talk him into coming back that when he said no, she'd flip entirely.

But that was tomorrow's problem. It was now nearly ten-thirty. I had a four-hour drive in front of me in the morning, not to mention all the attendant emotional baggage that would accompany me to my hometown. Right now, I just wanted to drink a final glass of wine, and take one of the herbal sleeping pills I use whenever I sense a restless night coming on. But there was the little matter of twenty-eight term papers . . .

I opened the first, written by Jamie Benjamin—a total knucklehead who spent much of my class sending notes back and forth to a girl named Janet Craig, whose daddy owned a Toyota dealership out near the Maine Mall, and who seemed destined, before she graduated next year, to get knocked up by a useless jock like Benjamin (he played tight end on the school football team, and though he always acted like Mr. Macho, he always got creamed by the opposing defense in every game I ever saw).

I read Benjamin's opening sentence.

"Evangeline is a very, very unhappy woman."

I don't know why, but I started to cry. Maybe it was the lateness of the hour, the three glasses of wine, the phone call with Lizzie, my fast-asleep husband down the corridor, the terrible, repetitive inanity of teaching the same stuff year in, year out, to kids who increasingly don't really seem to care a damn about any modestly articulate sentence that comes out of my mouth. Or maybe it was being fifty-three and trying to fight the thought that, at best, I am in the final third of my life, and what does all this mean? And the sad realization (which has been there for ages) that it simply adds up to your little life, nothing more . . .

Whatever the reason, I covered my face in my hands and let go. I must have cried for a good five minutes—the first time I'd had a long, unhinged weep since . . . well, since my mother vanished into the netherworld.

When my crying finally subsided, I stood up and went into a bathroom down the corridor, threw some water on my face, and avoided gazing at myself in the mirror (something I don't particularly like doing these days). Then I returned to my study and sat down at my desk. I reached for my cigarettes, lit one, and took a deep, pleasurable drag of smoke, drawing it way down into my lungs. As I released the smoke, I pulled the pile of term papers back in front of me. And I thought, *At moments like these, there is only one solution: go to work.*

ELEVEN

THE DRIVE FROM Portland to Vermont is long and wonderful. I should know, I've been doing it for several decades. As there's no direct interstate route, it's all back roads and two-lane blacktops—a slow cavalcade through small towns and lakelands and the best alpine terrain in the Northeast. I must have driven it over one hundred times since we moved back to Maine in 1980. Though I know every meander and bend of the route—the prosaic flat stretches, the deep woodlands, the sublime White Mountain vistas, the deep verdancy that announces the arrival of the Kingdom of Vermont—it never bores me. I always discover something new along the way every time I drive it—a reminder that, by looking closer, you can often find the unfamiliar amid the habitual.

But this morning, I wasn't paying particular attention to the passing landscape. My mind was elsewhere. I'd finally finished the term papers at two-thirty, then scribbled a note to Dan asking him to reset the alarm (after he got up) for eight-thirty, and to call me on my cell phone when he had a chance. I slept badly—a toxic combination of worry, nine Marlboro Lights, too much pinot noir, and the thought that Lizzie might ring me in the middle of the night. When I woke, Dan was gone, and there were no messages on the voice mail. I showered and dressed, made coffee, and put a call through to Lizzie's office in Boston. I wanted to speak with her directly to make sure she was all right, but I knew she'd probably get annoyed with me for checking up on her. One of her colleagues answered, and when I asked for "Ms. Buchan," he said that she was in the morning staff conference. Any message? "None," I said. "I'll call back."

I was relieved that she had made it to work, and knew that I'd be thinking all day about her meeting with Mark McQueen, which, I presumed, was scheduled for early evening, after they both got off work.

Maybe I should leave a message on her cell phone, telling her to call me on my cell phone as soon as . . .

No, she might think I'm crowding her. Anyway, she might not meet him until late. They might go out for dinner (no, he'll want to get it over with as fast as possible), or they might be talking for a long time. Maybe she will have arranged to see a girlfriend afterward (wishful thinking—she's expecting to fall back into his arms and pull him off into bed). Or perhaps she'll try to work off her upset in the gym. Anyway, if she's very upset, I'm sure she'll call me, and . . .

Stop. There's nothing you can do until you hear from her. The fact that she's reported for work is a good sign. It's out of your control. Get on with your day—which, under the circumstances, is going to be difficult enough.

I drank two mugs of coffee, then started coughing heavily. *Nine cigarettes.* I vowed not to smoke today or tomorrow. Then I filled the thermos mug with more coffee, grabbed my overnight bag, and was out the door by nine. I drove over to the school, turned in my midterm grades to the registrar, picked up a couple of pointless internal memos in my mailbox, and was gone from the place ten minutes after I first got there, giving silent thanks that I wouldn't be back for another ten days, when school reconvened after the Easter break.

Then I negotiated my way through Portland's mishmash of residential areas—a little pocket of remaining High Colonial architecture on Park Street, leading to Depression-era apartment blocks (which I used to write off as kitschy, but which I now recognized to be retro-cool). Then the usual low gray-shingle houses that seem to characterize the old blue-collar section of every modest New England city. Then the subdivisions near the highway. Then, in a matter of minutes, empty country. That's one of the many things I love about Maine—the sense that the land always dwarfs the population, that the wilderness is never more than a few miles from your front door.

I picked up Route 25 heading west. Thirty minutes later I saw signs for Sebago Lake, Bridgton, and Pelham.

Pelham. I hadn't been back there since . . . well, since we left the damn place in the summer of '75. Even after we finally got out of that wretched apartment and into the house of Dr. . . . What was his name again (thirty years is such a frighteningly long time)? . . . *Bland!* . . . Yes, even once we moved into Dr. Bland's house, Pelham still convinced us both that we'd never, *ever,* live in a small town again. Of course, I was so racked with guilt after that business with . . . (even now, after all this time, I don't like recalling his name) . . . that I simply kept my head down and got on with being the perfect doctor's wife and mother, somehow convincing myself that as long as I kept Dan happy and didn't make trouble, he might just stand by me when the feds finally came to pick me up, and the conservative Maine newspapers turned me into the Madame Defarge of the Weather Underground, and I was facing two-to-five for aiding and abetting a fugitive from justice.

But the feds never showed up, and the assorted catastrophic scenarios I painted in my head never came true. No one around town ever mentioned my visitor again. And poor Billy (I wonder if he's still alive?) was as good as his word and never talked about what he saw that night. I beat myself up for a long time afterward, telling myself that there had to be a punishment for what I had done, and constantly waiting for it to arrive at my door. But winter gave way to spring, and nothing happened—except that Dan's poor father finally died, which, after over six months in a coma, was a relief to both of us. Shortly afterward I finally made my first visit to New York. During that long, crazy weekend with Margy (during which I kicked myself for waiting so long to get to that mad marvel of a city, which, even at the height of its mid-seventies dinginess, still struck me as the great testament to everything dynamic and *out there* in American life), the question finally arose one drunken evening. We were at a jazz joint up near Columbia University, listening to a fantastic boogie-woogie pianist named Sammie Price. After the final set—it was about one-thirty in the morning and we were both a little ripped—Margy asked: did I ever tell anyone else about the things that happened when Tobias Judson (there, I've said his name) came to town?

"You're still the only person who knows," I said.

"Keep it that way," she said.

"No worry about that."

"You still feel guilty about it all, don't you?"

"I wish I could just shake it off, like flu."

"Flu doesn't last six months. You've got to stop punishing yourself. It's all in the past now. Anyway"—she lowered her voice to a conspiratorial tone—"say he did somehow get picked up in Canada by the Mounties, why would he suddenly tattle on you? It would get him nothing. By this point, he's probably forgotten all about you. You were just a little adventure, someone he used to get out of the country. Trust me, he's using someone else by now."

"You're probably right."

"You still giving your dad the cold shoulder?"

I nodded.

"You've got to forgive him."

"No, I don't."

I continued to refuse to forgive him—for almost the next two years. He did try to call me again, several times, but I always cut him off, always told him I would never speak to him again. On the few occasions when we were together as a family, I was civil but distant with him. Dan noticed this gulf between us, but said little about it, except, "Everything okay with you guys?" But he accepted my vague excuse that we were just going through a slightly disenchanted phase with each other right now.

Of course, Mom constantly tried to find out what was going on—but I refused to explain. I know she also hassled Dad—because he eventually cracked and confessed what he had done. God knows what sort of fireworks followed this admission. What I do know is that Mom called me up one day at the library and said, "All right, I have finally been told what this rift is all about—and I think your father is walking bent over right now because I've just torn him a new asshole."

Mom really did have such a subtle turn of phrase. She went on.

"If I were you, I'd be angry, furious, rabid. At the very least, he should have told you the guy was on the run . . ."

"Mom . . ." I said, "I don't know what you're talking about."

"If that was for the feds, don't sweat it. I'm not on our home phone and I called you at work, to make sure nobody was listening to any of this. But what I want to tell you is this: your dad made a wrong call . . ."

"He made a terrible call," I said.

"Okay, a terrible call—and he dropped you into a situation you shouldn't have been dropped in. Still, the thing is: you did decide to drive the guy into Canada, which was both honorable and gutsy . . . You could have easily told him to take a hike."

No, I couldn't have—because he virtually blackmailed me into helping him flee. But if I told her that, I would have to explain *why* he had me in a corner—and that would have meant entrusting her with a secret that, bar Margy, I knew I would never share with anybody. Anyway, the idea of confiding in Mom was anathema to me—because I knew that she'd somehow use this information against me. So I said, "That's right—I could have told him to take a hike. But having been landed with him—and as I was there when he discovered that the FBI were on his tail—what choice did I have?"

"A lot of people would have taken the easy way out and refused to have anything to do with it. You didn't—and I genuinely admire you for that."

It was the first time my mother had said she admired me for anything.

"Dan never found out, did he?" Mom asked.

"God, no."

"Well, keep it that way. The less people know the better. But you're going to have to forgive your father . . ."

"That's easy for you to say."

"No, it's not. He's done plenty of things over the course of this screwy marriage that I've found hard to excuse, but eventually, I have forgiven him. Because he's forgiven me stuff too. He may be a jerk sometimes, I may be a jerk sometimes . . . but we're jerks in this together. It's the same thing now with you. Your father's tried to apologize to you—he feels bad about what he did to you—but you still refuse to forgive him. And it's eating away at him."

I held out for another year. By this time, we were settled in Madison—Dan doing his orthopedic residency at University Hospital, while I was substitute teaching at a local private school, and heavily pregnant with Lizzie. One afternoon, at our rented house (a Gothic revival dump—very Addams Family), the phone rang—and Dad was on the line. "I just called to say hello."

No, there wasn't a Movie-of-the-Week denouement to this scene. I didn't suddenly break down on the line, telling him how much I missed him (which I certainly had), or saying the magic words: *I forgive you.* Nor did he get choked up and burst out with something lachrymose like:

You're the best daughter in the world. That wasn't our reserved Yankee style. Instead there was a long pause after his first sentence, during which the realization came to me that I simply wanted to start talking to my dad again; that, though what he had done was wrong, I was also punishing him for my own bad judgment.

So I simply said, "It's nice to hear from you, Dad." And we started to chat about general things—like Jimmy Carter's chances of beating Ford in November, and Nixon's pardon, and the news that I was going to be a mother again, and my work as a teacher. We kept the conversation light, we laughed at each other's jokes, we ended the breach between us by silently agreeing to dodge the matter. After all, what more could we say? So gradually, over time, we were able to find a way back to the relationship we once had. Looking back on it now—especially in the light of my knotty dealings with my own kids—I do appreciate that, like most interesting people, Dad is a very complex, contradictory guy, one who, back then, was never completely able to balance his public persona and his private life. In his own tangled way, he tried to do the best he could as a father, amid his own immensely tricky marriage to my mother.

Still, we never brought up the Toby Judson business again, even after it was widely reported in the newspapers that, following five years on the run in Canada, he had cut a deal with the federal prosecutors. In return for his testimony against the two Weathermen who had planted the bomb in Chicago (and whom the FBI had finally apprehended in New Mexico), Judson was able to return to the States and receive a suspended sentence for harboring fugitives. The trial, in 1981, was covered as a "Good-bye to All That" kiss-off to the era of sixties radicalism. None of the commentaries I read—even in what was left of the underground press—ever criticized Judson for ratting on his former comrades. Murder was murder—and the killers both got life, courtesy of Judson's testimony. Afterward, when he was asked how he felt about his radical years, Judson said, "I'd like to be able to blame it all on youthful folly, but I realize now that my politics were simply wrong. By harboring those killers, I denied justice to the families of the innocent men killed in the bombing. I hope that, through my actions now, I will bring some sort of closure to the loved ones of these brave men—though I know that their deaths will be on my conscience for the rest of my life."

Oh, he has a conscience now, I thought at the time. And then decided to think no more about it. Life moved on, and after his brief public reappearance at the trial, Judson disappeared into obscurity.

Sebago Lake suddenly came into view. Though the water hadn't frozen, its banks and surrounding country were frosted with last night's freak snowfall. It looked sublime. For a nanosecond I saw myself thirty years ago in a canoe on the lake—Judson rowing us along, Jeff and me sitting in the stern, the surrounding hills awash with autumn colors, me falling for Mr. Revolutionary's bullshit charm. Oh God, the naiveté of it all—and the terrible guilt that followed. Guilt that finally abated, but can still catch me unawares. But I made good on the bargain I cut with myself on the trip back from Canada: I stuck with the marriage, even when I felt totally frustrated by it. And I was never unfaithful to Dan again. And the payoff was . . .

Stability? I suppose so. *Avoiding the roller coaster of divorce that so many of my friends have been through?* Okay, that's a plus point—because no one I know has a good thing to say about the fallout of a conjugal bust-up . . . even those who were in rotten marriages. *A secure home environment for our children while they were growing up?* Absolutely . . . but look at them now. *Knowing that Dan is there at night when I get home?* I always get home before him. *A life without much in the way of emotional danger?* Is that a virtue?

The road turned a corner, Sebago Lake disappeared from view. My cell phone started ringing. I flipped the speaker switch and answered it.

"Hey," Dan said. "How's it going?"

"Not great," I said.

"I saw your note. Something wrong?"

"I have a confession to make," I said. "I've been keeping something from you, something that Lizzie asked me to keep to myself."

Then, in as abbreviated a way as possible, I told Dan the story of Lizzie's affair with Mark McQueen. To my husband's infinite credit, he didn't first demand to know why I hadn't informed him about this before now. Instead, he asked, "Do you think she might hurt herself?"

"She reported to work this morning, which is something, I guess."

"And when is she meeting the doctor?"

"Today sometime. Listen, I'm sorry I didn't tell you until now."

"A secret is a secret, I guess. Still . . ."

"You're right. And I feel shitty about it."

"I hope Lizzie doesn't feel I might judge her. Because you know I would never do that."

"Of course I know that. And I'm pretty damn sure she knows it too. But that's not what's going on here. I think she feels ashamed of her erratic emotional behavior and worries that you might be embarrassed by it. Between ourselves, *I'm* embarrassed about it . . . and I'm worried as hell."

"Did she say she'd call you today?"

"I've asked her to, but can't say whether she will or not. I suppose it all comes down to how the good doctor handles it."

"When do you think you'll reach Burlington?" he asked.

"In about three hours."

"And you're going straight to the home?"

"That's right."

"You're really looking at a delightful day, aren't you?"

"I'll get through it. And I'll be a lot calmer once I know how things are playing with Lizzie."

"As soon as you speak to her . . ."

"Don't worry. I'll call the moment I hang up."

"And I can always drive down to Boston tonight if she's in a bad way."

"Hopefully, that won't be necessary."

"Okay. Call me after you've finished your visit."

"Roger Wilco."

"Love you."

"You too."

I felt better after the call. Not because anything had changed, but because Dan was in this with me now—and I didn't have to guard Lizzie's secret anymore.

The road gained altitude as I approached the New Hampshire border, the peaks of the White Mountains defining the horizon toward which I moved. The snow was deep here, the driving slow. But I didn't care, as National Public Radio was broadcasting a performance of Brahms's *German Requiem*. I didn't know the piece, but was immediately intrigued when the announcer explained that the work grappled with that most profound and difficult of personal realizations: the fact that one is completely mortal and, as such, ephemeral. The stunning power of Brahms's music hit me full force—the profound gravity of it all; its magisterial sadness tinged with a solemn optimism. Even the settings of liturgical texts were remarkable in their refusal to talk about a paradise beyond this one. Brahms was a man after my own heart. Vis-à-vis temporal life, he understood that, like it or not, this *is* it.

And this got me thinking how our life as we live it always seems eternal. Though we might rationally be able to grasp the idea that we will die, there is still something incomprehensible about our own mortality; that, one day, we will be nothing; that, verily, we are all just passing through. I have often wondered if all the trouble we make for ourselves and others is nothing more than a response to the realization that everything we do, everything we achieve, largely vanishes once we are dead. I remember something Margy once told me, when she took a vacation with Husband Number Three in South Africa around four years ago . . . how they ended up for a few days in this "fabulous" (her favorite word) little town called Arniston, right at the bottom of the African continent.

"There wasn't much there, except some holiday homes for the Cape Town bigwigs, and some shabby cottages for the workers, and miles and miles of empty beaches, and one really fabulous little hotel, where Charlie and I stayed. Anyway, opposite the hotel was a seawall, on which a plaque commemorated the sinking of some passenger ship—traveling from India back to England in the 1870s, filled with the wives and children of all those guys who ran the Empire. Around two miles off the coast of Arniston, the ship got into trouble and sank, and over two hundred passengers drowned.

"Now here I was in 1999, looking at this plaque, and then staring out at that big watery emptiness where everybody died around one hundred and thirty years earlier. At the time, all of these deaths must have been such big international news. Now it was just a long-forgotten event, commemorated on a simple plaque in some isolated South African town. Even worse was the thought of all the grief and trauma all those deaths caused back then. Two hundred women and children. Think of the devastated spouses and the parents and grandparents and siblings they left behind. Think of how all those lives were marked by this tragedy and how now, all traces have completely disappeared. That's what got me the most—the recognition that all that suffering and pain, which probably carried over into two subsequent generations, has vanished completely. Because everyone who was ever touched by that tragedy is dead."

Margy. Unlucky with men (one bad husband followed another—she really had a knack when it came to choosing deadbeats). Lucky in her professional life (since 1990, she'd been running her own hugely dynamic PR agency in Manhattan), even though she always regretted the fact that she'd never forced her way into journalism. Just as she also regretted that she never did the child thing ("When you marry losers—and are also in a business that demands sixteen-hour days, six days a week—bringing a kid into the midst of such a crazy life just wouldn't be fair"). After all these years—after countless setbacks and reversals and personal griefs (and a few big professional successes)—she still managed to maintain her skewed, amused outlook on everything.

"You know that life is nothing more than one big fight," she said after she jettisoned Husband Number Three upon discovering that he had embezzled $50,000 from her to pay for a secret investment in a shoddy dot-com company. "But what else can we do but keep on fighting? There's no other choice."

But now Margy was in the middle of the biggest fight of her life. Four months ago, she had been diagnosed with lung cancer.

She announced this devastating fact to me in typical Margy fashion. It was a few days before Christmas. We were in the middle of our weekly phone call. I was telling her about a conversation I'd just had with Shannon, in which she informed me that she would be bringing her own special chestnut stuffing for the turkey and that she had already spent two weeks perfecting the recipe before unveiling it to us over Christmas. As I was cracking wise on how depressing it was to have a daughter-in-law who put so much effort into closing down abortion clinics *and* making the perfect chestnut stuffing, I dropped a hint that Margy would be very welcome for Christmas, knowing full well that, in the wake of her divorce and with no surviving family, she'd probably be spending the holidays alone.

"Hey, I'd love to come to Maine and do the whole Currier-and-Ives Christmas thing with you," she said. "But it seems I'm otherwise engaged over the holidays."

"Is that a euphemism for . . . ?"

"That's right," she said. "I have a new man in my life."

"And would you mind revealing who the lucky guy is?"

"Sure," she said. "He's my oncologist."

She was so matter-of-fact about this—so initially *haha* dismissive—that I first thought this was Margy's idea of a very black joke.

"That's not funny," I said.

"You're right," she said. "It's not fucking funny at all. Lung cancer never is. And the most diabolical thing of all is that it's so damn sneaky. As my new significant other—Dr. Walgreen . . . yeah, just like the cheap-ass pharmacies—as Doc Walgreen said, what makes lung cancer so diabolical is that it remains largely undetectable until it starts to affect another part of the anatomy . . . like the brain."

"Oh Christ, Margy . . ."

"Yeah, I could probably use His help right now—that is, if I could get my head around the idea that He and His Father actually run the behind-the-scenes show on this screwy planet of ours. Right now, I'm having a hard enough time getting my head around the idea that I have lung cancer . . . though the good news is that it *hasn't* gone to my head, so to speak."

She explained that the cancer was discovered on an X-ray when they were looking for something else.

"I got back from a business trip to Honolulu, pitching for the state of Hawaii tourism account. That town bills itself as the capital of our Pacific Paradise, but it also happens to be Smog City. And when I returned to Manhattan after a week there, I was suffering from this terrible cough. Since I'd had that bout of pneumonia a couple of years ago, I thought that maybe I was having a little relapse . . . even though I had no fever or any other signs of infection. After a couple of days, I called my doctor and he sent me to New York Hospital for what he called 'a little picture.' What the chest X-ray showed was an ominous gray cloud of *something* at the place where the bronchus splits into two branches, one that goes to the upper left lobe of the lung, the other to the lower lobe. There were actually two X-rays—one from the front and the other from the side, which is how they could locate the tumor so precisely. What the X-ray could not show is that the upper left lobe of my lung had collapsed, which is what was causing the coughing, because gunk collects in the collapsed lobe and keeps seeping into the bronchial tube, which the body keeps trying to clear by coughing. And hey, do you think I could get a job writing for *The New England Journal of Medicine*? Because only a week or so into this 'adventure,' I'm already beginning to sound like one of those medical geeks who gets to know everything there is to know about the disease that's going to kill her."

"Don't say that."

"Why? Because it offends your inherent need to be optimistic about everything . . . even though *I*—your best friend—know that, between the lines, you're an opinionated pessimist just like me?"

"Selfishly speaking, I just don't want you to die, that's all."

"Well, that makes two of us—and the good news is that I have the *kinder, gentler* sort of lung cancer . . . the kind that doesn't mean an automatic death sentence."

As she started talking about the bronchoscopy, I reached for a pad of paper and started taking notes—knowing that I would want to go over all this later on with Dan, and also because, instinctually, it was easier to focus on the *facts* than the underlying *reality* of what had befallen my friend. "Well, I just got the initial verdict yesterday evening," Margy said. "And the first major reasonable discovery is that I have what is known as a 'large-cell' tumor, because in the world of lung cancer, the really lethal tumors are 'small cell.' The second is that the tumor has all but completely blocked off the upper bronchial tube and is now threatening to close the lower bronchial tube as well. But the other important discovery is that the tumor is actually *tumorlike,* rather than a lesion. Dr. Walgreen is really pleased about this—and I have to say this, though I have not had any experience of cancer doctors before this, he is one cheerful oncologist. As he explained, the harder the tumor or lesion is, the less likely that the cells from it will have made their way into the bloodstream and lodged in other organs of the body."

By the time we got off the phone, I was already making plans to fly down to New York after finishing my classes on Friday—the day after Margy's surgery.

"Hey, what's the point of you schlepping all the way down here?" Margy asked. "I'm not going to be the best of company."

But I went anyway. I had run through everything Margy told me with Dan, who in turn talked with a heart-and-lung colleague at Maine Medical, who confirmed that though her large-cell tumor was the better sort of lung cancer, it could still prove fatal.

"Once they've got the tumor out," Dan explained, "they have to 'stage' the tumor to determine how far the cancer has progressed. Margy will be able to live with one lung. But if they discover that the cancer has progressed into both lungs, well, she might be able to buy a little time with a lung transplant. But . . ."

He opened his hands to avoid saying the unsayable. Then, after a moment, he said, "One of the many things I like about orthopedics is that you are rarely dealing with life-and-death stuff like this."

When I reached New York Hospital on Friday evening, I expected Margy to be in a postoperative comatose state. But though she was hooked up to assorted tubes and monitors, she was sitting up in bed, watching CNN. She looked desperately pale and tired, but managed an acerbic smile before saying, "I hope you brought me some cigarettes."

I spent most of the weekend in her room, only leaving to avail myself of the bed in her apartment. (When I said I'd find a hotel, she insisted that I stay at her place, "Because it looks like I will not be sleeping in my own bed for the next couple of weeks.") Margy amazed me that weekend. She refused to indulge in self-pity, and she made it clear that she was planning to adopt a "scorched earth" approach to the cancer.

"After three bad husbands, I'm well used to excising shit from my life. And when I fight, I fight *dirty*."

At night, back at her place, I couldn't help but worry that this show of gutsiness was for my benefit. I could see in her eyes the fear she refused to express. Margy never really liked to show her vulnerability—even to me. Just as she didn't ever articulate the loneliness I knew that she often felt—a loneliness that really hit home during the two nights I spent alone in her apartment. I had stayed at her place many times before, but this was the first visit when the apartment wasn't filled with Margy's oversized personality. So I was finally able to look at length at her small, faceless one-bedroom place—located in one of those white-brick 1960s buildings that have the appearance of a high-rise refrigerator and so dominate (from my limited experience of the place) the skyline of the East Seventies near the river. It always surprised me that she lived in such a petite apartment. After all, didn't she run this big-deal PR firm? But it was a "boutique firm" (herself and a staff of three), and she didn't take an enormous salary because cash flow was always an issue, and she was out and about most nights, and spent as many weekends as possible visiting friends in the Hamptons or western Connecticut. So her apartment was really just a place where she slept, changed clothes, and tolerated the occasional evening in. She had bought the apartment twenty-five years ago with the little money left over from her mother's estate—and sublet it during each of her marriages ("On all three occasions," she once told me, "I think I subconsciously knew that I was making a bad call, so I insisted that I move into the guy's place . . . because it let me eventually walk out with less hassle, knowing that I had my little co-op as a getaway"). But walking in from the hospital—the calm, sanguine front I had put on for Margy now replaced by numbing aftershock—the terrible silence and sterility of the apartment hit me. It was simply decorated—a sofa and an armchair covered in plain oatmeal fabric, a small dining table, an ordinary queen-sized bed. But it was completely devoid of decorative flourishes or a sense of style, let alone a hint of a personal life. There were no family photos, no quirky or interesting art on the walls—just two or three Whitney Museum posters. There was a stereo, but only twenty or so compact discs—light classics (Andrea Bocelli, The Three Tenors) and golden oldies. There was a television and a DVD player, and a bookshelf with assorted paperback best sellers of the past five years. There was a 1970s liquor cabinet—in which I now found a bottle of J&B and several packs of Merits. I poured a drink and sipped the scotch, giving quiet thanks for the medicinal pleasures (in moderation, I boringly hasten to add) of alcohol. I stared at the nowhere decor and wondered why I hadn't noticed its facelessness before, and why I hadn't grasped the disconnection between the chic, street-smart public woman and the lonely, impersonal world she retreated into. We rarely glimpse the true private realities of our friends. Or maybe we filter out the stuff we don't want to see, because we prefer to buy into the life more interesting than our own. Which is what I did for years with Margy—privately envying her such a metropolitan existence, the latitude when it came to travel or falling into bed with whomever, and (most of all) the privacy and time alone that was denied me until the kids had grown up and fled. I could tell, whenever Margy visited us in Maine (especially when Jeff and Lizzie were young), that she watched the family chaos—all boisterous voices and constant child demands—with a certain quiet envy. We always want what we don't have. We regret, in part, the lives we create for ourselves—no matter how successful they might be—because there's a part of us that can never be satisfied with our own reality, the place where we have ended up. Looking at Margy's bare apartment didn't suddenly make me give thanks for my long marriage, my domestic setup. But it amplified all the questions I have about the nature of choice and the inability ever to be really content. Just as it also told me there was so much about this woman—my friend for over thirty-five years—that I simply didn't know.

The next day at the hospital, Margy said, "Bet you found the apartment lonely last night."

"Not particularly," I lied.

"You don't have to soft-pedal me just because I've got the Big C. It's real Early Nothing, my place—and it's my own damn fault. A testament to my inability to expend energy on anything but the here and fucking now—the next meeting, the next deal, the next schmooze session with some hack who writes for an in-flight magazine. That's the sum total of my existence—the peripheral, the inconsequential, the—"

I put my hand on hers and said, "Don't do this."

"Why not? I love self-flagellation. More to the point, I'm good at it. My mom always used to say that my biggest problem was that I saw things far too clearly."

"I would have thought that a strength."

"It leads to ongoing four-in-the-morning dread."

"We all deal with that sort of thing from time to time."

"Yeah, but I do it six nights a week."

"And on the seventh night?"

"I medicate myself with enough scotch to conk out for eight straight hours and wake up with the mother of all hangovers the next morning. Jesus, will you listen to me? Little Ms. Self-Pity on top of everything else."

"Considering what you've just been through . . ."

"No, hon—the self-absorption has nothing to do with the cancer. I put it down to a lack of nicotine. You don't think you could smuggle me in one of those nicotine patches they sell to junkies trying to kick the habit?"

"Somehow I think your oncologist might not like the idea."

"Fuck him. All the surgery and the chemo-dreck to come is just damage control. This thing is going to get me."

"Yesterday you said you'd beat it."

"Well, today I'm celebrating the Power of Negative Thinking. It's weirdly comforting, feeling doomed . . ."

"Knock it off," I said, sounding stern and schoolmarmish. "You have the good kind of cancer."

"And you've just uttered the biggest fucking oxymoron going."

I had to fly back to Maine the next night, but called Margy midday on Monday at the hospital once the results of the biopsy were in.

"Well, they're pretty certain the cancer hasn't metastasized into other parts of the body," she said.

"That's fantastic news."

"No, it's bad but it could be worse, and they're going to have to run about a half-dozen more tests to make certain there isn't any metastasis they haven't caught. The final upshot of everything is that I will be starting chemotherapy just as soon as I am completely over all my postoperative shock. And if you fucking tell me that all this is very encouraging, I'm going to hang up, got that?"

The news, in fact, *was* encouraging. Dan—bless him—had his lung surgeon friend at Maine Medical call Margy's oncologist in New York (they'd been at Cornell Medical together) to get the complete inside dope on her case (I needed to know the actual nuts-and-bolts realities of what she was facing). They felt they had gotten all of the tumor out during surgery—and though they would only know after tests if any cancer cells had invaded the other lung, they were pretty confident that metastasis hadn't taken place. But—oh yes, that great medical *but*—they couldn't completely rule out metastasis, and they were going to run vast amounts of tests to see if the cancer might have traveled elsewhere.

And so, over the next few weeks, Margy endured assorted procedures—including a course of chemotherapy to zap any rogue cells. As

Margy explained it, chemo involved sitting in a recliner all afternoon while they dripped poison into her arm. I flew down to see her a week after the first course. She was back at home, but had hired her housekeeper to come in every day to cook and shop for her, as she was incredibly weak from the chemo. Her hair had started to fall out, her skin had taken on a yellowy tinge, and she complained of pain in just about every joint in her body.

"Otherwise, I feel fucking fabulous."

Amazingly, she had started to work again. There were client files spread across her bed at home. When I wondered out loud if this was a good idea, she said, "I've got nothing better to do—and anyway, what else is there in my life but work?"

Her resolve was astonishing. As the first course of chemo was successful, two subsequent series were ordered. By this point she was back at the office, and merely took off a couple of days to get over the appalling side effects. Just a month ago, she had to go back into the hospital for another week for a surgical procedure known as a lobectomy—to remove the scar tissue in the upper bronchus of her lung that had resulted in a lot of catastrophic coughing.

"However, as I'm certain you saw on CNN this morning," Margy said a few days after the operation, "my lower bronchus turned out to be undamaged, which means that I get to keep my lower lobe of my lung. Sounds like a game show, doesn't it? *Too bad that you didn't win our grand prize of an Amana Fridge/Freezer with a built-in ice cube maker, but you still get to keep the lower lobe of your left lung!*"

I laughed. But before I could make a comment, Margy said, "And don't tell me how great it is that I have kept my sense of humor. I don't find any of this funny at all—except the irony that I only started smoking at fifteen because I thought it looked sexy. But I bet every damn oncologist has heard that line before from some lung cancer loser, bemoaning the fact that they reached for their first Winston because they were insecure about how they looked and hoped it might get them laid. Anyway, the thing is—and this is really a diabolical admission after all the medical fun I've been through—I'd still kill for a cigarette right now."

The *German Requiem* faded into static. I was deep in the White Mountains. Up ahead, I could see the grave, stern silhouette of Mount

Washington—and remembered how I had once climbed it with Dan right after our final exams in . . . good God, could it have been 1970? Hiking up it was his idea. I complained frequently during the initial ascent—a boring, steep trek through woodlands. But then, just as I was about to suggest that we return to base, we turned a corner, the forest vanished, and there in front of us was this immense ravine. It was shaped like a bowl and veiled with thin cloud. There was a small glacier in the middle. To the right of it was a rocky trail—free of snow. Above that was a boulder field, which led to the summit—all 6,288 feet of it. I felt a stab of fear as I looked up at that ravine. Fear mixed with a strange sense of exhilaration, because how often in life do you get to do something as challenging and extreme as climb a mountain? Dan must have read my mind, as he said, "Don't worry, you'll make it to the top."

We did get to the summit—even though, halfway up the ravine, we got caught in a hailstorm, accompanied by a nervy half hour of high winds. I lost my footing at one point, and nearly took a three-hundred-foot fall that would undoubtedly have resulted in my death. What saved me was instinct and luck. As I slipped, I grabbed for some sort of support. In front of me was a thin rock, jutting out near my left hand. Had it given way under my weight, I would have been sent sailing southward. But it held—and saved my life.

The whole incident couldn't have lasted more than five seconds—the misstep, the moment of panic, the mad grab for anything stable, my left hand connecting with the rock. Dan was up ahead of me and saw nothing. I needed a minute to collect myself, then continued the ascent. When I caught up with Dan around fifteen minutes later and he asked me how I was getting on, I made light of what had just happened. "Lost my footing back there and nearly went over the side . . . but otherwise, no sweat at all."

"Okay. Just watch your step, eh?"

Watch your step. Story of my life. And with two exceptions, I had done just that. But whereas the business with Toby Judson was an instance where I had let dumb romantic impulses rule my head, the misstep on Mount Washington was just a bit of bad luck that could have proved fatal, if the instinct for self-preservation had not taken over. And I'd like to believe that, as hard as this life is, most of us want to cling on to it. Like me grabbing for that rock. Or Margy showing an inner ferocity against the cancer that may have been self-inflicted, but had now become an enemy to be vanquished before it vanquished her. Or Mom . . .

The Vermont border was up ahead. The snow was thinner here—the hills gentle, understated. My native state has none of the epic grandeur of New Hampshire's alpine terrain or Maine's jagged coast. Its scenic pleasures are serene, subtle ones that always sit well with me—because they invariably let it be known that I am home.

I hit the scan button on the radio and found the Vermont NPR station. On it, there was a *Talk of the Nation* discussion about family fallingouts over politics—and the wide dichotomy that existed between old sixties radicals and their more conservative children.

How about grandchildren? I thought, remembering how horrified Dad had been when he was down in Boston one weekend and took his granddaughter out for dinner, and she insisted on picking up the tab. And when the chivalric old school gent in him politely told her that grandfathers are supposed to pay for dinners out, she said, "But hey, I'm earning $150,000 a year—so it's not like I'm a student."

Dad was shocked at the size of her salary. He'd never made anything like that in his life, and it went against all his egalitarian principles. But Lizzie turning into a corporate type was nothing compared to Jeff becoming such a Bush-loving Republican. That was simply beyond Dad's comprehension. He asked me once or twice what Dan and I had done to make him so conservative. All I could say was, "It's not like he decided to mutiny because he was raised in an ashram, or by a pair of potheads. And we didn't exactly send him to the Emma Goldman Camp for Young Trotskyites every summer. Hell, you know how straight Dan is—and how undemonstrative he is about political stuff. Jeff, on the other hand, seems to be the original True Believer. America is God's preferred country, and the Republicans stand for all the right upstanding values. Personally, I sometimes think it's like he's having the teenage rebellion he should have had years ago."

Dad really took Jeff's conservatism personally. He saw it as a complete refutation of everything he stood for. When he joined us for Christmas last year—still amazingly vigorous and sharp at eighty-two—he tried to get Jeff engaged in a political discussion, because if there's one thing

Dad loves, it's a good debate. But Jeff refused to be drawn in, always changing the subject whenever Dad went into an anti-Bush tirade, or even walking out of the room.

"Why won't you talk to your grandfather?" I asked him after Dad tried to raise a question about the Patriot Act.

"I was talking to him," he said.

"Oh, please. The moment he brought up your beloved president, you excused yourself and went upstairs."

"I wanted to check up on Erin. And, by the way, Bush is your president too."

"There's a school of thought that says that Al Gore was actually elected president."

"There you go again, spouting the usual liberal bias."

There you go again. Didn't Reagan score a knockout punch with that comment during one of his debates against Carter?

"I didn't know I spouted liberal bias, Jeff."

"Everyone in this family does. It's in the blood."

"I think you're exaggerating . . ."

"All right, I know Dad isn't a raging lefty—"

"He's a registered Republican."

"But he still supports candidates who are pro-choice. And when it comes to dear old Granddad, well, his history and his FBI file speak for themselves."

"So should the fact that he's an eighty-two-year-old man who happens to think the world of you . . ."

"No, he thinks the world of the sound of his own voice. And I've read all about his 'heroic' role in the 'struggle' against this country's institutions in the sixties."

"But that was more than thirty-five years ago, before you were born. Anyway, if you had been a student then, you would have been out on the barricades with him."

"Don't be so sure of that," he said. "My political views aren't based on fashion."

Well, isn't it fashionable now to be a conservative? I felt like telling him. *Hell, you and your "friends" dominate the media. You've got your own all-news channel to tell you exactly what you want to hear. You've got your own very loud commentators who shout down anyone who disagrees with them. And the country is so damn jumpy since 9/11 that if you even dare question the administration, certain folks . . . like you, my dear son . . . will immediately question your patriotism.*

Patriotism . . . what a peculiar obsession.

"Look, Jeff," I said. "It's Christmas. And as a practicing Christian, surely you know it's essential to be tolerant of others, especially . . ."

"Please stop talking to me as if I were twelve years old," he said. "And I really don't appreciate being lectured about Christianity by an atheist."

"I am not an atheist. I'm a Unitarian."

"It's the same thing."

Later that evening, after Jeff and Shannon had gone to bed, and Lizzie had headed off with friends to some downtown Portland bar now popular with the city's young professionals, and Dan had retired to our room to watch *Nightline,* Dad sat by the fire in our living room, sipping a small whiskey ("My doctor says one a day will keep the blood flowing"), the melancholy showing.

"Do you think that the great central sadness of old age isn't just the realization that the end can come at any time," he said, "but also that the world has fundamentally passed you by?"

"Doesn't everybody over a certain age think that way?" I asked.

"I suppose so," he said, sipping his J&B. "I suppose all lives are like political careers—at best, they end in regret; at worst, in failure."

"You're morbid this evening," I said.

"Your sonny boy's to blame. What's wrong with that kid?"

"That kid is now nearly thirty, and he thinks he knows all the answers."

"Conviction is a terrifying thing."

"But you always had strong convictions, Dad."

"True, but I never thought I had the answers. Anyway, back then, we had a legitimate grievance against a corrupt government running a corrupt war. Now we also have a legitimate grievance against a corrupt government, but people are reluctant to get on the barricades."

"Everyone's too busy making and spending money," I said.

"You have a point there. Shopping has become the central cultural activity of our time."

"Don't say that to Jeff. His company is—how did he put it?—'the biggest worldwide corporate insurers of retail units.' And he won't have a word said against them because as far as he's concerned, they're spreading the gospel of good American consumerism, blah, blah, blah."

"He really despises me, doesn't he?"

"No, Dad. He despises your politics. But don't take it personally. He despises anyone who doesn't see things his way. And I often wonder, if we had raised him as a strict Assemblies of God Christian, refused to let him have anything to do with godless folk, and sent him to a really tough military school . . ."

"He'd probably now be reading Naomi Klein and going on antiglobalization marches," Dad said. "Oh, and by the way, there is no such thing as a lax military school. Your tough military school is a tautology . . ."

"Ever the pedant," I said with a smile.

"You sound like your mother."

"No, she would have said, 'Ever the *fucking* pedant.'"

"That's true."

"Have you been over to see her recently?" I asked.

"Around two weeks ago. No change."

"I feel bad about not making the effort to see her more."

"She wouldn't even know who you were, so what's the point? I'm only twenty minutes from the hospital, and I can only face it every two weeks or so. Frankly, if they had legalized euthanasia in this damn country of ours, I'm certain that Dorothy would be much happier not to be here now. Alzheimer's is so damn cruel."

I swallowed hard and felt tears welling up. In my mind's eye, I could replay our last visit to the nursing home where she lived now. A frail, hunched old lady, sitting up most of the day in a chair, staring off into a bottomless void, not aware of anything around her, unable to make the simplest connection with anyone in the room. Someone whose entire spirit had been erased, the memory of everything that she had done over her seventy-nine years of life wiped clean. Five years ago, when the Alzheimer's arrived, it was like watching a light gradually diminish—the occasional burst of illumination in the midst of an ongoing series of electrical short circuits. And then, just two Christmases ago, came the final blackout. Dad arrived home from the university one afternoon—he still kept an office there—to discover my mother had vanished. Oh, she was physically present in their living room, but her mind had closed down. She couldn't speak, couldn't make eye contact, couldn't even respond to stimuli like touch or the sound of someone's voice.

He called me immediately in Portland. I asked the headmaster at my school to find a substitute for a few days and drove straight to Burlington that night. Though I had known for some time that this day would eventually arrive—Alzheimer's always has the same dreadful denouement—I still broke down when I reached the house and saw my mother sitting on the end of the sofa in the living room, mentally conquered by her illness. In those first horrible moments, when I found myself crying uncontrollably, all I could think was how she had always been such a torrential, troubling, essential force in my life—and how she'd been reduced to this empty shell who would now have to be fed and changed like an infant, and how I somehow wished that we'd been able to take it easier on each other, and how so much human argument is irrelevant.

"You know," my father said, shifting me back to the here and now, "one of the strangest things about our marriage was that there were at least ten, fifteen, *twenty* moments when one of us said, 'That's it . . . I've had enough,' and was on the verge of bailing out. We put each other through a lot of grief—in our own different ways."

"So why didn't either of you leave?"

"Well, it wasn't as if we stayed together out of convenience, or because we were too scared to change. I guess, in the end, I couldn't imagine a life without Dorothy. Just as she couldn't imagine a life without me. It was as simple, and as complex, as that."

"Forgiveness is a curious thing," I said.

"If eighty-two years on this damn planet have taught me anything, it's that forgiveness—and being forgiven—is the most crucial thing in life. We all endlessly mess things up for those closest to us."

A small look of acknowledgment passed between us, and then we moved on to other things—only the second time in all these years we had almost mentioned the breach that came between us.

The phone on my dashboard started to ring. I hit the speaker button.

"Hannah?"

It was my father.

"Dad? What's wrong?"

"Why should there be anything wrong? I was just calling to see where you are."

"Just past St. Johnsbury."

"Well, if you wouldn't mind picking me up at the university, we can go to the Oasis for lunch," he said, mentioning a little local place he ate at most days.

"No problem. I should be there in around seventy-five minutes," I said.

"And we don't have to spend too much time at the home this afternoon," he added.

"Fine by me," I said. Dad knew that I found these visits to Mom difficult.

"You don't sound great," Dad said.

"Sleepless night, that's all."

"Are you sure?"

Dad hated when I kept stuff from him. So I said, "Lizzie's in a bad place." When he asked to know more, I hesitated, not wanting to recount the entire sad saga on a cell phone speaker. So I promised to fill him in on everything over lunch.

Dad was standing outside the History Building when I pulled up. Though his shoulders were now a little bent and his hair had moved from silver to serious white, he still retained his patrician bearing—and was dressed, as always, in the uniform of his professional life: a green Irish tweed jacket with suede-patch sleeves, gray slacks, a blue button-down Oxford shirt, a knit tie, polished cordovan shoes. As I pulled up, he smiled—and I immediately looked at his eyes, making certain (as I now did when visiting him) that they were still acutely alert. Ever since Mom's mind vanished, I've become extravigilant about Dad's mental condition—monitoring every phone conversation we have for signs of verbal hesitancy and using these monthly visits to Burlington as a chance to be sure that he's holding up. What continues to amaze me is that he is still so damn sharp, as if it has become a point of belligerent principle for him to defy the aging process. But as I returned his smile and leaned over to open the car door, I thought (as I frequently do now) that human biology is damnably inevitable, and I will lose him soon. Though I constantly try to accentuate the positive—telling myself how lucky I am that he's lived this long, and has remained in such a robust state, and how he might live on for some years to come—I still can't accept the fact that, one day before too long, he might not wake up.

Dad seemed to be reading my mind. After sliding next to me in the car and giving me a fast kiss on the cheek, he said, "If we were in Paris, I'd say you were gripped by existential doubt right now."

"And since we're in Vermont?"

"You probably just need a grilled cheese sandwich."

"Ah, so it turns out that grilled cheese is the solution to life's massive uncertainties."

"If accompanied by dill pickles," he said.

We drove over to the Oasis Diner—where we ordered Vermont cheddar grilled cheese sandwiches with extra dill pickles, washed down with proper iced tea (none of that powdered nonsense). As soon as we had ordered, Dad said, "Lizzie," and I spent ten minutes telling him the whole story. After I finished, Dad swung into adviser mode—a role he'd loved to play since his teaching days.

"She needs to get this doctor out of her life now," he said.

"You're right about that. And I know that bastard would love to permanently excise Lizzie . . . especially as she's now threatening to ruin his marriage, his career, his crappy television show, *everything.* Not that he doesn't deserve it."

"I hope you're not blaming yourself."

"Of course I'm blaming myself. What's eating me the most is the idea that, somewhere along the line, Dan and I did—or *didn't*—do something that—"

"Created all this neediness, this desperate search for love?"

"Uh-huh."

"You know that neither of you has been deficient in that department."

"Then why is she so dangerously off the rails when it comes to love?"

"Because that's how she is. Or that's what she's developed into. But you know what the real problem is here: Lizzie can't stand what she does."

"True, but she does like the money."

"No she doesn't—and we both know it. The money, the fancy apartment, the fancy car, the fancy vacations . . . she's told me all about them, and what I've been hearing from her is Faustian bargain despair. And I know all about her 'plan'—ten years in the money game, make a killing, retire, and do what she wants at thirty-five. But what she's found out is that the money game sucks everyone dry. It's social Darwinism writ large—and if you can't play survival of the fittest . . ."

"The thing is, she plays it very well. She's been promoted twice in the last eighteen months."

"But it's still corroding her. Because unlike the people who play that game for keeps, Lizzie is not shallow. On the contrary, she's very self-aware, very conscious of her own place in the world and the limitations she's put upon herself."

"Like mother, like daughter."

"Hannah, you might not like to admit it, but you are your own woman. Lizzie is also her own woman—who has managed to convince herself that earning all that money will set her free . . . which, in her private heart of hearts, she knows is complete BS. So the way I see it, this desperate search for love—this need to *land her guy,* even if he is a married fool—is a manifestation of the self-loathing she feels for carrying on in a financial world she hates. The moment she leaves the job and finds something she actually likes to do, she'll cast off this manic behavior—which, to me, sounds like the onset of serious depression."

I had to hand it to Dad. His analysis was spot-on—and brimming with the sort of penetrating cogency which so distinguished his work as a historian.

"Would you talk to her?" I asked.

"I have been talking to her."

"What?" I said, sounding genuinely shocked.

"She's been calling me two, three times a week."

"Since when?"

"The last few weeks. She just called me late one evening—well after midnight—and started crying on the phone. We must have talked for around two hours."

"But why did she call you?"

"You'd have to ask Lizzie that. The thing was, after we spoke that first time—and I essentially talked her down off the ledge, because this was right after the breakup and she sounded very shaky—she started phoning me most days. Then, after I helped find her a psychiatrist . . ."

"She's seeing a psychiatrist?" I said.

"A very good man on the staff of Harvard Med School. Charles Thornton—the son of one of my Princeton classmates, and one of the leading specialists in obsessive-compulsive disorders . . ."

"I'm certain he's a genius, Dad. You do only know the best. What flabbergasts me is that you haven't just kept all this from me, but that you played along today as if you didn't know anything."

"You're right to be angry with me. But Lizzie made me swear that I'd never tell you we were talking—and, like you, I always keep a confidence."

I said nothing in reply to this—though I knew what he was talking about, and couldn't help but wonder if family life wasn't one long tangle of *Don't tell Mom/Dad . . . Keep this to yourself . . . He/She doesn't need to know . . .*

"Then why did you break that confidence today?"

"Because you broke yours to Lizzie."

"But I only did that because—"

"I know. She's on a knife edge right now, and you knew I'd figure out something was eating at you, and you don't like keeping stuff from me, because, unlike your father, you've never really had much talent for the clandestine."

He met my eyes as he said that, and I didn't know whether I should shout at him or admire his ongoing complexities—someone who seemed able to compartmentalize his life and live comfortably with his manifold contradictions. Such as his need to admit something only after he was found out—like my little discovery last summer that, in the two years since Mom had been living under "managed care" at the home, he'd been seeing a younger woman named Edith Jarvi. By younger, I mean she's a mere sixty-seven years old (jailbait to an octogenarian like Dad). Like all of his women, past and present, she's an intellectual class act (I wonder if he's ever slept with someone who *hasn't* subscribed to *The New York Review of Books*). She's a recently retired professor of Russian who's still married to the university's former provost, but has been spending much of her time with Dad since . . .

Well, when I finally found out about it, he was rather cagey about how long they'd been together, which made me wonder if it had been going on before Mom's Alzheimer's had finally vanquished her mind. Even the way I'd discovered their affair was classic Dad. One evening last June, I rang his house just to say hello, and a woman picked up the phone.

"Is this Hannah?" she asked, throwing me a little off balance.

"Uh, yes it is. And to whom am I speaking?"

"I'm your father's friend Edith. And I'm looking forward to meeting you the next time you're visiting John."

John.

When she turned the phone over to Dad, he sounded a little sheepish.

"So that was Edith," he said.

"So she said. She's your 'friend.'"

"Yes, that's right."

"Just a 'friend'?"

A pause. Then, "No, a little more than that."

I had a near fit of the giggles.

"I am impressed, Dad. At your age, most men roll over and play dead in that department. Whereas you . . ."

"This only started after your mom . . ."

"Sure it did. Anyway, I don't really care."

"Then you're not upset?"

"Well, it would have been nice if you had mentioned something before now."

"It's all rather new."

God, why did he have to always stretch the truth? It was this inability to be completely straight with me that had sparked that rupture thirty years ago. And yet, just as I was about to explode into the phone, I stopped myself out of the knowledge that, at the age of eighty-two, my dad's shortcomings in the truth department were not going to suddenly correct themselves. This is who—and what—he was. Take it or leave it.

"So when can I meet your friend?" I asked. When I came up to Burlington a few weeks later, a very civilized dinner chez Dad was organized by Edith Jarvi. She was, as I expected, a most cultivated woman. She had been brought up bilingual in New York by first-generation Latvian immigrants. She'd received a doctorate in Russian literature and language at Columbia, had been a professor at UVM for thirty years, and (yes!) was an occasional contributor on things Russian to *The New York Review of Books.* During the course of the evening, she dropped the fact that her husband—the retired provost—was now living half the time in Boston (no doubt, with some exotic Croatian mistress), and that they had a sort of open arrangement when it came to their marriage. I took this to mean that the provost didn't mind the fact that his wife was sleeping with my father, which they almost certainly did on the night I visited them. I was a bit disturbed when, around ten, Dad and Edith excused themselves and went upstairs. I know it shouldn't have upset me, as Mom's condition meant that Dad was almost technically a widower, and I was of course aware that Dad hadn't been a model of fidelity during his marriage. Maybe it was the idea of this woman sharing the bed that Dad once shared with Mom. Or maybe I just couldn't handle the idea of being under the same roof while my dad was having sex with Edith (if, that is, they *were* having sex tonight). Or maybe it was just the casual presumption that I wouldn't mind them sleeping together while I was visiting. Or maybe Dad was just treating me like a fiftysomething grown-up who shouldn't be bothered by such things.

Anyway, when I woke in the morning, Edith was already up and insisted on making me breakfast. As she poured me a cup of very strong coffee, she studied my face and said, "May I be direct about something?"

"Uh . . . sure," I said, tensing myself for the revelation to come (at least she couldn't be pregnant).

"You don't approve of me, do you?"

"Why would you think that?" I asked diplomatically.

"Hannah, I know how to read faces—and yours reads: thumbs-down."

"I am very impressed with you, Edith."

"Perhaps, but you still disapprove of our romance. And that's what it is, Hannah: *a romance* . . . and a very providential one at that, for both of us."

"Well then, I am pleased for you both," I said, hearing the stiffness in my voice.

"I would like to believe that, Hannah. It's rather futile to be Puritan about such things, *n'est-ce pas*?"

For his part, Dad never asked me what I thought of Edith—though, after I got over my initial uneasiness (I guess I really am a Puritan about such things), I did approve of her, and came to quickly see this romance as a good thing in my father's life . . . because, among all its other obvious benefits for him, it also meant that there was someone looking after him at home.

"Try not to be upset," he said, bringing me back to the Oasis Diner and the untouched grilled cheese sandwich still in front of me.

"I'm not upset. I'm just completely thrown by Lizzie's behavior, and the fact that she was telling you not to say anything to me, and telling me that I couldn't even tell her father what was going on."

"She's irrational—and therefore will spin her own web of intrigue to augment the melodrama she's creating for herself. Does Dan know now?"

"Of course—and he was very good about the fact that I'd kept it from him. Did she tell you about sleeping in her car outside the doctor's house?"

"Oh yes—and the good news is that, last night, she did stay at home and did manage to get six hours' sleep—which for Lizzie isn't bad right now."

"How did you know that?" I asked.

"She called me first thing this morning."

"How did she sound?"

"Desperately optimistic, which might be an oxymoron, but in Lizzie's case seems an accurate assessment of her state of mind. The one good thing is that she's managed to get an emergency appointment with Dr. Thornton this afternoon. That's something, I guess."

"I said I'd phone her tonight."

"And she said she'd phone me tonight," Dad added. "Does she know you're visiting me in Burlington?"

"No, I hadn't mentioned that."

"Then you call her first—and I'll await her call."

Dad was right: Lizzie was on a knife-edge, and until we heard from her again, there was nothing either of us could do about it.

So we moved on to the next difficult bit of family business: Mom.

The home was located in a quiet residential area around a mile from the university. It occupied a functional modern building. The staff were highly professional and caring in a fixed-smile sort of way. And Mom's private room was tastefully done in a Holiday-Inn-Meets-Ralph-Lauren-Meets-Geriatric-Facility style. Despite its cozy attributes, I could only take about thirty minutes within its walls. Not that Mom minded the brevity of my visit. When we came into her room, she was seated in an armchair, staring off into the distance. I sat down next to her.

"Mom, it's Hannah," I said.

She looked at me, but didn't register my presence. Then she turned away, gazing at a nearby wall.

I took her hand. Though warm, it was limp within mine. In the past, I had tried talking to her—bringing her up to speed on her grandkids' work and activities, giving her news of Dan's career and of my life as a teacher. I stopped this after around a month—it was so clear that I wasn't getting through to her and was therefore doing this for my own benefit. But since I wasn't benefiting at all from these banal monologues (which only seemed to accentuate the awfulness of the situation), I cut them out. Since then, I looked upon these visits as my opportunity to support my dad, as the strain upon him was enormous. He worked very hard not to show it—maintaining a stoic calm as he sat opposite her. He put one of her hands between his, and simply maintained physical contact with her for around ten minutes. Then he carefully drew his hands away, stood up, leaned down, lifted up her chin with his forefinger, and kissed her softly on the lips. No reaction from Mom. As soon as my father removed his forefinger, her chin dipped down to her chest and stayed there. Dad blinked and strangled a sob, then turned away from me for a moment until he calmed himself. Reaching into the pocket of his trousers, he brought out a handkerchief, dabbed his eyes, took a deep, steadying breath, and turned back to me. Though I wanted to go over and hold him while he was crying, I knew from experience that Dad needed to be left alone at moments like this. He didn't cry during every visit, but when he did lose his composure, he didn't want to be consoled. Dad had never been the most tactile of men (the old WASP training), and he considered crying in public to be awkward, if not a little demeaning. So I let him be, taking his place in the chair opposite Mom, holding her hand again until Dad cleared his throat, turned back to me, and said, "Um . . . shall we?"

I leaned over and kissed Mom good-bye. I stood up and followed Dad to the door. I looked back one last time. Mom's eyes had glassed over, making her seem even more detached. I fought off a shudder.

"Let's go," I said, and we left.

Outside in the car, Dad sat quietly for a few moments, his eyes shut. When he opened them again, he said, "I cannot tell you how much I hate these visits."

"I know it's horrible to say, but you can't help but wonder if they couldn't give her something to help the end along."

"We're not as enlightened as the Netherlands on that front. Too many right-to-lifers screaming legalized murder whenever you mutter the word *euthanasia*. The same right-to-lifers who scream murder whenever someone mentions stem-cell research as a possible cure for Alzheimer's . . . because it means fusing an egg and a sperm in vitro. And meanwhile, Dorothy sits there, mentally dead—"

He broke off and let out a large sigh.

"And do you know what really gets me? The two hundred thousand that Dorothy still had in trust from her parents—money she was planning to bequeath to Jeff and Lizzie—is simply ending up in the pockets of that goddamn home. Forty thousand a year to keep her alive. For what purpose, what aim? And I know she'd hate the idea that the money she so wanted to go to her grandkids . . ."

"Jeff and Lizzie are doing just fine in the money department, bless their free-market souls."

"Well, it still galls me . . ."

"Dad, let's get a drink, eh?"

"Let's get two," he said.

I drove us to an old, no-frills bar he liked in downtown Burlington (his ability to drive was still a point of pride to him). Two drinks became three, accompanied by old-fashioned bowls of unshelled peanuts of the sort you don't see anymore. I can't remember the last time I drank three vodka martinis, back to back—but God, were we both hammered by the time I got the bartender to call us a cab. Despite his age, Dad really could hold his booze—by which I mean that, though clearly smashed, he managed to remain eloquent throughout, especially when he went into an extended rant about our current president ("The Fratboy in Chief," as he called him) and his "junta."

"You know, these days, I'm actually starting to get nostalgic for Dick Nixon—which, believe me, is something I never thought I'd do during my lifetime."

The taxi dropped us back at Dad's house around six. I staggered into the kitchen, rooted around the pantry and the freezer, and found the makings of a spaghetti Bolognese. As I somehow managed to throw dinner together, Dad went to his office, sat in the rocking chair next to his desk, and promptly passed out. I discovered him there when I walked in to inform him that dinner would be served in about twenty minutes. But he was so out of it that I decided I wouldn't put the spaghetti on to boil until he came around.

But just as I was turning to leave his office, my cell phone went off. Dad jumped awake. I simply jumped.

Lizzie.

But when I glanced at the LCD on the phone, the number that came up was a 212 area code.

Margy.

I hit the answer button.

"Hey there," I said. "You were on my mind today."

"Is this a good moment?" she asked, sounding serious.

"Sure," I said. "I'm at my dad's place in Burlington. Something up?"

"Can you find a place to talk privately?"

"Has the cancer come back?"

"No, but thank you for jumping to horrible conclusions. Listen, I can call back later."

"No, don't hang up, I'll just . . ."

I pulled the phone away from my ear, and explained that it was Margy on the line, and that I needed to vanish for a moment or two.

"Don't worry about me," he said. "I'm still sleeping off the martinis."

I wandered back into the kitchen, closed the door, stood over the pan of Bolognese sauce, picked up a wooden spoon, and started stirring as I put the phone back to my ear.

"We can talk now," I said. "You sound bad."

"Well, since you asked, I did cough up a little blood this morning, which required a lightning dash across town to my friendly neighborhood oncologist, who dispatched me immediately to a radiologist for a little photograph. It turned up nothing, which meant that I squandered an entire morning and simultaneously had the shit scared out of me. Then, when I got back to the office, a parcel was waiting for me. You know, my company's started handling writers now—things are that bad. No, I'm joking . . . but a lot of New York publishers are outsourcing certain authors to certain PR companies, and we've started to be sent the occasional proof for consideration.

"Anyway, and this is the point of this call, a conservative publisher, Plymouth Rock Books . . . they've gotten rather big over the past few years, surprise, surprise . . . contacted me two days ago, saying they were handling this Chicago talk-radio pundit who had developed quite a following around Lake Michigan, and who they were now hoping they could break out nationwide. He's written a book that they are certain will be a coast-to-coast best seller. It's the story of his radical years in the 1960s, all his subversive activities, his flight to Canada, and his Pauline conversion on the road to Damascus that has made him recant his radical past and turned him into the Great American Patriot—and Serious Christian—that he is today."

I stopped stirring the sauce.

"Tobias Judson?" I asked.

"Yes."

"And have you read the book?"

"I'm afraid so."

I turned the gas burner off, walked over to a kitchen chair, and sat down.

"You know what my next question is going to be," I said.

"Yes, I do," Margy said. "And yes, you're in the book. In fact, he devotes an entire chapter to you."

TWELVE

MARGY WANTED TO spill the beans and tell me everything that was written about me in Tobias Judson's book. But I was so knocked sideways by the news that I wasn't thinking clearly. Acting on instinct, I refused to let her give me a précis.

"I don't want to hear what dirt he's dished," I said. "I want to read it myself."

"You sure you don't want a little hint about . . . ?"

"I'll go berserk if you tell me, and then worry all night until the book arrives."

"You'll worry all night anyway."

"True, but at least I'll know I won't be able to get wound up about what you said *he* said."

"The good news is that he doesn't use your name."

"Which means that, from my perspective, there's plenty of bad news."

A long pause.

"Your silence is just a little telling," I said.

"I'm saying nothing. But I will FedEx it to you first thing tomorrow. You're back in Maine then, right?"

"Uh-huh."

"Well, it will arrive the next morning."

I flinched. Dan usually took Thursdays off—and though he'd never open my mail, if a FedEx package arrived for me, he'd ask who it was from and wonder out loud about its contents. And then I'd have to lie . . .

"Send it to me at the school," I said.

"I hear you," Margy said. "Listen, once you've read the book, I want you to call me right away. Without giving too much away, you might need what's known in my trade as 'professional representation'—better known as a loudmouth to refute . . ."

"Stop, *please.* Once I've read it, I promise I'll call you immediately and we'll talk. Before then, I can't really say anything . . ."

"You're taking this all rather coolly," she said. "Like, if it was me, I'd be bouncing off the walls."

"I've got larger concerns right now."

"May I ask?"

So I brought her up to speed on Lizzie, spelling out, for the second time today, the entire vexing story—only now adding into the mix the fact that my father had been counseling her for weeks. When I finished, Margy said nothing for a while. Then, "You know what the worst thing about all this is . . . or at least, from where I sit? It's the fact that you and Dan have been such solid damn parents. No divorce, no professional or domestic chaos. And from what you've told me over the years, you were always there just about every night for them when they were growing up. And despite all that care and loving attention—"

"It doesn't work that way, Margy. You can only do and provide so much. After that, it all comes down to . . . God, I don't know. We all hope our kids will get off lightly in the 'life is hard' stakes . . . but it doesn't always turn out that way. All I can think about is how horrible things are for Lizzie right now. She's unhinged by unhappiness . . ."

"Don't say that, hon."

"Why not? It's the truth."

"She's just having a rough passage."

"Margy, don't try to soft-sell this to me. Lizzie's stalking a married man. She's sleeping in her car outside his front door—and when she talks about what's going on, her voice takes on this strange, distorted, supercalm tone, as if what she's doing is the most natural, understandable thing in the world . . . whereas the truth of the matter is: she's heading straight into psychological free fall."

"At least your dad got her to see a shrink."

"But so far, he hasn't exactly brought about a miraculous recovery."

"Hey, take it from one who knows: therapy takes years . . . and even then it doesn't completely change everything."

"The state she's in right now, Lizzie doesn't have years. I'm scared for her, Margy."

"And now I am truly appalled with my shitty timing. Dropping this other thing in your lap . . ."

"I had to know about it. Anyway, it's best I hear it from you, rather than find out by other means."

"All going well, none of what he wrote about you should ever get out."

"You're giving the game away again."

"Sorry, sorry. Me and my big yenta mouth."

"Shut up. You're the best friend imaginable."

"When do you expect to hear from Lizzie?"

"Tonight, I hope."

"You'll call me afterward?"

"Promise. Are you still at the office?"

"I'm afraid so."

"Won't your oncologist slap you around for pushing yourself too hard?"

"I'm his poster girl for lung cancer. The bitch who beat the odds . . . so far anyway."

"If they say they've got all of it, you're in the clear."

"Now it's you who deserves to be trampled on for soft-selling a shitty situation. Dr. Drugstore—my new name for Walgreen—said they got virtually all of it, but note his qualifying use of the word *virtually*. Anyway, I've spent hours on the Mayo Clinic website, reading up on my charming self-afflicted illness. The fact is, secondary, tertiary, and . . . is *quadruplary* a word? . . . anyway, the blunt fact is that, after all the MRI scans and radioactive sugar drips I've endured, they can't be a hundred percent sure they've found everything."

"You've beaten it, Margy."

"*Virtually* beaten it."

After I hung up, I found myself pacing around the kitchen, willing myself to calm down, telling myself there was nothing I could do about Tobias Judson (yet again, even thinking his name made me shudder) and his damn book. And since I wouldn't be in receipt of said book until next week—as the school was closed for Easter vacation until then—I'd have to completely block it all from my mind.

Yeah, right.

All right, I knew I was going to be worried sick about this for the next week, but I couldn't say anything to my father. Because that would provoke massive guilt and recriminations in him and raise that entire damn business again—and the last thing I wanted to do was to bring him grief . . . especially at his age and with the ongoing calamity of my mother weighing on him all the time. So . . .

"Hannah, you off the phone yet?"

This question was accompanied by a light rapping on the door.

I took a deep breath, tried to rearrange my face, then said, "Coming now, Dad."

I opened the door. My father immediately went to the stove and started stirring the pan of sauce while the pot of spaghetti boiled nearby.

"Didn't mean to hassle you," he said, "but the spaghetti's just about done."

"No problem. I'd just finished up."

He studied me for a moment.

"You okay?"

"Margy's had some ups and downs recently."

He knew about her cancer, as I'd told him about it when she was diagnosed just before Christmas, and had been giving him regular updates since then.

"Poor Margy," he said. "In the great scheme of things, lung cancer is about as bad as it gets."

"That is the truth. And I suppose one of the things about getting older is the way you start to bargain with fate all the time . . ."

"As in: *Please don't end my life in an undignified, monstrous way*?"

"Exactly. And, I suppose, one of the big problems with not believing in an all-controlling God is that, when terrible stuff happens to yourself or to those closest to you, you can't console yourself with the thought that it's all down to some divine plan."

"Religion, 'That vast moth-eaten musical brocade created to pretend we never die.'"

"Is that original?"

"I wish. An English poet: Philip Larkin. Something of a misanthropist, yet also rather brilliant about life's big, unspoken fears. Or perhaps the one big unspoken fear that haunts everybody: death. 'Most things may never happen: this one will.'"

"Isn't that spaghetti ready to go?" I asked.

Dad smiled.

"That's a very Italian response," he said.

"To what?"

"To mortality. When seized by thoughts of your own ephemerality, the only solution is: eat."

Over dinner, we managed to work our way through a bottle of red wine that Dad had found in a cupboard. I would have happily downed methylated spirits if it had blocked out all my fears. We both glanced several times at the kitchen clock on the nearby wall, wondering when and if we'd hear from Lizzie.

"What time did she say she was meeting him?" I asked.

"After work. So that could mean seven, eight . . ."

"If she hasn't called by ten, I'll give her a ring . . . even though she'll hate the idea I'm checking up on her."

"Under the circumstances . . ."

By nine, the bottle of wine was empty and there was still no word from Lizzie. The postmartini nap had revived my father. He was talking at full steam, telling me an extended but rather amusing anecdote about getting very drunk in London during the war and finding the address of T. S. Eliot's flat, and rolling over there with a Harvard friend and knocking on the door.

"It was eleven-something at night, and he was in his pajamas and bathrobe. He was just a little bemused by these two American servicemen, standing outside his front door, clearly smashed. He got rather indignant and said, 'What is it you want?' I remember how cut-glass English his accent was—and how, even in his nightclothes, he had the demeanor of a great man. Anyway, he'd asked a question which obviously demanded an answer, and I was so out of it, all I could say was, 'It's you!'

"He slammed the door right in our faces, and my buddy, Oscar Newton, turned to me and said, 'Well, April *is* the cruelest month.' Three weeks later, Oscar was killed in France . . ."

The phone rang. We both jumped. Dad answered it. His expression showed disappointment.

"Hi, Dan. Yes, she's here. And no, we haven't heard from Lizzie yet."

He handed me the phone.

"Not a word at all?" Dan asked.

"We're still waiting."

"You've obviously filled your dad in."

"No, Lizzie did that already," and I explained how she'd been calling him for several weeks. I expected Dan to be further wounded by this revelation, and to ask why she hadn't turned to her own father for advice and support. But in true Dan style, he kept whatever hurt he felt to himself.

"It's good that she's talking to her grandfather. I just wish we knew what was going on."

"That makes three of us. Listen, as soon as she rings . . ."

But by the time Dad began to fade, around ten-thirty, there was still no word from her. So I called her cell phone and was connected to her voice mail. I left a message, simply saying that I was wondering how she was doing, and telling her to call me back when she could . . . and that my cell phone would be on all night, so if she needed to speak with me, I'd be on immediate tap. I thought about ringing her apartment, but worried that she might interpret too many messages as interfering. So I turned to Dad and said, "I think we should call it a night."

"She's occasionally called me in the middle of the night," he said. "If she rings . . ."

"Wake me up."

"I just feel like jumping into my car, driving down to Boston, just to make certain she's all right."

"If we don't hear from her by midday . . ."

"I'll hold you to that," Dad said.

I went up to the guest room, undressed, put on the nightshirt I'd brought with me, climbed into bed with a copy of some early Updike stories I found on one of Dad's bookshelves, and tried to focus on his elegiac depictions of a childhood in Shillington, Pennsylvania, hoping it would send me into the sleepy oblivion I craved.

But sleep was hard to come by. I turned off the light, clutched the pillow close to me, smelled the astringent bleach that Dad's very old-fashioned housekeeper used on the sheets (who else uses bleach these days?), and waited for unconsciousness to hit. Half an hour later I sat up, turned on the bedside light, and returned to Updike's limpid reflections on adolescent longings during football season.

Two hours went by. I got up and went downstairs to make myself a mug of herbal tea, in the hope that it might act as a soporific and grant me a few hours of unconsciousness. When I reached the kitchen, I found Dad sitting at the table, reading this month's edition of *The Atlantic.*

"I was wondering if you'd make it through the night unscathed," he said with a smile, also remembering the other white nights I'd suffered while staying here.

"Well, glad to see I've got someone else to share the worry with me until dawn," I said.

"Oh, even when I've not got something on my mind," Dad said, "I don't sleep much these days. It's the thing about getting older. The body doesn't need as much sleep as it used to—because it knows it's going to die."

"That's a real upbeat late-night thought."

"Well, when you've crossed into your ninth decade, blah, blah, blah. Funny, isn't it, how all the big thoughts about life and death are fundamentally banal. The thing is, even though I know it's coming sooner than later, I still can't imagine being dead. Not being here or anywhere—simply no longer existing."

"Remind me never to sit up with you at this hour again."

He smiled.

"I'll tell you one thing, I do envy Christian folk like my grandson: when the end comes for someone you love, their faith must provide a great deal of comfort."

"And meanwhile, before you shuffle off to your eternal reward, you can fill up your time on Planet Earth telling other people how to live their lives."

"Don't be too hard on Jeff . . ."

"Hang on, he's the one who's always hard on you."

"It's very difficult, figuring out somebody else's political anger. I often wonder what I've done to that boy—bar having a somewhat radical past that he seems to be ashamed of."

"I'd like to say something comforting and corny like, 'I know he still loves you,' but—and this is a real late-night admission—I don't even know if he loves *me* anymore. And you know what really disappoints me more than anything? The fact that his intolerance is bound up in such unkindness. He's so terribly judgmental and pitiless. I still love him, of course—but I've actually stopped liking him . . . as horrible as it is to admit that."

"Do you think Miss Shannon is to blame for his newfound reactionism?"

"She certainly 'brought him to Jesus'—which, as you may remember, were the exact words he used to describe his religious awakening. And you know all about her militant pro-life stance, not to mention the fact that her father is some bigwig evangelical. And Jeff's so totally bought into their born-again thinking that I sense he'll never be free of their clutches."

"Maybe we can arrange to get him caught with a prostitute on a business trip . . ."

"Dad!"

"We'd make it a very upscale call girl, of course—and someone who would show him a very good time, to let him know what he's missing with Shannon."

I couldn't believe what I was hearing, and stared wide-eyed at my father. He went on.

"Now we wouldn't want him to lose his job or anything over this, so we'd have the call girl admit that she was paid by 'an unknown party' to seduce him—make it seem like some prank thought up by a couple of his colleagues—and also say that she slipped something in his drink which made him lose all judgment and succumb to her charms. His firm would keep him on—from what you've told me, he makes them too much money to be dismissed for some minor sexual transgression. But with any luck, Shannon will throw him out. And though it will be hard on the kids, Jeff will come to his senses, renounce his insane fundamentalism, quit the corporate jungle, move to Paris, rent a garret in some seedy arrondissement, and start writing pornographic novels for a living . . ."

"Will you shut up, *please*," I said, resisting the temptation to laugh.

"Don't tell me you disapprove of my fanciful imagination?"

"I simply don't know if I should be appalled or amused."

"I did have you thinking I was on the level, didn't I?"

My dad was beaming with pleasure. And I couldn't help but think: *Bless him for still being so profoundly subversive and mischievous.*

We staggered off to our respective bedrooms just before five. Finally, exhaustion kicked in and I blacked out. The next thing I knew, a high-pitched beep was invading my unconsciousness. I jolted awake. Light was seeping through the thin bedroom curtains and my cell phone was ringing. I reached for it.

"Hello," I said, sounding full of sleep.

"Did I wake you, Mom?"

Lizzie. Thank God.

"No," I lied. "I was just dozing." I glanced at my watch. It was seven-twenty. "How did it go with Mark, hon?"

"That's what I'm calling about," she said, sounding incredibly upbeat. "I have the most fantastic news."

I tensed. "And what's that?"

"Mark asked me to marry him last night."

Now I was completely awake.

"Well, that's a surprise," I said, adopting a careful tone.

"You don't sound pleased for me."

"Naturally I'm pleased, Lizzie. I'm just also a little . . . amazed, I guess, considering that yesterday he seemed to want to end things."

"I knew he'd change his mind once I spoke with him."

"And, if you don't mind me asking, what did you say to Mark that made him change his mind?"

She giggled—the sort of high-pitched giggle I'd usually associate with a teenage girl in the throes of first love.

"That's between me and my guy," she said, sounding coy. When she giggled again, my BS meter suddenly entered the deep red zone—and a chill caught me between the shoulders. She was making all this up.

"Lizzie, hon, I still don't get it."

"Get what?"

"Get how you managed to talk Mark around."

"Are you saying you don't believe me?"

"Of course I believe you. I'm just . . . impressed by your powers of persuasion and I wondered how you managed to . . ."

"Mark hasn't been happy with his wife for years. In fact, he's often said that the marriage was one huge mistake. But he felt guilty about abandoning his kids. So . . . and I really shouldn't be telling you this, but as you insist . . . what I said to him last night is that there's no problem by me if the kids want to live with us, especially as Ruth, that's his wife, keeps talking about wanting to go to Ireland and be a writer. So what we're going to do is sublet my loft, find a big house for the four of us, and live happily ever after."

Then, as an afterthought, she added, "Joke!"

I quickly felt huge relief.

"So you *are* pulling my leg," I said.

"No!" she replied, all petulant. "The joke was the happily-ever-after bit. I'm not that naive to think that life with two young stepchildren will be easy. Still, I know I'll do my best with Bobby and Ariel . . ."

He has a daughter named Ariel?

". . . and with my own baby on the way . . ."

Now I really did feel as if I were in free fall.

"Did you just say . . . ?"

"Yes, I'm pregnant."

"Since when?"

"Since last night. It was all planned, of course. Like, I'm right in the middle of my cycle—and as it's something we've both so wanted for so long, what better time to make a baby than on the night when we've reconciled and realized that our destiny is to be together . . ."

Think, think. But all I could think was: *Play along, keep the conversation going . . .*

"Now that all sounds very wonderful, hon . . ."

"So you are pleased for me, Mom?"

"Completely pleased. But the thing is: you do know that, just because you're in the middle of your cycle, the chances of getting pregnant . . . though good . . . aren't a hundred percent certain."

"Oh, I *know* I'm pregnant. Because the sex we had last night—"

She broke off for a moment, then giggled again.

"Mom, can I ask you something? Have you ever been so intensely fucked that you actually thought you were having an out-of-body experience? Well, that's what it was like last night with Mark. It was as if we were both *fused* together. It was so pure, so beyond the realm of any sensation I've ever experienced with him or any other man in the past. And that's why I'm so certain that I'm pregnant. Because when he came in me, I could feel his seed . . ."

"Hon—"

I broke off, unable to complete the sentence.

"Sorry, Mom, I didn't mean to get graphic," she said with another giggle. "It's just . . . I can't tell you how happy I am right now. Like, this is a once-in-a-lifetime moment. And I know when the baby I'm carrying is old enough to understand these things, I'm going to tell him or her about how he or she was made in a moment of pure passion, pure love, pure . . ."

I had tears in my eyes—and they were not because of the romantic drivel she was currently spouting.

"Lizzie, hon, where are you right now?"

"On my way to work."

"You feel up to working today?"

"You mean, after all that fabulous sex last night?" she asked, giggling again. "Like, I haven't slept much, but with a kid on the way, I better keep the money coming in."

"And have you got anything planned for tonight?"

"I'm going to really need to sleep."

"Well, here's an idea. I'm at your grandfather's now . . ."

"Hey, can I talk to him? Haven't told you this, but I have been talking with Granddad quite a bit about Mark and stuff—and I know he's going to be so pleased to hear that it's all worked out."

"Granddad's still in bed right now. But here's the thing: why don't I drive down tonight and take you out for a celebration dinner?"

"Like I said, Mom, I'm kind of operating on no sleep . . ."

"But I'm sure you can catch a little nap after work. And anyway, how often do I get the chance to toast the arrival of another grandchild?"

"That's true, but you know I won't be able to drink any alcohol, now that I'm expecting."

"Well, I'll do the drinking for the two of us. So how about it?"

"You really want to drive all the way down here just to toast my baby?"

"You're my daughter, Lizzie . . ." As I said that, I felt a burning in the back of my throat. My eyes filled up with tears. I had to pull the phone away so Lizzie couldn't hear me stifle a sob. My poor little girl. "And there's nothing I wouldn't do for you. So come on, let's do that dinner tonight."

"Well . . . I don't know . . . I'm kind of—"

She broke off. Then, "No, I'd better not, Mom."

"I could come tomorrow, then."

Another pause . . . and I knew that she couldn't face me right now; that all the fantastical bluster about her miraculous reconciliation with the doctor was just a fragile veneer which would crack when we came face-to-face.

"I've got a lot going on tomorrow, Mom."

"Say I called you later today?"

Silence.

"Okay," she said, sounding hesitant. "I should be home after seven."

"Hon, you really sound exhausted. Why don't you just call in sick today, go home, and . . ."

"Mom, I've got three big client things happening before three. So call me tonight, okay? Got to go now."

And she hung up.

I put down the phone. I put my head in my hands. My mind was reeling. I tried to think clearly. I glanced again at my watch. Seven twenty-eight. I phoned Dan at home. No answer. I called his cell phone. No answer. He must have had an early-morning surgery scheduled for today. I left a message, asking him to call me back asap. Then I got out of bed and walked down the hall. Dad's bedroom door was still closed. It was pointless waking him with disturbing news that was best chewed over after some sleep. So I went down to the kitchen, filled the old-fashioned percolator with coffee, and put it on the stove. As I waited for it to percolate, I fought off the urge to panic, telling myself that what I needed now was a clear plan of action to stop Lizzie from . . .

No, I didn't want to go there yet. Or, at least, not until I was certain that what she had told me was complete tripe. There was a part of me—an irrationally hopeful part of me—that wanted to believe she was telling the truth. But there was only one way to verify such a fact—so I went back upstairs, dug out a business card from my wallet, and called Dr. Mark McQueen on his cell phone.

He answered on the second ring—and his tone indicated that this was a man who was not in a particularly happy place right now. After hearing my voice he said, "It's not even eight yet, and you're already calling me."

I ignored that comment and said, "I've just been on the phone with Lizzie and—"

"You're trying to plead her case with me . . . or tell me that, after what she pulled last night . . ."

"What did she pull last night?"

"You mean she didn't say?"

"No, she didn't."

"Well, what did she tell you?"

"Just that you met and . . ."

"Yeah?"

I chose my words with care.

"That you seemed to have reconciled."

"She said that?"

"Yes, she did."

"Anything else?"

"She seemed very happy, that's all."

"Happy? Happy?" His voice was raised. "That's un-fucking-believable. Beyond crazy. And let me tell you this: I don't know what you or your husband did to that kid while she was growing up, but she has turned out to be one crazy bitch . . ."

I wanted to tear into him, but I held back—because I needed information.

"What did she do last night, Doctor?"

"You really want to know? I'll tell you. I agreed to meet her in the bar of the Four Seasons Hotel, right off the Common. When she walked in, she had this completely beatific, loony smile on her face, and gave me this big deep kiss in front of everyone, and started going on about how she knew things were going to work out between us, how she knew I was *her one and only,* how she wanted to get pregnant by me and suggested we go straight out to the reception desk, get a room upstairs, and make a baby there and then.

"Well, as you can imagine—or maybe you can't imagine it, because you consider me the heavy in this story, the big bad married man who fucked up your precious little daughter . . ."

"I just want to hear the story, Doctor."

"I tried, very patiently, to explain to Lizzie that I was a man with responsibilities—toward my wife and my kids. And yeah, I know that sounds like major married man cliché stuff, but that was the truth of the matter. And yes, I had once said that I saw my future being with her—and maybe it led her to believe that I would leave my family to be with her—but now, sadly, I saw that I had to do the right thing, blah, blah, blah. Believe me, I said all this in as gentle a way as possible. I even rehearsed it with . . ."

He stopped himself—and I was certain that the sentence was going to finish with the words *my shrink.* He continued.

"Well, Lizzie didn't exactly take this news very well. In fact, she pulled a complete crazy number, in which she started to cry, telling me that I just had to reconsider. Once again, I patiently tried to explain that my position was final: I was staying with my family. And that's when she went ballistic. She started screaming, yelling, threatening me. I tried to calm her down, but that only seemed to enrage her. She threw a glass of wine in my face, overturned our table, and went completely out of control. It got so bad that hotel security was called. But as soon as they showed up, she went all calm again and agreed to be escorted out, hissing at me that I was going to pay big-time for . . ."

He stopped, almost losing it himself. "Do you know what your crazy daughter did next? She drove straight out to my house in Brookline, pounded on the door, pushed past my wife, stormed straight into my den, where my kids were watching TV, and started telling them that she was going to be their new mommy . . . that their daddy loved her, not *their* mommy, and that they would be moving in *with us* in some new home that . . ."

He stopped again, his voice cracking. I didn't know what to say, I was so thrown by what he was telling me.

"Ruth . . . my wife . . . handled things as best she could—and told Lizzie that she should leave immediately or she'd call the police. When she refused—"

"She refused . . . ?"

"Yeah, the demented bitch refused. So Ruth did call the cops. Right before they arrived, Lizzie actually tried to get my kids to leave with her. Understandably, they were hysterical—and Ruth had to restrain your daughter physically and get the kids into another part of the house, away from her. Just before the cops showed up, she fled and—"

"Do you have any idea where she is now?"

"You can't be serious . . ."

"She needs help!"

"Fucking sure she does. Because the police are looking for her now. And my lawyer is working on a restraining order while we speak. And my wife has vowed that if Lizzie ever comes near our kids again—"

"That won't happen. You have my word on—"

"I don't want your fucking word. I just never want to see your insane daughter again. And I don't want to hear from you again either. Got that?"

The line went dead. I stood up. I raced down the hall to where Dad was sleeping. I banged on the door.

"Daddy . . ." I shouted.

Daddy. When I was a kid, I only used that term when I was frightened.

"Hannah, you okay?"

The door opened. He looked at me. The story came out fast. He too couldn't believe what he was hearing. When I was finished, he said, "Call Lizzie now."

I went back to the bedroom, grabbed my cell phone, hit her number, but was connected to her voice mail. So I rang the office. One of her colleagues answered the phone.

"She's not in," he said. "In fact, nobody knows where she is right now. Who's this?"

"Her mother."

"Well, I don't want to freak you out, Mrs. Buchan, but we've had two calls from the Brookline police this morning. They're looking for her too."

I gave the guy my cell number and asked him to ring me if he heard from her or learned if the police had found her. There was one last possibility: her apartment. I hit the number on my cell phone. It rang out. I hit the off button, turned to Dad, and said, "I'm going to Boston."

"I'm coming with you," he said.

Twenty minutes later, we were in my car, heading down Route 93. Around the time we crossed the border into New Hampshire, Dan phoned. I gave him the full chain of events—from Lizzie's telling of the tale to McQueen's horrifying revelations. Dan always goes very quiet in a crisis. When I finished speaking, he said, "I'm getting into my car now to meet you in Boston."

"Good," I said.

"Before I leave, I'm going to call the Brookline police, explain that we're both en route south, and that we want to help them find Lizzie. I'll also see if they have an update about her whereabouts. Has your dad called his psychiatrist friend—Thornton—the one who's taken Lizzie on as a patient?"

"We tried him ten minutes ago. He hasn't heard from her yet, but he has been briefed about what's going on, and he has my cell number in case she does call him."

"All right, then. I'll phone you from the road."

"Dan, do you think she'd . . . ?"

"I don't know."

That was also typical Dan. He never tried to sweeten the pill, never tried to pretend that something was right when it was very wrong. But now, what I really needed to hear were lies and reassurances that everything would be all right. Even though I knew that everything would definitely not turn out well.

Ninety minutes later, when we were around fifty miles from Boston, the cell phone rang. It was Dan. He had spoken to the Brookline police. There was still no word of Lizzie's whereabouts. They'd checked her apartment. They'd checked her office again. They had someone posted outside McQueen's house. They had obtained a photograph from her employers and had emailed every local police department around Boston and Cambridge. They were very much on the job.

"The detective I spoke to said that they were primarily treating this as a missing persons case—that the doctor had come clean to him about their affair and he didn't want a lot of publicity about him having to get police protection for his family after his ex-lover . . ."

"That son of a bitch," I said. "His career is more important than poor Lizzie's whereabouts."

"I also managed to speak to her psychiatrist."

"You did?"

"Well, you did give me his name yesterday. After you phoned me, I called Cambridge Information and got his number. Luck was on my side. He was in. Better yet, he seemed like very good news—and he was naturally very concerned. He did sound one optimistic note. From the few sessions they'd had so far, he didn't think she'd do something extreme like take her own life . . . that her condition was delusional, but not brimming with the sort of appalling self-loathing or depression that would make her see suicide as the only way out. At the same time, however, his worry was that she might attempt something that was an extreme cry for help."

"Like what?"

"Well, like *attempt* suicide, in the hope that the man who spurned her would feel so guilty that—"

"I get the scenario," I said.

"The doctor is very hopeful that Lizzie might call him," Dan added. "Whenever things got too much for her recently, she always picked up the phone and rang him. So . . ."

"Let's hope."

"Yeah. Hope."

I brought Dad up to date on this new—and not particularly encouraging—news. He listened in silence. Then, "I feel a lot of this is my fault."

"But why?"

"Because I should have contacted you straightaway when she started talking to me about the affair. At least we would have been able to exchange notes on her mental state, and maybe . . ."

"Stop this now."

"The thing is, Hannah, I loved the fact that she was confiding in me . . . that she was entrusting me with this big secret."

"So you should. You're her grandfather."

"But I should have picked up on the fact that she was starting to come apart . . ."

"You didn't sit on your hands. You found her a psychiatrist. You did the right thing."

"I didn't do enough."

"Dad . . ."

"I didn't do enough."

When we got to Boston, we drove directly over to Lizzie's apartment in the Leather District. Dad looked at the new loft developments, the hip furniture shops, the latte bars, the twentysomethings in suits, and said, "Back in the sixties, urban renewal was about improving poor inner-city neighborhoods for their residents. Now it's about getting the young professionals with money to buy up the housing stock and raise the real estate values."

The concierge at Lizzie's apartment was on duty. He had last seen Lizzie yesterday morning when she went off to work. Since then . . .

"You know, the cops showed up with a warrant and asked me to open her place. They looked around, but didn't turn the place upside down or anything like that. They said it was a missing persons thing, which, I guess, is why they didn't go gangbusters through the place. They found her car in the basement garage, where she has an allotted space . . . and we've got CCTV down there twenty-four-seven, so we'll be able to see her if she comes back to claim it."

"Is there any chance we could go up to her place?" I asked.

"I'm afraid I can't be letting anyone in without permission of the owner. And since Ms. Buchan isn't around . . ."

"I'm her mother and this is her grandfather . . ."

"Nice to meet you. And I really wish I could help you, but the rules are the rules . . ."

"Please let us in, sir," Dad said. "There might be something there that we'd see that would perhaps indicate where she might have disappeared to . . ."

"If it was my call, we'd be up there now. But my boss is a toughie—

and I'd be out on my keister if he found out I let you look around without the owner's permission."

"We'd just be five, ten minutes, no more," I said.

"Really wish I could help, ma'am. Because between you and me, your daughter's about the only polite, nice person in this building. The rest are yuppie scum."

We found a Starbucks nearby. As we drank two cups of milky coffee, Dan rang. He had just arrived in Boston and was heading directly to the police in Brookline. When I told him that we'd been refused entry to Lizzie's loft, he suggested we call the management company that ran her building to plead our case.

"Can you also get in touch with her boss at work," he asked, "and see if we can schedule an appointment to see him tomorrow morning?"

"We're going to find her before then."

"I'm sure we will," he said, in such a matter-of-fact, dismissive way that it was clear he didn't believe it but was saying it for my benefit.

"Now, I've talked to our travel agent in Portland and she's found us two rooms at this new hotel near North Station called the Onyx. The area's a little seedy, but . . ."

"I'm sure it's fine," I said, thinking: *The few times I've ever seen Dan in distress, he's always managed it by staying busy, focused, taking charge.* So I let him talk about the good hotel deal, the free parking they were arranging, and how he thought we should fan out across Boston to help in the search for her.

By nightfall a considerable amount had been accomplished. Dan had had a long interview with a Detective Leary of the Brookline PD who was handling the case—and who impressed Dan with his resolve to crack it quickly. Already, he'd put a tag on all her credit cards and bank accounts—and had had one small breakthrough: she'd withdrawn one hundred dollars yesterday and today from two different ATMs in the Boston area, one in Central Square in Cambridge, the other in Brookline, at a location around five minutes' walk from the doctor's house.

"Leary thinks she could still be stalking him, or clandestinely watching his kids," Dan said. "Which he's happy about . . . from an investigative standpoint only . . . because it means that she should turn up soon near his office or his home. And thanks to the ATM withdrawals, we know she's still in the Boston area."

Dan imparted this information in the bar of the Onyx Hotel. It was eight in the evening. We'd just checked in. Dad had already gone up to his room. He was exhausted, and the strain of worry had been so evident on his face that I insisted he get to bed. But my God, how he'd thrown himself into the detective role that afternoon, heading off on his own on the T to Cambridge to talk to Lizzie's psychiatrist. He had no new insights, though Dad seemed pleased by the doctor's reassurance that she wasn't displaying telltale suicidal tendencies, and his confidence that, when she was found, her delusional condition was very treatable, with a high chance of a cure. He'd also called the management company of her building—and after some gentle arm-twisting, he received approval from the head guy there for us to be admitted to her loft the next morning.

While Dad had been in Cambridge, I'd been in the downtown financial district, speaking to Peter Kirby. He ran the division of the mutual fund where Lizzie worked. He couldn't have been more than thirty—fit, well polished, highly preppy, full of concern about my daughter's whereabouts, but also—I sensed—very much wanting to get through this meeting with me as fast as possible, so he could get back to the business of making money.

Still, in the fifteen minutes we had together, he was genuinely solicitous, telling me that Lizzie was one of the best members of his team—"someone who always gave two hundred percent and was incredibly goal-oriented."

"Everybody here," he said, waving his arm in the direction of the large floor of open-plan offices beyond the plate-glass windows covering his own, "is seriously motivated. You have to be to survive in this milieu. But Lizzie always exceeded everyone else here just by her sheer need to win all the time. It wasn't enough for her just to close a deal or get a client a seven percent return on investment. She had to try to push it up to nine percent, or she had to close three deals at once. And the hours she put in were phenomenal. The security guys would often report back to me that she'd been in all day Saturday and Sunday two weekends a month. A manager can't ask for more dedication than that. But, if I can talk openly here . . ."

"Please," I said.

"I always worried that Lizzie was heading for some sort of burnout or meltdown. You just can't sustain the sort of intensity that she displayed all the time. I kept encouraging her to find other outlets . . . like the cycling club I know she joined, because that's where she met Dr. McQueen."

"You know about him?"

"The police filled me in on the details. But to be honest with you, I'd heard stuff on the office grapevine about her being involved with a married man. Not that it's any concern of mine . . . or, for that matter, this company's . . . unless it becomes public information."

"And if that happens?"

"To be honest with you, Mrs. Buchan, if word gets out in the newspapers that your daughter has gone missing after threatening Dr. McQueen and his family, I think that her position in the mutual fund world will no longer be viable. Which would be tragic, because she's a great performer."

"In other words, you won't be taking her back."

"I didn't say that, Mrs. Buchan. If she's found soon—and if, after the appropriate medical intervention, she's given a clean bill of mental health—I will fight very hard to have her reinstated. But if this entire affair goes public, well, honestly, I think her position with us will be untenable. We are, I think, a very humane company when it comes to our employees . . . especially valued ones like your daughter. But the board is also quite conservative as regards the company's public image. And given that we're living in rather conservative times, I would be engaged in an uphill battle with my superiors to keep her on. I'm sorry to sound such a pessimistic note, but I'd rather not pretend that it will be easy to get her reinstated."

As I recounted this conversation to Dan over a glass of wine in the Onyx bar, I found myself thinking: *Lizzie the great team player . . . Ms. Two Hundred Percent?* It was so unlike the young woman who, during college, often mocked the sort of student obsessives who spent eight hours a day studying and were in thrall to the success ethos. And now . . .

"I never knew she put in such time," Dan said. "They were obviously very impressed with her."

"Stop talking about her in the past tense."

"I'm talking about her former employers. You know they're going to let her go."

"That's no bad thing."

"From where you sit. From where Lizzie sits . . ."

"It helped drive her to where she is right now. She's always hated the work."

"She never mentioned that to me."

"That's because she's never really talked to you about all this."

"What does that mean?"

"Just what I said. She didn't raise this with you."

"Because?"

"Because she didn't."

"You're getting at something here, aren't you?"

"Come on, Dan . . ."

"Come on *what*?"

"I don't want a fight over this."

"Over what, Hannah? Are you implying that I haven't been there for my daughter when she's needed me?"

I tensed. We hadn't had one of these child-based arguments in years. And I knew that, on the rare occasions that Dan got mad about something, it was impossible to get him off the subject.

"Dan, we're both very tired and very scared . . ." I said.

"But you still think I was never there for my daughter, and that's the reason why she's gone off the deep end . . ."

"Don't accuse me of something I haven't said . . ."

"You don't need to say it. It's evident that it's what you think."

"No, what's evident is that you are taking your own guilt about your absences during Lizzie's childhood and turning it into—"

"*There*—you said it. *My absences*. I was off, building up my practice, bringing in the money, giving us the life that—"

"Dan, why are you going down this road?"

"And because I wasn't there, she could never confide in me . . ."

I put my hand on his. He pulled it away.

"I don't need your solace. I need . . ."

He turned away, biting hard on his lip, his eyes wet with tears.

"I need Lizzie," he whispered.

I touched his shoulder. He flinched.

"Danny, don't beat yourself up . . ."

"That's easy for you to say. You had the relationship with her."

He stood up.

"I'm going for a walk," he said.

"It's cold out there."

"I don't care."

And he grabbed his coat and stormed out the hotel front door.

I didn't run after him—because I knew that when Dan got into one of these angry, guilty-conscience phases, he needed to be left alone. But—and this was a big *but*—I couldn't help but be saddened and unnerved by his remorse; his sense that he had let Lizzie down during her childhood by being so often otherwise engaged.

And yet did he really damage her by being away so much? Lizzie always adored her father, even during her manic adolescent years when I was, in her eyes, the maternal anti-Christ. There were never any major conflicts between them. So why should he now think himself a bad father, and blame himself for Lizzie's breakdown?

Because that's what parents do, I guess. They privately fret that they haven't gotten it right—that, deep down, they are to blame for, well, *everything*. You're so grateful to have children in your life. And yet you feel this undercurrent of ambivalence, this sense that, truth be told, life would be so much less rich . . . but so much easier . . . without them. And this, in turn, begs the question: why do we entangle ourselves in lifelong commitments that also bring such pain?

I finished my glass of wine. I signed the bill. I went upstairs to our room, undressed, got into bed, and, for around the tenth time that day, rang Lizzie's cell phone and her apartment. No answer. Having already left five messages, I added another one—giving the number of the Onyx Hotel and telling her to call us at any time, day or night.

Then I flicked mindlessly through thirty channels of televisual crap. I'm such an infrequent viewer—the news, the occasional old movie or series on HBO—that I'd forgotten just what a wasteland it could be. Eventually I could take no more. I snapped off the television, went into the bathroom, dug out an herbal sleeping pill from the bottle I always travel with, downed it, and returned to bed. I looked absently for a while at a copy of *The Boston Globe* I'd picked up at reception, until the chamomile fogginess of the pills crept over me and I passed out.

The next thing I knew, the bedside light was snapped on and Dan was crawling in beside me. I squinted at the clock radio on the bedside table. One-eighteen.

"You've been out all this time?" I asked.

"Needed the air."

"But four hours?"

"Ended up in a bar over in Back Bay."

"You really walked all the way to Back Bay?"

"I was looking . . ."

He stopped himself, turned away from me.

"Looking for Lizzie?"

He nodded his head.

"Whereabouts?"

"Around the Common, where there are a lot of homeless. Went to every hotel I could find, asking if a Lizzie Buchan had checked in. Then there were all the bars and restaurants toward the top of Newbury Street. Eventually, when I got up around Symphony Hall, I decided that what I really needed was four or five malt whiskeys . . ."

I reached over and put my arms around him.

He pulled away and said, "I really don't feel like being held right now, okay?"

He punched up his pillow, put his head into it, and passed out. I sat up in bed for a very long time, looking at my sleeping husband, thinking about how he was sometimes so easy to read and sometimes so damn opaque; and how, after all these years, there were parts of his life, his mind, that were completely closed off to me.

The wake-up call I'd requested woke us at seven-thirty. Despite his hangover, Dan was the first out of bed. He staggered into the bathroom. When he emerged a few minutes later, accompanied by the steam from the ultrahot water he always showered in, he looked at me with downcast eyes and said one word, "Sorry."

"Okay," I said.

"I just couldn't face . . . uh . . . things got a little on top of me and . . . look, it was the wrong way to . . ."

I held up my hand.

"Like I said, Dan: it's okay."

He managed a sad smile. "Thanks."

When we went downstairs for breakfast, Dad was already there, a *New York Times* open in front of him, alongside a yellow legal pad filled with his completely illegible writing.

"Did you sleep as badly as I did?" he asked.

We both nodded.

"Well, get some coffee into yourselves. I've taken the liberty of drawing up a plan of action for today . . . if, that is, you don't mind me doing this, Dan."

I knew Dan minded, because I also knew that he'd be thinking: *She's my daughter, so I should be in charge. Because when I'm in charge, I feel like I can exercise a little control over stuff that is really beyond my control.* But he simply sipped his coffee and said, "I don't mind at all. What do you want us to do?"

Dad's program of action took three days to execute and essentially involved looking into every possible corner of Lizzie's life. It was comprehensive and very rigorous—my father also attempting to keep his own anxiety under control by playing general and setting out a battle plan to trace his granddaughter. Men really do need to believe they can *take command* and *solve the problem.* It allows them to mask their own desperate fear that they are as helpless as everyone else.

Still, over the next few days, we all ended up finding out enormous amounts about Lizzie. The landlord who finally let us into her apartment told us that, upon learning that one of the concierges had a six-year-old daughter who had leukemia and was undergoing an experimental bone marrow program that wasn't covered by health insurance, Lizzie wrote him a $2,500 check as a contribution to a fund they'd set up to pay for the treatment. When we got inside her loft, her grandfather was quietly shocked by the lack of books on her shelves.

"She used to be such a great reader," Dad said, looking sadly through her thin collection of glossy paperbacks. "What happened?"

"She started working fifteen-hour days," I said.

More surprising was the discovery I made when I opened one of her closets and discovered box after box, shopping bag after shopping bag, of unopened clothes and shoes. There must have been nine pairs of unworn designer jeans, four boxes of different Nike running shoes (all of which still had the brown packing paper stuffed inside), a dozen or so bags from cosmetics and specialty shops like MAC and Kiehl's filled with unused compacts and lipsticks, and innumerable other shopping bags from places like Banana Republic and Armani Jeans and Guess, Gap, and . . .

It so distressed me, looking at all this untouched *stuff.* It spoke so much of her despair. Even Dan was shocked by this back-of-the-closet trove of consumerist paraphernalia.

"Jesus Christ," he said under his breath, looking at all those bags.

Dad said, "Dr. Thornton did mention to me that she talked about being a compulsive shopper . . . someone who constantly had to be buying things, even though she'd never use most of the stuff. It's the same sort of obsessional disorder that affects gamblers or even drug addicts . . ."

I said, "And I'm sure he told you that it's all desperately symptomatic of profound unhappiness and low self-esteem."

Dad looked away into that closet full of shiny detritus.

"Yes, that's pretty much what he said."

I managed to obtain an appointment with the guy at First Boston who handled Lizzie's financial life. He was a quiet, chubby man in his mid-forties named David Martell—and he made it very clear from the outset that he wouldn't be able to give me exact facts and figures about what Lizzie had in her accounts and assorted savings plans.

"I'd be breaching several laws if I did that, Mrs. Buchan. But I understand from the police that she has gone missing, so if I can help in any other way . . ."

"Without divulging the exact amount in her checking account, would she have enough money to, say, float for a while, or even set up a new life for herself elsewhere?"

He thought for a moment, then turned to his computer monitor, typed in some numbers, and turned back to me.

"Put it this way, she could probably last about three or four months if she lived carefully."

"That's all?" I asked, genuinely surprised.

"Without giving you hard numbers, Mrs. Buchan, the truth is that your daughter was always having money problems."

"But how could that be? She earned a huge salary and she got a large bonus every year."

"Well, I did discuss this with her on a regular basis—the fact that she was running through money. Even after her mortgage and her car payments, she still had a considerable amount of disposable income per month, but she was always edging toward being overdrawn, and she never saved anything."

"Didn't she have any mutual fund investments or IRAs or anything like that?"

"She did, but six months ago, when she hit a cash flow problem, she cashed most of them in. There is one IRA left, which would give her the three- or four-month comfort zone you asked about. Otherwise, her sole assets are her apartment and her car."

"What the hell did she spend all that money on?"

Mr. Martell shrugged.

"I've got plenty of clients like your daughter. They have big jobs in the financial sector, they make impressive salaries—and they often have little to show for it in terms of financial assets. Their money goes on eating out, shopping, expensive weekends away, more shopping, personal trainers, health clubs, cosmetic dental work . . . diversionary stuff, if you want my opinion. At least Lizzie invested in property, which means there's something for her to fall back on."

Mr. Martell assured me that if Lizzie tried to liquidate her IRA account, the police would be informed immediately. Just as the cops were also continuing to monitor any ATM withdrawals she was making.

"I've got a daughter who's just started Boston College and another who's a junior in high school," he said. "So I just want to say that I really sympathize with what you're going through right now. It's every parent's worst nightmare."

"Yes," I said, "it is."

While I was at the bank, Dad had inveigled his way into Lizzie's office and managed to speak with three of her colleagues, including a woman named Joan Silverstein, who turned out to be her in-office confidante . . . even though Lizzie had never mentioned her to me before.

"It seems," Dad said, "that Lizzie kind of got mixed reviews from her coworkers. She could be very supportive and simultaneously cold and arrogant."

"That's a new one," I said.

"It seems that a couple of the people who worked directly under her did complain to her boss, a Mr. . . ."

"Kirby."

"That's it . . . Anyway, they said Lizzie could be extremely demanding and didn't tolerate mistakes. She fired a young trainee after she messed up a transaction that cost the client around $10,000—money Lizzie then made back for him the next day. And once, when she was let down on a big deal, she actually threw her computer monitor across the room. She was reprimanded about that by Mr. Kirby and paid for a new one herself. She also made a point of giving everyone who witnessed that event a bottle of vintage champagne as an apology. That was a pretty expensive way of saying sorry."

"She had this habit of throwing money around," I said, and explained what I had learned about her finances from Mr. Martell.

"Well, that doesn't totally surprise me. All of her colleagues commented on just how generous she was—always picking up the tab, lending cash to people in the office who were short, giving considerable amounts of money to charities, especially this pro-choice group, the Massachusetts Women's Health Organization."

"That's a fact we'd better keep from her brother and, most especially, her sister-in-law. Any idea why she chose this women's health group for a contribution?"

Dad looked me directly in the eye.

"She had an abortion three months ago."

This took a moment to sink in. I was stunned—not by the discovery that Lizzie had terminated a pregnancy, but by the realization that I had never known about it.

"Who told you this?"

"Her friend Joan Silverstein."

"She just volunteered this information out of the blue?"

"After Mr. Kirby allowed me to have a little seminar at the office with her colleagues—where I convinced them to speak openly to me. I asked Joan, who seemed to know her best, if she'd like to get a bite with me. A lovely young woman, Joan. Harvard educated, a postgraduate year at the Sorbonne, fluent French, and a delightful sense of humor."

I heard myself saying, "Let me guess. You asked her out for a date tonight?"

Dad winced—and I felt shitty.

"Sorry," I said, "that was uncalled for."

"Anyway," he said, "over lunch I asked Joan if there was anything else about Lizzie that might hint at her whereabouts. It took a little friendly persuasion, but then she told me about the abortion. Lizzie had confided in her. It happened around three months ago. McQueen was the father, and he insisted that she terminate the pregnancy, but also swore to her that, when he left his wife and kids for her, they'd have a baby together."

I felt ill. Sick with anger that McQueen, the bastard, had promised her a baby, and had also convinced her to terminate her pregnancy. Even then he was probably thinking of ways to jettison her while simultaneously spinning this lie of a future life together to keep her sweet and keep her sleeping with him. No wonder poor Lizzie created this pregnancy fantasy: she'd been deceived into thinking that a baby was in the cards with the wonderful Dr. McQueen.

"Did this woman tell you how Lizzie dealt with the abortion?"

"She had it done over lunchtime and asked Joan to go with her for moral support. As soon as she came out of the post-op room, she acted like nothing had happened, and insisted on going back to work . . . though Joan tried to get her to go home. But she returned to work and put in another eight hours. And for the rest of the week, she did these crazy long days. Then, just before they were all about to leave for the weekend, Joan went into the bathroom at work and heard this woman howling her head off in one of the stalls. It was Lizzie. Joan said it took about twenty minutes to calm her down—and then Lizzie begged her not to tell anyone. On Monday, when they all came back to work, Lizzie acted like nothing had happened.

"There's something else you should know, Hannah. After lunch, I called the Massachusetts Women's Health Organization and asked to speak to their public relations office—a woman named Gifford. She didn't at first believe me when I said I was Lizzie Buchan's grandfather, and asked me a lot of questions about her because, as she explained to me, the organization was constantly getting threats from pro-life lunatics. But when she figured out that I was who I said I was, she didn't mention anything about Lizzie's abortion—patient confidentiality and all that, thank God—but she did say that she had made one of the biggest personal contributions to the organization that they had ever received."

"How much exactly?"

"Twenty thousand dollars."

"You're serious?"

"Well," Dad said, "it is supporting a very good cause. Still, it is a rather breathtaking sum of money. They must have helped her enormously."

This conversation took place back in the bar of the Onyx. It was a little after six, I was operating on around five hours' sleep, my nerves felt shredded, and my little girl was still missing. This new revelation felt as if it were going to split my head open. All I wanted to do was disappear and be alone.

"Dad, I'm going upstairs to lie down for a while."

"Are you all right?"

"No. I'm not all right."

"I'm not surprised."

"When Dan shows up, please tell him everything you just told me."

"I will."

Upstairs, I kicked off my shoes, stretched out on the bed, and stared up at the ceiling. I suppose this was the moment when I should have broken down and cried, weeping for my lost daughter and the desperate sadness that drove her to come apart. But I just felt a deep, terrible numbness—the same sort of numbness that accompanied my mother's Alzheimer's diagnosis. But at least my mother had had a full and complicated life by the time the disease began to seize her mind. Whereas Lizzie . . . Lizzie was still so young, still just trying to find her way. Her story was still evolving. That's what so unnerved me about her disappearance—that she somehow considered this disaster with the doctor to be the end of things. In her delusion, she staked her entire future happiness on an opportunistic shit who took advantage of her breakneck need for love.

But another thought struck me: just how much I didn't know about Lizzie. And no, it wasn't the same thing as realizing that there were hidden compartments in my husband's brain to which I would never have access. This was *my daughter:* someone I raised; someone who always—until very recently—told me everything that was going on in her life; someone whom I thought I fundamentally understood. To discover all these other terrible and extraordinary things about her . . . the shopaholism, the chronic money problems, the extreme generosity, the angry outbursts, the demands she made on others—and, most tellingly, on herself—the abortion . . .

That really shattered me—the fact that she'd kept this huge decision to herself . . . or, worse, that she couldn't bring herself to tell me about it. And it wasn't as if I would have gotten judgmental about it. She knows how pro-choice I am, and how I would stand by her in any situation. I could only begin to imagine the lonely grief she suffered afterward, especially when she realized that McQueen was going to renege on his promise of having a child together, a life together.

Oh God, why had she been so naive? And why did she squander such love on a married man, someone who was so clearly unworthy of her?

But it was clear to me now that there were several sides to Lizzie which had simply eluded me . . . or, maybe, which I knew were there but never wanted to see.

I stared up at the ceiling for, well, I lost track of time. Then the room door opened and Dan came in, looking drawn and sapped. He said nothing for a moment, just flopped into the armchair opposite the bed. I sat up.

"You okay?" he asked.

"Not really. Did you see Dad downstairs?"

He nodded.

"And did he tell you what he found out about Lizzie today?"

He bit his lip and nodded again. Then, in a near whisper, he said, "I am going to get that shit McQueen."

"It's all just so damn unreal. And now it's my turn to wonder why she couldn't call me . . . why she was scared of letting me in on this big thing in her life."

"Maybe the abortion wasn't a big thing at first. Maybe it only became so after McQueen dumped her."

"But giving twenty grand to that women's health group? That's a huge sum of money no matter how much they helped her through the abortion. And all the useless stuff she bought herself . . ."

"Sad people with a bit of money often shop," Dan said.

He covered his face with his hands, took a deep breath, pulled them slowly away, and said, "When I was sitting in Leary's office at the Brookline Police Department this afternoon, the thought struck me: this nightmare really isn't happening. I'm in some alternative reality, and any moment now, someone will flick a switch and I'll be back in my so-called normal life."

"When Lizzie turns up, that switch will be pulled."

He looked away from me.

"There are couple of things you need to know," he said.

"Tell me."

"The first is that, if Lizzie isn't found by Sunday, they're going to start dragging the Charles."

All I could say was, "So soon?"

"Leary says it's normal procedure in a missing persons case. The second thing is that they are now treating McQueen as a suspect in her disappearance."

I felt as if I had been slapped hard across the face.

"They think he harmed her . . . killed her?" I asked, my voice shrill.

"They're not saying that. And they still have good reason to believe that she's gone missing through her own volition. But they can't rule out the possibility that McQueen was so worried about being exposed by her that maybe—"

He broke off, biting hard on his lip.

"As Leary told me, it's not exactly a new scenario: the married man silencing his mistress when she starts to threaten his family. But what's worrying them is the fact that they spoke to the guy who worked at the Seven-Eleven on Causeway Street near North Station—that's where the first ATM withdrawal was made—and though he can't completely remember, he's pretty damn sure that he didn't see a woman come in and use their ATM at the hour when the bank registered a withdrawal from her account."

"Have they shown him McQueen's photograph?" I asked.

"Of course. But the guy couldn't say for certain it was him."

"Don't they usually tape all ATM withdrawals?"

"Yeah, but not in the little machines you see in convenience stores. And unfortunately, both of the withdrawals were made in convenience stores."

"Isn't Causeway Street right nearby?"

"Half a minute's walk from the hotel. I went into the Seven-Eleven myself before coming back. Showed the woman behind the counter Lizzie's picture. She'd never seen her, but she also was working largely in the back on the night the withdrawal was made. I also went around, talking to a lot of the street people hanging near North Station. No one recognized her, though everyone I spoke with hit me for a couple of bucks."

"Why would a rich doctor like McQueen be using Lizzie's ATM card to get money?"

"I asked the same question to Leary. He said that McQueen might be trying to muddle the trail—to make everybody believe that Lizzie is still alive because she's withdrawing money . . ."

"That makes sense. Have they questioned McQueen yet about this?"

"They haven't mentioned the ATM. They want to see if there's another cash withdrawal—and if they can somehow trace it this time. Or maybe they hope that whoever's taking out the money might slip up and use a cash machine with a videotape facility."

"McQueen would be too clever for that."

"They still haven't ascertained that it *is* McQueen, and though he's under surveillance, they haven't even intimated he's a suspect, just in case he gets nervous and tries to flee."

Lizzie *murdered*? No, I couldn't accept that, couldn't believe that. As much as I hated McQueen, I remember his upset and anger during our phone call. Surely if he had killed Lizzie, he would have acted more cagily, would have played dumb. But maybe he was also putting on an outraged act for my benefit, to further deflect attention from himself as the prime suspect. After all, if he could convince the police that the last time he saw Lizzie was in the bar of the Four Seasons when she went ballistic, then how could they link him to her subsequent disappearance?

I articulated this theory to Dan. He shrugged and said that Leary had essentially posited the same idea. The detective now wanted to meet me face-to-face in order to hear my description of that phone call with McQueen and to conduct a general interview with me, and one with Dad too.

"The way he figures it, either of you might tell him something that you don't think significant but which could help him. He suggested nine-thirty tomorrow."

"Okay. I do want to meet him."

"He's a good guy. But he also gave me another bad bit of news. Some journalist on the *Boston Herald* is on the case—and though Leary has been able, so far, to keep it out of print, he says it's just a matter of days before they run with it. And when they do . . ."

Oh, I could see it all now. Because this story had all the angles the tabloids loved—wealthy, highly respected doctor; big-salaried, well-educated young career woman; illicit sex; a terminated pregnancy; the reneged promises of a future life together; the way she stalked him, the big scene in front of the doctor's wife and kids; and, best of all, the fact that she had vanished. *Could it be murder? Could this well-known dermatologist* (they'll love the fact that he's a dermatologist—with his own TV show) *have cracked and, in a moment of deranged rage . . . ?*

And I could see some grainy vacation snapshot of my poor daughter being blazoned across an inside page of the *Herald* with the subtitle "Yuppie Executive Elizabeth Buchan Had It All . . . Except for the Celebrity Doctor of Her Dreams."

"Dan, do you think he killed her? And don't say no just to keep me calm. Do you think he went that far?"

"No, I don't. It doesn't make sense—and Leary says that McQueen can account for his whereabouts in the hours after Lizzie's disappearance."

"Then why is he treating McQueen as a suspect?"

"Because he's a cop, and I guess cops never rule anyone out until they can be ruled out . . . and also because if he's looking for someone who would want Lizzie disappeared, McQueen is the guy."

"We have to call Jeff," I said.

"That thought did cross my mind, especially if it's going to blow in the papers at any moment. If he got the news secondhand . . ."

He'd go berserk. And he'd be right to go berserk. This was news he had to know.

"I'll make the call if you like," Dan said.

"No, I'll do it."

I really didn't want to do it, because, like Dan, there was a part of me now that feared Jeff. Feared his anger, his judgmental tone. But I also knew that, unlike his father, I'd be better at deflecting any crap he threw at me. Dan hates confrontation, especially with his kids.

So I reached over and picked up the phone and dialed Jeff's house in West Hartford. Shannon picked up. In the immediate background, I could hear loud cartoon voices from a television.

"Oh hi there, Hannah!" she said in that relentlessly cheerful voice of hers, which ended every sentence in an exclamation point. "You've kind of caught me at a crazy moment . . ."

"I could call back when Jeff's home."

"No, he's here. We've just gotten back from church."

"On a Friday?"

"It's Good Friday today," she said coolly.

Somehow this fact hadn't registered with me.

"So it is," I said.

"I'll get Jeff."

I could hear her shout his name . . . followed by him shouting back, "I'll take it in the den," then him picking up the phone and Shannon hanging up the extension, and all that ambient family chaos suddenly vanishing from the line.

"Hey, Mom," he said pleasantly. "How are things up in Maine?"

"I'm in Boston. And I'm here with your father and grandfather."

"Didn't know you were all spending Easter weekend together in Boston."

"Nor did we."

A pause.

"What does that mean?" he said.

"Jeff . . . I have some difficult news. Lizzie has gone missing."

And then I told him everything. He didn't interrupt me once. He just listened. When I finished, he said, "I'm coming to Boston."

"There's no real need," I said. "The police seem to be doing a pretty thorough job, and we're leaving tomorrow."

"Do you think that's wise?"

"No. I would prefer to scour every street and knock on every door in the greater Boston area if it meant finding Lizzie. But your dad has three operations scheduled for Sunday . . ."

"He's operating on Easter Sunday?"

"Not everyone's an evangelical . . ."

"Why do you have to make a crack like that at a time like this?"

"Because I'm beyond stressed, that's why. Okay?"

Something in my voice told him to back off. He did.

"Okay," he said.

"So your dad has to operate the day after tomorrow, and I have to get Granddad back to Burlington and then drive back to Portland . . . so if you want to come to Boston, fine. But we won't be here. Because we won't want to be here when the story breaks in the *Boston Herald*—even though Detective Leary assures us that the paper will, no doubt, send one of their reporters up to Maine to snoop around and try to get us to give a tearful interview all about Lizzie, and probably get her high school friends to talk about what a nice kid she was . . . *is* . . ."

I caught a cry in my throat and squelched it before it turned into a howl.

"Mom, are you okay?"

"Why does everyone keep asking me that?" I shouted. "How can I be all right . . . ?"

"What's this doctor's full name again?" he asked, all business.

I told him.

"And the detective in Brookline handling the case?"

I gave him Leary's name and phone number.

"I'll see what I can do about keeping this out of the papers. We don't want the publicity."

"We?"

"The family . . . and especially Lizzie. When people find out she's had this affair and the scene with his kids and the abortion, her career will be over."

"Her life might be already over, Jeff."

"You can't think that way."

"Why the fuck not?" I yelled.

"Is Dad there?"

"I'll put him on."

I tossed the receiver on the bed.

"Your sanctimonious son," I said to Dan.

He picked up the phone and walked toward the window and talked quietly with Jeff for some minutes. Then he turned back toward me and said into the receiver:

"Of course I'll tell her . . . okay . . . right . . . call me whenever."

He replaced the phone in the receiver.

"All right," I said, "tell me I handled that badly."

"You handled that badly, but Jeff wanted you to know that he understood why."

"Well, that makes me feel real good all over."

"Hannah, I know you've got your problems with Jeff, but . . ."

"You know why he really wants to keep this all out of the papers? Because it means he won't be publicly embarrassed by the fact that Mr. Pro-lifer's sister had an abortion while screwing a married man . . ."

"He's very shaken, just like the rest of us. And very worried for Lizzie."

"And for *his* career, of course."

"If he can somehow keep it out of the papers, that's just fine by me. None of us needs the intrusion this will bring. And you need to try to get some sleep tonight."

"How am I going to do that?"

"I have a prescription pad in my bag. I'm sure there's a late-night pharmacist somewhere in Boston. I could get the concierge to run over a prescription for something that doesn't leave you too groggy in the morning."

"So you think I need to be knocked out, do you?"

"Yes, I do—and quite frankly, I want to take a couple as well tonight."

He called the concierge. He came upstairs for the prescription. An hour later, he returned from the late-night pharmacy, proffering a small bag. Dan thanked him with a $20 tip. I was already in bed—determined to get an early night. I accepted two of the pills from my husband and chased them with a glass of water.

"You coming to bed?" I asked.

"In a little while."

He started putting on his shoes.

"Where are you going?" I asked.

"I need another walk," he said.

"You're heading out to look for her again?"

"Do you have a problem with that?"

"I just don't want you wandering the streets all night, getting yourself more troubled. Anyway, weren't we supposed to get drugged up together and pass out for the night?"

"Just give me an hour."

"I'll be asleep by then. Anyway, you won't find her."

"Don't say that."

"But it's the truth."

"It's worth a shot," he said.

"If it makes you happy."

"It's not about making *me* happy," he said sharply. "It's about finding Lizzie."

"I'm not trying to start a fight here."

"Then don't say stupid stuff," he said, grabbing his coat. "I hope you sleep. You need to."

So do you, I wanted to add, but stopped myself. As soon as he was out the door, I felt desperately guilty. *If it makes you happy.* I didn't mean that to come out sounding catty, and yet that's exactly what happened. He was right: it was a stupid thing to say. And if wandering the streets made him feel he was doing something in the search for Lizzie, so be it.

The pills had their desired effect, pulling me out of waking life a few minutes later. The next thing I knew it was morning—seven-ten, according to the bedside clock. My brain felt chemically fogged in. It took me a few moments to overcome the initial postsleep grogginess and get my bearings. But at least I had slept.

Dan was already up, showering in the bathroom. When he emerged after a few minutes, he said, "You didn't seem to move at all last night."

"Didn't you take a couple of pills as well?"

"I had a few drinks when I was out. Sleeping pills and booze are always a recipe for disaster."

"What time did you get in?"

"Late."

Again? I felt like asking . . . but stopped myself.

"Where'd you end up this time?"

"The Theater District, Chinatown, South Station . . . then took a cab over to Cambridge and walked all around Harvard Yard. A lot of people sleep rough there at night. That's where I found this bar . . ."

"Another scotch night?"

"Bourbon."

"I wish I could drink whiskey. It just doesn't sit with me."

"It has its uses."

A pause.

"I'm sorry," I said.

"For what?"

"For making that stupid comment last night."

"It doesn't matter."

"I still shouldn't have said it."

"Don't you have a nine-thirty appointment with Detective Leary?"

Dad and I drove out to Brookline together.

"You look like you slept better last night," he said.

"It was drug-induced. Did you sleep?"

"Intermittently. But maybe that's because I also got a phone call from my grandson around ten last night."

"Jeff rang you? Was he friendly?"

"Not unfriendly, but a bit forensic when it came to questioning me. Still, I was pleased he phoned. He's worried—and, I suppose, he wanted to get my perspective on what had happened. He's going to come up here on Monday."

If it makes him feel better . . .

Detective Patrick Leary was in his late thirties—a big, slightly disheveled man wearing a suit that could have used a pressing. But his eyes were sharp and highly focused—and though his manner was a little unceremonious, I liked his professionalism and his no-nonsense decency. He didn't ooze sentiment about what we were going through. He didn't make rash promises about leaving no stone unturned—because he struck me as someone who, by his very thorough nature, would do everything necessary to find my daughter . . . but also wouldn't toot his own horn by telling me how much he was doing. I felt an immediate confidence in him, even after he started asking me some very awkward questions.

When we arrived at the Brookline station house, he came out to greet us both—and then asked if we didn't mind being interviewed separately.

"I find people talk a little easier when there isn't another family member in the room."

We agreed—and operating on the principle of ladies first, he led me down a corridor to a faceless interview room: dirty cream walls, fluorescent lights, white ceiling tiles, a steel desk, two hard chairs. He offered coffee. I accepted. As it was being made, he asked a lot of general questions about Lizzie's childhood and adolescence—whether she ever showed any signs of instability before ("not until she came to Boston and started working in mutual funds—though, from the moment she got interested in boys when she was around fifteen, she was always something of a romantic"), and was she someone who'd had reasonable amounts of friends ("she wasn't a great joiner—and she hated cheerleader types who hung together in cliques—but there were always pals at school and around the neighborhood").

Then, out of nowhere, he asked, "Would you say that Dr. Buchan and yourself have had a happy marriage?"

"I don't really see what that has to do with Lizzie's disappearance," I said.

"I'm just trying to piece together a psychological profile, see if there's something in her past that might have triggered a reaction during the breakup and sent her . . . I don't know . . . back to a place she used to spend time in during childhood. Often when people go missing, they are acting, on one level, irrationally. At the same time, they frequently head back to places that have certain past associations for them . . ."

"I still don't see what this has to do with my marriage."

"Are you afraid to talk about your marriage?"

"No, not at all. At the same time, though . . ."

"It's an invasion of your privacy?"

"I wouldn't put it so strongly."

"I posed the same question to your husband."

"And what did he say?"

"That's not for me to reveal," he said. "A police interview is always strictly confidential. What do you think he said?"

"Knowing Dan, he probably thinks we have a very good marriage."

"And would you agree with his opinion?"

A pause.

"Yes, I think that, compared to many couples I know, we have a good marriage."

"But not a *very* good marriage?"

"A good marriage is a good marriage."

"By which you mean . . . "

"It's survived. Both parties have kept their nerve, stuck with it, despite . . ."

"Despite what?"

"Are you married, Detective?"

"Divorced."

"Then you understand what *despite* means."

He favored me with a small smile.

"So Lizzie grew up in a stable household? No ongoing domestic warfare, no major bust-ups, no public exhumations of skeletons in the closet?"

"No, nothing like that at all."

"And you were both supportive, loving parents?"

"I think so, yes. But where are you going with this, Detective?"

He reached for a file kept in the briefcase he'd brought in for the interview. Upon retrieving it, he opened it.

"I'm sorry to have to bring this up, but I think it's relevant. One of her work colleagues told me that Lizzie once confided in her that she never felt that her parents were a happy couple. Civil with each other. Accommodating. Totally noncombatant—and completely stable. But never, in her mind, really happy with each other. And that made her worry that, perhaps, the reason why she herself never felt totally at ease with herself—and was always desperately searching for happiness—is because she never felt she came from a particularly happy family."

"That is such absolute crap," I said.

"I am just reporting—"

"But *why* are you reporting this? I don't see the relevance."

"I apologize if this line of questioning seems a little too personal, Mrs. Buchan. All I'm trying to work out is whether her disappearance is a simple running away or a suicide. And that's why finding out about her family background is so important, especially as she's now passed the crucial seventy-two-hour mark."

"What's that?"

"In most missing persons cases, the individual is either found or comes in out of the cold after three days. But if they haven't returned home by then, the disappearance is usually—and I have to stress that there is no straightforward rule here—because that person really wants to vanish, either through the act of running away or suicide. However, suicides usually aren't searching for something else—other than a way to end their pain. In Lizzie's case, she's still searching for a Prince Charming figure, someone who's going to whisk her away from all the bad stuff in life. The fact that McQueen has dumped her—and the fact that, even after that big scene in the Four Seasons bar, she still told you he was going to leave his wife and kids and get her pregnant again—means she's still traveling hopefully, so to speak. And the fact that, in her eyes, her parents didn't have the happiest of marriages means that, in her own psychoneurotic way, she's probably searching for the next guy who, she thinks, will make things right for her. If your marriage had been a disaster or blissfully happy, she might have reason to despair, thinking she'd never find such happiness or that all intimate relationships are toxic. The fact that yours was functional gives her something to play for—a chance to find the storybook romance she's still dreaming of.

"Or, at least, that's my take on it . . . and I could be totally wrong."

Pause.

"Are you a psychologist, Detective?"

"That's what I trained to be . . . before the police got me."

"It shows. And your theory about Lizzie is very persuasive, although I never knew . . ."

"What?"

"That Dan and I exuded so much . . . *functionality* as a couple."

"Like I said, it's just a secondhand report of what she said. And you're right—even in their twenties, kids want their parents to be picture-postcard happy and can never understand when the reality is a little grayer than that. Don't beat yourself up about it—and sorry again if I made you uncomfortable with my rather personal line of questioning."

"So you don't think McQueen could have killed her?"

"We haven't ruled that out completely, though we've checked out his movements in the days after the scene in the Four Seasons, and he seems clean. Who's to say, for example, that he didn't hire someone to do the job for him? But I'm just entering the realm of forensic hypothesis here. Because between ourselves, my take on this is: Mark McQueen might be an asshole, but he's not a murderous asshole."

The interview over, I went outside and waited while Detective Leary interviewed Dad. That one phrase—*she never felt that her parents were a happy couple*—kept thundering through my brain. So this is how she saw us. And if that was Lizzie's take on our marriage, Jeff must have seen this too. And then there were all our friends, our neighbors, our respective professional colleagues—did they too all think: *Hannah and Dan have a pretty damn loveless marriage?*

Dad's interview with Leary lasted over forty-five minutes—almost three times the length of my short, sharp shock of an interrogation. He emerged with the detective—the two of them very chummy.

"I gather you're driving your dad back to Vermont now," Leary said. I nodded. "And you'll be back home in Maine tomorrow?"

"That's right."

"Well, I have all your numbers there and will call as soon as I hear anything." He handed me a card with a number scribbled on the back. "Here's my cell phone number if you can't get through to me here. Feel free to call whenever. I know how anxious a time this is. And get your dad back safe to Burlington. We need more guys like him right now . . . even if I completely disagree with most of what he says."

"Only half," Dad said, proffering his hand to Leary, who shook it warmly. "And remember, we've got a great minor-league team in Burlington, so I'll expect to see you for a game come summer."

In the car, I said, "So you and Leary seem to be new best friends."

"He's a very impressive young man."

"What's this about some minor-league team?"

"Don't you remember the Vermont Expos, our local baseball team?"

"Oh, right."

"Turns out Leary is a big baseball fan—and loves minor-league ball. Thinks it's purer than what's played in the majors, which is how I see it too. Anyway, I told him about the Expos—how they're the farm team for Montreal and play right in the great little stadium in Burlington—and invited him up to catch a game."

"What else did you talk about?"

"Lizzie, of course."

"And?"

"It was mainly background stuff—though he did seem particularly interested to know if I felt she had any major gripes against her parents."

"What did you say?"

"That all kids were screwed up by their parents, but that you and Dan had screwed her up less than most."

"Thanks for the high praise, Dad."

"He really is a most interesting policeman," Dad said.

"He told me he trained as a psychologist."

"Oh, he mentioned that to me as well. But did he tell you that he spent three years before that in a Jesuit seminary?"

"That explains a lot," I said.

As arranged, Dad and I left the Brookline PD directly for Vermont—Dan having already departed back to Portland. It was a wrench and a relief to get out of Boston. Leaving was an acceptance of our failure to find Lizzie. The relief was being forced away from the place where she disappeared. Boston is, by and large, such a low-key city. Courtesy of its patrician hangover, it is not associated with the sort of emotional extremes or edginess of a New York or a Chicago. But from now on, I'd see it as the place from which my daughter fled into the void, and I knew I'd always hate it for that reason.

The traffic out of town was light. We crossed the Tobin Bridge and hit Interstate 93 in record time. It was a straight shot north to New Hampshire and the turnoff to I-89 just beyond Concord. Then another ninety minutes to Burlington. If the route from Portland to my hometown was indelibly etched in my brain, so too was this road from Boston to the shores of Lake Champlain—a stretch of highway I'd covered so often during my student years and those summers when Dan was working in Boston. As we drove north—little conversation passing between Dad and myself—all I could think was how I once shot south for a weekend in '69 with Margy; the two of us crashing on the tiny dorm room floor of one of her prep school friends now at Radcliffe, and smoking a joint with her near the statue of John Harvard, and buying some ridiculous tie-dyed gauzy shirt in a hippie boutique in Cambridge, and ending up at some dorm party and talking to this rather intense Harvard guy named Stan who was a sophomore and told me he'd already written a novel and wanted to sleep with me that night, but I wasn't in the mood, even though I did find him pretty interesting, and on my way back to Burlington I really regretted not sleeping with him, and how, around ten days later, I met Dan Buchan and our entire history got under way, even though neither of us realized at the time that this was the start of a shared destiny.

Now here I was, thirty-four years later, trying to be as brave and positive as possible in the midst of my child's disappearance, and suddenly, out of nowhere, I'm thinking back to that freshman weekend in Boston, and wondering just how my life would have turned out if I had slept with that would-be writer. No, I'm not naive enough to think I'd still be with him now. But I can't help hypothesizing: say I had gone to bed with him—would I have been particularly receptive or interested when this freshman med student from Glens Falls, New York, crossed my path? Might I have turned him down when he suggested a beer at some student dive? And if that had happened, I most certainly wouldn't be sitting in this car now, attempting to keep it all together as I try to tell myself that Detective Leary is right (he's an ex-Jesuit, after all): Lizzie doesn't fit the suicide profile.

"Penny for them," Dad said.

I just shrugged, not wanting to share Lizzie's comments with Dad, even though I wondered if Lizzie saw what I couldn't—wouldn't—

accept: that my marriage was one enormous falsehood. If I had opened up to him, Dad would have reassured me, of course, telling me that no one except the two central participants can ever really understand the complex internal geography of a marriage. But I was so emotionally frayed right now that I just couldn't bear the idea of a father-daughter heart-to-heart. So we said little on the drive back to Burlington. Vermont Public Radio broadcast a concert of Haydn and Schubert—and the hourly news bulletins came and went without comment from us. We were both talked out—any conversation we made would have been overshadowed by thoughts of Lizzie.

When we reached the Burlington city line, Dad said, "I spoke with Edith before we left the hotel. She said she'd make dinner tonight for us."

"That's nice of her."

"She's very concerned about Lizzie."

"You know, Dad, I think I might head straight back to Portland after I drop you off."

"Oh, I see," he said, sounding uncomfortable. "This doesn't have anything to do with Edith being there, does it?"

"No, it really doesn't."

"But you don't approve."

"I just don't want to have to explain everything about Lizzie to someone else again."

"Edith wouldn't demand that from you. She's not the prying type."

"That's not the problem, Dad—and, in fact, Edith is definitely *not* the problem. The thing is, I just want time alone now. Don't be offended."

"Understood," he said, but I was still pretty certain he did take my decision to leave personally. I'd always so wanted my father's approval when I was growing up, and I had started to realize that he now wanted mine.

Fair play to Edith—upon reaching the house, we discovered that she'd had the entire place cleaned while we were away, had completely stocked the refrigerator, and had a pitcher of martinis and a plate of cheese awaiting us.

"Hannah isn't staying," Dad said to her.

"I really need to head back to Maine," I said.

"I tried to get her to stay, but . . ."

"If Hannah needs to leave, she should leave," Edith said. "I know I'd want to be alone at a time like this."

Bless you, Edith.

"I still don't like the idea of you driving that road at night," Dad said.

"She's an adult, John," Edith said.

"And a parent is always a parent," Dad said.

Before I left, Dad did something out of the ordinary. Instead of giving me his usual cursory I'm-not-very-tactile good-bye peck on the cheek, he hugged me. He didn't offer me words of comfort, or the predictable I'm-sure-she'll-turn-up bromides. He just held me for a few moments.

I departed shortly afterward. I drove east through declining light—leaving the Interstate for a splendid two-lane blacktop that threaded its way through a string of untouched small towns. I concentrated on the road, the frosted hillsides, the domestic detail of the houses I passed. I played the radio. As darkness fell and NPR switched from *All Things Considered* to jazz, I cranked up the volume and let Dexter Gordon's melancholic saxophone carry me eastward. Occasionally I'd glance at the cell phone on my dash, willing it to ring and for Lizzie's voice to be there when I answered. But whenever such agonizing, wishful thoughts crossed my brain, I blacked them out, repeating, mantralike: *There is nothing you can do . . . There is nothing you can do . . . There is . . .*

At St. Johnsbury, I picked up Route 302. New Hampshire arrived. An hour later I was at the Maine border. Twenty miles outside of Portland, I called home but got no reply. So I tried Dan's cell phone—and when voice mail kicked in there as well, I left another message, telling him to expect me shortly. I glanced at the clock on the dash. Eight-seventeen. Dan probably went to the gym at the Woodlands Club for a late workout. When 302 dovetailed with 295 (American automotive life is one long series of recollected numbers, isn't it?), I headed north and took the Bucknam Road exit in order to do some shopping at the big Shaw's Supermarket right off the highway.

I ran up over one hundred dollars' worth of groceries at Shaw's. The kid who was packing the bags wheeled the cart out to my car. He couldn't have been more than seventeen—and as I watched him put everything into the trunk, I remembered that, when she was between sophomore and junior year in high school, Lizzie lasted two weeks one summer as a checkout girl at a Rite Aid pharmacy in this same strip mall.

"I can't do retail, Mom," she said when she came home one afternoon and announced she'd quit. I recall liking the fact that she refused to put up with an intolerable situation. So why had she put up with her intolerable mutual funds job for so long? And why had she stuck with an intolerable married man—and couldn't see that his promises were empty ones? When had she lost that ability to walk away from something she just didn't like?

"You okay, ma'am?" the checkout kid asked me.

I touched my right cheek. It was wet.

"Not really," I said.

Then I reached into my bag, fished out five dollars, and thanked him for helping me.

Home was shuttered, dark. Nine-twelve. This was quite a late workout by Dan standards. Before unpacking the groceries, I checked our voice mail. Nothing of importance vis-à-vis Lizzie—just Jeff confirming that he'd be heading to Boston on Monday and had arranged to see Detective Leary.

"He assured me that he could hold off the *Boston Herald* hack for a few more days. Over the weekend I'm going to talk to a few colleagues and see if there's any legal avenues we can travel down to stop publication."

Fat chance. And though part of me appreciated Jeff's efforts to curb First Amendment rights in this case, there was another unpleasant part of me that thought that what he was really motivated by was his desperate need to suppress the fact that his sister had had an abortion—which simply wouldn't play well with Shannon's right-to-life chums.

I read my email. Mainly junk—but there was a Greetings from ChemoLand dispatch from Margy:

> Hey hon
>
> Just came home from another top-up chemo session. Seems Dr. Drugstore found a little something gray and amorphous in the lower lobe during my last

MRI a few days ago and wants to zap it. Nothing too sinister, he feels—but, in true oncologist style, he is being ultracautious. So, having just spent the afternoon with an IV tube of poison dripping into my system, I'm home now, watching crap television—some moronic reality program about six couples who get locked up in a disused maximum security prison—and just wondering why you've gone so quiet. Have you read the dreaded book yet? If so, please call me asap so we can talk strategy.

Missing you—and wish we could down a couple of martinis right now . . . the best anesthetic going.

M xxx

More chemo . . . and *something gray and amorphous in the lower lobe.* Oh Jesus, that didn't sound good at all. And to hell with the book right now. Compared to everything else going on, it was small potatoes . . . or, at least, that's what I was going to tell myself tonight.

As I was firing back an email to Margy I heard a car pull up into the driveway. I finished the email and went downstairs. Dan was just coming in the door. He seemed surprised to find me home.

"Weren't you due back tomorrow?" he asked.

"And a big hello to you too."

"Sorry, I just wasn't expecting . . ."

"Didn't you get the message?"

"Forgot to turn my cell on after the gym."

"You were working out until now?"

"Met Elliot Bixby at the club. We had a beer afterward."

Elliot Bixby was the head of dermatology at Maine Medical—and something of a pompous ass.

"I couldn't stand being anywhere near a dermatologist right now," I said.

"Yeah, that thought did cross my mind, but he was there in the locker room and when he proposed a drink, and . . . I wasn't ready to come back to an empty house. Any news from Boston?"

I shook my head.

"How'd your interview go with Leary?"

"He asked some tough questions."

"Like what?"

"Did I think we had a happy marriage?"

"He asked me that too," Dan said.

"So he told me. And what did you say?"

"The truth."

"Which is?"

"Well, what do you think?"

"Tell me."

He glanced down at his shoes.

"I said we were very happy. And you?"

A pause. He continued to look away from me. I said, "I told him the same thing. It's a happy marriage."

THIRTEEN

THERE WAS NO news from Boston over the weekend. I continued to ring Lizzie's cell phone—and continued to get her voice mail. Then, suddenly, on Sunday afternoon, somebody answered. "Yeah, waddya?"

It was a man of indeterminate age. He didn't sound sober.

"I would like to speak to Lizzie Buchan, please," I said.

"Who the fuck is this?"

"This is her mother. Who are you?"

"That doesn't matter."

"Where's my daughter?"

"Fuck should I know?"

"Do you have her?"

"That's a good one."

"Are you holding her somewhere?"

"Are you crazy, lady?"

"Where is she?"

"Hey, stop yelling."

"Where is she?" I yelled. "What have you done with her?"

"You're gaga. I've done nothing . . ."

"Then why do you have her phone?"

"Found it."

"Where?"

"On the street."

"Where on the street?"

"Boston."

"Where in Boston?"

"Lady, what's with the third degree?"

"My daughter's gone missing. This is her phone."

"And I found the phone in the Gardens."

"The Public Gardens?"

"You got it."

"And did you see a woman around twenty-five, shortish brown hair, medium build . . ."

"Lady, I just found the phone. Okay?"

The line went dead. I hit redial but was connected with a busy signal. Immediately I phoned Detective Leary's cell phone, apologizing for calling him on a Saturday. When I explained what had just happened, he said, "Give me a couple of minutes. I'm going to check in with the team."

He called me back an hour later to say that the call had been traced to a guy who lived rough in the Boston Public Garden. He'd been picked up by a squad car and was already swearing up and down that he'd simply found Lizzie's cell phone discarded close to where he'd been sleeping.

"If this checks out, we might get lucky and find her also using the Gardens as a dormitory. Our people are doing a sweep of the place as we speak."

But the sweep turned up nothing, and the man they picked up was well known to the local cops. He was also considered pretty harmless, as he was ripped most of the time.

"We showed Lizzie's photo to everybody crashing in the Gardens," Leary told me. "No one made her . . . but the fact that her phone was recovered today means that she might have been in the vicinity during the last day or two. That's not definitive, but I'd bet good money that she dropped the phone less than twenty-four hours ago in the Gardens. This deadbeat swears he found it under a park bench . . . and as much as I'd like to nail the son of a bitch, I think he's telling the truth."

The next morning, the phone rang at eight a.m. I grabbed it. It was Detective Leary.

"We caught somebody using Lizzie's bank card," he said.

This stopped me short.

"Who was he?" I asked.

"Actually, it was a woman—another street person. The cops who work the Common know her well. They found her withdrawing two hundred dollars on Lizzie's card at an ATM near the Haymarket T station."

"How did she get the card?"

"I've just come out of an hour-long interview with her—and she keeps swearing that Lizzie gave it to her . . ."

"You're kidding me."

"I wish I was. According to this woman, Lizzie was sleeping rough next to her on the Common for the last two nights—and when she complained of having nothing to eat, she alleges that your daughter gave her the cash card and even wrote down the PIN number for her. The thing is, the woman showed me the piece of paper on which Lizzie supposedly scribbled the PIN number. We had it matched with a sample of her handwriting we had in our file. It checks out."

"Maybe she coerced her out of it."

"That thought crossed my mind too, until a woman named Josiane Thierry—I'm sure I'm pronouncing it wrong—anyway, this French tourist got approached by a woman this morning whose description very much matched Lizzie, near South Station. She said that this woman—who looked pretty dirty and haggard—came up to her, and when she discovered that she was French, she started speaking to her in her native tongue. Lizzie does speak pretty good French, doesn't she?"

"She spent a year studying there."

"Well, this Thierry woman was certainly impressed with her French, especially as it came from someone she described to our translator as . . . what was the word again? A *clocharde* . . . that's French for . . ."

"A vagrant, a tramp."

"That's it, I'm afraid. Anyway, she said this woman was pretty incoherent—and simply handed her a wallet and told her she could have everything in it. Before the French woman could say anything, she ducked into the subway station and disappeared. Anyway, the French woman was a good citizen and brought the wallet to the nearest police station. Every precinct in town has been flashed Lizzie's picture—they all know she's the big missing persons case right now. And the sergeant behind the desk took one look at the driver's license in the wallet and called me."

I fell silent, trying to take all this in.

"You still there, Mrs. Buchan?"

"Just about."

"I know this is pretty difficult stuff, but at least we have verifiable proof that Lizzie is alive, and was in Boston this morning."

"Yes, but if she's giving everything away . . . couldn't that mean she's decided to kill herself?"

"I won't say that's beyond the realm of possibility. But why give away her cards and money before doing it? We do know from her work colleagues that she is impulsively generous. But the fact that she's been sleeping rough for a while . . . we can verify at least two days . . . and seems to have been in a very preoccupied, absent state, according to the Frenchwoman, convinces me that she's suffered some sort of breakdown. Does this mean that she's a candidate to kill herself? Perhaps. But what I know about this sort of depressed dementia is that she probably doesn't understand exactly what she's doing right now . . . which makes her do wayward things like crashing in Boston Common when her apartment is only a mile away, or giving her card and PIN number to that drunk."

I tried to imagine my Lizzie among the sad, cast-off souls who haunted the public parks. And I was worried now about what she was doing for money. Oh, Lizzie, just get to a phone, give me a call, and let us rescue you.

"There is something else you should know," Detective Leary said.

"More bad news?"

"I'm afraid so. Much as I've tried to hold them off—and I gather your lawyer son has been working this angle too—I'm afraid that I just got a call from the reporter working the case for *The Boston Herald*. His name is Joe O'Toole, and his editor doesn't want him to sit on the Lizzie story any longer. So they're planning to run it tomorrow—and you should expect a call from him in the next hour. When he called me to see if there were any further developments, he said that he'd be wanting a comment from either yourself or Dr. Buchan. I asked him to let me tell you that he'd be calling . . ."

"Say I refuse to answer his questions."

"That's your prerogative. However, in my experience, I think it's always best to work with the press, especially since, in this case, the fact that they'll be publishing Lizzie's photograph means that somebody might see her on the street. So the *Herald* guy does have his uses . . ."

After the call I went downstairs to the basement, where Dan had his entire vintage watch collection laid out on his desk. He was polishing each timepiece—a minor domestic chore that he was using as a way of coping with the uncopable.

"That was Detective Leary," I said, and went on to recap what he'd just told me. Dan put his polishing cloth down and stared blankly at the flat oak veneer of his desk. All he said when I explained that a *Herald* journalist would be calling shortly was, "Would you mind talking to him? I've got to get to the hospital this afternoon."

"Well, I don't want to speak to him either."

"Just answer his questions as best you can."

"Dan, I really wish you'd deal with this."

He looked away from me and said, "I don't think I can handle it."

"Okay," I said. "I'll take the call."

Joe O'Toole rang around half an hour later. I was expecting some fast-talking hack—maybe I've seen too many movies—but he turned out to be a slightly hesitant man who, despite the halting conversational style, still managed to be frighteningly direct. He didn't commiserate with me, nor offer any solace regarding Lizzie's absence. Instead, his first question to me was, "Do you think this is the first time your daughter had an affair with a married man?"

I felt a stab of panic, but told myself that I should simply try to answer his questions directly.

"Yes, I do think that."

"Um . . . how can you be certain?"

"Because she was always very open with me about her private life."

"You were good friends, then?"

"Very."

"So you knew that she was reprimanded last year by her employers when she stalked a partner in an associate bank?"

"I don't know what you're talking about," I said, and I was sure I sounded scared.

"The gentleman's name was Kleinsdorf. Your daughter was setting up some financing deal with him. They had a brief fling—and when he ended it after around a month, she phoned him day and night, and even showed up twice at his office in New York."

"I didn't know . . ."

"But you . . . um . . . said that she . . . um . . . was very open with you about her private life."

I chose my words with great care.

"My daughter obviously has some very major problems."

"Do you . . . um . . . blame yourself for these problems?"

"Are you a parent, Mr. O'Toole?"

"Yes."

"Well, then you know that all parents feel a certain degree of guilt if their child has psychological difficulties. Lizzie was raised in a relatively stable, happy family. But depression is a malady—and that is what my daughter is suffering from: an illness that has caused her to act obsessively and . . ."

"Terminate a pregnancy?"

"That was a decision she made with Dr. McQueen . . ."

"According to McQueen, the only reason he encouraged her to have an abortion was because he felt she wasn't psychologically stable enough to . . . um . . . 'withstand the demands of motherhood' . . . and that's a direct quote . . ."

"That's a complete lie. McQueen didn't want to leave his wife and children. That's why he coerced her into having the abortion."

"Oh, so you think coercion was involved?" he asked.

This was going very, very wrong.

"I think my daughter terminated the pregnancy because McQueen asked her to . . . with the promise that they'd have a baby together after his divorce."

"Your daughter told you that?"

"I'm just surmising . . ." I heard myself saying.

"I see . . ."

"But I know that Lizzie so wanted to have children that she'd never *just* terminate a pregnancy . . ."

"But under these circumstances, do you approve of your daughter having an abortion?"

"If it was the right decision for her at the time—and if it was one she made free of outside pressure—then yes, I approve."

"Still, she never explained to you why she was terminating the pregnancy?"

"I only found out about the abortion after her disappearance."

"So she did . . . um . . . keep a lot of secrets from you."

"Only since she became so ill."

He went silent for a moment or two. I could hear him scribbling away on a pad, transcribing my words. I dreaded to think how they'd be manipulated.

"Well . . . um . . . thank you for your time, Mrs. Buchan. If I have any further questions I'll get back to you."

I wanted to say, "Please don't do her any harm . . ." But I stopped myself from making such a plea—knowing it could be taken down and used against us. Anyway, before I even had a chance to answer, O'Toole had hung up.

Panic, panic, and more panic. I wanted to pick up the phone and tell Dan how badly I'd responded to O'Toole's questions, how he'd caught me completely off guard, and how I wished that my husband hadn't passed the buck by asking me to handle the interview. But before that, I needed to attempt a little damage control. So I phoned Leary back on his cell phone and told him just how disastrously the interview had gone.

"I don't want to sound callous," he said, "but like I said earlier, in a missing persons case, the more sensational the story, the better chance we'll have of getting someone to spot the person who's vanished . . ."

"But say Lizzie really goes off the deep end when she reads this?"

"*If* she reads this. The fact is, given her abnormal behavior so far, she's probably not paying much attention to the media. That's just a supposition, of course."

"From the way he questioned me, I'm pretty damn certain that O'Toole is going to completely twist the story to paint Lizzie as a harridan."

"I'm sympathetic, but despite the efforts of some of our finer Republican politicians, we still have a free press in this country, and there's not a damn thing I can do about what O'Toole writes. More to the point, if I get on the blower and ask him how he's angling the story, he could go to his editor, who could go to my boss and have me drawn and quartered for trying to influence the press. So let's hope the article has the desired effect and Lizzie is found quickly and the media loses immediate interest and everything blows over."

I so wanted to believe this—although I doubted things would turn out this way.

"Your son is coming to see me tomorrow," Leary said. "He's not going to be pleased with the abortion stuff, is he?"

"How did you know that?"

"I'm a detective. And I know how to Google someone. Jeffrey Buchan—chairman of the Connecticut Pro-Life Coalition, leading light in the local Evangelical Free Church, father of two, married to the former Shannon Moran, co-chairperson of the Connecticut Pro-Life Coalition and someone who was arrested and released without charge last year during a march on an abortion clinic in New London."

"I never knew that."

"It only made the local Connecticut papers—and it was a pretty small item."

Still, Jeff should have said something. I knew so little about my children, whom I thought I knew so well.

"Anyway, I don't want to interfere in a family matter, but if it would be easier for you, I'm happy to call your son up now and let him know the *Herald* is running the story tomorrow."

"I would appreciate that."

"Consider it done, then."

"Detective, one last thing: O'Toole told me about the other harassment case. You obviously knew about this."

"Yes."

"Then why didn't you tell me?"

"I figured you've been coping with enough difficult stuff recently . . ."

I went online after the call and emailed Margy:

> Hon:
>
> Are you around?
>
> H xxx

As soon as I sent the email, another one ricocheted back from Margy's server: an out-of-office reply informing all correspondents:

> I will be off hiding somewhere bucolic and rural this weekend and will only be returning to the office

on Tuesday morning. If it's an absolute emergency, call my assistant, Kate Shapiro, at (212) 555-0264.

It was an absolute emergency, but I still couldn't bring myself to hunt down her assistant and then have her disrupt Margy's weekend away from work, chemo, and all the attendant traumas of lung cancer. Part of me wanted to call a local friend—like Alice Armstrong—and tell her the entire goddamn saga and cry on her shoulder. But though I was desperate to talk about it, another part of me simply wanted to flee—to avoid all the conversations and problems and pressures that I knew would arise as soon as the story hit tomorrow's papers. So I got up and scribbled a note to Dan saying I'd taken myself off for the afternoon and would probably be back in the early evening. Then, placing my cell phone on the kitchen counter (I wanted a few hours where I was completely out of contact), I picked up my car keys and the Sunday *New York Times* from the kitchen counter, left the house, pulled my vehicle out of the driveway, and pointed it north.

An hour later—courtesy of the coastal interstate and assorted back roads—I pulled into the parking lot for Popham Beach State Park. It was around three p.m.—and as it was a wintry day in mid-April, there were only two other cars in the big lot. I turned the collar of my jacket up against the cold and walked down the path to the beach, the sand crunching under my hiking boots. The sky was the color of light cigarette ash—a small patch of blue peering out from behind the dome of clouds. But I didn't mind the overcast gloom. Popham Beach—three uninterrupted miles of sand fronting the Atlantic—was mine. I was alone, and I had two and a half hours of daylight left for a long, mind-emptying ramble. The tide was out and, thanks to the low temperatures, the sand was hard enough to walk right down by the water's edge. So I turned left and started heading northeast. The air was tangy with salt, there was a breeze at my back, the horizon, though dark, seemed limitless. Mom always used to say that water was the best psychiatrist going. Whenever she was depressed or simply suffering from the everyday blues (which, in Mom's case, was, at best, a thrice-weekly event), she'd take herself down to the banks of Lake Champlain and stare out at its watery expanse until she felt calmer. I remember one Christmas Eve, a few years ago, she got into one of her black moods while chopping onions for the turkey stuffing. I'd arrived the day before. Dan was due that evening. Ditto our kids, and Dad was off hiding in his office on campus—so Mom and I were alone in the house. Suddenly her chopping became manic—and increased at such a staccato rate that I said, "Hey, take it easy there."

Without warning, she shoved the chopping board off the kitchen counter. The diced onion went everywhere.

"Don't you fucking tell me to take it easy. Don't you—"

She broke off and stiffened, then seemed to have a moment of mental absence accompanied by a rapid twitching of the head. It only lasted a couple of seconds, and when it ended, it took her a moment or two to figure out where she was. The episode over, she looked at me like someone still reeling from an out-of-nowhere slap and said, "What did I just say?"

"It doesn't matter, Mom. You okay?"

"There are onions on the floor."

"Don't worry, I'll clean them up."

She nodded and left the room. When she came back a few minutes later, she had her overcoat and hat on.

"I'm going down to the lake," she said. "Want to come too?"

We got into my car and negotiated the icy gray streets.

"Remember when we used to have proper winters in Vermont?" she asked quietly. "Now the snow's so damn sporadic that we just have four months of cold, overcast gloom."

"You sound like a character in a Russian novel."

"I *am* Russian," she said crossly. "And in Russian novels, there is always fucking snow."

I smiled, relieved to hear Mom back to her old cranky self. We drove down to a small beach right on the lake, parked the car, and walked onto the narrow strip of sand. Mom immediately sat down, clasped her knees to her chest, and looked out at the Adirondack skyline way across the lake in New York State. Though her hair was completely gray and she needed heavy prescription lenses to see the world, her posture on the beach was that of a young girl, staring out at the water, wondering what the future would bring her. Until she said, "You know what I regret most in my life? The fact that I don't do happy."

"Does anybody?" I asked.

"Yeah, I think there are a lot of people out there who are reasonably content. Or, at least, I want to think that. Because I've never been content, never been—"

She broke off again, losing the train of thought, blinking into the thin winter sunlight covering the lake. Three months later, she was diagnosed with Alzheimer's—and she began the long, slow descent into silence.

I don't do happy.

Staring out at the Atlantic from the prospect of a sand dune on Popham Beach, Mom's words came back to me—and I couldn't help but think that I don't really do happy either. It's not that I'm discontented with everything . . . it's just that I've never really felt that ongoing exhilaration that you hope will accompany life. Oh, there have been moments of pleasure, of fun, of a sense that everything is just fine. But these have been largely occasional; episodic flashes amid the day-to-day stuff that constitutes a life. And no, I'm not a gloom merchant who thinks she's had an unhappy life. But still . . . the idea of waking up enthused, of battling against all the everyday stuff, and seeing the little time you have here as a great adventure . . .

No, that's not exactly been me. All right, I've maintained a certain curiosity, I try to remain optimistic, but . . .

I don't do happy.

Does Dan? He never seems cheerless, but he also never comes across as greatly enthused. It's just not his thing. He keeps it all so *level,* so controlled. He doesn't do happy either.

And Jeff? The angry man, always railing against whatever doesn't fit with his rigid point of view, so insanely concerned with appearing to be the Great Husband and Father, Mr. Family Values, Mr. Corporate America. *Does he do happy?*

And then there's Lizzie—my poor lost girl who once seemed to be in such splendid control of her life, so determined to avoid all the pitfalls that land so many people in professional and personal culs-de-sac from which it is very difficult to escape.

And now . . .

Oh God, here we go again.

I felt the tears sting my eyes and tried to tell myself it was a reaction to the salty air. I forced myself to keep walking, to raise my eyes above the sand and keep them focused on the ceaseless roll of the Atlantic. So much for emptying my head of everything that was tearing me apart right now. But how could I really expect to void all thoughts of Lizzie at a moment of such desperate uncertainty, when I didn't know if she was alive or dead or sleeping in some gutter or . . .

I kept walking, pushing myself up the beach, past the shuttered summer cottages, and the great colonial revival homes that defined the farthest corner of Popham, keeping up a brisk pace until I reached that point where I was directly opposite an imposing lighthouse, several hundred yards out to sea. I checked my watch. Four-forty p.m. Time to hightail it back to the parking lot.

Thanks to my pressing concern about getting off the beach, the sense of being besieged by grief lifted for a little while—and for the first time since this nightmare began, I could exist in the moment without the crushing weight of Lizzie's disappearance impinging on my every thought.

I reached the car just as night fell. A low fog was rolling in off the sea, so I had to peer over my headlights as I drove slowly back to the interstate. By the time I reached I-295, it was well after six. But instead of heading home, I decided to turn north, driving another thirty minutes up the coast to Wiscasset—one of those postcard-perfect New England towns of white clapboard churches and sea captains' houses with widow's walks. It was packed in the summer with tourists and blessedly empty at this time of year. But there was a small restaurant on the main street, which I gambled on being open. I won the wager—and basically had the place to myself. The waiter gave me a booth, leaving me plenty of space to spread out the endless sections of the Sunday *New York Times* while I ate clam chowder and scrod, drank two glasses of sauvignon blanc, and quietly reveled in this time by myself and the simple pleasure of lingering over food and newsprint for a couple of hours.

By the time I got back to Falmouth, it was after nine. As I approached the Bucknam Road exit, I was tempted to keep on driving. I didn't want to go home, didn't want to tell Dan about the bad interview, didn't want to hear bad news from Detective Leary. I just wanted to stay on this road.

But there was already one runaway in this family—and I knew that, like it or not, unpleasant stuff must always be faced (the old New England sensibility always kicks in). So I made the turnoff and pulled into our driveway ten minutes later.

The lights were off downstairs, but I could hear the bedroom television. I went upstairs. Dan was already in bed, watching some History Channel documentary on Stalin. Why do so many middle-aged men have such an addiction to the History Channel? It wasn't, I felt, a thirst for knowledge—rather, a need for some sort of visceral experience beyond their own day-to-day grind. Dan looked up as I entered, raised the remote control, and lowered the volume.

"So where did you disappear to?" he asked quietly.

I told him.

"Sounds nice," he said, turning his attention back to the screen. "We had a couple of calls while you were out."

"Detective Leary?"

He shook his head. "Just your dad, wanting an update, and Jeff, sounding pretty damn upset that the *Herald*'s running the story tomorrow."

"He certainly won't be pleased with what they reveal about his sister."

Dan said nothing. He kept looking at the screen.

"And I'm a bit worried that the stuff I said to the journalist might be taken out of context."

He still didn't look over at me.

"I'm sure it won't be too bad."

"I really didn't like the way the interview went."

"Did he ask some tough questions?"

"Yes, he did."

"Well, if you answered them reasonably . . ."

"That's not the point, Dan. The guy's a tabloid journalist—he's going to sensationalize everything. And the way he was questioning me, I'm pretty damn sure he's going to twist everything to . . ."

"Well, if you knew the guy was a tabloid hack, why didn't you exercise a little caution?"

"Are you kidding me?" I said, trying to keep my anger in check. His eyes remained fixed on black-and-white footage of assorted Russian gulags.

"I'm just saying . . ."

"Do you have amnesia?" I asked.

"What is that supposed to mean?"

"You asked me to handle the interview, remember?"

"Yeah, but don't go getting angry at me because it all went wrong."

"Oh, thanks a lot . . ."

"Hey, lose the tone."

"I will not lose the tone—and I'd really appreciate it if you'd look at me while we're having an argument."

He clicked off the television, pulled down the covers, and got out of bed, grabbing the robe that he'd left on a nearby chair.

"You're the one having the argument here, not me."

"Don't try to play your usual passive-aggressive games."

He stopped and looked at me coldly, but his voice was dry, unemotional.

"Passive-aggressive? Since when did you start talking in psychobabble?"

"See? You're doing it right now!"

He walked toward the door. I said, "I'm not going to let you just leave without . . ."

"Well, I'm not fighting with you over nothing."

"What is going on right now is hardly *nothing*. Our daughter is missing."

"And you are understandably distraught. And I am going to cut you a wide berth and sleep downstairs. Good night."

He shut the door behind him. My first instinct was to chase after him and demand a confrontation. But I was so infuriated by his pass-the-buck comments—and his usual cunning avoidance of a showdown—that I forced myself to stay put, knowing that all the fear and sorrow I was feeling right now might come out in a vindictive deluge. And there was a big part of me that always worried what might happen between Dan and myself if I ever told him what I really thought about everything to do with us.

So I couldn't face Dan right now. Just as I couldn't face a phone conversation with Jeff (anyway, Shannon complained if I ever called after nine). And I frankly didn't want to try to calm Dad's anxieties when I couldn't calm my own. All I wanted to do was sleep.

But sleep was elusive. I woke twice during the night, and didn't dare take a second sleeping pill for fear of being groggy in the morning—something my students would see and mock. By six, I gave up, tossed aside the book I was reading, and started getting ready for the day.

When I came downstairs twenty minutes later, I saw that Dan's car was gone from the driveway. There was no note saying he'd headed off earlier—and I was surprised that I didn't hear him pull out during the last two hours of this *nuit blanche*. Maybe he'd driven off during one of my dozy moments. My stomach was tense. I hated fights that ended inconclusively, without some sort of détente. Just as I hated myself for rising to combat last night.

I picked up the phone and punched in his number. No answer—just his voice mail. That was strange, him forgetting to turn on his phone, especially given that the hospital always needs to have access to him. No doubt, the stress was making him neglectful too.

I grabbed my gym bag and briefcase and left the house. The sky was still black, a sharp chill to the air. I drove into downtown Portland and parked in front of the gym. Even though there is an excellent gym at the Woodlands Golf Club, where Dan is a member, I've never really been able to stomach the country club atmosphere of the place. When the kids were still at home, I couldn't really stand all the soccer moms who used the gym there . . . largely because they always looked down on me for not being a stay-at-home type like themselves. So I found this basic, utilitarian gym in the business district a few years ago—and I try to work out at least four times a week. It's a regimen that I find boring but effective when it comes to keeping the weight off and telling yourself that you are stalling the ravages of time—as Margy once noted after we both turned fifty, "From now on, it's all about damage control."

Today, however, my half hour on the StairMaster—followed by another twenty minutes with light free weights—was all about trying to dampen down the effects of insomnia and stress. But as I climbed more than a hundred floors on the dreaded machine, all I could think was,

How can you engage in something so banal and self-serving while your daughter is still missing?

I knew that my overriding feeling of helplessness stemmed from the fact that, without scouring every park and flophouse in Boston, there was nothing more I could do in the hunt for Lizzie. And in the middle of the endorphin rush that followed the workout, I also resolved not to read *The Boston Herald* until the end of the working day. After all, bad news doesn't have to be ingested immediately.

So, on my way to the school, I pulled over to a 7-Eleven and bought that dreaded tabloid, refusing to look at the front page and immediately folding it in half and tucking it into my briefcase. I got back in my car and drove over to the school. It was now seven-thirty. I had just over an hour until my first class. There wasn't much accumulated mail in my box, but the expected FedEx package from Margy was there. I picked it up and retreated to my little cubicle of an office. I shut the door, took off my coat, sat down behind the metal desk, and opened the package. Inside was a hardcover book, around three hundred pages in length. There was a Post-it from Margy attached to its front cover, with a simple message: *Read chapter 4, then call me.*

I removed the Post-it and found myself staring at the title:

I Ain't A-Marching Anymore: Memoirs of a Reformed Radical

Below this was the cover illustration, a split image. On one side was a photograph of the then long-haired author, aged twenty-two, hectoring a crowd of fellow long-haired radicals while somebody burned an American flag in the background. The other side showed the author, now in his fifties, with horn-rimmed glasses and thinning hair, dressed in a sober suit and tie—shaking hands in the Oval Office with a certain George W. Bush. I don't know which version of Tobias Judson appalled me more.

I fought the urge for a cigarette. I lost. I stood up and opened the window behind me all the way. Then, sticking my head outside, I plugged a Marlboro Light in my mouth and lit up. I smoked it quickly, hoping that a backwind didn't send its fumes into my office (smoking on school property is a serious offense, especially for staff members).

When I had sucked the cigarette right down to its filter, I stubbed it out on the windowsill and tossed it into a drain conveniently located in the ground below.

I retreated back into the room. I shut the window. I sat down again at my desk. I breathed deeply—my head buzzing with the first nicotine jolt of the day. It gave me just enough chemically induced courage to pull the book toward me again. Once again, I started nervously tapping its cover.

Come on, get it over with.

I picked it up, opened it to chapter 4, and started to read.

FOURTEEN

Chapter 4

Love on the Run

When the phone call came, I was sitting on the floor of my apartment with George "the Lynx" Jefferson—the Chicago-area "Information Secretary" for the Black Panthers. It was around ten a.m. George had stopped by for an early-morning rap, but back then, after the usual coffee and Danish, no day could begin among comrades without a little taste of the old bong. So we sat cross-legged on the floor, listening to Ornette Coleman's weird jazzy syncopations while George filled the bong with Panama Red—some of the best grass on the market back then. We were discussing recent "Pig Activity" in the Chicago area—how the cops had just busted Brother Ahmal Mingus for attempting to sabotage all U.S. mail leaving the Chicago-area FBI headquarters—when the phone snapped into life. I exhaled a lungful of Panama Red and answered it.

"Yo," I said.

"That Groucho?" the voice on the other end asked.

"Hey, if I was Harpo, I wouldn't be talking," I said.

"Jack Daniels here. How about picking up a newspaper for me? But come prepared."

Within moments, I had grabbed my coat and was out the door. "Groucho," you see, was my code name in the Weather Underground, because I had always been their most outspoken advocate of Marxist economics. "Hey, if I was Harpo" was the coded exchange I always used whenever "Jack Daniels"—the head of my Weatherman cell—called to verify that he was speaking with me. "And how about picking up a newspaper for me" meant only one thing—it was an order to walk to a public phone on the street, where I was to await a call that couldn't be tapped.

"But come prepared" was coded language for: pack a bag and be ready to split.

So I did as commanded: I threw some clothes in a backpack, grabbed the $300 in cash and false ID I kept hidden away for just a moment like this, and told George he too had to split right now. Without even looking around to see if I'd left the stove on or the fridge open, we both snuck out a back door, scanning the street to check if we were under pig surveillance. The coast clear, we gave each other the clenched revolutionary salute . . . and started walking in different directions.

The phone was just three streets away from the main gates of the University of Chicago—now, as then, the sort of institute of higher learning that embraces a Left Bank–style disdain for American values.

I reached it just as it started to ring.

"Groucho?" Jack Daniels asked.

"Hey, if I was Harpo . . ."

"Affirmative," he said. "I'll be fast. The Man is onto your roommates for the past couple of days."

"How on?"

"I'd say you should clear the area now."

"Are you talking about a hop and a skip?" I asked, code for jumping the border into Canada.

"Let's not go drastic yet, especially as they could be watching all such exit points. Why not hit the road for a while? Get lost somewhere quiet, out of the range of media attention. And when you've found a safe haven, call me on the secure line and let me know your whereabouts. Happy trails, Comrade."

What had happened was this: after the bombing of the Department of Defense by another Weatherman cell, Jack Daniels contacted me and said that, as the police and the FBI had thrown a virtual blockade around the city, I would have to let these comrades hide out with me until the heat was off. Now, thanks to my radical indoctrination, I didn't think once of questioning the idea of harboring two murderers—men who, through their violent, egocentric actions, had been responsible for the deaths of two upstanding citizens: Wendall Thomas III and Dwight Cassell, both African-Americans, both veterans of Korea, and both family men with five children between them. But did I think about the innocent death of these men, guarding a government department responsible for the security of our nation? To me—the great Marxist—they were simply collateral damage in the struggle for revolutionary change.

Now, however, the Man—better known as the Federal Bureau of Investigation—had worked out that the two bombers had stayed with yours truly in the aftermath of the attack, and I was wanted for aiding and abetting, a federal felony that carried a maximum sentence of twenty years. I had no choice but to get out of Dodge—and to do so right now. So, figuring they'd be watching all the bus stations and airports, I got on the Green Line out to Oak Park. Why Oak Park? Hey, it was Ernest Hemingway's birthplace and I also decided that the one place they wouldn't be looking for me would be out in the suburbs. I found a little motel on the edge of town and checked in.

Once night fell, I went out under cover of darkness and found a phone in the street. I called the operator and asked to make a station-to-station call to Burlington, Vermont. I chose station-to-station so no names would be used. She asked me to deposit $2.25 for three minutes. I held my breath and—even though this was years before I ever understood the real meaning of prayer or Christian witness—I said a little entreaty that James Windsor Longley would answer the phone.

James Windsor Longley (like so many people in this memoir, I am using a pseudonym to protect his real identity). Can you imagine a more patrician-sounding name? Then again, James Windsor Longley was just that: a true Boston Brahmin who, back in the sixties, went through something of a long-overdue adolescent rebellion when he discovered radical politics.

To describe James Windsor Longley as a mere radical really doesn't do him justice. He was that much tougher breed of revolutionary: the intellectual ideologue playing Johnny Reb against his class and all the privileges that his country had bestowed upon him.

I got to know Professor Longley as a fraternal fellow traveler in the antiwar movement. He was in his early fifties at the time—and he was a big draw at any rally or demonstration, because he cut such a curious figure: the aging preppy professor who nonetheless spoke the language of radical political change. The kids loved him. To them, he was their dad turned revolutionary. The women especially loved him. And like all the rest of us in the movement, he considered sexual conquest without consequence to be one of the rewards of espousing antiestablishment rhetoric (and I should point out here that, when it came to free love back then, I was as much of a vagabond as the next lefty. The difference between myself and James Windsor Longley at the time was a straightforward one: he was married).

Anyway, I looked upon James Windsor Longley as something of a mentor whose counsel I always sought whenever the heat got too hot. And boy, was I in one smoking kitchen right now. So I was hugely relieved when he answered. Without giving too much of the game away—I sensed that his phone was bugged too—I simply hinted that I was in need of a quiet place to lie low for a little while. He asked a few indirect questions—"Does this relate to recent news from Chicago?"—that made it clear he knew I might have been somehow involved in the recent Department of Defense bombing there. Then he hinted that coming north to his place in Burlington might not be the coolest of ideas, especially as he suspected that the feds were always keeping an eye on him.

But then he said, "You know my daughter, Alison [also a pseudonym], is living in Croydon, Maine [not its real name]. And I know her husband is out of town right now—so I'm sure she'd put you up for a day or two. From what I gather, it's pretty quiet in Croydon . . ."

And as nowhere in Maine was more than a few hours from the Canadian border, that definitely appealed to me too.

"Thanks, Comrade," I said after I took the number.

"Good luck" was his reply.

I made a call to Greyhound and found out that there was a bus heading east. Three days later—following an obscure Greyhound route through minor cities, and crashing every night in nowhere hotels—I was deposited in Bridgton, Maine.

It was around five in the evening. I went to the only phone booth in Bridgton and called the number that James Windsor Longley had given me. His daughter, Alison, answered on the second ring. She sounded pleasant, welcoming—until I spun her some jive about how I was bumming around the country, researching a book I might write about The Radical United States of America (hey, I was beyond arrogant back then), and how I needed a place to crash for a couple of days. She sounded hesitant—and told me she'd have to call her father and her husband first before saying yes. "What a square," I thought to myself—but said nothing. I needed to get off the road fast and hide out until I got further word from Jack Daniels about my next move.

Twenty very long minutes passed until the public phone started ringing. It was Alison.

"Okay," she said, "my dad said you're cool, and my husband's own father is dying, so he's out of town and has got other things on his mind. And quite frankly, it's pretty lonely here in this small town, so I could use the company."

Croydon was just seven miles from Bridgton. I found the one and only cab company in town and dropped five bucks on the ride. En route the driver asked me what I was doing in Croydon. "Visiting an old college friend" was my reply.

Alison told me that the house they were supposed to be living in had been damaged due to a burst pipe, so they were temporarily squatting in an apartment above the doctor's office. It wasn't hard to find. Croydon, Maine, was a one-street town, a blink-once-you-miss-it sort of place.

But I did more than just blink when Alison opened the door. Ever heard the French expression *coup de foudre*? It means "love at first sight"—and a proper *coup de foudre* hits you like a slap across the face. I looked at her, she looked at me, and although the only words we exchanged were awkward greetings, I could tell immediately that the attraction wasn't one-sided. It was very mutual.

Of course, I noted right away that she was holding a little baby in one arm. Not that I gave such detail a second thought. I was the Great Revolutionary—the advocate of free love. And from the moment our eyes locked, I knew that Alison and I were destined to become lovers. Because what I saw in her deep, sad gaze was longing—a longing to escape from the small-town dead end she'd found herself in.

The apartment was poky—three small rooms stuffed with furniture too big for its small dimensions. Alison apologized for the cramped conditions.

"Hey," I told her. "No need to go all bourgeois on me."

She laughed, then said, "That's the first time somebody's used a two-syllable word in my presence since we moved to this burg!"

We hit it off immediately. Within an hour we'd put away most of a bottle of wine and were sliding into a great spaghetti and meatballs dinner she'd made us. Her little son, Baby Jeff, played in his playpen while we ate, drank, and had a heavy conversation about things political and the meaning of life.

"I haven't talked about this sort of stuff since college," Alison admitted. "My husband is a good man, but he really isn't up to much in the big ideas department."

She touched the top of my hand as she said that—and looked at me longingly with her big liquid eyes. Even though I was totally attracted to her—and was of the immoral opinion back then that monogamy was for squares—a small part of me (the part, I think, that years later allowed me to be open to Jesus's love and guiding hand) stopped me from going any further. I could also sense that Alison was torn between desire and responsibility . . . and, this evening anyway, I decided that it was best to be prudent and not take things any further. So she fixed up a few sofa cushions for me on the floor, helped me spread out my sleeping bag, and wished me a good night. What she didn't realize was, after three nights of nervy travel, her great warmth of spirit made me feel safe for the first time in days. I was no longer just a radical on the run. I was a man falling in love.

The next day, Alison showed me Croydon. Though I smugly thought to myself that this place was the original boring Mom's Apple Pie small burg, now I can see what a unique place it was—and how rooted Croydon was in the great American tradition of small-town communal spirit and strong family values. Alison worked in the library—a quaint, well-stocked place, filled with loads of local children learning an early love of books. And I also fell for the local diner and the great general store, where all the great local characters also met to discuss the affairs of the day. And after she finished work that afternoon, we picked up Baby Jeff from the lovely old lady who looked after him while Alison was at the library, and we drove over to one of New England's great natural wonders: Sebago Lake.

It was the perfect autumn day—and the Maine foliage was putting on the best show imaginable. We rented a canoe and—with Baby Jeff held tightly in Alison's arms—I paddled us out in the middle of the lake. Had

I known God then, I would have realized that He was shining His light upon us and hinting that, in such a beautiful, bountiful world as our own, we must not overstep that big moral border we both so wanted to traverse.

"You know, Toby," Alison said to me when we were out in the middle of the lake, "Gerry is a very good husband: kind, decent, loyal. But—I hate to admit this—there's no charge between us, no passion, no intensity, no romance. And I'm still so young, so full of possibility. Surely there's something beyond all this."

There are times when you speak before thinking. This was one of them.

"Why don't you run off with me?" I said.

She blanched. "You mean that?"

"More than I've ever meant anything in my life," I said.

"But we've only known each other . . ."

"I know—less than twenty-four hours. And still—"

I broke off, finding it difficult to put into words what the heart was saying.

"Tell me . . ." she said. "Try."

"Certainty like this comes once in a lifetime," I said.

"That's beautiful," she said.

"That's the truth," I said.

"But I'm married."

"I know . . . Just as I know that the feeling I have right now is one that will never leave me."

"Oh, Toby . . ." she said quietly. "Why did you ever come into my life?"

"I'm sorry . . ."

"I'm not. And yet, life would have been so much easier if—"

Now it was her turn to break off and turn away from me.

"Tell me, my love," I said.

". . . if I hadn't set eyes on you and known immediately that you were the one I was meant to be with."

We said nothing for a long time thereafter. Alison rested her head against Baby Jeff's head. Then, after several minutes, she looked up at me and said, "I think you should leave tonight."

I was privately crushed by the news—just as I was also worried about where I could head next and avoid detection. But though I knew that, by leaving, I was putting my freedom in jeopardy, I suddenly did something totally unusual for me: I made a selfless decision and decided that if, by leaving, I would make things easier for Alison, then so be it . . . even though it meant walking away from the woman I loved.

I paddled us back to shore. We loaded Baby Jeff into the car and then drove off to Croydon in silence. We got there just after sunset. Upstairs, Alison bathed and fed Baby Jeff while I repacked my knapsack and phoned Greyhound in Bridgton to find out the next bus to . . .

Well, truth be told, I had no idea where I'd be going next.

While I was on the phone, Alison brought Jeff into the bedroom and put him to sleep in his crib. When she returned, I said, "There's a bus from Bridgton to Lewiston at eight p.m. I think I'll try to make that."

"But where will you go?" she asked.

"It doesn't matter. You're right: I have to go. I have to—"

I never got to finish that sentence, as we were suddenly in each other's arms, locked in the deepest, most passionate embrace. We couldn't keep our hands off each other—and within moments, we had stumbled into the bedroom.

Around an hour later, as we lay together naked, curled up in each other's arms, I couldn't help but think: I've had sex so many times with so many different women, but this was the first time I have truly made love. At the end of our bed, Baby Jeff slept soundly, oblivious to all that had happened right in front of him. Alison and I said nothing to each other. We just kept gazing into each other's eyes. Then, out of nowhere, the phone began to ring. Alison tensed and got up, throwing on a bathrobe. She went into the next room and answered it.

"You want to speak to whom?" I heard her asking, followed up by, "I'm sorry, but there's no Glenn Walker at this number . . . really, you must be mistaken . . ."

I was suddenly out of the bed, pulling on my jeans and saying, "That's for me."

Alison pulled the phone away from her ear, and looked at me with something approaching total shock—the sort of shock that comes with discovering that someone has totally betrayed your trust.

I took the phone from her. I immediately heard a voice I knew all too well on the other end.

"Groucho?"

"Hey, if I was Harpo . . ." I said. Alison's puzzlement deepened.

"Affirmative," Jack Daniels said. "And, as always, I'll be fast. Our friends seem to know that you are somewhere in New England—as some ticket guy at Greyhound in Albany saw your mug in the local rag, called our friends, and told them he remembers selling you a ticket to Maine just two days ago. So I'd suggest a hop and a skip tonight. Understood?"

"Affirmative," I said.

"Good. And our real friends up above will rendezvous with you in the town of Saint-Georges. I've been studying your whereabouts—and this is about a seven-hour drive from you . . . and, for them, the easiest place to meet you. Do you think you can get access to wheels?"

"Not tonight. But maybe tomorrow I can rent a car."

"Tomorrow might be pushing it. Talk to your hostess. And expect a call from me again in fifteen minutes."

The line went dead. I put down the phone. Alison came over to me and took me by both hands.

"Alison, my love . . ." I started to say, but the words became choked in my throat.

"You have to tell me," she said.

"I don't want to involve you . . ."

"I am already involved," she said, "because I love you."

"I never meant to hurt you."

"Toby, please, tell me the truth . . . no matter how horrible it is."

She led me over to the sofa. She sat me down. She looked deep into my eyes . . . and I told her everything. I spared no details. I made no excuses for myself. Just as I also explained that there was a split-second moment after Jack Daniels had told me to harbor the bombers that I came very close to telling him, "This is wrong. I can't do it."

"But," I explained to Alison, "if I had told him that, they might have killed me. Once you're in a Weatherman cell, you can't get out. And all betrayals may be punishable by death."

"Oh, my poor darling," Alison said. "What a terrible choice you had to make."

"And I now realize I made the wrong choice. And I really want to go to the authorities, give myself up. But I know if I do that, I am looking at twenty years in a federal penitentiary. Whereas if I make it across the border to Canada, I will have more leverage when it comes to bargaining with the FBI. I know that sounds cynical, but . . ."

"I understand. Because, as you know, my dad has been harassed by the feds for years. And if they get you on this side of the border, they will show you no mercy. So, yes, you must flee tonight."

"But how? I don't have a vehicle."

Without hesitation, she said, "I'll drive you."

"You can't do that," I said. "You'll be immediately implicated. If they caught us, you could go to jail. You'd be separated from Baby Jeff. I won't let you . . ."

"Do you have identification in the name of . . . what did that guy call you?"

"Glenn Walker. And yes, I have ID in that name."

"Well, if we leave now, we'll get to the border in a couple of hours, and they won't stop a man named Walker traveling with his wife and child."

"You're going to bring Baby Jeff?"

"He won't notice. And anyway, I can't leave him here."

"And say your husband calls while you're gone?"

"If I call him now, he won't ring me back tonight. It's not his style to check in a lot."

"I still can't let you . . ."

"I have to do it."

"But why?"

She gripped my hands tighter.

"Even though I abhor violence, especially directed against innocent civilians, I do so loathe this terrible war we are fighting in Southeast Asia. I've always stayed on the sidelines—out of fear, perhaps . . . or maybe my own inability to show commitment. But do you know what I have learned over the past twenty-four hours from you? The fact that deep, abiding love is the most important commitment there is. And as I know that you too were a nonviolent activist coerced into harboring violent men, I have to help you escape."

"I don't know what to say, Alison."

She leaned over and kissed me deeply.

"There is nothing to say, except: let's be ready to leave in a half hour."

I dashed back to the bedroom, had a quick shower, got dressed, and made the bed. Alison, meanwhile, threw some baby stuff—diapers, milk bottles, spare clothes, and pacifiers—into a small bag. She also dug out her passport and Baby Jeff's birth certificate as identification. The phone rang. She answered it and handed it to me. It was Jack Daniels.

"Groucho?"

"Hey, if I was Harpo . . ."

"Affirmative," he said. "What's the state of play?"

"I'm ready to hop, skip, and jump."

"With or without assistance?"

"With."

"Reluctant assistance?"

"On the contrary. Like father, like daughter . . ."

"Right on. Okay, here's the meeting point . . ."

He gave me specific directions where to meet my contact in the Quebec town of Saint-Georges, and reminded me that, if there was any trouble at the border and I was apprehended, I must not break the Weatherman code and collaborate.

"We will get heavy if that happens—and no matter where you are, we will find you."

For the first time ever, I suddenly saw through Jack Daniels's radical posturing, his right-on, workers-of-the-world-unite propaganda. He wasn't really into political activism for change. He was a gangster. And looking at Alison's brimming, nervous eyes—eyes that told me, "I will get you through this . . . even though it will kill me to let you go"—I suddenly realized that it was the love of a good woman that had made me change my way of seeing, that had swept away the revolutionary cobwebs and made me realize that there was more to life than the dangerous antiestablishment games I was playing.

But, for the moment, I had no choice but to make a run for the border. Alison called her husband, Gerry. They spoke for around five minutes. She hung up with a simple "Talk to you tomorrow." No terms of endearment, no dedication of love. This knowledge—that hers was a sterile marriage—gutted me. Because I knew that, in a few short hours, I would be forever separated from the woman whom I now knew had been put on earth for me.

When she hung up, she bit her lip and said, "If it wasn't for Baby Jeff, I'd vanish with you right now."

"If it wasn't for Baby Jeff," I said, "I wouldn't let you go."

We got in the car and set off in the dark. It was about five hours to the border. Baby Jeff slept soundly. Alison and I talked nonstop all the way north, telling each other the story of our respective lives, desperate to find out everything we could about each other before we parted.

We stopped just once for gas. Before we knew it, the miles had vanished behind us. We were at the town of Jackman, Maine. Up ahead was the frontier. We switched places and I drove us slowly past the U.S. Customs Post, holding my breath, expecting that, at any moment, a police car would pull out in front of us. But the road remained clear—and within moments, we had entered a narrow no-man's-land that separated the U.S. from Canada.

"Bonsoir," said the French-Canadian customs official. "What brings you to Quebec?"

"Visiting friends in Quebec City for the weekend," I said.

"You're traveling late," he said.

"Well, I just got off work and the baby sleeps best at night."

"Oh, boy, do I remember all that," he said. "Might I see some ID?"

I handed over my false passport. He scrutinized it for a moment or two, then asked me if I was bringing any food or drink into Canada. When I answered no, he handed me back my passport and said, "Mr. Walker, I hope you and your family have a pleasant weekend in Canada."

We drove off.

"You and your family," Alison said quietly after we cleared the border. "If only . . . if only."

Twenty minutes later, we were in the town of Saint-Georges. I followed Jack Daniels's instructions to a small closed gas station on the edge of town. When we pulled in, I saw another car parked there, its headlights off. I cut the engine and flashed my headlights twice. The other vehicle flashed me back with its light—the agreed sign. I turned to Alison and took her hand.

"It's time," I said.

"Take me—us—with you," she said.

"I can't," I said. "Because I will be on the run for months, maybe years . . ."

"That doesn't matter. We'll be together. That's all that counts."

"Alison, my love, every vessel in my heart wants to say yes, but my head tells me otherwise. Because this will be no life for you or Baby Jeff."

She started to weep, burying her head in my shoulder. We held on to each other, like fellow shipwrecks on a life raft in high seas. When her crying finally subsided, she gave me one long, deep kiss and whispered one word: "Go."

I reached behind me and touched Baby Jeff's sleeping head. I got out of the door and retrieved my knapsack from the trunk. I came back and looked at Alison for one last time.

"I'll never forget you, Tobias Judson," she said, her face wet with tears.

"I'll never forget you, Alison Longley," I whispered back.

Then I turned and started walking toward the parked vehicle in front of me. My years in exile were about to begin—years when my every move was haunted by the loss of Alison. Later on, after I had received the redemption of Our Lord, Jesus Christ, I was still shadowed by a sense of shame at having committed adultery with a married woman. And yet, what I now realize is that Alison's love put me on the road to fundamental personal and spiritual transformation. And I've never forgotten her—because how can you ever forget the person who changed your life?

FIFTEEN

I SLAMMED THE book shut and shoved it away from me with such force that it landed on the floor. I didn't retrieve it. Had somebody just beaten me around the ears, I would have felt less trauma than I did now. All I could do was sit rigid with shock.

It wasn't just his disgusting lies that so appalled me—the way he fabricated just about everything, bar the sex we had together. It was also the way he made me seem like a coconspirator, someone who willingly drove him across the border. And the way he turned our dumb little fling into a gooey romantic fiction . . . brimming with fabricated comments about Dan, about the state of our marriage back then. All right . . . I can't remember exactly, thirty years wipes out so much from memory . . . but I'm pretty sure I did talk about how thwarted I felt in Pelham, and maybe how I got married too young. But all that crap about having a *coup de foudre* with Toby Judson . . . my tears when I realized I'd never see him again. The son of a bitch coerced me into driving him to Canada. In fact, coerced is far too nice a verb. He blackmailed me, pure and simple. And now he was attempting to rewrite history for his own deceitful gain. But who would believe my version of the story against his? Especially as he was now the reformed radical who had embraced his great friend Jesus Christ and was such a zealous conservative that he was shown being glad-handed by George W. on the cover of his damn book. And according to his reconstruction of events, I was so smitten with him that I was willing to break the law to help my beloved. And then there was all the horrible stuff about my dad . . .

My cell phone started ringing. I glanced at my watch. It was around eight-twenty. My first class began in twenty-five minutes—and I wondered how I'd now be able to get through it without suddenly retching in front of all my students . . . who'd probably think it was way cool to see me barf: *Teach must've tied one on last night . . . and I thought she was some kinda stiff . . .*

The phone kept ringing. I answered it. Before I managed to speak, Margy said, "I've just seen the *Boston Herald* article. Oh shit, Hannah, I can't even imagine the worry . . ."

"I've just read that asshole's book," I said.

"Fuck him. Lizzie's more important. And after what that hack in the *Herald* wrote about you and Dan . . ."

"What did he say?"

"You mean, you haven't read it yet?"

"Couldn't bring myself to."

"Do you have a copy of the paper nearby?"

"I'm afraid so."

"Read it now."

"Is it that bad?"

"Read it."

"I don't want to."

"Hannah, you have to face up to . . ."

"Okay, okay," I said, reaching into my bag and retrieving the paper. "Do you want me to call you back?"

"I'll stay on the line. The story's on page three."

I opened the paper and felt like I'd just been kicked again in the stomach. The story took up *all* of page three. There was a horrible grainy photograph of Lizzie, taken at some Christmas party by an office colleague, that made her look vaguely deranged. Next to her was a sober professional head-and-shoulders shot of McQueen in a white doctor's coat. The headline read:

BOSTON WOMAN BANKER DISAPPEARS AFTER FAILED AFFAIR WITH LEADING BROOKLINE DOCTOR

The story was lurid in the extreme—Lizzie painted as this big-salaried mutual fund whiz (described as "very driven and very edgy" by one associate), living this über-yuppie lifestyle in a downtown loft (also described in loving designer detail), with a string of bad romances behind her (her stalking of that banker guy Kleinsdorf got considerable mention). McQueen, on the other hand, was described as "a pillar of the medical community" and "the dermatologist to the stars" who, though providing a credible alibi, "has not been completely ruled out of the investigation." Then the story detailed Lizzie's first encounter with McQueen on the bicycle trip—and how a brief fling soon escalated into what McQueen was quoted as calling "her major obsession."

She became my worst nightmare—phoning me day and night, showing up at my office, sleeping outside the front door of my house in her car. Then, out of nowhere, she informed me she was pregnant and wanted to have the baby. When I expressed concern at whether she could handle motherhood, given her emotional instability, she went nuts, screaming at me and vanishing for three days. When I next heard from her, she told me she'd terminated the pregnancy. I was shocked beyond belief.

Oh, you dirty little liar. Poor Lizzie's nowhere to be found, so you can say what you want—spin the story to make you look like the reasonable party here—and no one will refute what you say.

My eyes moved down to the next line.

According to Ms. Buchan's mother, Hannah, a teacher at the Nathaniel Hawthorne High School in Portland, Maine, "I think that my daughter only terminated the pregnancy because McQueen asked her to . . . with the promise that they'd have a baby together after his divorce."

But Dr. McQueen emphatically denies this charge, citing the fact that, for over ten years, he has been an active antiabortion campaigner as well as a senior medical adviser for the Archdiocese of Boston.

"I have confessed all to my wife, who has been far more understanding about all this than I deserve, just as I have asked for forgiveness from my church. As to the absurd idea that I would ever even think of condoning an abortion . . . it just shows the deranged state of mind that Ms. Buchan was in."

Hannah Buchan, however, states that she wasn't aware of her daughter's termination until after she went missing. But she condones her decision: "If it was the right decision for her at the time—and if it was one she made free of outside pressure—then yes, I approve."

Hannah Buchan also admits that, though her daughter's upbringing was "relatively stable," she still blames "parenting mistakes" for her daughter's disappearance, stating that, "All parents feel a certain degree of guilt if their child has psychological difficulties."

"Parenting mistakes"? I never said that. *Never.*

The rest of the article recounted the scene in the Four Seasons bar when Lizzie went ballistic, and how she had been spotted sleeping with the homeless since then. There was stuff about McQueen's TV show, and a quote from Detective Leary, talking about how the police were still hopeful of finding her in the Boston area, although he did admit that he wasn't dealing with someone of sound mind.

"She is not a danger to the public," he said, "but she is definitely a danger to herself."

Now the *Herald* followed that damn book onto the floor. I put my face in my hands, pressing my fingers hard against my eyes, wanting to black out the world. But then I heard Margy's voice on the cell phone.

"Hannah, hon, you still there?"

I picked up the phone.

"I'm afraid so," I said.

"You finished it?"

"I never said we were bad parents, and he also twisted the whole abortion quote way out of proportion. He makes Lizzie sound deranged."

"Hon, why didn't you call me days ago when she disappeared?"

"Because I figured that, having found something else on your lung, you had other stuff on your mind."

"Hannah, this is major stuff. And best friends are there for best friends during major stuff."

"Jeff is going to go ballistic when he reads that article. Dan too."

"Dan will understand. And Jeff will just have to lump it."

"Jeff never lumps anything. He takes everything so personally when it offends his moral worldview. But what's now completely scaring the crap out of me is the effect that the book is going to have when people figure out it's me."

"When did you read it?"

"Ten minutes ago."

"At least you haven't been sweating it for the last couple of days. But here's the thing: I'm pretty damn certain that the asshole's book is going to remain low on everybody's radar."

"How can you be so sure of that?"

"To begin with, it's being published by this second-rate right-wing press: Plymouth Rock Books. They make the John Birch Society look like a bunch of Ted Kennedy Democrats. They do have the muscle to get their books well publicized, but this piece of shit is so atrociously written—and so damn soppy, especially when it comes to Judson's personal relationship with Jesus Christ—that I don't think it will attract any public attention. And what about all the crap he wrote about you . . ."

"You don't believe any of that, do you?"

"What do you take me for? Like I was saying, what really offends me about his book—besides all the lies regarding your little fling—is his born-again bullshit. Take it from a Semite—there is nothing more appalling than a Jew for Jesus."

"Say it does go public . . . ?"

"Now I'm going to put on my professional PR hat and tell you that, from where I sit, this clown is very small potatoes. And I've come to this conclusion after running a background check on him. After Judson cut a deal with the Justice Department and returned to the U.S. in the late seventies—in exchange for turning state's witness on his former comrades—he spent around twenty years as a minor-league academic in a string of junior colleges around the Chicago area. He's been married for the last fifteen of them to a woman named Kitty, who has been a big *macher* in some 'No Smut on TV' family values pressure group. She's also from a serious Bible-thumping family in Oklahoma, which isn't exactly the most enlightened state in the union. God only knows how—or why—Judson hooked up with her. I found a photograph of her on his website . . ."

"He has a website?" I said, sounding appalled.

"Hon, every idiot has a website these days. You can find his at www.tobiasjudson.com. And besides learning all about Judson's redemption through Christ and his denunciation of his bad-boy past, you can also check out the family portrait gallery. They've got two kids—Missy and

Bobby, don't you love it?—who, to be politically correct about it, could be kindly described as circumferentially challenged. But the wife, well, excuse my lack of subtlety, but she's what's known in Brooklyn as 'a fat fuck.'

"Anyway, the thing is, Judson's been trying to climb out of his junior college prof purgatory for the last couple of years by shilling himself as a conservative commentator: the Talmudic Rush Limbaugh. Only recently he's started having a bit of minor-league success: a column in some freebie Lake Shore suburban rag and a gig on a small talk-radio station that mainly beams out to redneck Illinois. The book is his big play for national attention—which ain't going to happen, because (a) it's crap, and (b) it's crap without an angle . . . and if there's one great rule of American life, it's this: you can always sell crap as long as you've got an angle. Add this to the fact that he gave you and your dad a pseudonym, and also disguised the name of the town, and let's keep our fingers crossed that nobody's going to trace it back to you. I certainly wouldn't tell Dan or your dad about it. In fact, when it got passed my way, there was a part of me that didn't want to bring it to your attention."

"I had to know."

"That's what I figured you'd think—and that's why I sent it to you. But now, with a real nightmare staring you in the face, I wish I hadn't."

The school bell started to sound, signaling the first class of the day.

"I've got to go—but what do you think I should do about the article?"

"For the moment, you can't do anything until we see what kind of heat the story generates."

"But is it going to generate 'heat'?"

"Hon, I'll be blunt here. The media love nothing more than a story of illicit sex among the professional classes where the woman goes missing and there's a whiff of murder in the air, and if the chief suspect is a doctor with a TV show, they're going to be all over this in a heartbeat. Sorry . . ."

"No, it's what I figured too."

The bell sounded again.

"That's the last call."

"I'll get my people in the office to monitor how things break this morning. I'll call as soon as I hear anything."

"I can't believe I'm in the middle of all this."

"The *only* important consideration right now is Lizzie—and the hope that this might just flush her out, or that someone will spot her because of all the publicity."

"I suppose that's true . . ."

"Courage, hon. And remember: I'll be running damage control for you."

By noon that day—somehow having managed to make it through my classes on autopilot—I was in serious need of damage control. As soon as I turned on my cell phone at lunchtime, there were six messages. Dan: "Call me as soon as possible?" Margy: "Can you call me as soon as possible?" A reporter from *The Portland Press Herald* named Holmes: "Can you call me as soon as possible?" A reporter from *The Boston Globe:* "Can you call me as soon as possible?" A reporter from the local Fox News affiliate: "Can you call me as soon as possible?" And, finally, my son Jeff, sounding furious. "Mom, I'm in Boston with Detective Leary. He's just shown me the *Herald* article—and, quite frankly, I am appalled that you made that comment sanctioning Lizzie's decision to terminate her pregnancy. I've just spoken to Dad and decided to come to Portland tonight. I will see you then."

Oh God, this can't be happening . . .

The cell phone started ringing again. It was Dan. He sounded exceedingly tense.

"Hi, it's me. Has Jeff spoken to you?"

"Dan, hon, I was completely misquoted in that article. I promise you I never said we were bad parents. And that shit of a journalist completely twisted my words about Lizzie's abortion . . ."

"It doesn't matter now," he said flatly.

"What do you mean by that?"

"The damage is done."

"Dan, he took what I said and—"

"My office has been flooded with phone calls this morning—largely from news agencies and television stations, all asking for a quote, an interview. And there must be around fifteen messages on our home phone from the same damn journalists, all wanting to invade our lives and talk about our poor tragic, crazy daughter who may or may not have been murdered by her doctor lover, and whose foot-in-mouth mother condoned her abortion and also admitted that she was raised badly."

By the time he had reached the end of this sentence, Dan was sounding very angry. I said nothing for a moment, the phone shaking in my hand.

"Are you still there, Hannah?" he asked.

"I'm here—and I won't be scapegoated for this."

"Why the hell didn't you tell me about that abortion comment?"

"I tried, but you weren't interested . . ."

"Don't tell me you're playing that pass the blame game again . . ."

"'Again'? What you do mean, 'again'? I don't make a habit of passing the blame . . ."

"No, you just refuse to take responsibility for your actions."

"Like when?"

"Like now."

"Dan, I'll say it again: *I tried to tell you* that the interview went very wrong. You pooh-poohed it."

"Don't try to get out of it, Hannah."

"If you hadn't been such a damn coward and had handled the interview—"

"Fuck you," he said, and the line went dead.

I sat down at my desk, I put my head in my hands, I didn't know what to do next. The cell phone started ringing again.

"Mrs. Buchan, it's Rudy Warren here of the *National Enquirer* . . ."

"I have nothing to say at this time," I said, and closed the phone. Now my desk phone sprang into life. I answered it, immediately saying, "Can you call me later?"

"Uh, well, I was hoping to see you now, Hannah," said a voice I knew all too well. It was the headmaster, Mr. Andrews.

"Sorry, Mr. Andrews, I'm having a terrible morning."

"I can well imagine that you are. If it's a bad moment . . ."

"No, sir, I'm free."

"Well, would you mind dropping down to my office for a few moments, please?"

Carl Andrews was a man who made everyone feel uncomfortable. He was an ex-marine who quietly boasted about the fact that he ran a tight ship, and was known for having one of the strictest public schools in Maine. Adolescent insubordination was never tolerated—though it broke out regularly—and Andrews encouraged a distant relationship between himself and his staff. He was the commanding officer, we were the ground troops, and he made it known that he was "Mr. Andrews" or "Sir" to us. None of that cordial first-name collegiality in his school. Yet he was able to get away with such aloof protocol by being absolutely fair in his dealings with all of us and, in several instances, defending his staff.

I walked down the corridor to his office, hoping he'd show his customary fairness toward me. Because I certainly knew why he wanted to see me.

He was seated behind his big steel desk—his office decor was very simple, with an American flag in one corner, his Marine Corps discharge and U. Maine diplomas framed on the wall, and a photograph of him receiving Maine Educator of the Year from the governor a few years back. There was a copy of that morning's *Boston Herald* in front of him.

He greeted me with a nod and motioned for me to sit down.

"First, I just want to say how sorry I am about your daughter's disappearance. No matter how old the child may be, she's still your child, and the worry must be enormous. And I want you to know that you have the school's complete support during this very trying time. If you need to take a few days off . . ."

"That's very kind of you, sir," I said, "but I'd prefer to keep working."

"Understood," he said. "Now I must raise a couple of things with you. The first is media attention. The school has already received seven calls this morning from assorted journalists, asking for a comment about you, whether you're a good teacher and did we think you raised your kids well, since some of the TV and newspaper people had found out they went here. I've issued a statement—very simple, very straightforward—and am about to send out a memo to all staff, informing them that they are not to talk to the press and that they should inform Mrs. Ivens about any approaches from the media. Anyway, here's the statement."

He handed me a photocopied piece of Nathaniel Hawthorne School–headed notepaper, on which there was one neatly typed paragraph, in which Mr. Andrews said that I had been a teacher at this school for over fifteen years—"an esteemed member of our faculty"—and that the school was fully supporting me during this time of difficulty. He also stated that Jeff and Lizzie had been students at Nathaniel Hawthorne, where they distinguished themselves academically and were well known to be stable, well-reared children. In closing, he asked that both my privacy and that of the school's be respected—and that the school would not enter into a debate about the rights and wrongs of my statements regarding my daughter's private life.

"I think I'd better explain that final sentence," Carl Andrews said. "As you may know, we have several parents here who are devoutly religious. You probably remember Trisha Cooper, who tried to get us to stop teaching the theory of evolution in science class. I have no doubt that, once she reads about your support for your daughter's termination, she will organize a campaign against you. I'm not telling you this to scare you—rather, just so you know what you could be up against. Because there are at least two dozen Trisha Coopers who are parents in this school. As far as I'm concerned, they are perfectly entitled to hold their views, just as you are perfectly entitled to hold yours. But if they start telling me that I shouldn't be employing a teacher who doesn't toe their line on certain things, that's when I bring out the heavy artillery."

"Thank you, Mr. Andrews."

"May I give you a piece of advice, Hannah? No matter how much they badger you for an interview, just issue a simple statement and tell them you have no further comment. If you take their bait, they will definitely eat you alive."

Margy said the same thing when I spoke to her directly after this meeting. Something about Carl Andrews's reassurances—his resolve to protect me should certain Bible thumpers start calling for my head—calmed me down slightly. "Okay, here's the bad news," Margy said. "It's a slow time, mediawise, right now, so the news channels and the tabloid press will have decided that Lizzie's disappearance has all the right ingredients for a big story. Remember that pregnant housewife who vanished in California around a year ago—and her preppy husband kept denying he had anything to do with it, until her body was fished out of the drink and it turned out he'd been shtupping some real estate agent? Well, excuse my streetwise crudeness, but from what the people at the office have been telling me, the folks at Fox News and the *Enquirer* and

People and all those other bastions of free speech think that this story is picture perfect for a long run—especially since McQueen hired legal counsel this morning."

"Is he admitting that he . . . ?"

"Don't jump to the worst conclusions. It's just that, with all the accusations swirling around him right now, he figures he needs an attorney, and you know what? He's right."

"Good God . . ."

"According to the statement released by McQueen's lawyer, which I've just had emailed over to me at home . . ."

"Margy, you should be resting right now, not worrying about all this . . ."

"Fuck off," she said with a laugh. "As Uncle Sigmund Freud once said, 'Work is the closest thing to sanity,' especially when you're undergoing chemo."

"That's the second time this hour someone has told me to fuck off," I said, recounting Dan's blowup on the phone.

"He's understandably tense," Margy said. "And he probably feels guilty about passing the buck to you by making you do the interview . . ."

"No, he's looking for a scapegoat . . . and I'm it."

"If you want me to talk to him—"

"I can fight that battle myself . . . but thanks for offering. When it comes to the press, however . . ."

"I want you to go home and put a message on your voice mail saying that all press inquiries are being handled by Margy Sinclair Associates—and leave our New York phone number on the message. And I want you to screen all calls and *not* answer the phone if some journalist calls. Tell Dan to do the same thing—and get his secretary to send all interview requests to us. You guys just lie low and let us take the heat. And I'm going to email you over a prepared statement I've drafted on your behalf. What was the name of the shrink she was seeing in Boston?"

I gave her Dr. Thornton's number in Cambridge and said that I'd phone him right away and ask that he give Margy any assistance she needed.

"I'm also going to need to talk with the detective handling the case. Can you tell him I'm legit and in your corner?"

"Of course."

"The important thing here is that you try to remember one crucial thing about this entire shitty business," Margy said. "Once the press have worked out that neither you nor Dan will speak with them, they will back off. Hopefully, we'll be able to keep this thing as contained as possible."

By the end of the day, containment seemed a fantasy. When I arrived home from school, there was a Fox television crew on my doorstep. As soon as I stepped out of the car, a young aggressive woman shoved a microphone in my face while a cameraman pressed in close behind.

"Mrs. Buchan, any comment about your daughter's disappearance?"

Instinctually, I put my hand over my face and said, "I have nothing to say at this—"

The journalist cut me off.

"Do you believe that Dr. McQueen might have murdered her?"

"I have nothing to say . . ."

"And how many abortions before this one did you sanction?"

Without thinking, I shouted, "How fucking dare you . . ."

Then I shoved her out of my way. But she kept pursuing me, saying, "And is it true that you consider yourself a bad mother who . . ."

I turned back, yelling, "Leave me alone," then rushed toward the door, managing to slam it in her face just as she started asking if I knew that three of Lizzie's ex-boyfriends had just come forward to say that she stalked them. As soon as I was safely behind the door, the phone began to ring. I reached for the extension near the front door.

"Mrs. Buchan, it's Dan Buford from the *New York Post* . . ."

"Please call Margy Sinclair at Margy Sinclair Associates. She's—"

"But Margy told me it was okay for me to speak with you directly."

"She didn't say anything to me."

"Did you know that Dr. McQueen had to surrender his passport this afternoon and that they're currently dragging the Charles—"

"I hope that bastard gets whatever he deserves . . ."

"So you do think he's behind your daughter's disappearance?"

"Please call Margy Sinclair at—"

"Why have you hired a publicist, Mrs. Buchan? It's pretty unusual for a Maine schoolteacher, isn't it? Unless you have something to hide . . ."

I hung up. There was banging on the door. And shouting, "Mrs. Buchan . . . Hannah Buchan . . ."

I peered out of the blinds, only to find the same Fox cameraman with his lens up against the glass. I could feel my face contort before I slammed down the blind. Then my cell phone started ringing again.

"Will you please leave me alone!" I yelled into the receiver.

"It's Dad."

"Oh, Christ, I'm sorry, I'm . . ."

"I've just seen the *Herald* piece, and Margy just called to let me know that the press vultures are descending, and I could get a call or two . . ."

"It's been hideous here," I said, and brought him up to date on everything that had happened so far today.

"Don't worry about the abortion thing," he said. "There are a lot of people who will privately applaud you for taking that stance."

"Unfortunately, those people don't work for tabloid newspapers and their television counterparts."

"Your headmaster sounds like he's a good man."

"Yeah—ex-marines can occasionally surprise you. My husband, on the other hand . . ."

"Let him calm down a bit."

There was now more banging on the back door.

"Hannah Buchan . . . Hannah Buchan . . . Just a few questions . . ."

"I'm under siege here," I told my father.

"Margy told me not to answer any questions."

"Well, if this keeps up, I'm going into hiding . . ."

"No news from the detective?"

"One of the reporters told me they're dragging the Charles and that McQueen has had to give up his passport."

Even on the bad cell phone line, I could hear my father's sharp intake of breath.

"That means nothing," he finally said.

"Let us pray."

I hung up and moved to the kitchen, and looked at the answering machine. The message counter listed twenty-four voice mails. I fast forwarded through them—almost all from news media, with the exception of Alice Armstrong calling me to offer solidarity and say if there was anything she could do . . .

How about gathering up every attack dog in Portland and positioning them on my front lawn to keep the hacks away?

I rerecorded the message on our voice mail, informing all journalists to contact Margy Sinclair Associates . . .

Then I braved a call to Dan's office. His secretary answered.

"Oh, Hannah, God . . . what a business," she said. "We had a film crew here and I must have logged over twenty calls."

"Did Dan speak to any of the journalists?"

"He's been with patients all afternoon. And he's operating right now. Anyway, I got a call from a Margy Sinclair who said she's running interference for you . . ."

Bless Margy for her superefficiency.

"That's right," I said.

"She also said that the doctor shouldn't talk to the press."

"Correct. And when my husband gets out of surgery, would you also tell him that he shouldn't come home, as there's a television crew outside?"

From the kitchen window, I could see an NBC affiliate truck pull up.

"And tell him to call me as soon as he's free."

I knew that I had to flee the house but I realized that this would require a certain degree of subterfuge. So I called the local cab company and asked if they could send a taxi over to my home. I told the dispatcher that I wanted him to drive down an adjoining side street and wait for me in front of a large colonial house with the name Connolly on the mailbox.

"But you're Mrs. Buchan who lives at number eighty-eight Chamberlain," he said.

"That's right."

"So why can't I send my guy to your front door?"

"I'll explain that later."

"Okay, what time do you want him there?"

I glanced out the window at the encroaching darkness.

"Say, half an hour."

I hung up. I called the Hilton Garden Inn downtown and booked two rooms for the night, one in my name, the other in Jeff's. Then I rang Dan's secretary and asked her to tell "the doctor" that he should meet his wife at the Hilton Garden Inn—and that I'd explain all when I got there. After that, I took a deep breath and phoned my son on his cell phone. His tone was distant, punitive.

"I'm in a rented car, outside of Wells," he said, mentioning the town on the Maine/New Hampshire border. "I should be with you in around forty-five minutes."

"Well, I want you to meet me and your father downtown," I said, giving him the name of the hotel and explaining why he couldn't come to the house.

"How did this thing develop into a three-ring circus?" he asked angrily.

"Blame *The Boston Herald,* Jeff."

"Your comment about abortion certainly didn't aid things either."

I was about to get very angry but stopped myself and said, "We'll talk about all this later at the hotel."

Then I hung up.

I went upstairs and packed a bag with enough clothes for several nights. Then I went to my office and put my laptop computer into my travel bag. Margy rang just as I finished.

"You won't believe what's going on here," I said, glancing out the window. The ABC affiliate truck had also pulled up outside. "It's like there's a media feeding frenzy . . ."

"I know all about it—you were on Fox News around five minutes ago."

"But I refused to give them an interview," I said, sounding shocked.

"Yeah, they showed that."

Oh, God . . .

"Did they also show when I—"

"Told their reporter to fuck off? Of course they did. It's Fox News—they love messing up people's lives . . . though being oh-so family values, they censored the 'fuck.'"

"I looked demented, didn't I? Completely loony tunes."

"Don't sweat it."

"That means you thought I was a disaster."

"You looked frazzled and upset and pissed off at the press intrusion, but who gives a shit? Your child is missing—you have a right to feel and look disturbed."

I told her about my escape plan.

"Good idea. I'll call you in a couple of hours—to talk through some stuff. The phone's been hopping at the office all day."

"I don't like the sound of that."

"This is the worst part of the ordeal. In a couple of days, attention will move away from you and Dan completely. Good luck with the getaway."

I checked my watch. It was five-thirty p.m. I turned off all the lights, except one in the bedroom, hoisted my two bags, and went downstairs to our basement. Beyond Dan's playroom was a passage that led into an old apple cellar in the garden. We had renovated it, building a connecting passage from the house and installing lights so we could use it as a storage area. It was piled high with boxes and old bicycles—but it also contained the original doors that led out into the garden. When I reached it, I found the key for the inside lock on the shelf above the fuse box. The doors were directly overhead, and we kept a small stepladder handy for those rare occasions when we opened them. I climbed the ladder, undid the lock, and using all my weight, pushed open one of the doors. It landed with a thud on the outside ground. A blast of cold air hit me. I waited for a moment to see if the opened door attracted attention or if any of the journalists had been sleazy enough to stake out the garden. But as far as they were concerned, I was still upstairs in the lighted bedroom. So I climbed down off the ladder, turned off the storeroom lights, picked up my bags again, climbed back up the ladder, put them on the ground, then hoisted myself up. Once on terra firma, I shut the door, glancing around nervously to see if I could be spotted. I was in the clear. I lifted my bags and walked quickly into the trees at the rear of our acre of land. I threaded my way through this wooded outcropping, emerging at the back of a house owned by a couple named Bauer, with whom we had absolutely no contact, bar a Christmas card once a year. I was relieved to see that both cars were gone from their driveway and all lights in the home were off. I walked briskly past their outdoor swimming pool, negotiated the downhill curve of their lawn, and ended up in the cul-de-sac where they lived. Up ahead was the taxi. I walked over to it and knocked on the window. The driver got out, took my bags from me, and put them in the trunk. I climbed into the backseat. He slid behind the steering wheel, looked at me in the rearview mirror, and said, "Don't you live over on Chamberlain Drive?"

"I'm on the run."

"From all those television vans out in front of your place?"

"I'm afraid so."

"What did you do, kill someone?"

"No such luck," I said, thinking of Mark McQueen.

Twenty minutes later I was shown to my room at the Hilton Garden Inn. It was, as requested, of decent size, since I didn't know how long we might be camped out here. After I unpacked, there was a knock at the door. It was Jeff. I hadn't seen him in a few months, and tried to disguise my shock at his appearance. He'd struck me as a bit chunky over Christmas, but since then he'd piled on more weight and I couldn't help but think that he was looking ten years older than he should. As always, he seemed tense. Even if this hadn't been a desperately difficult time, Jeff would still have appeared stressed. Being under strain had become his natural state.

"Mom," he said quietly, kissing me on one cheek.

"Did you check in?" I asked.

"Yeah," he said, coming inside. "Where's Dad?"

"He'll be here soon."

"I just got a call from Shannon. She said she saw you on Fox News. She's pretty upset."

"Because her mother-in-law blew up at a reporter and used the f-word?"

"She said you looked crazy."

"An accurate description of how I feel."

"I don't know why you've allowed all this to escalate. And if you hadn't made that comment about Lizzie's termination . . ."

Once again, I tried to stop myself from getting angry. This time I failed.

"The only reason several television crews are parked outside my front door is because your poor sister has disappeared, and that creep of a minor celebrity doctor is under suspicion. For you to say that it's all to do with my comments about abortion . . ."

"All right, all right," he said. "I'm just a little wound up about all this."

"Well, join the club."

"And Shannon's gone ballistic since she read the *Herald* piece this afternoon. She's really furious at you, Mom."

"That's her prerogative."

"Yeah, but she's furious at me at the same time."

"And that's my fault?"

"Look, you know our feelings about the right to life of an unborn child . . ."

"I was asked a tricksy question by some hack journalist about whether I backed Lizzie's decision to terminate her pregnancy—and all I said was, 'If it was the right decision for her at the time—and if it was one she made free of outside pressure—then . . . yes, I approve.' Now what is so damn fiendish about that? You know—and I know—how much Lizzie loves children. As I said before, I am absolutely certain that McQueen sweet-talked her into having the abortion by promising her they'd have a child after he left his wife. That's what Lizzie told your grandfather."

"Why was she talking to him?"

"Because they happen to be close . . . and what's wrong with that?"

"He's not exactly the person I'd turn to for moral advice."

"And do you know what, sonny boy? You're not the person I'd turn to for moral advice either. Nor would your sister—because we both know just how rigid and dogmatic and uncompassionate you've become."

"Don't pass the buck to me for your slack parenting."

The comment caught me like a slap to the face . . . even though part of me was expecting him to drop it.

"I won't accept that from you," I said.

"Too bad."

"What the hell is wrong with you, Jeff? When did you become so mean? And why?"

He flinched—like someone caught by a counterpunch. But before he could reply, there was a knock on the door. Jeff opened it. Dan walked in. He proffered his hand to Jeff, who also clasped his shoulder and gave him a conciliatory nod. Then he turned to me.

"I don't see why we have to hide out here," he said.

"Because I was under siege there. And because Margy suggested—"

"Since when is Margy running the show?" Dan asked.

"Since she offered to this afternoon."

"You could have consulted me," he said.

"You were otherwise engaged in the operating theater at the time—and since we are suddenly the object of major media attention, I was more than happy to let her assume the role of spokesperson and media flak-taker for us . . . she *is* one of New York's leading PRs."

"She might not be the right person to handle this," Jeff said.

"And why is that?"

"Because what I think is needed now is someone who can deal with the likes of Fox News."

"Margy is perfectly capable of—"

"Issuing a statement rescinding your comments on abortion?"

I turned away for a moment, my fists clenched. Then I faced my son again and said, "If I wanted to rescind that comment, Margy would issue a statement to that effect. She would not—as I think you're implying—oppose it on political grounds."

"Margy's a deep-dyed New York liberal."

"She's also Jewish."

"That has nothing to do with . . ."

"Yeah, right. Anyway, the thing is: I don't want to rescind that statement, because (a) it would be disloyal to my daughter, and (b) I stand by what I said . . . even if—"

"I know, I know," Jeff said, "you were completely misinterpreted by that hack. Well, a statement from you will end the misinterpretation."

"You didn't hear what I just said: I am not rescinding it."

"What do you think of that, Dad?" Jeff said.

"What Dad thinks about it," I said angrily, "doesn't matter—because it's *my* statement, *my* daughter . . ."

"Lizzie is my daughter too," Dan said, "and I agree with Jeff—but perhaps for different reasons. A comment like that plays right into the hands of the media moralizers who just love to trample on a liberal Easterner who thinks it's okay that her daughter—"

"To hell with what they think. I'm not rescinding it."

"Will you *please* think about Lizzie here?" Dan said.

"What do you think I have been doing every damn moment of every day? Anyway, my opinions about her abortion aren't exactly going to impede the police's effort to find Lizzie. But I do think that, if she sees that I have rescinded the statement, it might push her further away from us . . . and I'm sure Detective Leary would agree with me. Did you see him today?"

Jeff nodded.

"He's good news, I think," I said.

"He's not getting results," Jeff said.

"He's doing everything he can," I said.

"I want to hire a private investigator," Jeff said.

"That's unnecessary—and it could impinge on Leary's investigation."

"We use several investigators in the firm who are superprofessional and don't tread on the toes of the cops."

"We have Leary on our side," I said.

"Big deal."

"Let me ask you something: if Leary was a 'committed Christian,' would you feel differently?"

"Hannah, that's not necessary," Dan said.

"Yeah, but it's totally predictable," Jeff said. "You always have to get the little dig in, always have to make the nasty little atheistic point . . ."

"The one and *only* reason why I make this point is that you choose to wear your Christianity like protective armor and act like you have all of life's answers . . . which, in fact, you don't."

"All right, Hannah," Dan said, "that's enough."

"No, it isn't enough—because, once again, instead of trying to bind together as a family, we're at each other's throats. And it's your insane piety that's—"

"I'm not listening to this," Jeff said. "Because you have completely messed up this situation with your inappropriate comments, to the point where Shannon told me today that if you don't rescind what you say, you can forget about seeing your grandchildren in the near future."

I looked at him in shock.

"You wouldn't do that."

"Yes, I would."

"You'd keep your parents away from their grandchildren because you disagree with a statement about abortion?"

"I'm not talking about keeping Dad away from them," Jeff said.

I looked at him with a mixture of disbelief and contempt, then asked, "Did you hear what you just said, Jeff?"

"Shannon thinks you're a bad influence."

"On a two- and a four-year-old? As if I would even dream of saying anything about *that* to my grandchildren . . ."

"The choice is yours," Jeff said.

"No, Jeff," I said, "the choice is actually yours."

My cell phone rang. It was Margy.

"Is this a bad moment?"

"Yes, it is."

"Are you with Dan and—?"

"Jeff," I said.

"Who is that?" Jeff asked.

"Margy."

"Tell her I'd like to see the family statement she's preparing," he said.

"Did you hear that?" I asked Margy.

"Indeed I did. And you can tell your charming son that it's been emailed to your computer. But listen . . . I need to speak with you in private for a moment. Can you invent some excuse and call me back, but away from them?"

"Okay," I said.

I hung up.

"I've got to go downstairs and collect a fax."

"Couldn't the concierge bring it up?"

"I feel in need of a cigarette," I said.

"I can't believe you still use that drug," Jeff said.

"It's very occasional usage," I said, "and it's a very good friend."

Then I grabbed my coat and said I'd be back in around ten minutes.

Once downstairs, I stopped at the front desk and asked for the hotel's general fax number. Stepping outside, I lit up, dragging down a lungful of smoke before calling Margy. She answered immediately.

"Are you still at home?" I asked.

"Yeah, my bedroom's been general command center all day."

"Any chance you have a fax there?"

"Of course I have a fax. Why?"

"I need you to fax over that family statement I approved today—it was the excuse I used to come downstairs."

"No problem. But look, hon, the family statement is pretty small potatoes right now."

"Why's that?"

"Ever heard of someone named Chuck Cann?"

"Isn't he that right-wing guy who runs a news website?"

"Bull's-eye. Chuck Cann's Canned News. The biggest disseminator of mud-slinging conservative propaganda going—and, believe me, he's got a lot of competition in that field right now. Remember how he went after Clinton? The guy's another reformed revolutionary who now hates anything and everything to do with the sixties. And the third-lead story he's posting tomorrow on his website is about Tobias Judson's book—which, no doubt, some publicist like me got into his nasty little ultra-Republican hands.

"And, hon, it's not easy to tell you this, but I'm afraid that Cann or one of his henchmen did a little research, and he found out . . ."

I pulled the phone away from my ear. Because I knew what was coming next.

SIXTEEN

IT'S A STRANGE sensation, sitting on a time bomb. I've always wondered what goes through the mind of one of those kamikazes who board a bus in Tel Aviv or Baghdad with a jacket full of explosives and a detonator within easy reach. Does he look at his fellow passengers, going about their day-to-day business, with the cool, ruthless objectivity of a fanatic—someone who is so convinced of the justness of his cause and his heavenly destiny that he doesn't consider for a moment the lives he is about to destroy? Or is there a terrible instant of psychic horror when he realizes the evil insanity of the deed he is about to perpetrate? Does he think, *The only thing about going through with this is that I won't be around afterward to see the horror of what I've done*?

That evening, over dinner in a restaurant near the hotel, there was a moment when I couldn't help but think: *Our lives are about to detonate.* And it's all my fault. One long-ago transgression suddenly gets excavated and is about to be made public. And as our lives are already public news because of poor Lizzie's disappearance, the interest in this dirty little tidbit from the past will be, as Margy explained to me, multiplied by the power of ten.

"The only good thing about something like this," Margy said when she broke the news on the phone, "is that the public attention span is very short. There will be a flash of interest, which we will do our best to control, and then it will die away. And I'm saying this now, hon, because when you're in the thick of it, you have to keep remembering that it will not be a permanent state . . . that, like all nightmares, you will eventually wake up out of it."

"In other words," I said, "I am about to walk into a nightmare."

A pause. Then, "I'm not going to lie to you, hon. From where I sit, this all looks pretty bad. There's a lot I can do to limit the damage, but the big problem really is . . ."

The man sitting opposite me now at dinner. My husband for the past thirty years. The guy with whom I decided to spend my life. And now, tucked inside the bag underneath this restaurant seat, was a printed copy of a news story that would be posted online tomorrow morning and would demand, at minimum, some serious explanation. But that was a "best case" scenario. The other problem was the second man sitting opposite me: my hard-nosed son who now viewed the world in strictly black-and-white terms. It's a terrible feeling, realizing that you and the child you raised—and for whom you've only ever wanted the best—no longer get along. How does such a close, lifelong relationship unravel . . . especially when there's never been a single defining, deal-breaking incident to cause such disaffection between you?

That's what so astonished me about the current state of play between myself and Jeff. Nowadays, after less than a half hour in each other's presence, we couldn't help but argue.

I glanced over at my son, in mid-conversation with his father. They were talking about Portland property prices and whether Jeff should invest in a chunk of land north of Damariscotta. Jeff caught my eye for a moment, then quickly turned away, his lips tight with distaste. I had to fight hard to keep from bursting into tears. It wasn't just my daughter who had vanished, it was also my son, who was now threatening to bar me from seeing my grandchildren because of an out-of-context opinion. But even if I could somehow now bring him around—and create some sort of rapprochement between us—all that would evaporate in an instant once he learned of Tobias Judson's book. I couldn't even begin to imagine how he would react to his mom playing Madame Bovary *and* Emma Goldman to a onetime radical . . . not to mention bringing "Baby Jeff" along while happily transporting the alleged "love of my life" to political exile in Canada . . . and breaking about five federal laws in the process.

Then there was Dan. How would he react to the news that I had betrayed him all those years ago—sleeping with another man while he was out of town with his dying father? If that wasn't enough of a betrayal, then how would he take Judson's lies that I fell madly in love with this dashing young Jacobin, while complaining bitterly about being trapped with a stiff of a husband?

And there was no way that Dan and Jeff were *not* going to find out about this. That was one thing about which Margy was absolutely clear.

"The badass fact of the matter is that you've been outed by that schmuck Chuck Cann. As soon as you get off the phone, go to his website and read the article. And though we can come back with a counterpunch about you being misquoted and Judson totally fabricating stuff, there's absolutely nothing, legally speaking, we can do. If this was England, where the libel laws lean heavily in favor of the victim, we could slap an injunction on Cann's ass in a New York minute . . . and we could crucify Judson for defaming you, even though he used a pseudonym. But this is the good old USA, where, for better or worse, we believe that you can sling mud without cost . . . even if you've fabricated much of what you've said. So, we'll just have to cope with the fallout."

"What the hell am I going to tell Dan?"

"Tell him that most of it is a lie . . ."

"I did sleep with that guy, Margy. That is no lie."

"Okay, but it happened thirty years ago. Surely that makes it way beyond the statute of limitations."

"I just don't know how he'll take it."

"He doesn't want to lose you, hon. You've stuck it out. You've done okay together. You have no reason to split up. Especially since—dare I say it—you're both in your fifties. Anyway, this fling was a onetime thing. No repeat business, right?"

"You know I've been completely faithful since then. I would have told you otherwise."

"Then I honestly think that Dan—in his own phlegmatic way—will be philosophical about it."

"Margy, don't go Pollyanna on me here."

"All right, he might be upset about Judson's contention that you fell deeply in love with him, but once we come out with a contradicting statement, and once we attack Cann for invading your privacy . . ."

"Dan will still hate me."

"Don't go there just yet. He might just surprise you. He has a lot at stake here too—and he'll have to back you up. More than that, he'll *want* to back you up—show the world a united front."

"How am I going to tell him?"

"That is a real tough one, sweetheart—and I don't envy you the task for a minute. But you're just going to have to get it over with tonight . . . because by tomorrow morning, this story will be everywhere. He has to hear it from you first. He must get your side of the story before he reads Cann's trash, and before he gets his hands on that fucking book."

After I hung up I lit up another cigarette. Fear is such a strange emotion. It's all bound up in the terror of being found out, exposed, shown up for what you really are. I've lived so much of my life according to the edicts of fear. It kept me from going to France (fear of losing Dan). It kept me in the marriage (fear of being alone). It kept me from saying what I thought at work or in social situations (fear of being ostracized). It kept me from upsetting the steady equilibrium of my little life. And now . . .

Now I knew that everything was about to be upended. That was the worst sort of fear—the dread of loss . . . and entering a terra incognita where everything you hold dear is suddenly in jeopardy.

I finished my cigarette, shrugging off a nasty look from a woman who shook her head at me as she passed me by—like I was still a thirteen-year-old who was stupid enough to smoke in public. I went back into the hotel and asked the concierge if they had a place where guests could read their email. He directed me to their business center on the second floor. The woman behind the desk there powered up a computer in a small cubicle for me and asked if I'd like tea, coffee, or water. Neat vodka seemed more appropriate.

As soon as she left, I sat down and typed: www.canned-news.com.

I hit enter. Within seconds, I was connected with the website. Canned News: The Truth Behind the Lies. Under this banner was a quote from *The New York Times:* "Whether or not you like its extreme politics, the fact is: Chuck Cann's website breaks more stories than any other news organization in the country and has become the site everyone in the media reads every day." Great.

I moved on from this bit of self-advertisement to the index. After all the big news stories of the day, I saw the following headline:

CHICAGO TALK JOCK TELLS A MADAME BOVARY STORY FROM HIS REVOLUTIONARY PAST

I clicked on the story. I shut my eyes. I forced them open. I read:

Give the guy an A+ for ambition. Tobias Judson is doing his best to become the Rush Limbaugh of the Midwest.

*Judson—who has been making an impact on WBDT in the Lake Michigan area—was a self-described "onetime Lefty Pinko" who even graced the FBI's Wanted List when he harbored two of his Weatherman comrades after the fatal bombing of a Defense Department office in Chicago. Now a dyed-in-the-wool Republican and evangelical Christian, he has written a big tell-all book—*I Ain't A-Marching Anymore*—detailing his mad, bad years in the Weather Underground. Though he isn't exactly Hemingway—and his account of being born again as a solid, God-fearing family man is supersaccharine—there is enough down-and-dirty inside dope on the dangerous revolutionary games played by the Weathermen and other sixties purveyors of anti-Americanism to keep you turning the page.*

But, without question, the most riveting chapter of the book is "Love on the Run," which describes Judson's brief, intense affair with the wife of a married doctor in a small New England town; a young woman frustrated by being a housewife and wanting to engage in the same left-wing politics practiced by her famous antiwar professor father.

In the book, Judson tactfully uses pseudonyms for the woman and her lefty dad—calling the prof James Windsor Longley and his daughter, Alison. He also renames the town in which they conducted their steamy affair—calling it Croydon, Maine. But as Judson assures us in the introduction to this book, everything he describes happened—including "Alison" declaring her love for Judson after a torrid two-day sexual romp and driving him to Canada to escape apprehension by the federal authorities.

Now, after a bit of investigative legwork, Canned News can reveal the identities of the major players in this little drama. The radical professor was none other than the University of Vermont historian John Winthrop Latham, now retired, but back in his Summer of Love heyday a hard-line antiwar activist, even though his family background is as American aristocratic as they come. A little checking around also revealed that Win-

throp's daughter, Hannah, was indeed living with her doctor husband, Daniel Buchan, in a small Maine town—Pelham—back in '73 when Judson came breezing through town.

Hannah Buchan is now a schoolteacher in Portland, Maine, where her husband is head of orthopedics at Maine Medical Center. Could Mrs. Buchan now be liable for prosecution under federal law for aiding and abetting a wanted man? Watch this space.

The strangest thing about reading this was the fact that I didn't go into extended shock or rage. I was simply numb.

I printed the article, folded it up, and put it in my bag. I logged off, went downstairs again, stepped outside, lit up my seventh cigarette of the day, called Margy, and told her my side of the story from beginning to end, refuting point by point every lie in Judson's book. She said she'd spend the next hour writing up a release and would email it to me so I could show it to Dan later—after I broke the news to him.

Then I went upstairs and found Dan and Jeff deep in conversation. Dan gave me one of his low-key guilty looks when I came into the room, which indicated that they had been talking about me.

"Where have you been?" he asked.

"Took a walk," I said. "I needed the air."

Jeff made a sniffing sound with his nose.

"How many cigarettes, Mom?"

Ten minutes later, we were in a nearby restaurant and I was going through that awful guilt fugue, exacerbated by Jeff catching my eye, then turning away in distaste. Dan and Jeff talked among themselves while I picked at a shrimp salad and worked my way through three glasses of sauvignon blanc. Jeff did speak with me when I ordered the third glass.

"You're hitting it hard tonight, Mom," he said.

"Three glasses of wine doesn't exactly qualify me for a twelve-step program, Jeff."

He put his hands up.

"Hey, it was just a comment."

"No, it wasn't."

"Look, if you want to give yourself liver damage by the time you're sixty . . ."

"I am having three glasses of wine in an attempt to dampen the despair I'm feeling right now about your sister. And if you start lecturing me about using booze as a crutch . . ."

"I don't have to lecture you, Mom, since you're clearly already aware of the way alcohol deadens feeling . . ."

"You know what?" I said, standing up. "I'm going outside to have a cigarette." Then, turning back to Dan, I told him I'd see him back in the room.

I walked down to the docks and sat on a bench and smoked, and felt terrible about smoking, and looked at the waters of Casco Bay, and tried to concentrate on the gentle undulation of the surf but simply found myself too deeply under mental siege to find that "little moment of calm" that all those self-help books talk about. I stamped out the cigarette and headed back to the hotel, dreading what was about to unfold . . . yet determined to get it over with.

When I came into the room, Dan was sitting in the armchair, staring out the window. He looked up at me as I entered, then turned his gaze back outside.

"Why did you have to cause a scene?" he asked quietly.

"I didn't cause a scene," I said, my voice also temperate. "I just left."

"You pick a fight with Jeff every time you see him."

"Bizarrely, I thought it was the other way around."

"You are so damn intolerant."

"*Me* intolerant? Don't tell me you haven't noticed the fact that our son has turned into what could be politely described as a Christian bigot."

"You've just proved my point."

"I'd rather we get off this subject."

"Why? Because you don't want to admit that I'm right?"

"No, because it's pointless arguing about this. And because—"

"You'd rather dodge the issue."

"Dan, please . . ."

"Fine. Dodge the issue."

"I have to talk to you . . ." I said.

"I don't really feel like talking right now. It's been a long, unnerving day."

"I am aware of that, but . . ."

"And the house is still surrounded by reporters."

"How do you know that?"

"Called a neighbor," he said, glancing out the window again.

"Who?"

"The Colemans," he said, mentioning a couple who lived down the road from us, and with whom we had little contact.

"Really?"

"Why do you sound surprised?"

"Because we hardly talk to the Colemans."

"They were the only people nearby I could get hold of."

"You tried everyone on the street?"

"The Bremmers, the McCluskeys, the Monroes," he said, mentioning our nearest neighbors. "No answer."

"Well, it is ten at night. The Colemans didn't mind you calling so late?"

"They were okay about it. But they did say that we were still under siege."

"I'll get Alice to run by tomorrow, if she's free, and give us an update."

"Isn't she kind of under pressure right now with the new show?"

"How did you know that?"

"You mentioned it to me."

"Did I?" I asked, sounding confused myself.

"Yeah, last week. You reminded me that her show would be opening next month on the twenty-second . . ."

"I don't remember saying that at all."

"Well, you did."

"If you say so . . ."

"So what did you want to talk to me about?" he asked.

"We could do this tomorrow," I said, all nerves.

"Do it now," he said. "I'm wide awake."

"I'm kind of tired now . . ."

"If you said it was that important . . ."

I fumbled in my bag and pulled out my pack of cigarettes.

"This is a nonsmoking room on a nonsmoking floor," Dan said.

"I'll open a window . . ."

"Hannah . . ."

I walked over to behind where Dan was sitting and flipped the latch on the window and opened it, then sat down in the opposite armchair and lit up.

"I can't do this without cigarettes," I said.

"Can't do what?" he asked, looking directly at me.

"I have something difficult to tell you."

"Something about Lizzie?"

"Dan . . ."

"Did you just get a call from Leary?"

"There's no news about Lizzie."

"Then what is it?"

I took a long drag on my cigarette.

"Do you remember somebody named Tobias Judson?"

"Tobias who?"

"Judson," I said. "Years ago—1973—when your dad was dying—he was the friend of my father's who stayed with me while you were out of town. Remember?"

"Vaguely. So?"

Another deep drag on the cigarette.

"I had a two-day affair with him."

Long silence. Dan's face registered a moment of shock, then slipped back into his usual impassive mask, though I could tell he was working hard not to appear agitated, not to show any emotion.

"Why are you telling me this now?" he asked quietly.

"I need to first tell you about what happened and why," I said.

Then, with great care, I narrated what had happened on those two days all those years ago: how it was at a juncture of my then very young life where I was feeling trapped and limited; how Judson flirted with me and made me feel interesting and desirable; how we had too much to drink; and how we fell into bed with each other.

"I should have stopped it there and then, but these things have a strange momentum, and I wanted to keep it going for as long as he was there. It was dangerous and exciting and I was drunk on it—intoxicated by this risky game we were playing. But then Judson got a call out of nowhere . . ."

I took him point by point through what happened next, how he explained he was on the run, how he insisted I drive him to Canada, how I refused and he threatened me with exposure if I didn't do what he demanded, and how I had no choice but to load Jeff and myself in the car and drive him north.

Dan interrupted me.

"You brought Jeff into this?" he said, his voice barely above a whisper.

"I couldn't leave him there. Like I said, Judson was putting me under the worst sort of pressure—blackmailing me—and I had to think fast."

"So you drove him to Canada?"

I nodded.

"With our son in the backseat?"

"He was only six months old."

"I remember how young he was at the time. His crib was in our bedroom. Was he in the same room with you while you and that guy . . . ?"

I nodded again.

"You fucked him in our bed?"

I nodded again.

Long silence. I stubbed out my cigarette in the pack top I was using as an ashtray and lit up another one. Then I said, "I brought him to the place in Quebec where he asked to be dropped. I turned the car around. I returned home. And I vowed never to be unfaithful to you again. And I haven't been. Ever."

"Congratulations," he said quietly.

"I'm certain this will sound lame," I said, "but not a day has gone by since then when I haven't felt some stab of guilt."

"And that makes it all right?"

"No, it doesn't. I made a very wrong call. But it did happen three decades ago."

"You suddenly felt the urge to finally get it off your chest, to suddenly dump on me all the guilt you've felt for the past thirty years. Is it that?"

"I would never, *ever,* have told you if I hadn't learned that . . ."

"Learned what?"

"That Judson has just published a book about his radical years. And in it, there's a chapter about . . ."

Dan put his face in his hand.

"Oh, don't tell me that . . ."

"Yes," I said. "I'm afraid so."

Now I had the pleasant task of detailing, point by point, how Judson had embellished the story and spun fabrications about what I'd said, especially as regarded Dan . . . and how there was absolutely no truth to his assertion that I fell madly in love with him.

"He turns the whole thing into this cheap, florid romance. It's complete and utter bullshit, especially the stuff about me feeling thwarted and having a dull husband."

"But you just told me that you *did* feel thwarted at the time."

"All right, that's true. But I didn't come out and say that to him."

"Oh please, if you *felt* it, you must have communicated *something* to him. Just as you must have said that you were married to a bore."

"I never said that."

"No, that was just another of his embellishments, right? What else did he embellish? The sex? Don't tell me you didn't have sex with him, even though he's written that you did."

"No, we did have sex together."

"Was it good?"

"Dan . . ."

"Was it good?"

"Yes, it was good."

"And in this book of his, he writes about how good it was?"

I nodded again.

"And does he mention me by name in this book as well?"

"No, he's made up names for all of us—except Jeff. And he calls Pelham something else."

"Well, that's something, I guess."

"I wish it was," I said, and then explained about the Chuck Cann column. This time, Dan blanched.

"You're not serious," he said.

I opened my bag and handed him the article I'd printed out downstairs.

"This is why I was late coming back from my walk," I said.

He took it and fished out his glasses and slowly read it. When he finished he tossed it on the table in front of us. He didn't say anything for a few moments. Then, "Do you know how bad this is?"

"Yes."

"This is going to go everywhere. *Everywhere.* Especially since it ties in so perfectly with Lizzie's disappearance. The tabloids are going to love this. It will play right into their hands. *Her mother was a free-living hippie—no wonder she turned out bad.*"

"How long have you known about this?"

"A couple of hours. I found out when I went downstairs before dinner."

"You should have said something immediately."

"With Jeff there? He would have gone crazy."

"He will go crazy. And so will the board of Nathaniel Hawthorne High. Not to mention the powers that be at Maine Medical. And then there's the little matter of the FBI and the Justice Department. You did aid and . . ."

"I know what I did, but it was coercion. And the statement that Margy's drafting right now . . ."

"I want to see that statement."

"Fine, fine," I said, sounding very nervous. "She should have sent it to me by now. I can plug in my laptop and download it."

"Then do it."

"Dan, before that, I just want to say . . ."

I touched his shoulder. He shrugged me off.

"I really don't feel like talking to you right now."

"But can I explain . . ."

"No, you can't. I would like to see the book, please."

"It's late. And it's just going to upset you more. Why don't you wait until—"

"Do you actually think I'm going to sleep now? Get the book, please."

"Will you read Margy's statement first?"

"I don't see why that should matter."

"Just please read the statement first."

"Whatever," he said.

I got out my laptop, brought it to the little desk in the room, and plugged it into the data port. As soon as I was online, I checked my email. There were several messages from friends who had seen the *Boston Herald* story—even one from Sheila Platt, who wrote, "As a mother, I cannot imagine a worse nightmare than the one you are going through right now. Please know that I am praying for you and Dan, and especially for the safe return of Lizzie. And though I certainly don't approve of the 'F' word, I can completely understand your reaction to that horrible television reporter."

People do surprise you sometimes. I made a mental note to write a thank-you email to Sheila tomorrow. Then I clicked on Margy's email:

> Here it is, hon. Hope you approve. Call me back a.s.a.p. I want to work the phones first thing tomorrow to get this response covered in as many places as I can.
>
> Courage
>
> Love
>
> Margy

The press release ran for two pages and systematically trashed everything that Judson had written. It attacked Chuck Cann for invading our privacy by naming us as the people behind the pseudonyms. It did acknowledge that we'd had sex on two occasions, that I still felt tremendous guilt about this one betrayal of my husband, but that I saw the affair as nothing more than a foolish two-day fling—and that I certainly did not consider Tobias Judson to be the love of my life, nor did I ever utter a comment like "I will never forget you."

Where Margy really hit hard was in the section about his fleeing to Canada, saying that the assertion that I offered to drive him to Quebec was a complete invention.

Hannah Buchan refutes Mr. Judson's claim that she volunteered to help him flee the country. She wishes to make absolutely clear that Mr. Judson fabricated almost all the dialogue in the chapter in which she appears under the pseudonym of Alison. She wishes to state that Mr. Judson coerced her into driving him into Canada, saying that if she did not help him flee he would expose their affair and if captured in the United States by the FBI—he would implicate her.

"I am in no way attempting to make excuses for betraying my husband or trying to justify my actions back then. I made a series of wrong decisions—and I accept full responsibility for them. However, the assertion that I was motivated by political belief or love for Mr. Judson in helping him flee is an outright lie. He offered me a stark choice—either drive him or risk exposure. I was a young woman with a young child—guilty for what I had done and desperately scared. It was blackmail—and, under the circumstances, I felt I had no choice but to do what he demanded. It's a decision I have regretted ever since."

Margy followed this with a parenthesis for my attention:

(Hon: I know this is a complete mea culpa, but I think it's what's needed. Also: I spoke with the lawyers and they are completely cool about us having you call Judson an outright liar and a blackmailer. They feel he has no legal comeback—when he has made such absurd assertions about your role in the story. Now don't freak or be furious with me when you read the next paragraph, but I knew that I had to get a statement from your dad and figured that, under the circumstances, it was easiest if I approached him directly. I also went ahead and explained the shitty situation you found yourself in—and how he'd been implicated in Judson's book as well . . . just as you were now having to do some difficult explaining to Dan about all these past events. I was also able to get the offending chapter scanned and sent up to him by email—so he could read it and respond. I know this was a big liberty on my part, but as time is of the essence vis-à-vis getting this press release out, and you were dreading having to talk to your dad about all this, I decided to brave your wrath and tell him myself. I think I want to run off with your dad—if he doesn't think me too old. He couldn't have been more sympathetic—or more horrified on your behalf. He was going to call you immediately, but when I said you had to talk things over with Dan, he said he'd phone tomorrow.)

I was hardly angry with Margy. On the contrary, my relief at not having to explain everything to Dad was massive. All I had been doing recently was trying to explain everything to others . . . and, most of all, to myself.

I read on.

> *Hannah Buchan's father—the distinguished historian John Winthrop Latham (referred to in Mr. Judson's book as James Windsor Longley, but named in the Canned News feature on the book)—comments, "I have read the chapter in question of Mr. Judson's book and am shocked by his deceitful manipulation of past events for his own purposes, his wild departures from the truth, and his wanton cruelty."*

Dad then went on to refute everything in Judson's chapter about us. He stated that he knew Judson well in those days, but never shared his brand of coercive revolutionary politics.

> *"He always asserted he was in the Students for a Democratic Society, which was the political wing of the antiwar movement, whereas, as he now clearly admits, he was in bed with the Weathermen and their brand of violent protest."*

He also admitted he knew Judson was in "a bit of trouble," but that he never knew he was on the run from the FBI. So, yes, he did send Judson to me:

> *"A decision I have always regretted and one which subsequently caused a rift between my daughter and myself which, thanks to her decency and forgiveness, was repaired years ago. Had I known what he had been involved with, I would never have suggested he stay with Hannah."*

Dad even came clean on his unfaithfulness.

> *"My wife, who is now suffering from a degenerative illness, was aware of my adulterous behavior and was eventually able to forgive me. Our marriage has lasted fifty-three years—and I think that speaks volumes. Though I am appalled by Mr. Judson's callousness in exposing aspects*

of my private life, I will not attempt to soft-pedal my past actions. I was wrong. I would like to say that I am thoroughly appalled that Mr. Judson has seen fit to detail a brief romantic liaison with Hannah that happened thirty years ago—knowing full well that it could cause her and her husband enormous pain, even though it must now be considered nothing more than ancient history. Dishing the dirt on your past for personal gain may not be the most attractive spectacle, but it's a personal decision. But when you implicate other people in your story—knowing full well you are going to destroy their reputations in the process, decades after the events in question—you show yourself to be the worst sort of amoral opportunist."

The release then ended with the statement that, given the terrible strain under which Dan and I were currently living, considering the disappearance of our daughter, we asked that the media respect our privacy at this difficult juncture in our lives. There was a final comment in parentheses from Margy:

(The chance of any news organization heeding this final paragraph is somewhere between absurd and preposterous. But I still thought it had to be said. Delete all my little asides before you show this to Dan—and call me as soon as it's possible for you to talk. Hang in there.)

I did as instructed, deleting all of Margy's editorial passages. Then I turned to Dan, who was standing by the window, looking out into the dark night, and said, "You can read it now."

"You mean now that you've excised—"

"Dan . . ."

"Well, I did hear you using one key repeatedly. *Delete,* no doubt."

"I just removed a few editorial comments she made, that's all."

"Because you didn't want me to see them. Because you're hiding something, just like you've been hiding something for thirty years."

"Look, I know you are very angry at me right now. And you have every right to be. But please, try to remember—"

"What? That this all happened three decades ago, and I should just act like it never took place?"

"I'm not saying that—"

"Well, if you're looking for instant forgiveness right now, sorry . . . no sale."

He stood up and walked over to the closet and opened it and took out his coat.

"Where are you heading?"

"Out."

"Out where?" I asked.

"Does that matter?"

"No, but . . ."

"I am going out, Hannah, because I don't want to be in the same room with you right now."

Without thinking, I hung my head.

"Okay," I said quietly. "But don't you want to read . . . ?"

I pointed to the computer.

"Email it to me," he said.

He reached for Judson's book and shoved it under his arm.

"When will you be back?" I asked.

"I don't know," he said, walking toward the door.

"Margy needs an okay on the press release."

"I said: email it to me and I'll send you a reply."

I turned and reached for him.

"Dan, sweetheart, I'm . . ."

He dodged my hand.

"Hannah, I don't want to talk."

"Sorry. Truly sorry."

"I'm sure you are."

I felt my eyes fill up with tears.

"Dan, I don't want to lose . . ."

"Good night," he said, and walked out the door.

I didn't start to weep uncontrollably. I didn't fall apart. Instead, there was a very long moment where I stood by the door, not knowing what to do next.

Finally I sat down at the desk. I copied the press release and pasted it into an email and sent it to Dan. Then I turned off the computer and closed it shut. Again thinking: *What next?*

SEVENTEEN

DAN DIDN'T COME back that night. I waited up for him until three and twice called his cell phone. No answer. When I spoke with Margy at midnight—our second conversation of the evening—she counseled patience.

"The guy's in shock," she said, "as you would be if you got a piece of news like that. It's going to take him a little while to absorb it and realize that it did happen a long time ago and that you don't deserve to be hung, drawn, and quartered for it. At the same time, you've got to understand that he's probably scared shitless about how all the dirt that Judson dished will play with the board of the hospital, his clients, the asshole golf buddies at the country club."

"But he's going to come out of it all looking like the Wronged Man—whereas I'm going to seem like the harpy, the slut . . . and rightfully so."

"Don't start flagellating yourself just yet. If all goes well, we're going to be able to spin this favorably and show you to be a model citizen with a solid marriage, commanding great respect in your community as an educator, and all that other all-American crap people go for. You'll be seen as someone who made a youthful mistake that she now acknowledges and regrets all the pain she's inflicted on her loved ones, blah, blah, blah."

"You make it sound like such an easy sell."

"What you have to understand is that, in the eyes of the media, the only reason you merit interest is that your daughter is missing and her doctor lover has a TV show and is still under suspicion as the cause of said disappearance. That's it. Had Lizzie been found by now—had she never disappeared in the first place—there wouldn't be one-fifth of the attention there is now. They've got a hook, Missing Girl's Mom Was Onetime Lover of FBI Wanted Radical, and they're going to run with it. But, believe me, it's not a story with legs. It's a footnote—one that asshole McQueen will appreciate, because it will take some pressure off him for a couple of days . . . though until she's found, the media circus will still revolve around him.

"Did you speak to your dad yet?"

I had—and true to form, he was wonderful.

"Of all the major mistakes I've made in my life—and there have been a multitude," he said, "one of the worst was sending that appalling man to you."

"You can't blame yourself, Dad, for anything beyond that. It was my decision to sleep with him. Just as it was my decision to give in to his threats and drive him across the border."

"You're too forgiving."

"No, I'm not. But this is long-ago stuff. Anyway, you did your penance—as I did mine. Or, at least, I thought I had."

"The book is just a cavalcade of lies, not to mention execrably written."

"I don't think those 'fair and balanced' people at Fox News are going to worry too much about its literary style. All they're going to see is that it's a onetime Weatherman turned George Bush lapdog, an illicit affair, radical politics of the despised 1960s, and, best of all, the felicitous connection between the onetime adulteress and her missing daughter, who might have been murdered by her married celebrity doctor lover. Talk about history repeating itself . . ."

"I've told Margy I'll do anything she asks when it comes up—and I'd even be happy to take on the right-wing media in interviews or articles. We're not going to just sit there and let them savage you."

"I should have told you long ago about the affair," I said.

"What good would that have done? Anyway, your private life is your private life."

"It's a pretty damn *public* life now," I said.

I repeated what he said to Margy.

"Well, there you go—and among the many amazing things about your dad is that he is so quick to admit when he's gotten something wrong. Do you know how rare that is . . . especially in a man? Speaking of which, don't be surprised if you don't see your husband for the rest of the night."

"Why's that?"

"Because just while we've been speaking, he's emailed me his okay for the press release."

"What did he write, exactly?"

"I'll read it to you: *Dear Margy—press release ok by me . . . Dan.* Pretty straight and to the point."

"Did he say where he was emailing from?"

"Of course not—and why would he? He's probably at his office or maybe he snuck back home. My advice to you is give him some space. If you start calling him now, begging him to come back and forgive you, you'll just get his back up. He will get over it . . . but it might take some time."

I still tried his cell phone one more time after hanging up with Margy. When I got his voice mail, I said, "It's me. And I just want to say that I miss you being here tonight and that I have always loved you, and I will always continue to love you, and I am very, very sorry for all this. Please call me."

There was a part of me that felt I was being a little too beseeching and another part of me that thought I wasn't being beseeching enough. More than anything I wanted him back here with me, in this bed, safe and secure and all those things long-married people take for granted until they are suddenly taken away from them, and the specter of impending loss clouds the horizon, and they find themselves thinking: *Surely we're not going to fall apart now after all these years?*

I tried to sleep. It was impossible. I raided the minibar and drank two of those expensive airplane-sized bottles of vodka. Then I made the mistake of channel-surfing and found myself staring at myself on Fox News. The item was third from the top in the one a.m. headlines. First came a photo of Lizzie projected behind the blond talking head presenting the news. Over this, in a breathy, urgent voice, she said:

> *No new developments in the disappearance of Boston investment banker Elizabeth Buchan, last seen on April 4 when she stormed out of a downtown hotel after an argument with her married lover, celebrity dermatologist Mark McQueen. Yesterday, Boston police asked McQueen to surrender his passport, as he remains the prime suspect in the case, even though he has constantly protested his innocence.*

The camera cut away to a chunky, well-dressed man in his fifties speaking to a group of reporters. Under his image was the caption: *Bernard Canton . . . Lawyer for McQueen.* His sound bite lasted thirty seconds:

> *To show his complete willingness to cooperate with the police, my client has agreed to hand over his passport. He has clearly stated that he will continue to give all assistance demanded of him by those looking for Elizabeth Buchan. Dr. McQueen has witnesses on the evening in question who can vouch for his whereabouts at the time of Ms. Buchan's disappearance, so I do feel that the Boston police are grasping at straws by even hinting that my client is under investigation.*

They cut back to the talking head.

> *Today, in Portland, Maine, Lizzie Buchan's mother reacted angrily when reporters tried to interview her on her doorstep.*

The camera cut again, and there I was, getting out of my car, looking hassled and frightened and very pissed off, and then that young aggressive woman shoving a microphone in my face while a cameraman pressed in close behind. And when she asked me that question, *"How many abortions before this one did you sanction?"* I shouted, *"How f******* [they inserted bleeps here] *dare you . . . ,"* looking rather crazed.

Remember that movie where someone gets one day of their life replayed over and over again? Watching this clip was like entering that repetitive universe—especially as it was played again on the two a.m., three a.m., and four a.m. newscasts. Sometime after the five a.m. news I must have drifted off, because the next thing I knew, it was 6:48 a.m. and my cell phone was ringing. I answered in a completely groggy state.

"Bad moment?" Margy asked.

"Fell asleep on the bed fully clothed," I said.

"At least you got a little sleep . . . which is a good thing. Because all shit has broken loose. Turn on Fox News at the top of the hour. Then flip on your radio to the local Clear Channel affiliate—you know, the station that Ross Wallace broadcasts on," she said, referring to a right-wing talk jock who was popular among the rednecks of the northeastern seaboard.

"I think it's WHLM," I said, sounding half awake. "I make a point of *not* listening to Ross Wallace."

"Well, turn it on after you watch the news . . ."

"I've got to get to work."

"Then listen to it on the car radio. I've already heard the segment—and as he tends to repeat things, I've no doubt that he'll use it again around seven twenty-five . . . he's that predictable."

I jumped off the bed, stripped off all the clothes I had slept in, hurried in and out of the shower, and dried myself while standing in front of the television.

The item I was waiting for was ten minutes into the broadcast—by which time I was dressed and brushing my hair, having already called the concierge and asked him to have my car brought up from the hotel's basement garage. It took me a moment to realize that the anchorman had changed since last night.

> *In an intriguing new development in the Elizabeth Buchan case, a recently published book by Chicago radio talk-show host Toby Judson reveals that when he was a student radical and on the run from the FBI in 1973, he had a brief affair with Elizabeth Buchan's mother, Hannah, the wife of a Maine doctor who was out of town when the affair took place. What's more, Judson contends in his book that Hannah Buchan drove him into Canada to help him evade arrest.*

They cut away to a clip of Tobias Judson, sitting in front of a microphone in the radio studio where he broadcast. Though I'd seen a recent photo on the cover of his book, his plump, balding middle-agedness shocked me. And I felt such instant revulsion that I had to force myself to look at him. He spoke in a low, soothing voice, oozing unction and false decency.

> *I am very upset that Chuck Cann decided to reveal the identity of Hannah Buchan. It was never my intention that her identity become public knowledge—and I feel genuinely sorry for the publicity she is receiving,*

especially given the horror of her daughter's disappearance. Like everyone, I am praying for her safe return . . .

I bet you are, asshole.

The film cut away to . . . now this made me jump . . . Margy, of all people, standing under the awning of her apartment building in Manhattan, looking very pale and wan, though her eyes were ultrasharp in the glare of the television lights. Under her was superimposed the subtitle: *Margy Sinclair. Hannah Buchan's Spokesperson.* There were four boom microphones overhanging her head as she read, in her usual loud, no-bullshit voice, "This is a prepared statement from Hannah Buchan. 'I have read Mr. Judson's book with shock and disgust, because it is so full of lies and distortions . . .'"

She then gave the short sound-bite version of my statement in the press release, acknowledging the affair and also vehemently denying that I drove him to Canada of my own accord. "'Mr. Judson blackmailed me and left me little choice but to do what he demanded . . .'"

She ended with my statement that I regretted the pain I caused my family and, owing to the strain of my daughter's disappearance, I would not be making a public statement at this time.

They cut back to Judson, looking smug in front of the studio microphone. The off-camera reporter asked, "And how do you answer Hannah Buchan's charges that you blackmailed her into being your getaway driver into Canada?"

I can understand Hannah's anger at being exposed in this unjust way, just as I can appreciate her guilt. Because, God knows, I suffered tremendous guilt at my actions over the years—until I was able to admit my wrongdoing and move on. But for Hannah to repudiate the fact that she did offer to drive me into Canada, well, denial is a very human and understandable emotion. But the truth can never be denied—or evaded. I committed a crime. I fled the country—and so missed my country, and felt so guilty about what I had done, that I came back and faced the music. I urge Hannah to come clean about her role in this incident, as I have done.

Cut back to the talking head in the studio:

> *A spokesperson for the Justice Department said that they were currently investigating Hannah Buchan's role in Tobias Judson's 1973 flight from justice. Judson himself returned to the United States in 1980 and turned state's evidence against other members of the Weathermen organization. He received a three-year suspended sentence for harboring wanted criminals. Besides being a Chicago talk-radio host, Mr. Judson has recently been appointed to President Bush's National Commission for Faith-Based Charity Initiatives.*

I wanted to scream and shout and put my fist through the television. But I didn't have time to engage in such actions, as I had a class to teach in just under twelve minutes. I grabbed my briefcase and raced out the door. Downstairs, before heading out the door, I ran over to the guy at the front desk and said, "I'd like to keep the room for another day, and could you get housekeeping to please pick up the clothes I left on the floor and have them dry-cleaned for tonight?"

I charged into my waiting car, cranked it up and sped off, hitting the scan button on the radio until I found WHLM. It was now 7:22 a.m. As Margy had predicted, the item came on three minutes later. I had only heard Ross Wallace once before—and knew that he was an ex–Boston fireman who played the shock jock card every morning on some big megawatt station that broadcast from Washington to the most northern reaches of Maine. He promoted himself as "A Loudmouth Conservative in a Ninny Liberal State." That tagline boomed out of the car radio as a commercial break ended and he came back on the air.

> *Now here's a down-and-dirty development to that down-and-dirty Boston story about super-yuppie woman banker Elizabeth Buchan, who just couldn't take no for an answer when her married doctor lover ditched her.*
>
> *This grubby little tale now gets even grubbier. Because it turns out that Ms. Buchan's mommy was a onetime sixties radical who helped her revolutionary lover make a break for the border . . . even though she was married to someone else at the time.*

He then went on to give a breezy, Ross Wallace–sarcastic summary of the entire story. When he reached the end of it, he said:

> *Now, folks, the moral of this story could best be summed up as: like mother, like daughter . . . because affairs with married men seem to be standard operating procedure in the Buchan family. But, for me, what's most amazing about this story is that, in the other corner, you have Toby Judson—who, back in those crazy amoral years of free love and burning the American flag, believed in the violent overthrow of our way of life. But what happens? He runs away to Canada, and after a couple of years in that French-speaking socialist playground that dares to call itself our good neighbor to the north, he suffers a massive crisis of conscience. He has what is known in the Good Book as a Pauline conversion on the road to Damascus, and he realizes not only that he is all wrong about his brand of revolutionary politics, but that he also did wrong to his country. So he does the right thing. He contacts the FBI and says he wants to give himself up—and he comes back to the U.S. of A. and he faces the music. He is arrested, he's charged with his crime. And to show that he wants to make full amends, he tells the Department of Justice that he will testify against his two comrades who killed those innocent security guards while attacking Our Way of Life.*
>
> *And thanks to Toby Judson's testimony—in fact, due solely to him, because he was the only prosecution witness—those two dangerous radicals are serving life in a federal penitentiary.*
>
> *Now I don't know about you, folks, but my definition of a man is someone who can face up to his mistakes—who can say, "I got it wrong! . . . I love my country and I got it real wrong!" Which is exactly what Toby Judson did. And since returning to this great land of ours and taking his punishment like a man, Toby Judson has flourished. Our friends in Chicago know his voice on the air every morning. His friends in the Church of Christ know him to be a highly committed Christian who has done Trojan work coaching their Christian Little League team. And George W. Bush knows him to be a dedicated member of his team prying good works from the slimy hands of liberal charities and giving them to the churches . . . where they belong.*

Now compare and contrast Toby Judson's willingness to face the music with Hannah Buchan's actions. Think about it, folks—you're a twenty-three-year-old doctor's wife in a small Maine town. Your husband has to rush out of town to attend to his dying father—and what happens next? Your ultralefty dad—Ms. Buchan's father happens to have been one of the most notorious radical professors of the sixties—sends you one of his revolutionary comrades, saying he needs a place to stay while in Maine. Not only do you offer him a bed, you offer him your marital bed—and after two days, you tell him he's the love of your life. Then—and folks, here's where the story gets really nasty—when your lover announces he's on the run for being involved in a political murder, what do you do? You offer to drive him to the French-speaking socialist paradise to the north—and just to really undermine everything you hold dear, you bring your baby son along.

Now if there's any further proof needed that the sixties and the seventies nearly witnessed the downfall of American civilization, this story is it. Not only did Hannah Buchan break her marital vows, she also broke the law. Not just any old law. A federal law. Not only that, but she also passed on her lax morality to her daughter. When it comes to raising your kids with the proper values, remember this, folks: they often repeat your mistakes. That's certainly the case with Elizabeth Buchan. Even if she never knew about her mother's affair, something in the way she was brought up told her: "It's all right to do this. Because Mom did it." And if I was Hannah Buchan's husband right now . . . well, put it this way, I'm sure as heck glad I'm not her husband right now. But what I'd like to know is this: are you, Hannah Buchan, going to follow Toby Judson and face up to what you did? Are you going to say you're sorry? Not just sorry to your husband for your betrayal of him, but also sorry to your country? Because you betrayed her too.

And then he cut away to a commercial.

I had just driven into the school parking lot as Ross Wallace finished his rant against me. It was a surreal experience, listening to someone pull you apart on the air. It was like hearing him talk about someone else—some abstraction who had little relation to myself.

And yet, by the end of his rant, I was gripping the steering wheel so hard that I thought my knuckles were going to burst the skin. *Like mother, like daughter . . . It's all right to do this. Because Mom did it.* If Lizzie was anywhere near a radio and heard this, it might just tip her over the edge. The cell phone began to ring. It was Margy. She sounded hypercharged, hyperstressed.

"Did you see the Fox News thing?"

"I did."

"And did you hear Ross Wallace?"

"I did."

"Look, I don't have time to commiserate right now, because this whole thing has gone crazy, but know this: there are plenty of ways we can—and *will*—respond. What's more pressing is getting you to somewhere safe immediately . . ."

"I don't understand."

"Where are you right now?"

"Outside of school."

"Right, here's what I want you to do. Call the principal now on your cell phone, and inform him you're feeling unwell and you won't be coming in for the day. Then get back to the hotel, tell the front desk that you need anonymity and that they should not tell anyone you're staying there, and stay in the room until you hear from me . . ."

"Margy, I have to teach a class now . . ."

"Listen to me, hon. I just got a call from Dan. He was trying to get to your house this morning and found the place surrounded again. Then he drove to his office and discovered that a bunch of television crews were lying in wait for him there too. He's at the hospital now—and very pissed off and upset, because someone from his hospital board heard the Ross Wallace item when it first went out at six twenty-five and was demanding an explanation . . ."

Without thinking, I fumbled around in my bag, found my cigarettes, and lit one up.

"Anyway," Margy continued, "Dan wanted to know what he should do, vis-à-vis the press. And I told him what I'm telling you: stay indoors and out of contact. The thing with Dan is, he's got three surgeries this morning. The press may be a pack of vultures, but they won't storm a hospital. However, they will surround your school."

"I'm teaching the class, Margy."

"Now before you go all Joan of Arc on me, I promise you that, within an hour, the same crowd of reporters who are now around your house will work out that you're not there and will have moved on to your school. So do yourself a favor and—"

"Did Dan tell you where he spent last night?" I asked, interrupting her.

"We really didn't have time to go into that. But, hon, I'm imploring you . . ."

"I'll call you back after I've finished the class," I said, then clicked off the phone.

I gathered up my coat and briefcase, got out of the car, and walked with great haste toward the main entrance of the school, glancing nervously at my watch. I was five minutes late. I opened the door. The main corridor was empty. I raced up it, my heels resonating percussively on the linoleum. When I reached my classroom, I could hear my students being their usual rowdy selves. They quieted down as I walked in, tossing my coat on the back of the chair, opening up my briefcase, and scrambling for the copy of Sinclair Lewis's *Babbitt,* which I was supposed to be teaching. There was a low murmur among my students. I looked out at them.

"Something wrong?" I asked.

Jamie Benjamin, the class tough guy, raised his hand. I nodded.

"Any chance we could smoke too, Teach?"

That's when I realized I still had a lit cigarette in my mouth.

I tried not to act startled. I failed. I walked over to the window, stubbed out the cigarette on the sill, and tossed the butt outside.

"Isn't that littering?" Jamie Benjamin asked. There was a low rumble of laughter around the classroom.

"Touché, Jamie. And since you've caught me out, let me repay the compliment by asking you to explain to the class the contemporary relevance of *Babbitt.*"

"But it's not a contemporary book. It's all set in the 1920s."

"True, but surely you can find certain modern-day parallels between Babbitt's situation and America today."

"Like what?"

"Well . . . like if Babbitt was alive now, who would he have voted for in the last election?"

"George W. Bush, I guess."

"You guess?" I asked.

"No, I kinda know."

"And why do you know that?"

"Because Babbitt was a conservative dick."

Big laughter around the classroom.

"I think Sinclair Lewis would have agreed with you on that one. Does anyone else think that Babbitt was a conservative dick?"

The class began to gain its own momentum after this—the kids relaxing into a reasonably animated discussion about Babbitt's rigid, traditional, all-American values, and how the patriotic midwestern businessman whom Lewis was satirizing in his novel had plenty of 2003 parallels. This was what I liked best about teaching—when the students themselves took over the conversation and seemed genuinely engaged by the subject under discussion. Suddenly, I wasn't trying to force-feed them educational stuff that they filed away under *Boring*. Suddenly they seemed interested in debating an idea, in having a point of view, in seeing that there was relevance to be found in literature. Suddenly I was far away from everything that was happening to my life in the world beyond this classroom.

But then there was a knock on the door. It was the headmaster, Mr. Andrews. He hardly ever interrupted a class, but as soon as he walked in, I knew that he was aware of everything that had come out on the airwaves this morning. At the sight of him, all my students were immediately on their feet (he had everyone in the school trained well).

"Be seated," he said to the students. Then, nodding me to come over, he said, "We need to have a chat, Hannah."

"I've only got about five more minutes before the bell goes."

"*Now,* please," he said. Then, stepping away from me, he turned to the students and said, "Please continue whatever you were discussing among yourselves. Mr. Reed will be here for social studies in ten minutes—and if I find out that there was any goofing off during that ten minutes, there will be trouble."

He turned toward the door. As I followed him, he said, "Bring your coat and briefcase, please."

Everyone in the classroom heard this. There was a long quiet moment when they all stared at me packing up my things. I looked up at them. They stared back—all of them suddenly nervous, unsettled. None of them knew what exactly was going on, though I sensed they knew I was in some sort of very deep trouble. I finished packing my things. I raised my head again and looked out at that sea of faces. I tried to make final eye contact with each of my students. Then I said, "Good-bye," and followed Andrews out.

Once outside the classroom, he said, "We'll do this in my office."

Do what? I wanted to ask. But I knew the answer to that question already.

I followed him down the corridor, up a flight of steps, and into the outer office where his secretary worked. She gave me a nervous nod of the head as I walked behind Andrews into his inner sanctum. Once inside, he motioned for me to sit down.

"I've just had three calls from three different school governors, as well as several messages from very concerned parents. They've all either seen the item on Fox News or they've heard the Ross Wallace item. And it seems that all the local affiliates of the big networks had an item about you on the eight a.m. news."

I started to speak, but Andrews raised his hand, like a traffic cop telling me to halt.

"Let me say what I have to say first. Personally speaking—having known and worked with you for over fifteen years, if you tell me that the Judson guy coerced you into driving him into Canada, I'm going to believe you. Personally speaking, if you were unfaithful to your husband thirty years ago, my attitude is: that's between you and him, and it's none of my business. And personally speaking, I think the way that loudmouth Ross Wallace drew a connection between what happened thirty years ago and your daughter's current problems is loathsome. I might be an ex-marine and I might vote Republican, but I can't stand conservative showboaters like Wallace and that clown Rush Limbaugh because they're so damn petty and mean.

"Still, my personal sentiments don't have much bearing on the fact that the mess you found yourself in thirty years ago is now in the public domain. What this means is—"

"You now have a lot of parents and school governors screaming about having an admitted adulteress teaching here?"

"The adultery isn't the stumbling block. If that was all, I could have put my big foot down and told everyone to mind their own damn business. No, the problem here, Hannah, is that you helped a wanted criminal cross an international border to escape apprehension. You may have been forced to do it. You may have felt there was no choice but to do what he demanded. Nonetheless, you still did it . . . and on the CNN and Fox News websites there's talk of the Justice Department investigating whether you can be prosecuted for helping Judson flee. And sorry, but the idea of someone under investigation for a federal offense being allowed to teach here . . ."

"Do you want me to resign?" I said, my voice strangely calm.

"Let's not get ahead of ourselves here."

"If my resignation would make things easier for you, then you can have it now."

"You serious?" he asked.

"Completely serious," I said.

He looked at me with concern.

"Don't you want to keep your job?" he asked.

"Of course I do. I love teaching. You know that. But you also know that I might be prosecuted for aiding and abetting a onetime criminal. You also now know my side of the story—and that I will scream intimidation and arm-twisting in every damn court through which this case is dragged. My conscience is clear on this one, Mr. Andrews. All that really concerns me now is finding out whether my daughter is alive or dead. So if there is going to be a big nasty fight about whether or not I can continue teaching here, then I'd rather just make it easier for you and leave now."

Andrews said nothing for a few moments, drumming his fingers on the top of his desk. Finally, "There is no need for you to resign," he said. "However, I will have to ask you to take a leave of absence. On full pay, of course—and, trust me, I will raise hell with the board of governors if they object to this. I will issue a statement to the press saying that you requested leave, and that it is not a suspension. And if asked, I will simply say that you have been a long-admired and respected member of staff. But the board of governors are an ultraconservative bunch—and if the Justice Department does decide to prosecute you or the entire business spins out of control, I honestly don't know how long I'll be able to keep them acting reasonably."

"I'm certain you'll do whatever you can, Mr. Andrews."

"It's probably best if you leave immediately. I'll get my secretary to clear your office tonight. One last thing—there are about ten reporters gathered at the front door of the school. Do you want an escort out the back way?"

"That would be helpful."

"Is your car in the parking lot?"

I nodded.

"A navy blue Jeep Cherokee?" he asked.

I nodded again.

"Could you give me the keys, please?"

I handed them over. He walked into the outer office and returned a moment later.

"Jane will drive it around the back."

We waited two minutes in silence, then Mr. Andrews nodded for me to follow him. We went down a flight of stairs and out the back door. The car was already there, with Jane standing beside it. But just as I was about to step into it, an entire phalanx of reporters and cameramen came charging around the building. Immediately they surrounded us and started barking questions. Mr. Andrews tried to silence them, saying I had nothing to say at this time. But they shouted him down, their questions running together into one long din.

> *Mrs. Buchan, is it true that you helped Toby Judson escape to Canada? Did you know you were breaking the law? Did you want to leave your husband for him? Are you still a member of a subversive organization? Do you blame yourself for what's happened to your daughter? Did you tell her to have the abortion? Did you say it was all right to sleep with a married man?*

Those last three questions threw me—and I suddenly lost it, hissing at the journalist, "How dare you talk such trash."

"Hannah . . ." Carl Andrews said, but I ignored him, shouting, "My daughter is missing . . . maybe dead . . . and you make these vicious insinuations . . ."

One of the journalists shouted back, "So you're not going to apologize for what you did?"

"No way," I yelled, and somehow managed to climb in behind the wheel. Several of the reporters banged on the window, still bellowing questions, while the glare of television lights caught me full in the eyes. I gunned the motor, everyone jumped back, and I sped off like a mad getaway driver.

Two blocks away from the school, I pulled over, cut the motor, and started manically pounding the steering wheel. I was furious—not just at those merciless hacks, but at myself. I had taken their bait.

So you're not going to apologize for what you did?

No way.

How could I have been so stupid? I sat rigid in the car for several minutes, dazed and befuddled. Then I forced myself to drive back to the hotel. As soon as I let myself into the room, my cell phone went off. Margy.

"Okay, I've just seen it," she said.

"Margy, hon, I'm so sorry. I . . ."

"Didn't I tell you to go hide?" she said quietly. "Didn't I say—"

"I know, I know, I blew it . . ."

"It's not good, hon. It's not what we really need right now. And I've just had Dan on, fuming."

"Why didn't he call me?" I asked, thinking out loud.

"You'll have to ask him that. But he started getting really angry with me, telling me I shouldn't have let you off the leash."

"Were those his exact words?"

"Look, he's under a lot of strain too. He's been asked to go explain the situation to some members of the hospital board this afternoon—and he's worried about the impact this is going to have on his practice."

"And now the press is going to use that comment against me, over and over again."

"We'll do our best to respond. I might have to line up some interview with you and a simpatico journalist in an attempt to do a little damage control. We need to get your side of the story out there in the next thirty-six hours, otherwise Judson's version of things will stand. It's how it works now in the media—you've got a day-and-a-half window to hit back."

"I'll do whatever you ask."

"Well, you must promise me now not to leave the hotel. And if a journalist calls your cell phone, you should hang up immediately. I'll get back to you later."

I rang Dan as soon as I was off the phone with Margy.

"That was a great performance this morning," he said, his tone arctic.

"I'm sorry. I lost it. I—"

"It doesn't matter," he said in a way that made it very clear it did matter.

"Margy said you went by the house this morning."

"Yeah, thanks to you it was surrounded by journalists."

"Where did you sleep last night?"

"The office," he said.

"I see."

"Well, I couldn't exactly go home with all those hacks camped outside."

"Dan, is there any chance we could meet up now and try to—"

"I've got a very full day. And there's really nothing I want to say to you right now."

"Look, I know you're furious with me. And you're right to be furious with me. But—"

"I'll see you tonight. I'll come by the hotel around seven."

And he hung up.

I'll come by the hotel around seven. It sounded so formal—which, of course, was exactly his intention.

I made the mistake of turning on the television. On the top-of-the-hour news on Fox, I was the third item.

In yet another new development in the Elizabeth Buchan case, her mother, Hannah, took a leave of absence from her teaching job at the Nathaniel Hawthorne High School in Portland, Maine, after revelations came to light in a newly published book that she helped former Weatherman ter-

rorist Tobias Judson escape to Canada. Mrs. Buchan herself was unrepentant about her past actions.

Then they showed that clip of me going ballistic while getting into my car and turning on the reporter and then screaming that there was no way I'd say I'm sorry before appearing to roar off without the slightest concern for anyone in my way. Viewed coolly, you would have been forgiven for thinking that this woman was a full-fledged viper—evidently demented and morally suspect.

The final statement from the talking head reminded viewers that the Department of Justice was still considering whether I could be prosecuted and that the Boston police had no new details on the whereabouts of Elizabeth Buchan—though, in a recent development, Brigham and Women's Hospital in Boston had announced that Dr. Mark McQueen was going on leave of absence to "spend more time with his family." And Choice Communications, the production company that made his *Face It* show, announced that it was being taken off the air until further notice.

At least McQueen got the hospital to say that he was on leave.

Margy was on the phone again fifteen minutes later.

"I want you to do an interview this afternoon with a journalist from *The Boston Globe.* I took the liberty of giving her the green light before talking with you, because she got in touch with the office right after everything broke this morning and said that, if she could have access today, she could have her piece in by tomorrow. Her name's Paula Houston—I don't know her personally, but I had one of my people run a background check on her. Vassar-educated, very feminist, and seriously interested in what she called the 'Rashomon' aspect of the case—the fact that your version so completely contradicts Judson's. She's driving up to see you now. Traffic permitting, she should be at the hotel by noon."

"Margy, I've hardly slept and I look like a car wreck . . ."

"After what happened this morning, we're in damage control mode. Paula Houston can right some wrongs for us. You can't turn her away when she shows up. You have to do the interview today, hon."

"All right, all right . . . I'll do it."

"Smart girl—and I'm working on an NPR angle for tomorrow as well . . . though what I'd really like to do is find some more or less sympathetic conservative journalist who might just take Judson to task for digging up grubby personal stuff from his past for professional gain."

Margy was definitely in flat-out PR mode, and I was being treated now as the wayward client who needed reining in. All I wanted to do was run and hide, reemerging again when the parade had passed me by and fixated on someone else's scandal.

"How can anyone be so interested in my little life?"

This was the only question I posed during the hour I spent that morning with Paula Houston. Margy was right—Houston was superbright and very sympathetic, though not in a touchy-feely way. She was short, wiry, edgy. She had bitten nails and took notes with a pencil that also showed teeth marks. I had taught the occasional student like her over the years—bookish and intense; someone who had learned early on that the only way she was going to survive high school was by being brighter than everybody else . . . and who now, in adult life, used her intelligence as a bulwark against her own awkwardness.

"What's it like to have a daughter disappear?" she asked. It wasn't an aggressive question, rather one dropped out of nowhere, and it came with the sweeten-the-pill follow-up, "I haven't done the kid thing yet, so I can't even begin to imagine what you must be feeling right now."

We were sitting opposite each other in the two small armchairs by the window of my hotel room. Margy had insisted we do the interview in the room ("Portland's a small town—if anyone sees you in the hotel lobby or bar, word could get around and you'd have the network affiliates knocking on your door there"). I had called housekeeping as soon as I got word that Houston was arriving within the hour and had them tidy the room and remake the bed. I also fell into the shower and then tried to mask my lack of sleep by slapping on several layers of foundation. Looking at myself in the bathroom mirror, I thought: *Time isn't just relentless, it is also cruel.*

And now here I was—sitting opposite this nervy, highly intelligent young woman—trying to talk about Lizzie. And yes, we were very close. And yes, I simply have to continue to believe that she is alive. And no, I don't have the same sort of relationship with my son. Well, he is a rather conservative fellow, and his wife doesn't exactly share my pro-choice views on abortion. And yes, I do think Dan and I have a stable marriage—but, of course, things are difficult now.

"Were you in love with Tobias Judson?" she asked suddenly.

"Absolutely not."

"But you must have felt something for him . . ."

"I was young, I was living in a small town, I was a mother at twenty-three and felt as if I had denied myself the sort of latitude that most people have at that age. And Dan and I had been going through one of those periods in a new marriage when things weren't as stable as they could have been, and I was gripped by a lot of doubts, and along comes this guy—very assured, very worldly, politically savvy, and very raffish."

"Did he seduce you?" she asked, not looking up from her notepad.

"No, it was mutual."

"Was it great sex?"

"Do I have to answer that?"

"Let me rephrase it, then: was it bad sex?"

"No."

"And I know you've said in your press statement that you definitely did not offer to drive him across the border . . ."

"He forced me," I said.

"Would you mind taking me through the entire story of the drive to Canada—as you remember it."

I did as requested, explaining everything: the threats, his immense cynicism in the face of my distress, and how once we reached Quebec he told me I should forget all this ever happened.

"So you think his interpretation of events—"

"Is nothing more than an outright set of lies; an attempt to reinvent the past to sell his newfound image as a great patriot and a born-again."

"You could have turned Judson down back then—you could have held firm."

"I was scared."

"But ultimately it's your story against his, isn't it?"

"That's true. But I'm not peddling my story like he is."

We talked for a full hour. At one p.m. she looked at her watch and said that we had to wrap things up, as she had a four p.m. deadline for the interview and she was now going straight to a rented-by-the-hour office in the hotel business center to get it written in time.

"One last thing—outside of getting Judson to admit what you say is the truth, what would you like from all this?"

"You mean, besides Lizzie seeing this article somewhere and picking up the phone and calling me? I'd just like my life back as it was. In the great scheme of things, it's not a big important life—but it is *my* life. And I certainly wasn't dissatisfied with it."

She said nothing as she left—no "God, what a terrible story" or "I wish you luck" or "I will do my damnedest to see that truth triumphs," or any of the other comforting clichés I wanted. She simply shook my hand and thanked me for my time. Once she had gone, I paced the room, wondering if I had struck the right tone, if I had been overly demonstrative or said the wrong thing.

I stayed in the room for the rest of the afternoon—attempting to kill time with a Carol Shields novel that traced the very ordinary life of a very ordinary woman, a life with few moments of high drama, but which Shields somehow managed to make remarkable. *The extraordinary in the ordinary.* It was a theme I often discussed with my students—how we can never consider anybody's life "ordinary," how every human existence is a novel with its own compelling narrative. Even if, on the surface, it seems prosaic, the fact remains that each individual life is charged with contradictions and complexities. And no matter how much we wish to keep things simple and uneventful, we cannot help but collide with mess. It's our destiny, because mess, the drama that we create for ourselves, is an intrinsic part of being alive. It's a bit like tragedy: none of us can avoid it, as hard as we try. Maybe it's all a reaction against mortality—the cold, chilling, middle-of-the-night realization that everything is finite, that all the striving and ache and want and pleasures and disappointments of life vanish with us when we die. Can anyone really imagine their own death? No *you* on this planet, and the very absence of *you* noted by so few people. Which means the point to all the striving and suffering while we are here is . . . ?

But that's the ongoing imponderable question, isn't it? *What's the damn point?* How I envy so many people who have religious faith. I've never been able to make that leap—to accept the existence of a God and paradise eternal for those who accept Him. But even though I think it's all nothing but a fairy tale that adults tell themselves to soften the nullity of death, it must be wonderful to proclaim: *Yes, there is a point after all! Yes, I'm going to spend the rest of eternity with everyone I love . . .*

But will you also run into those whom you don't love . . . those who have done you wrong in temporal life . . . even though they call themselves Christian?

No wonder I'll never be a believer: you can't be sardonic about the Sweet Hereafter.

I couldn't concentrate on Carol Shields's deftly woven narrative. I couldn't stand being cooped up in this room anymore. I wanted to shoot off in my car and head north and spend the afternoon walking Popham Beach. But I was suddenly overwhelmed by a wave of tiredness. So I turned off my cell phone, stripped off my clothes, climbed in between the clean hotel sheets, and surrendered to the pleasure of the void.

The next thing I knew, the bedside phone was ringing. For a moment or two, I was completely dislocated, not knowing where I was or the hour of the day. Then my eyes focused on the bedside clock. Seven-thirteen p.m. *Damn, damn, damn.* I'd slept straight through the afternoon, and now night had arrived, and my brain was thick with stupor.

"Hi, it's me," Dan said, sounding tense and distant. "I've been trying to reach you on your cell phone."

I explained how a short nap had turned into a five-hour sleep.

"We were going to have a drink now," he said.

"Where are you?"

"The hotel lobby."

"Well, come on up," I said.

"I'll wait for you down here."

"That's silly," I said, suddenly awake. "You can wait for me up in the room."

"I'll be in the bar," he said, and put down the phone.

I got dressed quickly and hurried into the bathroom to attempt a new round of damage control with foundation. If he wanted me to feel scared and vulnerable, he'd succeeded admirably. *I'll be in the bar.* To which I wanted to shout: *You're my husband . . . why can't you come upstairs?*

But he'd already hung up before I could pose that question . . . because why should he act pleasantly to a woman who had betrayed his trust?

I was downstairs in five minutes. Dan was in a corner booth in the bar, out of public view. He already had a drink in front of him and was abstractly tapping the side of the glass with the plastic swizzle stick. He looked up as I approached, but then looked down at his drink again.

"I'm sorry I was asleep when you called," I said.

He shrugged.

"Do you want to order something?" he asked.

"A vodka on the rocks, please."

He called over the waiter and gave him our order.

"I really shouldn't be down here," I said lightly. "Margy wants me to stay out of sight."

"You mean, so you can't disgrace yourself again, like you did this morning?"

"That wasn't my best moment," I said. "And I'm sorry if I embarrassed you."

Another shrug.

"It doesn't matter," he said quietly. He lifted and drained his scotch, then caught the eye of the barman and indicated he wanted another.

"It does matter. I feel terrible about—"

"I was at the house this afternoon," he said, cutting me off.

"You were?" I said. "But I thought—"

"The camera crews have gone. They've obviously gotten what they want from you."

"Yes, I suppose they have."

The drinks arrived. Dan immediately slugged back half of his scotch.

"You're hitting it hard tonight," I said.

"So what?" he said.

"It was just an observation. Anyway, I've got the room for another night, so we might as well stay here."

"I'm not staying here."

"Dan—"

"I'm not staying here," he said in a vehement whisper.

A pause.

"Okay," I said, trying to stay calm. "You don't have to stay here if you don't want to. But please let me call you a cab when you head home."

"I'm not going home."

"I see."

"I've been home. I've taken what I need to take. I'm not going back home."

A long pause.

"I don't understand . . ." I heard myself saying, even though I did understand.

He drained the scotch.

"I'm leaving you," he said.

It took a moment or so before I could speak.

"Just like that?" I asked.

"No, *not* just like that. But . . ."

"Look, I know how angry you are right now. You're right to be. If it was you who had been revealed to—"

"You said all this earlier. It means nothing. I'm leaving you. That's it."

"Dan, please. What happened happened in 1973. I know I betrayed you then, but I never betrayed you again."

"Yeah, you've said that before too."

"You have to believe me."

"No, I don't. Why should I believe someone who announces publicly that there's 'no way' she's going to apologize for what she did . . ."

"That was taken out of context . . ."

"Only you know that. Everyone else who knows us—all my colleagues, all our friends—saw your 'I won't apologize' routine on the television this morning, and took that as completely *in context.* And while you've been asleep your little showstopper has been broadcast on every local news broadcast, not to mention hourly on Fox News. Two hours ago, I got a call from Tom Gucker. Do you know what he said to me? This is a direct quote: 'I just want you to know from the chairman of the board that you have the complete support of the hospital. I cannot imagine what it must be like to have a wife's infidelity broadcast everywhere, and to have her defending such actions while looking so clearly unstable.'"

"Don't you understand why I overreacted like that? Can't you see that—"

"What? That you're under pressure because of Lizzie's disappearance? Do you know what? So am I. But I'm not out there, disgracing myself in front of the television cameras."

"This will blow over, Dan. It will be forgotten in a couple of weeks . . ."

"Not in Portland it won't."

Silence.

"If you forgive me," I said quietly. "If we hang on together and don't let a thirty-year-old revelation undermine a very long, good marriage . . ."

"Do you really think it's good?"

"Yes, I do."

"Despite the fact that you consider me a bit of a dullard, not your equal when it comes to intellect, and someone who's held you back over the past three decades . . ."

"Do you really believe the crap in that man's book?"

"I don't have to believe it. It's there—and not just in his book. It's been there from the start."

"Dan, since 1969—"

"I know how long we've been together . . ."

"And, yes, of course, we have always been different people with different interests. But that doesn't mean—"

"I knew your mom never really approved of me. The small-town doc. The *steady-on-the-tiller* bore who could never be as erudite as the great John Winthrop Latham or as New York street-smart as Dorothy."

"Do you think I cared about what my mother thought?" I said. "I chose *you* because I loved you."

"Yeah, maybe, once upon a time. But I knew long ago that I was never that satisfactory for you."

"Then why the hell did I stay? *Why?* Do you really think I would have held on in a dead-end marriage?"

"I think you stayed for the same reason you never went to Paris during your junior year. Fear and the inability to articulate what you really want."

"Yes, that's exactly why I stayed. I admit it. But my junior year was thirty-two years ago . . . and the other reason I stayed was because I didn't want to lose you. Just like I don't want to lose you now."

"If you didn't want to lose me, you shouldn't have fucked that guy."

"All right, all right, guilty as charged. But still, *still,* can't you see that brief, stupid fling for what it was? A mistake made by a twenty-three-year-old who has lived with the knowledge and guilt of that betrayal ever since. But to say that I stayed with you just out of complacency . . ."

"Let me ask you something. Do you think I've just been the happy dullard, content in my nice little marriage to my nice little schoolteacher wife? You don't think I've dreamed of another life beyond hip replacements, and the family vacation in Florida, and making occasional, less-than-passionate love with the same woman since . . ."

"Welcome to marriage," I said.

"That's just like you, the condescending comment at the wrong moment . . ."

"Oh, is that another of my great failings?"

"Yes, in fact, it is. When in doubt, go caustic."

"Dan, I have never, *never,* felt the sort of rage toward you that you feel for me now."

"Maybe that's because you've never been publicly shamed the way I have been now."

"But this stuff you're throwing at me . . . it's been there for—"

"That's right, *years.* But I kept it nicely under wraps because I thought—"

"What? That I felt the same rage?"

"Something like that."

"Well, goddamn you, though I might have felt sometimes that life could have panned out differently, I still came to understand that one of the great virtues of a long marriage—besides continuity and stability and all that stuff—is a shared history. And the sense that any feelings either of us may have about the other's shortcomings is overridden by three-plus decades together. And, goddamn you again, it is not like we have fought our way through the past thirty-four years. On the contrary, we have—"

"Always kept things under wraps . . . always dodged the central issues, always—"

"Will you listen to yourself?" I said. "I have been under the impression that we've done pretty damn well together, that we were one of those couples who worked out how to deal with our disparate temperaments, who always cohabited well, who never had major disagreements about the kids, and generally had something to say to each other most nights. And now you tell me that, for you, it's all been a sham . . . that you've lived with this quiet, accelerating rage that I didn't really rate you, that I was feeling trapped so much of the time but was too cowardly to jump? Which just kind of leads me to believe you are using these current shitty events as a way of—"

"Don't go trying to shift the blame onto me. You didn't just betray me, you betrayed this entire family. And instead of doing the honorable thing and admitting—"

"I admitted it to *you*. I'll admit it again: *I was wrong*. I am desperately sorry for the pain I have caused you and Jeff. And I wish I had handled the press better. But I didn't—and now—"

"You expect me to forgive you and pretend like nothing happened?"

"I expect you to be angry and hurt and outraged and doubtful . . . but I expect you to still be in my corner nonetheless."

"That's asking a lot."

"After thirty-four years together? What's the betrayal here? I didn't fall in love with someone else—despite what that liar says. I didn't walk out on my husband and baby son. It was sex—two nights of sex back during the Nixon administration. And now, we have what Margy would call a 'public relations problem' and one which wouldn't exist if our poor daughter . . ."

"You think this is just a PR problem?" he said angrily.

"I think if this hadn't become public information, it would not be as big a deal as it is now."

"Well, that's just typical of you to attempt to sidestep responsibility."

"I have *never* sidestepped responsibility . . ."

"Yeah, go on, find another excuse for yourself."

I looked at him, wide-eyed.

"Dan," I said, lowering my voice, "do you realize what you're doing?"

"Yes, I'm leaving you."

"But it's more than that. You're telling me that our entire marriage was a lie."

"I should have jumped years ago—if I'd only ever owned up to what you really thought of me."

"But, as I've said before, I chose to stay with you because I *wanted* to stay with you."

"You *chose* to stay with me. Oh, thanks a lot. I'm flattered, honored, *touched*. I am so thrilled that, having fucked somebody else and helped him flee prosecution, you decided to stay with me. What a heartwarming finale to your little episode of betrayal. You can tell that to the court when the federal prosecutors are cross-examining you."

"That might not come to pass."

"You mean nobody's told you?"

"I've been asleep all afternoon with the cell phone off."

"Well, you should turn it on, because I'm sure there are plenty of messages waiting for you. It was all over the Maine news at five p.m."

"What?"

"The Justice Department announced that their legal team have decided there is a case to be answered, and they are taking the first steps to have you prosecuted. I'd get a lawyer now if I were you."

I drained my vodka, trying to take this in.

"Thanks for the advice," I said.

"And you think this is just a PR issue. Christ, Hannah, do you have any sense of the professional damage this has caused me? And Jeff is devastated by it—he has his partners raising the issue with him, worried about the impact that his having a felon for a mother will have on the firm."

I lowered my head. I said nothing.

"Cat got your tongue?" he asked.

"You're enjoying this, aren't you?"

"If you want to think that, fine. I'm going now. I've arranged for a moving company to come and pack up the rest of my clothes and possessions on Friday. I've also spoken with a lawyer who will be handling my side of the divorce. Her name is Carole Shipley of Shipley, Morgan, and Reilly."

"Dan, *please,* don't hit the detonate button just like that. Can't we try to—"

"You were the one who hit the detonate button, not me. As I said, my lawyer will be in touch—and we can start working out division of shared assets as soon as you've retained counsel."

"Where will you be living?" I asked.

He averted my gaze.

"I have a place."

"What's her name?"

"You would ask that."

"Where did you sleep last night?"

"At the office."

"I don't believe you."

He threw some money on the table and stood up.

"Don't lecture me on fidelity, Hannah."

I felt tears streaming down my cheeks.

"What's her name?" I asked again.

"As I said: expect a call from my lawyer."

"Dan . . ."

"Good-bye," he said tonelessly.

"You can't walk away from thirty years of marriage just like that."

"Watch me," he said.

And he turned and walked out of the bar.

EIGHTEEN

I WOKE UP the next morning to the sound of Ross Wallace taking me apart again.

Well, folks, some people just don't know when to keep their big ol' lip buttoned. Remember Hannah Buchan—adulterous mother of the missing Elizabeth Buchan? As anyone listening to the show yesterday will have heard, Hannah Buchan has just been outed in a book by Chicago talk jock Toby Judson as having an affair with him back when he was an unpatriotic radical on the run. She even helped him escape into Canada. What does the virtuous Hannah Buchan do yesterday when asked by a Fox News reporter whether she regrets her infidelity and her unpatriotic, felonious act? She says—wait for it, folks—"No way." That's a direct quote: "No way"! Memo to our great protectors in the Department of Justice: get this woman behind bars as fast as possible so we don't have to hear her talk drivel anymore.

That certainly woke me up—not that I had been asleep for long. After Dan left, I sat in the bar and drank three more vodkas. Then, feeling just a little blotto, I walked back down to the port and found a park bench and sat and smoked five cigarettes in a row while staring out at the choppy waters of Casco Bay.

The tears that had dampened my face before were now dry. The initial shock had dulled into quiet, profound trauma. Part of me wanted to ring Dan's cell phone and beg him to come back. But another corner of my head silenced all such supplicating pleas. This was the side that was so bludgeoned by what had just happened—and by everything Dan had said—that I still couldn't take it all in. I wanted to believe that he too was suffering from the turmoil of everything that had hit us recently, that his outburst in the bar was some sort of delayed reaction, a rage that, now vented, would transform into a mature realization that exploding our marriage would be an appalling mistake.

But this hope was overlaid by another deeply unnerving speculation: everything that he articulated last night was the truth; stuff that he had kept concealed for years (maybe even hidden away from himself) and which had suddenly geysered to the surface. But no, the idea of everything suddenly bursting forth was trying to soften the blow; to convince myself again that it had all come out in anger . . . whereas the truth of the matter was it hadn't emerged during a flare-up. He'd had over a day to think about all this. He'd packed up enough clothes to get him through the next week and had arranged for movers to come and clear the rest of his effects. And he'd either rented a place or . . .

And I was now pretty damn sure the *or* was a woman. But who? And when had it started? And why hadn't I picked up any clues beforehand?

A policeman walked by, then turned and walked back in my direction, sizing me up.

"Are you all right, ma'am?"

I straightened myself up from my slumped position on the bench and put out the cigarette that had burned down to the filter.

"Yeah, sure, Officer, fine," I said, the words slightly slurry.

"Have you been drinking, ma'am?"

"A little, yes," I said, sounding sheepish.

"A little?" he asked. "You seem to be somewhat beyond 'a little.' Are you driving tonight?"

"No, sir."

"Then how are you planning to get home?"

"I'm staying at the Hilton Garden Inn."

"Well, ma'am, I think it might be a good idea if you—"

He stopped and looked at me closely.

"Hang on, aren't you Mrs. Buchan who teaches English at Nathaniel Hawthorne High?"

Oh, great . . .

"Yes, Officer, that's me," I said.

"You taught my son, Jim Parker."

"I remember Jim," I said, even though his name swam in front of me. "Nice boy. Class of . . ."

"Ninety-seven. Went to U. Maine in Farmington. He's a teacher now up in Houlton."

"Please give him my best."

"He called me yesterday, asked me if I had seen all the stuff about you in the paper."

"Is this going to end up in the paper tomorrow too?"

He did not look pleased by this question. Immediately I said, "I'm sorry, Officer. That was stupid . . ."

"I could book you for public intoxication and add to your woes, if that's what you're thinking."

"Please don't book me, Officer. Things are bad enough as—"

I covered my face, on the verge of some sort of outburst. But I pulled back. When I took my hands away, I saw him looking at me dispassionately, thinking about what his next move would be.

"Please stand up, Mrs. Buchan," he finally said.

Oh Christ, here we go. I stood up.

"Are you okay to walk?" he asked. I nodded. He asked me to follow him. We turned away from the port toward the main road. I saw his parked cruiser awaiting us. But he touched my arm and directed me to cross the street. Two minutes later, we were in front of the Hilton Garden Inn.

"I want you to promise me that you'll go upstairs to your room and sleep this off, and that you won't leave the hotel until morning," he said.

"I promise," I said.

"If I find you out here before then, I will book you. Understood?"

I nodded and said, "Thank you, Officer."

"A piece of advice, Mrs. Buchan—and one which is probably none of my business, but which I'm going to give you anyway. It doesn't matter if it's all lies. You should still apologize. Everyone now thinks you've done wrong—and until you publicly say you're sorry, they're going to shun you."

Back upstairs, I did as ordered. I got undressed. I got into bed. I ignored the message light on the phone, unplugging it from the wall socket. Vodka-induced sleep quickly arrived. Seven hours later I woke with a jolt to the voice of Ross Wallace venting his anger at me. As soon as he was finished, I plugged the phone back in the wall and hit the message button. There were five—all from Margy, all sounding increasingly anxious about my whereabouts and asking me to call her urgently. Before I did, I rang the hotel front desk and asked them to send up a copy of that morning's *Boston Globe.* The interview ran an entire page and included the photograph taken of me yesterday. I looked awful. The article by Paula Houston followed this line of thinking, talking about how I was hiding out from encroaching media in a downtown Portland hotel, how I looked like I hadn't slept in a week, how my cuticles showed signs of being chewed (takes a nail biter to know a nail biter), and how I really did come across as a woman whose entire world had caved in on her.

It was a well-written piece that maintained a studiously neutral tone, though there were occasional flashes of partisanship toward me. "She is remarkably direct and forthright," she wrote, "even to the point of admitting that a rift has developed between herself and her son, Jeff, over the strong pro-life views he shares with his wife, Shannon. 'Though I respect their moral position,' Ms. Buchan said, 'I can't agree with the stridency of the anti-abortion movement and the way they always scream "murderer" if you have different views.'"

She also made the point that I seemed far more concerned with the welfare of my missing daughter than my now-damaged reputation.

As soon as I finished reading it, I phoned Margy. Before she could speak she started coughing violently.

"That sounds bad," I said.

"Well, I'm calling you from the swish confines of New York Hospital. Yesterday afternoon I started hacking up blood again."

"Oh God, Margy . . ."

"Hey, don't write me off yet. They did an MRI and essentially decided that some scar tissue from the tumor was to blame. But they decided to keep me in overnight for observation, just in case I started going stigmatic again. But, believe me, any worries about a little bloody phlegm were way overshadowed by the thought that you had done something drastic. Twice in the middle of the night I was on the verge of calling the night porter at the hotel and telling him to knock on your door and see if you were still alive."

"I had a bit of bad news last night," I said, and then explained the little bombshell that Dan had exploded. For one of the few times in her life, Margy was speechless. Finally she said, "I can't believe he said all that."

"What's that old cliché about never really knowing the people closest to you?"

"But Dan has always been Mr. Loyalty, Mr. Reliability, Mr. Solid."

"And now I've done something that has given him the excuse to rebel against all those labels—which, so he implied, he's been wanting to do for years."

"Who's the woman?"

"He won't say—and he all but denied there was someone else."

"There is definitely someone else," Margy said. "Because though Dan might be having a postadolescent rebellion against a lifetime of being so straight, he wouldn't be dumping you for a life by himself."

"Believe me, I know that better than anyone. Dan isn't that kind of independent guy. He needs someone to come home to."

"Any candidates?"

"I bet it's some damn nurse at the hospital—or maybe one of the women radiographers. There's one over at Maine Medical who's had her eye on him for years. It was a running gag between us—how he'd one day run off with Shirley-Rose Hoggart . . ."

"She's really called Shirley-Rose?"

"I'm afraid so. But he always used to say that she was this side of dull. Surely he couldn't have decided . . ."

"Maybe he'll get sense . . ."

"After what he said yesterday, I think it will be very hard for him to come back. He drove our marriage right off the edge of the cliff."

"How are you holding up?"

"Wonderfully, especially as Dan also told me yesterday I should expect to be arrested at any moment."

"That was another part of my message. Some Justice Department spokesman made an announcement yesterday that they were now moving toward the idea of prosecution, but they still haven't come out and definitely said that they'll be picking you up."

"Aren't they giving me the chance to flee the country?"

"My lawyer guy thinks they're reacting to all the publicity. Having said that, he also told me to advise you to get a criminal lawyer pronto. Do you know any in Portland?"

"Hardly, but I'll ask around."

"I'll get back to my guy here in New York and see if he has a suggestion or two. Now what are you up to this morning?"

"Hon, if you ask me to do a new interview today, I'm going to turn you down."

"I won't ask you to do another interview. In fact, after the *Globe* piece this morning—which I've just read online and think is pretty terrific—I'm going to be keeping you, PR-wise, under wraps. What I want now is some big television thing . . ."

"Please, Margy, I don't think I could handle—"

"Hear me out. The only way you'll be able to win the public relations side of this shitty business is by continuing to make your side of the case. Especially as Judson is booked today to appear on *The Rush Limbaugh Show* and on NPR's *All Things Considered.* He's just loving all the attention—and it's doing wonders for his book. It's already at number thirty on the extended *New York Times* best seller list—and no, I don't think he's going to give you a cut of his royalties."

I couldn't help but laugh. It was a classic Margy ploy—a wisecrack to chink the bleakness of the moment.

"Do me a favor. Get on home and try to get some rest, and keep your cell phone turned on, because I definitely will need you. Tell anyone from the press who calls to speak to my office. Even if they try to trick you by saying, 'We're just looking for a simple one-line quote,' tell them, 'No sale.' Understood?"

"Understood."

"One last thing: don't read today's *Portland Press Herald.* There's an editorial calling for your dismissal from the school."

"What else does it say?"

"What you'd expect it to say, 'Sets a bad example for the good young people of Maine . . . betrayed not just her husband, but her community . . . the fact that she has refused to apologize shows great arrogance . . . ,' that kind of predictable small-town horseshit."

"Maybe I should apologize," I said, and told her about the incident with the cop last night.

"Maybe you shouldn't appear on the streets again drunk," Margy said.

"There *were* extenuating circumstances."

"Hey, I'm not saying I don't understand why you got smashed. I'm just saying: thank God that cop had a big streak of decency in him. And I'm telling you: lay low now. We'll think about whether a *nuanced* apology might help things during the course of the day."

There were around nine messages on my cell phone—largely from Margy, but also from assorted journalists asking for interviews and one from my dad, telling me that he'd read the *Globe* piece and was very proud of my "dignified defiance."

I tried to ring Dad back, but there was no answer. So I left a simple message: "Hi, it's me. You need to know that Dan walked out on our marriage last night. Please call me asap." Then I had a fast shower, packed my bag, and—not wanting to have to show my face at the front desk, especially after that editorial in today's local paper—used the on-screen television checkout service to settle the hotel bill. Business completed, I took the elevator straight down to the basement parking lot, retrieved my car, and drove home.

When I reached Falmouth, I stopped at the general store right near our house. I walked in. Mr. Ames—the proprietor of the place for as long as we'd been living here—looked up as I came in. But instead of his usual "Hey, Hannah" greeting, he looked away. I picked up a basket and filled it with some basic necessities. When I got to the counter and put my basket up by the cash register, he picked it up and put it behind the counter.

"From now on, you're going to have to do your shopping elsewhere."

"But why?" I asked.

"If you have to ask that question . . ."

"Mr. Ames, there are two sides to—"

"As far as I'm concerned, I don't want a lawbreaker as a customer."

"I am not a 'lawbreaker.'"

"Well, that's your opinion. You can buy your groceries elsewhere."

"Mr. Ames, I've been a customer here since—"

"I know how long you've been shopping here. If I were your husband, I'd have you run out of town. Now if you wouldn't mind . . ."

He nodded toward the door.

"You are not being fair," I said.

"Too bad," he said, and turned his back to me.

I went home, passing by the house once without stopping, just to give the place the once-over and make certain there were no journalists lurking. I swung back around. But as I headed up the driveway, I saw something that made me hit the brakes—an instinctual reaction that had nothing to do with anything in my immediate path. Rather, it was the sight of my front door that provoked that sudden stop. It had been attacked by someone with a brush and a can of red paint. One word—*TRAITOR*—had been daubed across the entire width of the door.

I sat in the car, blinking with shock. For a moment or two I thought my brain was playing games with me, that this was some phantasmagorical extension of the ongoing nightmare. Then I got out and noticed that one of the windows near the door had been smashed. I hurried over to the door and opened it, fully expecting to find the house trashed. But in the living room all I found was a brick with a note attached to it, courtesy of a rubber band. I removed it. I stared down at a message scrawled in black crayon:

If you don't like it here, why don't you go back to Canada again and stay this time?

I was about to head to the phone and call the police, but thought better of it. If I involved the law, this incident would make the papers. If it made the papers, it would just augment my newfound atrocious reputation. So I walked through every room of the house (just to make certain there weren't any other broken windows I had missed), and came to an abrupt halt when I reached our bedroom and found Dan's closet door open and half his clothes gone. He'd also cleared out his chest of drawers, as well most of his shoes. I went immediately downstairs to the basement. His computer was gone. Ditto most of his DVDs and his precious titanium golf clubs. The rest of his stuff had been packed away in boxes, awaiting collection.

Moving out was no mere knee-jerk act of anger. He'd been planning this for a while—and judging by the amount of stuff he had taken, he hadn't checked into a hotel while searching for a new place to live. He'd headed to a preplanned destination—somewhere big enough to absorb all his things.

I picked up the telephone on Dan's desk and punched in the code for our voice mail. There were over twenty messages—the bulk of which were from journalists asking for interviews, and clearly ignoring the message I'd left, telling them to call Margy's office. I scrolled through them, stopping when I heard the voice of my daughter-in-law, sounding nervous yet stern.

"This is Shannon. Jeff asked me to call you, and to say that, given your appalling comments about us in today's *Boston Globe* and the way you made it very clear that, to your mind, we are fanatics because of our pro-life stance—we want nothing to do with you anymore. I won't even get into the revulsion I feel at what you've done to your husband, let alone your criminal activities—or the fact that you now refuse to apologize for such venal actions. All I will say is: you are not to contact us, or our children, again. Do not call. Do not write. If you do, we will simply hang up on you or delete your emails or tear up your letters. This is a decision that Jeff and I made in tandem. You're dead to us both now."

I hit the delete button on the voice mail and scrolled on to the next message—from Carl Andrews at Nathaniel Hawthorne High. "The school board met last night and unanimously voted for your dismissal. Personally, I tried to argue that we shouldn't be firing you until the Justice Department has decided whether or not to charge you with a criminal offense. But sentiment in the room was running pretty damn high, and I'm afraid even I couldn't stop the witch hunt atmosphere. Whatever your past actions, or whether or not you've committed a crime, I am a believer in due process, innocent until proven guilty, and other such quaint ideas. The only small bit of good news I can give you in all this is that I did force the board to agree to let you keep your pension, which, I know, isn't much after fifteen years of service, but is better than nothing, I suppose."

Strangely, neither of these calls threw me, because I was expecting bad news. And when you get what you expect . . .

Just what I was up against locally, however, was made clear to me when I phoned our local glazier in Falmouth to get him to repair the smashed window. Phil Post was also the local carpenter and had been doing work for us for years. But when he heard my voice on the phone, he turned distant, saying that he was far too busy today to do the job.

"Well, how about tomorrow?" I asked.

"Busy tomorrow too," he said.

"The day after tomorrow?"

"The truth is, Mrs. Buchan, I don't really need the work right now."

"You mean, you don't really need the work from me," I said.

"Something like that, yes," he said, then added, "Gotta go," and hung up.

I used the Yellow Pages and called a mobile glazier who was free this morning, and didn't seem to hesitate when I gave him my name and address. Maybe he didn't read the papers, or only listened to the sort of classic rock stations that didn't have news broadcasts. When I asked him if he knew anyone who was a house decorator, as my front door also needed to be repainted, he said he did that sort of work too.

"One-stop shopping," he said with a laugh. "See you in about two hours."

Now I needed to speak with someone nearby who could be counted on as a friend. So I rang Alice Armstrong on her cell phone.

"Oh hi," she said, sounding very nervous.

"It's great to hear your voice. You don't know the half of what is going on right now."

"Well, I do read the papers," she said. "And I did see you on the television news."

"Did you also hear that Dan has walked out on me? And that I've been dismissed from Nathaniel Hawthorne High? Or have the jungle drums not started rumbling on—"

"You know, Hannah, this is a really bad moment right now. Could I call you later?"

"Uh, sure, I guess. It's just, I'm really feeling a little isolated right now. And if you were free for dinner tonight . . ."

"I'm not," she said. "Listen, got to go."

And she hung up on me.

Now that was totally strange. Alice was probably the most left-wing person I knew, and someone who would have called me the moment

Tobias Judson aimed his neocon guns at me. Maybe I did just catch her at a bad moment. Or maybe she was with some people just now and couldn't be mouthing expressions of support with them nearby.

I had wanted to ask Alice about the names of any lawyers in town who might handle criminal cases (she knew everybody in Portland). Instead, it was Dad who came through on this one. I rang him after Alice and told him everything. He was so outraged on my behalf, especially at Dan.

"It's one thing to play around; it's another to walk out when your wife is under attack. It's cowardly—but, deep down, he knows that."

"Cold comfort."

"The way everyone's behaving, you'd think you'd helped Osama bin Laden to escape."

"It's now all come down to that snippet on television when I refused to say I was sorry. But as I explained in the *Globe* . . ."

"I saw what you said about only having to apologize to your family—and completely agreed. It was a good interview. You came out of it well."

"Well, I'm glad you think that. Because according to your grandson and daughter-in-law . . ." And I told him how I had been barred from seeing my grandkids.

"That won't be a permanent situation."

"Don't count on it," I said. "Jeff is very unforgiving, especially toward his mother."

"I suppose I could try to have a word with him myself, but I think he considers me to be the Trotsky of the family."

"Shannon is worse. To her we're all rabid fetus killers. And now, after all that's been revealed about my wayward past, and all that stuff in the book about you . . ."

"Does that 'stuff' still bother you?"

"It's a long time ago . . ."

"Answer the question," he said gently.

"It bothered me then, sure. I didn't like the idea of you being unfaithful to Mom, even though I understood back then that this is how things worked between you two. I guess, deep down, Mom was right about me—at heart, I've always been a small-c conservative. And with the exception of that one time with Judson . . ."

"I don't need to know this, Hannah. It really makes no difference to me anyway. If you'd had a lover on the side for the past thirty years . . ."

"I wish . . ."

He laughed. "Well, had that been the case it wouldn't have changed how I feel about you, or that I see you as a remarkable person."

"I am hardly remarkable, Dad. I haven't written books or become famous for a stand I've taken against the government. I've led a small life. Not a bad one up until now, but small nonetheless. And when it's over in twenty or thirty years, who will remember that I even passed through? You'll be gone. Dan will have long since shut me out of his mind. Ditto Jeff. Ditto his children—who will never have gotten to know me in the first place. And then there's Lizzie . . ."

I felt my eyes well up and my voice crack. I suddenly felt more tired than I had ever felt in my life and about to lose the battle I had been fighting for days—to somehow *not* fall apart. But there was a small, sane part of me that stopped myself from going over the edge, that bit down on a knuckle to halt the pending emotional torrent.

"Hannah, *stop,*" Dad said. "There are enough people kicking you right now. You don't have to add to the onslaught. Because, as far as I'm concerned, you've done nothing wrong . . ."

"Oh please . . ."

"*Nothing* . . . and believe me, I'd be the first to tell you otherwise."

No, he wouldn't. Dad never took me to task for anything. That was, I realized now, one of the many remarkable things about him. And hearing my father now, on the other end of a long-distance call, I could only think how lucky I was to still have him around . . . and how he would always defend me, no matter what the circumstances.

"Now if you wouldn't mind a little bit of paternal advice, whatever interviews you do next, I think it's best if you keep to the idea that you have already said sorry to the people who count, but that being bullied into something you didn't want to do doesn't merit a general apology to the nation.

"And I know this one lawyer in the Portland area who might be interested in handling your case. Ever heard of Greg Tolland?"

"Everyone in Portland's heard of Greg Tolland," I said. He was an aging, late-fiftyish radical attorney who'd been a thorn in the state government's side when it came to native land rights and corporate pollution by the big logging companies up in Maine's huge northern forest reserves. To say that Greg Tolland divided local opinion was the understatement of the new century. To that small coterie of local environmentalists and left-wing political activists in Maine, he was a hero. To the rest of the state, he was an old-style sixties troublemaker.

"Well, if he did take my case," I said, "it would cause a lot of talk around town. But since I'm already causing a lot of talk around town . . ."

"I'll call him now. And as much as I'd like to offer you safe shelter over here in Burlington, I really do think you have to stick it out in Portland—just to show the bastards that they won't intimidate you."

An hour later, the glazier showed up—a quiet, laconic guy named Brendan Foreman who looked at the word *TRAITOR* scrawled on the front door and said, "Glad I don't have your neighbors."

By mid-afternoon he'd removed all traces of the graffiti and had replaced the shattered pane of glass. As I wrote him a check for $300 and thanked him for coming so quickly, he said, "If they come back and write something nasty again on the door, just call me and I'll do the job for half-price. I don't believe in intimidation . . . especially when it comes to stuff that happened so long ago."

Then, with a sly wink, he headed off.

That encounter cheered me. So too did the phone call from Greg Tolland. He was phoning from the state capital, Augusta, where he'd been arguing a case in front of the Maine Supreme Court, and said, "Great minds think alike. I've been following everything that's been going down with you, and was wondering if you could use legal representation. You know, I was an undergraduate at UVM in the mid-sixties—and your dad was my adviser . . . so we go back a long ways. Now I'm stuck in Augusta until lunchtime tomorrow, but could you come and see me at my office tomorrow afternoon? Say, four p.m.? And here's my cell number—if anything happens before then . . . if feds come to your door with an arrest warrant or any such crap, you call me immediately and I'll be there asap. Otherwise, see you tomorrow."

That afternoon, I headed off to the local big supermarket, where nobody stopped me at the front door to tell me my patronage wasn't wanted. When I came back home, I braced myself for another bit of graffiti on the door—but then thought: *Nobody would attack my door in broad daylight.* I thought right. All was quiet at home.

Until the phone began to ring again.

"Hannah, hon, it's me," Margy said. "And do I have news for you."

"Good news?" I asked.

"*Interesting news.* Ever heard of Jose Julia?"

"Sure, the right-wing talk-show guy."

"Right wing is a little extreme. He's a real libertarian—*government out of our lives, nothing wrong with cigarettes as long as you don't blow them in my direction*—which makes him something of a Republican. But he's also very anti-Puritan and has often admitted that he's an atheist . . . and, as you probably know, he's got a big audience, largely as a scandalmonger . . ."

"He's been doing some stuff on Lizzie's disappearance, hasn't he?"

"Sure he has. And you know why?"

"*Married Celebrity Doctor possibly involved in disappearance of his Investment Banker Lover . . .*"

"It's right up his grubby alley, I'm afraid. But the guy's ratings are huge—and he doesn't like the religious Right, which is something in our favor. And he also has a thing about people who play the moral card, which means he could give Tobias Judson a very hard time . . ."

"I also remember reading in some crappy magazine that he has a fanatical thing against adulterous behavior, as he caught his first wife in flagrante with another guy—and, as it turned out, she'd been cheating on him for years . . ."

"Where'd you see that?"

"*People,* I think—and yeah, I only read *People* at the hairdresser's."

"Me too, but I'm a complete liar. Listen, here's the thing: whatever you think about Jose Julia's ex-wife, the fact is: he's huge, he's influential, everybody watches him, and he wants you to meet Judson face-to-face on his program."

"No way."

"I know it sounds tacky and tabloidy, but think of the possibilities. You get to present your side of the story. You get to take Judson on, to call him a liar, you get to . . ."

"I won't do it."

"Look, I can understand how the idea of even being in the same room as him . . ."

"I won't do it."

"And I also know how much you hate the sort of moronic television that Jose Julia represents. But if you score a knockout punch . . ."

"Margy, I've seen his show once or twice. He starts hectoring his guests, going all moral on them, waving an accusatory finger, telling them what bad people they are. And I have been through enough recently without subjecting myself to—"

"Okay, okay, I hear you. But you don't have to give me a definitive yes or no until—"

"It's a definitive 'no.'"

"Hear me out. The Jose Julia people will need to know by the end of tomorrow. Think it over—and think about how good it would be to show up that asshole in public, to really stick it to him. Anyway, we've got just over twenty-four hours before telling them, so . . ."

"All right, all right, I'll think about it. More important, are you still in the hospital?"

"Yeah, but they're sending me home tomorrow."

"You shouldn't be putting yourself under such pressure."

"What am I supposed to do? Sit here and keep worrying that every time I cough, blood will follow? Among other things, this takes my mind off the thought that this thing might kill me."

"Don't talk that way. The doctors told you they got it all . . ."

"Now they're starting to wonder if there was some secondary or tertiary tumor they hadn't caught."

"I'm sure you'll be okay."

"I'm not, but thanks for the platitude. I need all possible platitudes right now. Please tell me you'll give serious thought to the Jose Julia proposition . . . especially now that I've emotionally blackmailed you with my recurring lung cancer."

I laughed.

"I will think about it."

My plan for the evening was a straightforward one. I was going to make myself a light dinner, curl up in front of the television, and watch an old movie. I saw that one of the cable channels was showing Billy Wilder's *Ace in the Hole,* that wonderfully sulfurous story of American-style yellow journalism. It seemed appropriate viewing right now. But before I could settle down to this much-needed quiet evening, the phone rang again. I thought about ignoring it. Instead I answered it—a decision I instantly regretted.

"Hannah, it's Sheila Platt."

Just what I need.

"Hi, Sheila, and thanks so much for your message of support the other day. It was very welcome."

"Well, I'm afraid I—"

"Might we be able to talk tomorrow, Sheila. I'm awfully tired . . ."

"This won't take long," she said. "We had a meeting last night of the book group—and we overwhelmingly voted to bar you from it. I'm very sorry to have to be the bearer of this news . . ."

I started to laugh. Loudly.

"No, you're not," I said. "In fact, I bet you not only put the motion forward to kick me out, but you also volunteered to be the messenger."

A small pause. "Well, I've never liked you either," she said.

"I'm devastated," I said, "even though I actually considered you a class act when you called last week to offer your support."

"That's before I found out you betrayed your husband and your country."

"Well, thank you for only believing a Christian like yourself. And, speaking of belief, I can't *believe* that it was a unanimous vote, especially if Alice Armstrong was there."

A long nasty cackle of laughter from Sheila Platt.

"You can't be serious about Alice," she said.

"Why not?"

"You mean you don't know?"

"Don't know what?"

"You *really* don't know that your husband's moved in with her?"

It took a moment to register.

"You're lying," I said.

"You *wish* I was lying," she said.

I still couldn't believe what she'd just said.

"How long—" I started saying.

"—has it been going on?" she answered. "I have no idea. Why don't you ask Dan?"

Another bark of laughter. I hung up.

Without stopping to think, I picked up the phone again and dialed Alice's home number. After five rings, the call was answered.

"Hello?" Dan said.

The receiver started to shake in my hand.

"You cowardly little shit," I said, my voice tremulous, on the edge of a shriek. "You fire me from our marriage in a hotel bar, but you can't bring yourself to tell me the truth."

There was a silence, followed by a decisive click. The line went dead. Immediately I hit redial, but the line was engaged. I hit the redial button three more times. The ongoing busy signal said it all: he'd deliberately left the phone off the hook. I suddenly found myself grabbing my coat and car keys and storming out the door. Before I knew it, I was driving toward downtown Portland, fully prepared to slam the front of my vehicle into the front door of Alice Armstrong's house . . .

But another voice inside my head whispered, "Do that, and they'll have you committed for psychiatric observation, and then everyone will believe you really *are* totally gaga and wayward. *Go back home now.*"

I heeded the first part of the message. I ignored the second part. I kept driving. On through the center of Portland to the junction with I-95. I didn't really have a plan. I just decided to keep driving. I reached the interstate. I sped south. Within forty-five minutes I was at the state line. An hour later, I was on the outskirts of Boston. I crossed the bridge. I took the exit near the Fleet Center. I pulled up in front of the Onyx Hotel. I handed my keys to the doorman. I went inside and approached the front desk and said I'd like a room for the night. The desk clerk looked at me with some suspicion when I said I had no luggage. It was a last-minute trip, I said. I could see him studying my face. I couldn't tell whether he was wondering if I was a potential suicide or if he had seen my face somewhere before—like in the newspapers or on the television or perhaps the last time I stayed here. To stop his scrutiny I handed over my Amex card. He ran it through the machine, received approval, and handed it to me with a room key.

"You'll just be staying the night?" he asked.

"I don't know," I said.

I went upstairs. I opened the door of my room. I walked inside. I looked at the big bed and thought that I no longer had a husband to share it with. I sat down in the armchair near the bed. I wondered what the hell I was doing here. I checked my watch. Just after nine-thirty. I kept thinking: *Maybe I should start scouring the city again . . . an all-night expedition to find Lizzie. Or maybe, just maybe, she'd snuck back into her apartment in the Leather District and was hiding out there, living on ordered-in food. Or maybe . . .*

I suddenly dug out my cell phone and rang Lizzie's number. A man answered. A voice I knew.

"Who's this?" asked Detective Leary.

I told him who it was.

"Any reason why you were calling?" he asked.

"Desperation," I said. "Any news, Detective?"

"You would have been the first to know."

"Why are you answering this number? Are you at the apartment?"

"Hardly, but we arranged for all calls to Lizzie's number to be redirected to us over here. I just happen to be working late tonight, which is why I answered. You at home in Maine?"

"No, I'm in Boston."

"Oh yeah? Why?"

"I don't know," I said, and started to cry, suddenly letting go of all that pent-up rage and distress that I had been holding in for days. I must have cried for a good minute—unable to stop. When I finally got myself under control, I lifted the receiver again, fully expecting Leary to have hung up. But he was still there.

"You okay?" he asked.

"No," I said, sounding spent.

"Where are you right now?"

I told him.

"Listen, I'm just finishing up here. Give me a half hour and I'll meet you in the lobby."

"You really don't have to . . ." I said.

"I know I don't," he said, "but I will."

He was there, as promised, thirty minutes later. He looked around at the superchic, hypertech design of the lobby and said, "There's this Irish bar next door, which is a little more my kind of place."

We ended up in a corner booth. The bartender came over and shook Leary's hand, and told him the first round was on the house. He ordered us both double Bushmills straight up, with beer chasers.

"I'm not much of a whiskey drinker," I said.

"Take it from me, Bushmills is the best anesthetic going—and you need an anesthetic tonight."

The drinks arrived. We clinked glasses. I sipped the whiskey. The initial back-of-the-throat burn transformed quickly into a pleasurable buzz.

"That's not bad," I said.

"An Irish solution to all of life's problems, but hey, that's real Boston Mick talk."

He threw back his whiskey, reached for his beer, and nearly drained it too. Then he motioned for the bartender to bring him another round.

"It's been a long day," he said. "But it must have been a long couple of days for you. I've been monitoring you in all media."

"Then I'm surprised you'd agree to down a few with a future convicted felon, not to mention such an unpatriotic, adulterous . . ."

He nudged the whiskey glass in my direction.

"Drink up," he said.

I took a small sip of the whiskey.

"All of it," he said.

I threw it back in one go.

"Well done," he said, and motioned to the bartender for another whiskey.

My equilibrium was suddenly sent sideways—but then it subsided again and I felt myself back on terra firma, albeit it with a nicely numbing buzz.

"Okay," Leary said. "Tell me everything that's happened."

I did as commanded, even though it took around twenty minutes. Leary remained impassive during my monologue, studying my face with a certain professional detachment. When I finished, he said nothing for a moment. Then he waved his finger again in the direction of the bar, asking for refills for our now empty glasses.

"Sounds like you've had a hell of a week," he said, reaching into his pocket for a small notebook and a ballpoint pen.

"You could say that, yeah."

"And you say that the Jose Julia people want an answer by the end of tomorrow?"

"I'm not going to do the program," I said.

"I think you shouldn't make that decision just yet."

"Why?"

"Just a hunch. But first, tell me the name of the town you used to live in when Judson came a-calling?"

"Pelham, Maine."

He wrote this down.

"And who were the people you knew in Pelham?"

I gave him a few names—but, of course, as I hadn't been back to Pelham since leaving it, I had no idea whether any of these people were still alive.

"That's for me to find out," he said.

"But when?"

"I've got a day off tomorrow—and I've been recently thinking about breathing some country air. So maybe I'll just drive up to Pelham in the morning and see if anyone still remembers you there."

NINETEEN

GREG TOLLAND LOOKED like a scarecrow. An aging scarecrow—and one who was undoubtedly put together in the 1960s. He was around six feet four, stringbean thin, with long gray hair tied back in a ponytail. He wore tight, faded blue jeans, cowboy boots, and—this was an interesting sartorial touch—a blue blazer, a blue button-down shirt, and a Harvard Law School tie. The wardrobe and the hairstyle sent out a mixed message—late-middle-aged hippie who still came out of the establishment and could play them at their own game.

His office—on Congress Street in downtown Portland—was a rabbit warren of small rooms. The walls of this labyrinth were covered with assorted posters—from an old enlarged photograph of Martin Luther King, to an environmental group advertisement showing George W. Bush about to press a detonator and blow up the world, to historic *TROOPS OUT OF VIETNAM* notices, to more recent *NO TROOPS TO IRAQ* signs. There wasn't much of a staff—only four youngish assistants who seemed to be very engaged in assorted administrative tasks. One of them was manning a reception desk piled high with legal files and new mail. She was in her early twenties, wearing overalls and sporting big frizzy hair. I had a fast nostalgic pang for assorted vanished friends from college in the sixties who used to adopt the same splendidly no-style style.

"You must be Hannah," she said as I came in the door. "Greg's expecting you, please go right in."

There was no door on Greg's office—another political statement—so there was nowhere to knock. But he was on his feet and walking toward me as I paused in front of the doorless door frame.

"Hey there, Hannah," he said, extending his long bony hand in my direction. "I am so pleased to meet you—not just because, as I said on the phone, your dad is the last of the great progressives, but also because

I so respect the way you've been handling yourself during this entire shabby business."

"Even though I've refused to say I'm sorry?"

He motioned for me to sit in the wicker chair opposite his desk—a desk that seemed to be awash in paperwork. Filing was not a high priority in this legal practice.

"That was the smartest thing you did—and not just from a purely ethical standpoint. Had you apologized, you would have opened yourself up to the legal argument that you had admitted guilt. Instead, we're into a classic he said/she said situation. It doesn't mean that the feds won't go after you, especially with the attorney general's predilection for chasing after anyone with even the vaguest radical past. But it does make it harder when it comes to building a case against you.

"Now I went out yesterday and actually bought Tobias Judson's book—which, believe me, I didn't want to do, on the grounds that it was putting money into his sanctimonious little pocket. But I naturally needed to see what we were up against . . . besides, that is, bad prose. I'm not surprised that he could only get this piece of crap published by a right-wing goon house. To call it treacle is to insult treacle."

"But it's still selling—number twenty-eight in the Amazon Top Hundred yesterday . . . not that I've been checking these things."

"Well, it has been getting a considerable amount of publicity—and all due to your daughter's disappearance, from which Judson has immensely benefited . . . not, of course, that he'd ever think of doing something so cynical and callous as riding on the back of someone else's misfortune."

He raised his eyebrows like Groucho Marx. I decided that I was going to like Greg Tolland.

"Now, I'm certain you're sick of doing this, but it would be really useful if you could take me back through the entire story again—literally from the moment Judson popped into your life all those years ago."

Greg Tolland was very skillful in the art of cross-examination, especially when it came to peeling back the layers of my tale and exposing the hidden conflicts underneath.

"After you made love to Judson for the first time, did you mention to him about how guilty you felt?"

"Of course."

"And what was his reply?"

"He accused me of having 'bourgeois values.'"

A tight smile from Greg Tolland.

"That's one to drop during the face-to-face debate."

"I still haven't made up my mind about that one yet."

Another wry smile from Greg Tolland.

"Even though you know that it's your only real shot to stick it to him?"

"Did you ever have an abortion?" he asked.

"No."

"Do you think Jeff ever convinced a girlfriend to have an abortion?"

I was a little thrown by the question and said so.

"Sorry for my bluntness," Tolland said, "but in my experience, the real rabid pro-lifers often have some skeleton in the closet and have taken an extreme position because they have done something of which they are actively ashamed."

"Well, I know of no such skeleton in Jeff's past, but even if I did, I wouldn't let you use it against him."

"Even though Judson's side might enlist him against you?"

This stopped me short.

"I can't believe he'd publicly take his side," I said.

Actually I *could* believe it, especially after the conversation we'd had this morning. It was around eight-thirty and I was waking up in my hotel room in Boston, thankfully alone. Well, to be honest about it, I wasn't that thankful. After three shots of whiskey and three beer chasers, I ended up walking the half block back to the hotel on the arm of Detective Leary, who promised me that he wouldn't drive himself home (he was three ahead of me in the drinks stakes) and instead would be taking a cab back to his apartment in Brookline. As soon as we reached the front of the Onyx, I did something rather out-of-body and alcohol-induced. I leaned over and kissed him. Not a light little peck on the cheek—a proper, deep kiss. He responded with considerable enthusiasm—but then, after a moment or two, gently disengaged himself from our embrace.

"This is a good idea which is *not* a good idea," he said quietly.

I pulled him toward me again.

"Don't think, just . . ."

He held me by the shoulders.

"I want to. But—and it's a big *but*—we have pretty strict rules about getting involved with anyone who's part of a case . . ."

I kissed him.

"I won't tell," I whispered.

"Hannah . . ."

I kissed him again.

"It'll just be a night . . ."

"Hannah . . ."

"And I'll still respect you in the morning."

He suppressed a laugh.

"I have never, *ever* used that line myself," he said.

I kissed him again.

"Don't go . . ."

He took my hands in his, held them for a moment, then let them go.

"I'll call you in the morning," he said, "see if your hangover's a doozy."

Then, with a light kiss on the top of the head, he directed me into the hotel's revolving doors. As I started circling around, he waved good-bye and sauntered off.

I made it back to the room, managed to unlock the door, strip off my clothes, climb beneath the sheets, and pass right out. The next thing I knew, it was morning. Thin light was seeping in. The bedside clock said 6:52. My head felt as if it had been cleaved by an anvil. My guilt made whatever alcohol-induced pain I felt right now seem comparatively mild.

Don't think, just . . .

I pulled the pillow over my face. Trust me to make a drunken pass at an ex-Jesuit who just happens to be investigating my daughter's disappearance. Score ten out of ten for stupidity . . . especially with everything else breaking around me.

I rolled over, hoping sleep would whisk me off again for several hours. No such luck. I had left Portland in such a hurry that I had no book with me. So I turned on the television, snapping it right off again when I flicked onto Fox News and saw Lizzie's photograph fill the screen. *You can run, but you can't hide.* Margy was right: this thing was bound to keep on attracting media interest until Lizzie was found.

I got up. I ran myself a bath. As I lay in it, a strange realization clouded over me: I had nothing to do today. No job to go to, no husband to phone, no commitments, bar the meeting with Greg Tolland this afternoon. But other than seeing the lawyer who would try to keep me out of jail, my day was my own—an empty slate, on which was to be written . . . ?

What? That was a strange feeling, especially after decades of *always* having a task at hand, always privately moaning to myself about never really having enough time. Even after the kids left home, time still seemed chockablock. Preparing for classes, teaching classes, advising students, sitting on committees, running a house, keeping fit, attending the book group, reading, reading, reading, my work with the homeless, my work in adult literacy programs, making certain I saw every new movie of worth, making certain I got down to Boston once a month to hear a concert at Symphony Hall, making certain I stayed abreast of all current events, making certain I . . . filled the time.

Curious, isn't it, how so much of that time was filled *without* Dan. And yet, he was always *there*—the guy waiting for me when I got home . . . who called in the middle of the day just to say hello . . . who liked to surprise me with a night out at a big-deal restaurant downtown . . . who always seemed to be content with how things were between us . . . the man I still expected to be there with me . . . because, hell, we'd made it through all the tricky stuff—the early years of adjustment, the decades of child rearing, the usual postfortysomething midlife crap. We were the exception to the modern rule: the long-married couple who hadn't stayed together out of some grim duty or warped psychological neediness. We were still together because we still wanted to be together, despite the usual shortcomings. And how many couples can say that after . . .

We were still together because . . .

No, that was a reality that was no longer true. Now the sentence had to be changed to the past tense: *We had been together because . . .*

The past tense. How could we have ended up in the past tense? And how could Alice have . . . ?

No, don't go there. Because even trying to work out the mechanics of their affair—how they first hooked up, the tentative start, the first clandestine lunch or dinner, that moment when he put his hand on hers, their first kiss, the moment he started taking off her clothes, the . . .

Stop. This is a futile exercise—and one that is guaranteed to drive you into even greater regions of despair. Move on, now . . .

I got out of the bath. I dried myself, got dressed, and went downstairs to breakfast, hiding behind a magazine, and never once looking at the television news being broadcast on a flat plasma screen opposite me. At eight a.m., I returned to the room, sat down in the armchair by the bed, and made a call I'd been dreading.

"I don't want to talk to you," Jeff said as soon as he answered his cell phone.

"Are you really going to cut me off just like that?" I asked.

"You act like it's my fault this has happened."

"I am hardly saying that. I am just asking you to talk this through with me and consider . . ."

"*Consider? Consider?* You're asking me to *give thought* to this situation—when you obviously gave no thought to the effect your comments would have on your son and daughter-in-law when you gave that interview to *The Boston Globe.*"

"All I said was . . ."

"I know exactly what you said. I *can* read. And do you know what I read last night? Tobias Judson's lurid account of my mother having sex with a man who wasn't my father while I was sleeping in the same room. Now how do you think that made me feel, Mom?"

"I know, I know. I've told you how bad I feel . . ."

"How do you think this looks for me? You made love with him while I was right there. And then, you thought nothing of bringing me along while you drove getaway for your lover . . ."

"Jeff, sweetheart, you have to try to understand—"

"No, Mom, I don't have to understand *anything.* And if you start in on that 'He coerced me . . . I had no choice' stuff, I'll hang up. Because so many secrets and lies have come tumbling out the past couple of days, I don't know if the frontier between your delusions and what actually happened exists anymore."

"But whatever you think about my behavior at the time, can't you see that Judson is selling his side of the story in order to make a buck and also augment his public profile? And can't you also see that the only way he can really tell the story is by embellishing . . ."

"Just answer me this: did you sleep with Tobias Judson while married to my father?"

"Yes, but—"

"And did you bring Tobias Judson to Canada when he was on the run from the FBI?"

"Yes, but—"

"And did you smoke all the way to and from Canada while I was in the backseat of the car?"

"What does that matter?"

"Just answer the question," he said, sounding like the public prosecutor he briefly once was.

"Yes, but—"

"Do you know that I called my doctor this morning about this and he's scheduled a chest X-ray for Monday . . ."

"Don't you think that's just a little overcautious?"

"You would think that. Just like you'd try to deny the inherent dangers of secondhand smoke . . ."

"Jeff, this was thirty years ago. Surely . . ."

"*Surely* what? *Surely it doesn't matter?* Is that your lame excuse? Or maybe it's *Surely Jeff, you're being the little prig as usual?* Or how about, *Surely you don't believe a born-again idiot like Tobias Judson?* Well, guess what, Mom? I'm happy being a prig, just as I'm happy in my Christian faith. And I am going to hang up now before I blow up and say some very *un-Christian* things. Just know this: I am in complete accord with Shannon when it comes to keeping you away from our kids. And nothing you can say or do will change that."

Before I could reply, the line went dead. When I called back, I got his voice mail. I didn't leave a message.

Hours later in Greg Tolland's office, I related this conversation to him. He said, "May I give you a piece of difficult advice? No matter how desperate you are to speak to your son, let him be right now. From what I can gather, he's rather dogmatic—and, in my experience, once a dogmatic person adopts a hard-line position, he is loath to surrender it . . . because that means admitting he is wrong. If you are that doctrinaire, you are not going to back down, especially if, like your son, you have a wife who is very much part of the fanatical wing of the Evangelical Free

Church. I Googled her this morning—she's quite the poster girl for the antiabortion movement in Connecticut."

"It would be easy to blame her for the position Jeff's taken against me. But the fact is: he's a grown man . . . and not a stupid one. He knows what he's doing."

"Which is why the other side might use him against you."

"If that happens," I said quietly, "so be it."

He then told me he wanted to propose a counterstrategy to "scare the crap" out of the other side. He wanted to publicly announce that we were planning to sue Judson and his publishers for an excessive sum of money, on the grounds that he had defamed my character.

"Take it from me," he said, "the chances of us winning anything in a court of law are virtually nonexistent, because, as I said before, it's your word against his. Still, by simply announcing we're going to sue them for, say, $20 million . . ."

"Good God."

"It's a ridiculous figure, I know. But that's the idea—frighten them into thinking we mean business. They'll know it's all strategic on our part, but the public impact will be made. And it will also send a message to the Justice Department that we plan to mount a very robust defense of your position . . ."

My cell phone started to ring. I apologized for the interruption and answered it.

"How's your hangover?" Detective Leary asked.

"I've had clearer starts to the day," I said.

"Me too—and I hope you weren't beating yourself up too much this morning . . ."

"I'm always beating myself up," I said.

"So I gather."

"And I did an especially good job around six a.m. today. But listen, can I call you back? I'm with my lawyer right now . . ."

"Then my timing's spot-on, as I happen to be in Pelham, Maine, right now."

"You're kidding me."

"I wish I was. What a dump. Still, there are worse things to do with a hangover and a day off than drive up to the middle of Maine. And in the course of my snooping around, I happened to turn up something rather interesting."

He then explained what he had unearthed from the distant past. I listened with growing amazement.

"That really happened?" I finally said.

"So it seems," he said.

My brain was whizzing. I couldn't believe what I was hearing.

"That changes everything, doesn't it?" I said.

"I certainly think so."

"Listen, if I hand you over to Greg Tolland, who's agreed to take me on as a client, would you mind explaining to him what you've just told me? He needs to hear it too."

"Well, if he charges what most lawyers charge, my five-minute explanation will cost you fifty bucks."

"He's not that kind of a lawyer," I said. "Hang on a sec . . ."

I whispered to Tolland who I had on the line. I handed him the phone.

"Good afternoon, Detective . . ." he said into the phone, and then swiveled his chair away from me as he became engrossed in the conversation. He reached for a legal pad and took a lengthy stream of notes while he spoke. As the call progressed, he became increasingly animated, punctuating his questions with sixties jive: "You serious?" or "Well, that rocks" and—the real throwback word—"groovy." *I have a lawyer who talks like a roadie for the Grateful Dead.* Still, I was grateful to have him in my corner.

When he finished the call, he handed the phone back to me, flashed me a big smile, and said:

"We are going to soak those suckers."

And then he started to outline his strategy.

As soon as I left Tolland's office I rang Margy in New York and detailed the contents of Leary's discovery in Pelham.

"Holy shit," she said. "The people on *The Jose Julia Show* are going to love this."

"Do you think they'll buy into it?" I asked.

"Are you kidding? They'll completely eat it up. It's exactly the sort of crap that keeps the blood coursing through their sleazy veins. I'll get on to them straightaway, say we're ready to go when they are, see when they can slot us in next week."

"I'm still a little worried about how I'll stand up in a debate with the guy."

"When they fly you down to New York, we'll arrange for you to arrive here the day before and we can do a couple of practice runs, get you nice and prepared to take the bastard's head off."

And then she started to outline *her* strategy.

I drove home. As soon as I came up the drive, I slammed on the brakes. The front door had been attacked again by someone with a pot of red paint and a brush. Only this time the graffiti had somewhat altered. The word *TRAITOR* had returned . . . but beneath this had been added: *GET OUT NOW.*

This time, I didn't blink in shock. I simply seethed . . . especially when I saw that all the front windows had been smashed. I parked the car. I used the back door to enter the house. I tried to remain controlled and calm. I picked up the phone and called the glazier. He answered immediately and said that he was on his way. As I waited for him to arrive I suddenly, out of nowhere, had this deep, abiding need to be on my own; to walk away from everyone and everything to do with the situation.

So I called my dad and told him I'd be disappearing for a few days.

"Why don't you disappear over to Burlington?" he asked.

"I have to be on my own for a while," I said.

"I see," he said quietly.

"Please don't take it personally," I said.

"I'm not taking it personally," he said. "I just want to make certain you know my door is always open to you day and night."

"I know that, Dad. You have been so fantastic during all this."

"Every time I see another article about you and that appalling man—or I hear Judson's sanctimonious voice during yet another interview, talking about how Jesus forgave him his betrayal of his country—all I can think is: if I hadn't told him . . ."

"Dad, this is pointless—and does neither of us any good."

"Where will you go?"

"Somewhere I can't be found."

The glazier showed up around a half hour later.

"You're not exactly winning the local popularity contest, are you?" he said.

"I guess not."

"You planning to stick around now?"

"I think I'm going to give in to intimidation, and vanish for a little while."

"Then if you don't mind me making a suggestion . . . something that should ensure no one hits the front door with graffiti again . . ."

He told me his idea. I smiled grimly and said, "Do it."

While he worked, I packed a suitcase, including the clothes I'd need for the interview in New York in a few days' time. Halfway through this task, the home phone rang. I answered it.

"Is this a bad time to talk?" Alice Armstrong asked me.

"Yes, it is," I said. "I have nothing to say to you."

"I don't want to *explain,*" Alice said, "or ask your forgiveness. I just want to try and clear up why this happened."

"That sounds like an explanation to me."

"Neither of us ever thought this would turn into anything. But . . ."

"Let me guess. From the outset, you just thought it was a friendship. Or maybe you just considered Dan to be your fuck buddy?"

"We'd been having lunch for a couple of months . . ."

"Just lunch?"

"Initially, yes."

"If it had just been lunch at the start, Dan would have told me. What's lunch with a mutual friend, right?"

"All right, it wasn't just lunch after the second time."

"How did it start?"

"Hannah, you don't want to know this . . ."

"I'm asking the question, so I obviously *do* want to know. How did it start?"

"I had to see Dan about a recurring rotator cuff problem."

"A rotator cuff? Really?"

"Lots of illustrators suffer from it."

"And do lots of illustrators then sleep with their orthopedist—or does that only happen when the orthopedist is the husband of one of your best friends?"

"I didn't mean to fall in love. Neither of us did."

"Oh, it's love, is it?"

"Do you really think Dan would have just walked out on you like that?"

"How touching to know he did it for love."

"Look, I am *not* asking for your understanding. I just wanted to explain."

"You want my forgiveness, don't you?"

"I didn't say that."

"Then what's the actual point of this call?"

"I feel bad . . . I'm sorry . . . I'm . . ."

"Apology not accepted," I said, and put down the phone.

I sat down on the bed and bit hard on my index finger—in an attempt to stop me from screaming or reaching for the first inanimate object and hurling it through the window. But even though there was a glazier downstairs, ready to do the repair work if I started smashing glass, something stopped me. Maybe it was the fact that the initial urge to scream and cry was doused immediately by a cold numb rage.

I forced myself up from the bed. I finished packing. I went around the house, checking that all windows were locked. I wrote notes to the milkman and the newsboy, telling them that I wouldn't be needing their services until the middle of next week. I phoned Margy and said that I was heading off to points unknown in a little while.

"But you will be able to get to New York for Monday?" she asked.

"I'll be there."

"Well, don't run too far away. The show is set to be taped early evening on Tuesday, which means we'll have around thirty-six hours to get you primed to take on Judson."

"I'll be ready," I said.

"You sound terrible. Another sleepless night?"

I explained about the call from Alice Armstrong.

"Doesn't surprise me," she said.

"Why the hell not?"

"Because she's obviously suffering from terrible guilt, especially as she was your friend, which is probably making her guilt about ten times worse. As someone whose own husband left her, she's going to know what she's putting you through."

"That's cold comfort right now."

"Hon, nothing anyone is going to say or do is going to make this better. But you know that, don't you?"

"I'm afraid so."

"Go hide out for the weekend . . . but have the cell phone with you, so I can get hold of you at all times. You know what a control freak I am."

I brought my bag out to the car. As I did, I saw that Brendan had replaced all the smashed windows and had also whitewashed away the graffiti. In its place, as agreed between us, he was using a can of red paint to write: *YOU WIN . . . I'M GONE.*

"That will definitely keep them away from you," he said.

"How much do I owe you?" I said.

"Forty bucks will do it."

"But the last time you charged me three hundred."

"The labor's on the house this time."

"That's very generous, but not necessary."

"Yes, it is necessary."

I didn't flee far from home—just a few hours north to a little hotel on Mount Desert Island. As it was early May, it was still the off-season, so there was no problem getting a room.

The hotel was a little weather-beaten, and its decor was shabby. But the place was clean, there was a beach nearby and plenty of walking trails, and my room had a wonderful old armchair with a beat-up ottoman, which made it the perfect spot in which to collapse with a book. I arrived just before sunset. I checked in and hiked over to the beach and stood on the sand, looking out at the Atlantic, telling myself that, whatever happened next week, I would still carry on, still find something productive with which to fill the day. And yet, while convincing myself, mantralike, that *things would work out,* the words sounded hollow. I'd persevere. But with no one to go home to, no children to call, no close friends nearby, no . . .

Enough.

I walked the beach. I went back to the hotel, insisting that I attempt to concentrate on nothing; that I treat the next two days as "time out," and do my best to avoid thinking about anything.

Fat chance. But I still tried. I worked my way through three novels. I took long walks, including the gently inclined, but still lengthy, hike to the summit of Mount Desert. I never turned on the television, never opened a newspaper or magazine, and kept my little portable radio tuned to Maine's all-classical music station that made a virtue of never broadcasting the news. I found a small seafood place in Bar Harbor where I ate dinner each of the three nights, a book propped up against a wineglass, the owner asking me no questions about what I was doing here alone at the end of spring, but insisting on giving me a liqueur on the house every night.

I kept my cell phone off for most of the time, checking in with its voice mail twice a day to collect messages. There was a particularly persistent journalist from *The Portland Press Herald,* insisting that I agree to an interview—"You owe it to the people of Portland to set the record straight"—to which I could only think: *No, I don't owe them anything.* There was a crank call from some shrill woman who refused to identify herself, but hissed, "I'm glad they fired you from school. We don't want sluts like you teaching our kids." It was, thankfully, the only nutcase message, but it still unsettled me, and I couldn't help but wonder how she got my number. There were several worried messages from Dad, but when I called on Saturday evening, he seemed to accept that I was in all right shape and that, yes, once everything settled down, I would come see him and Edith soon.

Margy only called twice—once simply to say hi and see that I hadn't "checked into the Bates Motel," the second time to inform me of the travel arrangements that the Jose Julia people had made for me.

"They're also providing you with one hundred fifty bucks per night of credit at the hotel, to cover meals and stuff—though on Monday you'll be over at the apartment, eating with me."

"Why don't you let me take us out?"

"It'll be easier if we eat here," she said.

"By which you mean?" I asked, sounding suspicious.

"I want to eat at home, okay?"

Her tone was definitive. I decided not to push it.

"Whatever you want," I said.

"Ben, my assistant, will meet you at the hotel after you arrive and bring you over to the office for some coaching. He'll be assisting Rita, who's my number two here. You'll like her. She's this total hard-ass JAP from the Island who hates religious idiots and really wants you to stick it to Judson. So be prepared for some serious grilling from Ms. Rita.

"Oh, one final thing. I spoke with the Jose Julia people again about how everything will pan out. They've made all the arrangements now, gotten all the okays . . ."

"And do you think . . . ?"

"I called your Detective Leary again. He seemed to feel pretty confident that it will play our way. Of course, this kind of thing . . . it *is* risky. If it goes wrong, the whole thing blows up in our face. But if it goes right . . ."

"I'm getting nervous now," I said.

"That's understandable," Margy said, "as the next couple of days will definitely be nervous ones."

Still, I managed to sleep well on my last night at the hotel. I woke at seven, took a final walk on the beach, then headed south for the three-hour drive to Portland. Around ten miles north of the airport I checked my watch and saw that I still had a little time to kill, so I turned off the highway at the Falmouth Foreside exit and drove down Route 88, slowing down as I approached my house. I turned into the driveway. The graffiti—*YOU WIN . . . I'M GONE*—hadn't been augmented by anyone else. All the windows were intact. The tactic had worked. The house had been left alone.

I didn't stop to check the mailbox. I backed up and headed off straight for the airport. Once there, I deposited the car in the Extended Stay Parking Lot, wheeled my bag into the terminal, and checked in for the flight to New York.

I am not a nervous flier, but every small lurch of the aircraft today made my hand go wet and my stomach backflip. I shut my eyes and told myself I was being ridiculous. Computers run these planes—and they are built to withstand even a lot of turbulence. But it wasn't the moderate winds that were making me nervous. It was the days ahead.

At LaGuardia there was a man in a suit and a black chauffeur's hat holding up a sign with my name at the arrivals gate. We crossed the 59th Street Bridge, and that vast vertiginous cliff of buildings enveloped us as we plunged into Manhattan. I kept staring out at the streets, wanting to be excited about being in New York. But all I felt was complete dread.

When I reached the hotel, Ben Chambers was waiting for me in the lobby. He was a short, jumpy guy in his late twenties, who nonetheless radiated a certain take-charge charm.

"You're here, that's great, that's great. And we're all waiting for you at the office. So say we meet back here in thirty minutes. Thirty minutes ready to go, okay?"

My room was large, spacious, faceless—but with a great view toward midtown and the East River beyond. I unpacked quickly and was downstairs well before the half-hour deadline. Ben was pleased that I was early.

"This is good, this is good, we've got a lot to deal with. And we've only got two hours to deal with it, because Margy's expecting you for dinner at seven."

"How's she doing?" I asked.

A fast anxious shrug from Ben Chambers.

"Put it this way: she's one hell of a fighter."

That sounded ominous.

Margy's office was only two blocks away—and as it was a bright late-spring day, we walked. Or, at least, I tried to walk while Ben negotiated his way through the human traffic at a pace that could be best described as a take-no-prisoners canter. We crossed 6th Avenue and then entered an old squat 1940s office building on West 47th Street. Margy Sinclair Associates was a small suite of offices on the eleventh floor—four rooms with framed posters and photographs of past PR campaigns and assorted clients; the decor simple, sleek, *can-do*.

I was ushered into a conference room and came face-to-face with Rita. Unlike Ben, she was large in every department: a woman of size who seemed to wear her substantial girth with ease. Her voice was foghorn loud; her head a large Methuselah-like bundle of tight black curls. Her handshake was chiropractic, her stare positively forensic.

"You know what I thought after reading that asshole's book?" she said, motioning for me to sit down at one of the chairs around the long table. "There's nothing worse than a born-again Christian playing with skeletons in other people's closets."

Coffee showed up—and after about three sips, Rita said, "All right, let's get on with the show."

For the next two hours, I was subjected to the sort of grilling that left me feeling as if I had been pistol-whipped. With Rita in the role of prosecuting attorney—and Ben regularly interjecting with additional questions—they pried, probed, cajoled, and baited me. At first, the verbal assault was unnerving. So much so that I actually believed they were taking Judson's side. That was the point, of course. As they jolted me—continually throwing me off balance while picking apart all my arguments and excuses—they were simultaneously toughening me up, preparing me for the worst that Jose Julia and Judson could throw at me. The level of aggressive questioning sent me reeling. After ninety minutes of Inquisition-style tactics, Rita interrupted their interrogation and asked, "Having fun?"

"You have me scared," I said.

"That's the game plan. Scare the crap out of you now so nothing they toss at you tomorrow will seem that surprising."

"Do you think he'll really throw questions like that at me?"

"Are you kidding me?" Rita said. "Jose Julia is the reigning king of the sleazy question. There are only two reasons he wants you on his show: one, your missing daughter, and the fact that she might have been murdered by her married doctor lover, and two, to get you and your ex-lover into a mud-throwing contest about who did what. If he could get away with it, he'd probably ask you if you went down on the guy. As it is, he'll do his best to *imply* that."

"Oh, great," I said quietly.

"Now, don't you go getting scared on me," Rita said. "You didn't do too badly, considering the shit we just threw at you. The thing to remember is: your fifteen minutes of fame will only last ten minutes, and as long as you follow the strategy we're working out, you'll get your side of the story across just fine.

"Ready to start again?"

We went through the entire mock interview one more time, refining my answers, working out counterpunches and possible curveball questions, with Ben now taking charge on issues like my body language, my posture, my bad habit (as he pointed out) of gnawing on my lip when I was anxious.

"Under no circumstances can you do that during the interview," he said. "You'll end up looking apprehensive, which will make many people wonder if you have something to hide. Always look Judson straight in the eye. Never avoid his gaze—*meet it.* And with Jose, be as pleasant and relaxed as possible—even when he starts giving you a hard time. Because he *will* give you a hard time. That's what he's paid to do."

At six-thirty Rita glanced at her watch and said, "Time flies when you're having fun. We've got to dash, otherwise Her Royal Highness will be pissed with me for getting you to her place late. Her Royal Highness expects her minions to make certain her guests arrive on time."

"We'll pick this up again at ten tomorrow," Ben said. "And we'll do two more practice sessions before the taping at five. Do you want me to meet you at the hotel around nine forty-five a.m.?"

"I think I can make it over here myself," I said, with a small smile.

"Hey, she's from Maine," Rita said, "so she's probably packing a compass . . ."

In the taxi on the way uptown Rita said, "So, Her Royal Highness told me you're her oldest friend."

"Thirty-six years and counting."

"That's pretty damn impressive. Then again, she is about as loyal as they come."

"Even if she is 'Her Royal Highness'?"

"Oh, she knows we call her that. She even encourages it."

"I bet she does."

"The thing about Margy is, professionally, she always cracks the whip and terrifies everybody, while personally, she is a total softie . . . but you know that already."

"All too well. Can I ask you a direct question?"

"About her health?"

"You guessed it."

I could see her hesitating, chewing her lip in the same anxious way I did.

"She's been pretty adamant that we say nothing . . ."

"She can't leave the apartment now, can she?"

She nodded.

"How badly has the cancer come back?" I asked.

"Badly."

"How badly?"

She turned away and stared out the window.

"I really shouldn't . . ."

"She's my best friend and I promise I won't say anything."

"Believe me, she's acting like it's just business as usual, but she knows . . ."

"Knows what?"

"Six months maximum."

I shut my eyes and said nothing for a while. Then, "Did she tell you this herself?"

Rita nodded.

"She entrusted the secret to me. The thing is, everybody knows—because the few times she's come into the office, it's been so obvious how ill she is. And we're a small operation, so we've all been back and forth to her apartment with files and clippings for her, as she has completely refused to stop working."

"It's everything she has."

"When you see her tonight, you're going to freak a bit. But you have to try not to show it. She refuses to publicly acknowledge what's going on—even though you can see that, privately, she's terrified. Who wouldn't be? If it was me, I don't think I could deal with it the way she's handling it."

You don't know that, I felt like telling her. *Because none of us know how we'll act if we're faced with the diagnosis that, within six months, maybe a year, we will no longer exist.*

When we pulled up in front of Margy's building on East 72nd Street, Rita squeezed my arm and said, "You're going to do fine tomorrow, really."

"Don't be too sure of that."

As I rode upstairs in the elevator, I kept telling myself: *Act natural . . . pretend everything is normal . . . do not flinch.*

I hesitated for a moment outside her door, taking a deep, steadying breath before ringing the bell. From inside I could hear her voice shout, "It's open."

The strength of her voice reassured me—it sounded like the old Margy. But as soon as I opened the door, it was hard to fight my shock.

My friend sat on a sofa near the door—a small, shrunken woman, slightly hunched over as if she were suffering curvature of the spine, her cheeks emaciated, most of her hair gone, her eyes and skin tinged with a jaundiced yellow coloring. A canister of oxygen was standing alongside one of those portable hospital stands. Suspended from this was a bag of medicinal liquid, the tube of which ended up attached by a needle to a vein in one of her hands.

But in the midst of taking all this in—making sense of the way the cancer had completely decimated my friend—I caught sight of a dirty ashtray on the side table near the sofa. A smoldering cigarette was lying there, awaiting the next puff. Margy saw me do a double take at the sight of this smoking object. And said, "If you say a fucking word about the cigarettes, I'm throwing you out."

"All right, then. I won't say a fucking word."

A grim little smile from Margy.

"Okay, we're off to a good start. But if you come over here and give me a great big consoling hug, I am going to get annoyed. So no touchy-feely stuff tonight. Just go get me a vodka and find something for yourself while you're at it."

I went into the little galley kitchen and located the vodka by the fridge.

"Rocks?" I shouted from the kitchen.

"Who the hell drinks warm vodka?"

When I came back with the two drinks, Margy had the oxygen mask over her face and was noticeably wheezing as she ingested that pure air. Then she reached over, turned off the canister valve, and picked up her cigarette.

"Now I can smoke again."

I handed her the vodka. She drew down a small lungful of smoke. She didn't exactly exhale it. Rather, it seemed to leak out of her mouth, almost like someone drooling smoke.

"Go on," she said, pushing her pack of Marlboro Lights toward me. "I know you want one."

I fished out a cigarette and picked up the table lighter and lit up. "A great guilty pleasure, eh?" she said, reading my mind. "And you're not your usual positive self, hon."

"I've got a lot on my mind," I said, sipping the vodka.

"About tomorrow, you mean?"

"Not just that."

She wheezed and coughed and dampened down the wheezing with a slug of vodka, followed by a long draught of fresh oxygen. When she finally pulled the mask away, she saw my horrified expression and said, "Surely Rita told you the ground rules: no shows of concern, no displays of dismay . . ."

"She said nothing."

"Don't shit a bullshitter. She's a great kid, Rita—a fantastic kid—but she's taking all this far too hard. Anyway, before we get all tragic and lachrymose—hell of a word, *lachrymose*—know this: I'm not talking about it. And by 'it' I mean *IT.* I'm keeping *it* off the agenda until we get through with tomorrow. Even after that, there'll be nothing much to say about it anyway, because there's not much to say. We clear about that?"

I nodded.

"Good. On to other things. I've ordered in sushi tonight, because I figured you don't get much in the way of Japanese food in that rube state you come from. You got anything against raw fish?"

"Bizarrely, even a backwoods country girl like me has eaten sushi."

"I tell you, the progress we've made in this country . . ."

She took another sip of vodka. Then said, "Okay, next bit of business. See that file on the table over there," she said, pointing to a bulging yellow envelope on the dining table near the kitchen. "That's your clippings file. It's got everything that's been written on you in the past two weeks—most of which you've probably not seen, since you've mentioned to me that, for some strange reason, you've wisely turned off the media and the Internet recently."

"That's the truth. But I've obviously been missing a lot."

"Oh, this whole story has gone beyond stupid. Chuck Cann has gotten at least four more columns out of it, and every right-wing pundit in the country—from Coulter to Brooks to Kristol—has taken his or her turn bashing you and also pointing out that you represent everything that was immoral and hedonistic about the sixties. There have also been pieces chastising you for refusing to say you're sorry, analyzing whether our generation refuses to accept responsibility for our actions, and, amazingly, even one or two articles supporting you . . . but they're in left-wing small-beer publications like *The Nation* and *Mother Jones,* which are basically speaking to the converted. Anyway, I'd like you to read through them all . . ."

"I don't need to. I pretty much already know what they say. And I don't need to read about my sins anymore."

"Have it your way. I just want you to be completely up on everything that's been written about you, in case Julia or Judson dredges up some quote—"

"I've decided how to handle it."

"Tell me."

"They are entitled to write whatever they want about me. And though I might not agree with what they write, I accept it. But my conscience is clear about the legality of my actions."

She thought about this for a moment.

"Not bad, but this is trash television, not the Constitutional Convention of 1787, and if you start coming on like Thomas Jefferson, it won't fly. So here's what I suggest . . ."

We ran through the entire mock interview again—refining it, targeting potential weaknesses, brushing up my retorts and responses. The food arrived. We made small talk over the sushi. Without saying anything, we both deliberately decided to avoid the big stuff—Margy simply asking me once whether I felt better after the weekend in Maine, and wondering out loud if Dan might just have a sudden change of heart and return home.

"He's 'in love,'" I said. "Why would he run back to someone who hasn't just betrayed him, but has also made him a subject of derision at the country club?"

"He can't have done his local image much good by running off with your best friend."

"On the contrary, it shows he can pull a babe, and that he's being desired by two women. That will do wonders for his ego."

"You know, I always thought Dan was one of those rare men who didn't have much of an ego."

"He's a surgeon—of course he has an ego. The thing is, he always kept it under wraps. Until now, when I finally gave him the excuse to use it against me."

"You're beating yourself up again."

"So what else is new?"

We finished the sushi—washed down with more vodka—then ran through one or two more points about the interview. Around nine that evening, Margy began to fade—whatever energy she still had left suddenly deserting her.

"I think I have to get into bed," she said, leaning her head against a hand and suddenly looking even more shrunken than earlier.

"Let me help you," I said.

"No fucking way. Allow me to hold on to just a sliver of my dignity. But before you go, just remember two things when you're taping the show tomorrow. The first is: you are the victim here, but you have to walk a fine line between acting put-upon and being indignant. The second is: that other thing is still in the works and looks like it's going to come through."

"You mean it's not certain?"

"There have been a few last-minute hitches," she said, and explained them. "We'll know for certain tomorrow."

"And if it doesn't come through?"

"We'll just have to hope that the Court of Public Opinion sides with you."

As I was leaving, I tried to give Margy a hug. But she put up her hand like a cop stopping traffic and said, "You hug me, I'm going to do something stupid like get emotional. And I can't get emotional right now."

In the cab back to the hotel I found myself trying to imagine life without Margy; tried to think what it would be like to wake up some morning in the very near future, knowing she was no longer at the end of a phone line; knowing that that part of my life was over. Is that what getting older really means—the people you care about disappearing one by one until it becomes your turn to leave the scene?

The tears I thought would follow the meeting with Margy didn't come—though I knew they would eventually arrive later. As the cab sped crosstown, I hugged myself, trying to keep a deep chill at bay. The tiredness that had lifted during those three days by the sea suddenly returned—accompanied by the sort of stupefaction that often accompanies a confrontation with life's less bearable realities. When we reached the hotel, I went straight to my room and was asleep within minutes. I woke sometime just before dawn. I opened the curtains and peered out at the gradual emergence of light over Manhattan—a small pinprick in the darkness that eventually lengthened and widened, before parting like a curtain to expose the new day . . . a day that I dreaded facing.

I was back at Margy's office at ten for a final two-hour rehearsal. Rita and Ben pronounced themselves reasonably pleased with my progress, but still reminded me to keep my answers short and simple, and always to maintain crucial eye contact, no matter how distasteful the line of questioning became.

At noon they told me to get lost for a couple of hours—and I did just that, killing time in the Metropolitan Museum, looking at Old Masters and Egyptological remnants, and the subdued ethereal delicacy of French Impressionists, and trying somehow to keep my mind off things to come.

At two-thirty I grabbed a taxi back to the hotel. I returned to the room and changed into the simple black suit that Margy had told me to pack last week. I resisted the desire for a cigarette and took the elevator down to the lobby. Rita was already waiting for me.

"There's a surprise waiting for you in the car," she warned me. "Don't freak."

I got into the Lincoln Town Car and found Margy there. She was dressed up in one of her best business suits. It hung loosely on her diminished frame. She had also applied a little too much makeup to compensate for the ashen tone of her skin.

"Are you out of your mind?" I said.

"Completely—and yeah, my oncologist read me the riot act. But to hell with that *putz*. I wasn't going to miss this for anything. We got some good news this morning."

"About . . . ?"

"That's right. It's on."

"Are you sure?"

"Hey, I'm just going on what the Jose Julia people told me. But they said it was a slam dunk."

Rita climbed into the front seat next to the driver and we headed off westward.

"Do you really think you can be away from the oxygen for a couple of hours?" I asked Margy.

"Will you listen to my friend the Girl Scout," Margy said to Rita.

"We've got the canister in the trunk," Rita said.

"But hey, if I keel over in the studio, Judson-the-Schmuck can do the laying-on-of-hands bullshit and revive me, and then go on the road as a faith healer."

"You're a piece of work," Rita said, laughing.

"Too fucking true," Margy said in reply.

We took the Lincoln Tunnel and popped up again in the nowhere-land of New Jersey. The studios of *The Jose Julia Show* were located in an industrial park on the outskirts of Secaucus.

"This must be the place where God decided to give the world an asshole," Margy said as we pulled up to the stage door. "Rita, hon, if I start to go under here, you've got to promise me you'll get me back across the river before I expire. There's no way I'm dying in Jersey."

A hyperenergetic woman with a clipboard was waiting for us inside the stage door.

"You must be Hannah!" she said, pumping my hand. "Jackie Newton! Production coordinator for Jose!"

She also pumped the hand of Rita ("You must be the publicist!") and looked a little nervously at Margy, who was leaning on the arm of the chauffeur . . . the canister of oxygen under his other arm.

"I'm her mother," Margy said.

I was whisked off to makeup, where a large woman in spandex pants took over.

"You nervous?" she asked me as she started applying foundation to my face.

"Is it that obvious?"

"Hey, it's always a little nerve-racking doing TV. But honestly, Jose's a doll. A total doll. Now, you strike me as someone who doesn't use a lot of eyeliner or mascara . . ."

Ten minutes later I was sitting in one corner of the green room with Rita and Margy, trying to stay calm. Jackie Newton came bursting in, clipboard in hand.

"Okay, just about ten minutes to showtime! And our other guest is already here, so . . ."

"He's not coming in here, is he?" I asked, sounding desperately jumpy.

Jackie patted my arm. "Now, as they say in Jersey, I may be dumb, but I ain't stupid. And considering your 'shared history,' we thought it best you guys didn't meet until you were on the set. So, don't sweat it, Hannah. Anyway, just to run through some stuff you already know, your segment will be ten minutes exactly. We'll need you to sign the following release form. And the good news for you is that we've decided to make it the first item on the program, so there won't be a long wait. And Jose will be dropping by in a moment, just to say hello and make you feel at home. So hey, kick back!"

As soon as she was out of earshot, Margy said, "You know, I've never really trusted anyone who talks in exclamation points."

Then the green room door burst open and Jose Julia waltzed in. Naturally, I'd seen him on television before—he'd been around since the mid-seventies, first when he was a roving reporter for NBC and sported long hair, a leather jacket, and a big liberal conscience. Since then, he'd reinvented himself several times over—as an anchorman on assorted cable stations, then as a front man on a failed ABC newsmagazine, then as a wandering journalistic gadfly—before finding his niche, in the late nineties, as a scandalmongering rabble-rouser on cable. And though he always proclaimed himself to be "apolitical," the fact that he had done an extended stint on Fox News before switching to New America Cable News more than hinted that he had embraced his conservative paymasters. So too had the patriotic bilge he had spouted after 9/11—and the way he made headlines around the country after browbeating a Muslim cleric on his show and telling him, "You hate our way of life," a comment that won him a great deal of positive feedback in right-wing circles. This is what I dreaded most about Julia—the fact that he'd play the patriotic card with me and question my allegiance to my country.

"Well, hey there, Hannah Buchan!" he said, bearing right down on me.

I hate to admit it, but for a man edging toward sixty, he looked amazingly fit. Dressed in a very well-cut black suit, with an English spread collar shirt and a subdued polka-dot tie, he had a full head of thick, slightly ruffled black hair, a big Zapata-style mustache, and a thousand-watt smile. He exuded designer good taste and aerobic high maintenance.

"It is so great to have you here," he said, giving me a two-handed handshake. "Like just *so* great. You feeling good about being here?"

"Well, to be honest . . ."

"I know! I know! *That man!* Can't say I blame you—but once we're out there, mixing it all up, you'll have your chance to put the record straight—*and* on national television. So, hey, it's Dealer's Choice here, right? And the thing is, Hannah, the real object of the show . . . is to have fun."

Fun? Did he actually say *fun*?

"That's right, fun," he said, reading my mind. "Because even though we'll be touching on some pretty heavy personal stuff, well, confrontation and catharsis are a great kick, right? And one of the reasons why I've always wanted this show to be taped without an audience is because confrontation is always more forceful without the crowd from the Colosseum cheering the warriors on, right?"

I nodded.

"So, hey, if you want to get angry out there, you *get* angry. You want to tell him what you think of him, you tell him. Okay?"

"Okay," I said.

"You're going to do great. Just great. See you in five."

And he waltzed out.

I turned to Margy and hissed, "I'm leaving."

"No, you're not," she hissed back.

"It's going to be a freak show out there. Especially since he's probably told *him* the same thing as me. *'If you want to get angry out there, you get angry. Tell her off. Call her a harlot!'* I'm going to look like an idiot . . ."

"You can't get out of this now," Rita said, placing one of her big hands on my wrist and squeezing it very hard. "The die is cast. And you will do just—"

I stood up. Rita yanked me down again. And said, "Hannah, this is your one shot to set things straight. You walk out now, the cause célèbre multiplies by the power of ten. You do the show, you have the chance to close the deal, and get your life back. What's the better option here?"

Margy jumped in.

"And if you dare leave now, I'll die on the spot and haunt you for the rest of your life."

"That's not funny," I said.

"It wasn't meant to be."

Jackie returned, clipboard in hand, exclamation points bubbling out of her mouth.

"Moment of truth time, Hannah! Ready to rock?"

I stood up, feeling woozy. If I feigned a collapse, if I fainted . . .

I'd never forgive myself for not going through with it.

I shut my eyes. I tried to steady myself. I opened them again.

"I'm ready," I said.

Margy reached for my hand. "You'll be fine."

I followed Jackie into the studio. En route she said, "We can't invite your support team in here, as Jose likes to keep it strictly off-limits to everyone except the crew and the participants. Still, they'll be able to follow everything on a monitor in the green room."

The set was simple. A large thronelike chair for the host, with two narrow armchairs facing each other over a small coffee table. The logo, *JOSE!,* covered the plain blue backdrop. A sound technician approached me with a wireless microphone that he attached to my jacket lapel, then asked me to hide the battery pack in an inside pocket. I was shown to my seat, where I crossed and recrossed my legs in an attempt to get comfortable. A makeup woman arrived to patch up any gaps in the foundation base that might have shown up in the last half hour. I closed my eyes when she applied powder to my cheeks and nose. When I opened them, Tobias Judson was sitting opposite me. I tried not to flinch. I failed. Up close, he looked even stockier than the times I had recently seen him on television—his bald pate currently being dusted with powder, his rimless glasses catching the light. Our eyes met for a moment. He gave me a small curt nod. I nodded back and we both looked away. On the table in front of Judson were two books—his autobiography and a copy of the Bible.

Jose Julia came out, trailed by his own makeup lady and a producer who was whispering rapid-fire final instructions in his ear.

"Got it, got it," Julia said as he settled into his chair, studied his notes, did a sound check with the technicians, asked for the teleprompter to be brought forward two feet, checked his watch, and completely ignored his two guests.

Then, when the producer shouted thirty seconds, Julia looked at each of us, flashed a big smile, and said, "Showtime!"

"Twenty seconds, ten seconds, five, four, three, two . . ."

The set lights blazed on, the producer signaled Julia, who looked straight at the camera and started reading the teleprompter.

"Good evening, America! Tonight, the curse of an overweight woman whose affair with her personal trainer turned homicidal. And what happens when stepdaughters marry their stepfathers? But before that . . . say you had an illicit affair with a man thirty years ago—a man who you also helped to flee the country while he was wanted by the FBI. And say that man who has now reformed his ways writes a book about his past life, and talks all about that 'little' skeleton in your closet. How would you react? That's the dilemma that's facing Hannah Buchan, a married schoolteacher from Maine whose past life has been exposed in a new book by Chicago radio talk-show host Tobias Judson. And Hannah seriously disputes Toby's telling of the tale, saying he forced her into it . . . whereas he's saying she was so in love with him at the time she was only too happy to help him evade the strong arm of the law. It's a classic he said/she said situation, folks—and right after this message, we'll be back to find out: who's telling the truth here? Stay tuned!"

The lights went down again.

"Thirty seconds!" shouted the producer. Julia again avoided glancing at either of us as he took a sip of water. I looked up in the direction of Judson. I could see him watching me, noting my nervousness. He shot me a little sardonic smile, as if to say: *I am going to get you.*

"Ten seconds. Five, four, three, two . . ."

The lights came back up.

"Welcome back, America! In the right corner, Toby Judson, well-known Chicago radio host and author of a new book, *I Ain't A-Marching Anymore.* In the left corner, Hannah Buchan, schoolteacher from Maine, a married mother of two grown children, whose affair with Judson became national news in the light of her daughter's own affair with celebrity doctor Mark McQueen—and her subsequent disappearance. We've talked about the Elizabeth Buchan case on the show before. Before we get started, Hannah, can I just have your thoughts on whether you think Dr. Mark McQueen may have done your daughter harm?"

This was a question that Rita told me would certainly be thrown at me, so I knew exactly how to field it.

"Well, Jose," I said, making the all-important eye contact. "As every parent watching knows, there is no worse nightmare than your child disappearing. And until she is found alive and well, my life will be haunted by her absence. Having said that, I must believe that she is still alive and hasn't come to any harm."

"But do you think Dr. McQueen could have been involved in her disappearance?"

"That's a police matter, Jose."

"And the police still consider McQueen their prime suspect in this case. Toby Judson, considering the pain that Hannah Buchan is suffering right now due to her daughter's disappearance, do you think it was the appropriate moment to publish this book?"

A big smile from Judson toward Julia.

"Jose, let me say from the outset that my heart goes out to Hannah Buchan for her loss—and that I have prayed daily for Elizabeth's safe return home. But I also must point out that it was never my intention to expose Mrs. Buchan as the woman who helped me flee to Canada. I used a pseudonym in the book . . ."

"But surely you knew that someone would figure out that the woman in question was Hannah Buchan."

"The pseudonym was meant to protect her identity. If you want to point fingers, Jose, you should start with Chuck Cann, who revealed all on his website."

"Now, you were a real die-hard sixties radical, right?"

Another relaxed smile from Judson.

"The hardest of the hard left," he said, then began to quickly explain the circumstances that landed him in Maine, the way my dad had sent him to me, the *coup de foudre,* the baby in the bedroom as we made love (Jose loved that detail), and the way I insisted on driving him to Canada.

"Quite a steamy story there, Toby," Julia said. "Extramarital sex. Radical sixties politics. An accomplice to a serious crime. Love at first sight. And a midnight flit across the border. No wonder your book's already a best seller! Hannah Buchan, what does your husband think about all this?"

"He was understandably upset," I said, looking directly at him.

"So upset that he walked out on you after thirty years of marriage."

I was about to start chewing on my lip.

"I'm afraid that's the case, Jose."

"And no chance of reconciliation, since he's now living with your best friend. Or should I say *onetime* best friend. Never knew Portland, Maine, was just like Peyton Place! But seriously, Hannah, what do you think of Judson's account of your affair?"

"It is full of lies and misrepresentations. But the biggest misrepresentation . . ."

Julia cut me off.

"Hang on, your dad did send him to you, right?"

"Yes."

"You did fall for him, right?"

"It was a temporary infatuation—"

"Which led to you two sharing a bed together, right?"

"Uh . . . yes."

"With your baby son in the same room?"

God, this was not going according to plan.

"That's right, but—"

"And you did drive him to Canada, right?"

"All that is correct, Jose—I have never denied any of those facts . . ."

"You've just refused to apologize for them. Unlike Toby, who has written an entire book apologizing for his past deeds and proclaiming his patriotism and newfound Christian faith."

"I have apologized to the people who count in my life: my husband . . ."

"Well, your husband evidently didn't accept your apology."

"May I ask Hannah a question?" Judson asked.

"Be my guest," Julia said.

"Did you apologize to God?"

"Unlike you, I don't speak to God," I said.

"Maybe you should start," Judson said.

"And maybe you should stop writing lies," I heard myself say.

"You've just called Tobias Judson a liar," Julia said, delighted with this angry turn in the conversation.

"That's right—the stuff he wrote about me taking him to Canada is a total lie."

"But you've just admitted you drove him to Canada," Julia said.

"Under duress. He threatened to expose the affair, threatened to tell the FBI I was his accomplice if he was caught, threatened to—"

Judson cut me off.

"I will not sit here and be called a liar by a woman who has refused to accept her guilt, her . . ."

"Accept my guilt? Accept my guilt?" I yelled. "My entire life has been destroyed by you and your shabby little book, your defamation of my character, your . . ."

"See how out of control she gets when challenged," Judson said to Julia. "And yet, from a Christian point of view, asking forgiveness is the path to redemption."

"You are no goddamn Christian," I said. "You are . . ."

"I won't even deal with your use of blasphemous language. As to my relationship with Jesus Christ—and the way I was able to change my life through His redemptive powers . . ."

"Change your life?" I said, now really letting it rip. "You're just a huckster, a con artist, using your story of 'redemption' to further your career . . ."

"I really think this sort of talk is way over the line," Judson said to Julia.

"You certainly are one angry lady, Hannah," Jose said.

I clenched my fists and started chewing my lip. I tried to lower my voice, but I still trembled as I spoke.

"I was having a perfectly normal, quiet little life until this man came back into it with his cheap accusations, his . . ."

"It was hardly a *normal* life, Hannah," Julia said, "if your daughter's disappearance was front-page news everywhere. And don't you think we have to be responsible for our own actions . . . even if they did happen years ago?"

"Of course, but—"

"Okay, let's cut to the chase. You, Hannah, admit that you slept with this guy all those years ago. You admit that you drove him to Canada, but you're pretty damn firm on the fact that he forced you into it. Whereas you, Toby Judson, insist that she did it out of love for you . . . that she volunteered to do it. So who's right here, folks? Stay tuned after the break—and you'll find out. Because the Jose Julia Investigating Team have found a surprise witness who was there and who knows who was telling the truth! Don't go away!"

The lights dimmed. There was a flurry of activity as two stagehands brought out another armchair and positioned it near Julia's throne.

"What surprise witness?" Judson said angrily.

"You'll find out," Julia said coldly.

"I was never told about this," Judson said.

"Well, a surprise is a surprise."

"You can't just—"

"Thirty seconds," the producer shouted—and suddenly Jackie emerged from the wings holding the arm of Billy Preston. Though his hair was gray and the glasses were thicker, he hadn't changed enormously in the past thirty years. Same jumpy eyes, same goofy grin. He was dressed in the sort of tight, narrow blue serge suit that was a relic from the sixties and made him look like an old-time preacher at a backwoods Baptist church. His eyes lit up when he saw me.

"Hey there, Hannah!" he said.

"Hey, Billy," I said back. "Great you could make it."

"Hey, it's real cool being on television . . ."

Across the stage, Judson hissed, "*Him? Him?* He's not a witness. He's . . ."

"Fifteen seconds," the producer shouted.

"I won't sit here and . . ."

Judson started to get up, reaching for his lapel mic to pull it off.

"You walk out now," Julia said coolly, "I'll announce that you stormed off rather than face the surprise witness. You want that?"

Judson sat down again, shifting nervously in his chair.

"Five seconds. Four, three, two . . ."

Lights. Camera. Action.

"Welcome back, America! So who's telling the truth here? Toby Judson, who maintains that Hannah drove him to Canada voluntarily to escape prosecution? Or Hannah Buchan, who maintains Toby coerced her by threatening to expose their affair? Well, here's our star surprise witness: Billy Preston, who was there when all this happened over thirty years ago. Welcome to the show, Billy."

"Sure pleased to be here, Jose," he said, nodding his head rapidly.

"Now, Billy, you're a lifelong resident of Pelham, Maine, right?"

"Yup."

"And you suffer from a form of developmental challenge called autism, is that right?"

"I never think myself different from nobody."

"And, bless you, Billy, you're not. I only mention that so your credibility as a witness cannot be challenged. Because, though you do suffer from autism, you hold down a job, don't you?"

"I'm the Mr. Fix-It of Pelham, Maine. You got a problem with your drains, you need your house repainted, you call me."

"Now that's just terrific, Billy. Just terrific. You're a beacon of light for all people living with *challenges.* But the thing is, Billy, you've also got a terrific memory, don't you?"

"So my mom used to say."

"Well, let's test that memory. Who pitched the second game for the Boston Red Sox during the 1986 World Series against the Mets?"

"Roger Clemens."

"Sounds good to me. And who was the fourteenth president of the United States?"

"Franklin Pierce."

"How about that, folks! Well, Billy, if you've got such a terrific memory, you'll obviously be able to remember a conversation you overheard around thirty years ago . . . although you're going to have to come clean with us, Billy. Did you actually hear this conversation by putting your ear to a closed door?"

Billy blushed and turned all shy.

"Well, as George Washington once said, 'I cannot tell a lie,'" he said, laughing a little. "So yeah, I was listening behind a door when I heard—"

"Hang on there, Billy!" Julia said. "Let's not get ahead of ourselves here. Now, you knew Hannah Buchan when she lived in Pelham in 1973."

"That's right. I knew herself and Dr. Dan . . ."

"Her husband."

"Yeah, her husband. Hannah and me, we were friends."

"You liked her a lot."

Another blush and giggle from Billy.

"A real lot. Guess I kind of had a crush on her."

"So when this tall, dark stranger named Tobias Judson came to town while Hannah's husband was elsewhere . . ."

"Didn't like the fact that I saw 'em kissing one night."

"Really? You saw them kissing?"

"Yeah, in the window of the apartment she was living in at the time."

"And you didn't like that?"

"I didn't like it one bit."

"Did you see them kissing again?"

"No, but the next night I went back to the street in front of the apartment and looked up at the window and I could see the two of 'em arguing."

"The two people here with you tonight?"

"There wasn't no one else in that apartment."

"So when you saw them arguing, what did you do?"

"Well, there was a back entrance to the apartment up a flight of stairs. And I climbed 'em real slow and real quiet and stood outside the back door, and I could hear everything that was being said."

"And what, Billy, was being said?"

"I heard the man . . ."

"Tobias Judson?"

"Yeah, *him,*" he said, pointing to Judson. "I heard him say, 'You better drive me to Canada or I'll tell your husband.' And then I heard Hannah say, 'I can't drive you, it's against the law.' And then he said, 'If the FBI shows up here, I'll tell 'em you were my accomplice.' And then she said, 'Go on, tell the FBI.' And then he said, 'You want 'em to take your little boy from you? 'Cause that's what's gonna happen after I tell 'em you were my accomplice.' And then she started crying and stuff, pleading for him to let her alone, telling him that her little boy was the most important thing in her life, that she couldn't bear to be away from him. And he said, 'Then you better drive me to Canada, or . . .'"

"I cannot believe this crap," Judson thundered.

"*Crap*'s a bad word," Billy said.

"You expect the American public to believe these lies," Judson said.

"Ain't no lies," Billy said. "It's the truth. I was there. I heard you say . . ."

"Jose, this is outrageous . . ." Judson said.

"Sounds pretty plausible to me," Julia said. "Is that how you remember the conversation went, Hannah?"

Without a moment's hesitation, I said, "It's exactly how I remembered it. Billy really does have one fantastic memory."

"Hey, thanks, Hannah!" Billy said.

"Oh, for Christ's sake," Judson yelled. "Can't you see they've gotten together beforehand to get their story right?"

"I ain't seen Hannah since 1974," Billy said, all indignant. "And you really shouldn't take the Lord's name in vain . . ."

"How can you accept the word of a man with a mental defect?" Judson yelled.

"That's not fair!" Billy said, turning all red. "I ain't no retard. I'm just different, that's all. But I know how to tell the truth, Jose. And I'm telling the truth right now."

"And we believe you, Billy. We *truly* believe you. So there it is, folks—another wrong righted on *The Jose Julia Show*! But don't go away, there's so much more to come after this!"

Lights down. Judson was on his feet, ripping his microphone from his lapel.

"If you think there's an iota of a chance that this show will be aired . . ."

"Hey, I'm really quaking in my shoes," Julia said. "But if you want to take us on, be my guest. We've got a platoon of lawyers who will take great pleasure in bankrupting your lying ass. Thanks for coming on the show, Toby."

Judson stormed off.

Julia turned to Billy and said, "You did great."

"You think so?"

"Better than great. And you also got your friend here out of a lot of trouble."

"You're not mad at me, are you, Hannah?"

"Of course not."

"Even though I told everybody about what happened after you made me swear . . ."

"It's okay, Billy."

Jackie came and escorted us both offstage. When I went to shake Julia's hand, he gave it a brief squeeze and returned to studying his notes for the next guest. To him, I was now history.

Thirty minutes later, I was in the back of a Lincoln Town Car with Margy and Billy—while Rita sat shotgun next to the driver. Billy was staying at the same hotel as me, and I volunteered to look after him tonight in the city and also show him some of the sights before his flight back to Maine tomorrow evening. Up ahead, the Manhattan skyline came into view. It looked incandescent.

"Wow, is that a thing of beauty or what?" Billy said.

"We like it," Margy said drily.

"Never been on an airplane before," he said. "Never been out of Maine much, 'cept to New Hampshire and once to Fenway Park when I was in school. Can't thank you enough, Hannah."

"Don't thank me, Billy. Thank Detective Leary. He was the one who searched you out, didn't he?"

"Sure did."

He started to blush again, his eyes flickering fast. He asked, "Hey, you're not angry that I was standing at the back door, listening all the time while you and that guy . . . ?"

"No, I'm not angry," I said

"Promise?"

"Promise."

"Like, you know, I didn't quote you and Judson one hundred percent exactly, but I did give everyone the gist of what was said, didn't I?"

Margy came in here. "Kid, you saved our ass."

He smiled one of his big goofy smiles, then asked, "So we're still friends, Hannah?"

"Yes, Billy, we're still friends."

TWENTY

THE CALL CAME around ten in the evening. It was a few days before Thanksgiving. I was at home. I had just booked my flight to Paris and was compiling a checklist of things to do before I vanished in just three weeks' time. As I wrote item after item—shaking my head at the thought that I was the sort of person who needed to compile lists—the phone jumped into life. I reached for it.

"Hannah, it's Patrick Leary."

It had been around five months since I'd spoken to Detective Leary. He'd called me a few days after my appearance on *The Jose Julia Show* to see how I was doing. At the time, I was still in around three different minds about him—still embarrassed at that pass I made at him; still attracted to him; still wanting him to pull out a miracle and find Lizzie. When he complimented me for getting so angry on the program, I said: "I thought I'd nearly blown it."

"Nah, the anger worked, because everyone could see that it was a righteous anger, and completely justified."

A righteous anger. Once a Jesuit . . .

"It was Billy who saved my skin. Thank you for finding him."

"All part of the service."

He then changed the subject by telling me that he was getting engaged—to a schoolteacher he'd been seeing for over a year. He said this in a matter-of-fact way, as if he was reporting the fact that it was raining outside his office in Brookline. I answered in a matter-of-fact way, "How nice for you . . . I hope you're very happy." What else was there to say? A drunken fumble on a Boston street corner didn't exactly rank up there in the pantheon of mortal sins. I was suddenly no longer embarrassed. Rather, I was disappointed . . . and seized yet again by the loneliness that seemed to catch me unawares all the time now.

There was little else to talk about. He said he was following up a couple of new leads on Lizzie's disappearance, but the trail had gone cold. And they'd just done yet another "interview" with McQueen over the weekend, and he was as certain as he could be that the guy was innocent. "Like I said at the start of all this—he's a dirtbag, but not a homicidal one."

"So it's either suicide or alien abduction?" I said.

"Or she could be living somewhere under a new identity," he said. "It's a big country, it's not a hard place to vanish in. Anyway, if anything new happens on the case, you'll be the first to know."

And now, all these months later, "Hannah, it's Patrick Leary. Am I getting you at a bad time?"

"No, it's fine. But if you're calling me at this hour . . ."

"Yeah, something has come up. And as I promised you'd be the first to know . . ."

"Good news?"

"No."

A long silence.

"Is Lizzie dead?" I finally asked.

"We don't know that yet. But a body was fished out of the Charles yesterday. A woman in her late twenties, according to the forensic boys. Preliminary analysis of the body hints that she's been in the water for over seven months."

"I see," I said tonelessly.

"So far, there's absolutely nothing conclusive, and our database of missing persons in the Boston area has turned up at least thirty women around Lizzie's age. A quick question, though: did she wear any jewelry?"

"A diamond cross that she bought herself."

"Worn as a necklace?"

"That's right."

"Well, I hate to tell you this, but the woman they recovered was also wearing a diamond necklace."

I swallowed hard.

"They'll be doing DNA tests tomorrow, along with the autopsy. What would be useful is if you could come down here and maybe look at the cross and also check out some of the scraps of clothing that still remain."

"Okay."

"You up to anything tomorrow?"

"No, my days are pretty free right now."

"Would you like me to call your husband or will you do that yourself?"

"Would you mind calling him?"

"No problem."

Thirty minutes later, as I was sitting in an armchair, staring into the fire, still trying to take in the information that Leary had just imparted to me, the phone rang again. I picked it up and found myself talking to my ex-husband for the first time in five months.

Actually, we had spoken once before this—in Greg Tolland's office, late in July, when Dan arrived accompanied by his lawyer to discuss details of our divorce. The meeting had been Greg's suggestion—a straightforward discussion of who would get what—with most of the details worked out by our respective lawyers beforehand. There was little to go over—just the inking of a separation agreement. I was being handed ownership of the house, Dan would keep the stock portfolio and all other significant investments. There was to be no alimony—my insistence . . . I didn't need to be supported—but it was agreed that the interest of a trust we set up together in the early eighties would provide me an income. There was a little dickering on fine details, but it was, in principle, a fifty-fifty split, and one in which neither side emerged financially diminished.

Dan's lawyer didn't make much in the way of small talk. Greg Tolland, on the other hand, was being his usual outgoing "groovy" self—but he also turned out to be a stickler for detail, insisting on certain changes of language in the separation agreement and protecting my flank when it came to any liability owing to Dan's practice—he'd discovered that our house had been put up as collateral for Dan's mandatory malpractice insurance.

During the conference in Greg's office, Dan and I sat on opposite sides of a conference table, avoiding each other's eyes. When he first walked into the office, we exchanged nods and a nervous hello. When the conference ended—after we had both signed the separation agreement—he extended his hand. I hesitated, but then took it. There was a quick good-bye, and he was gone. Thirty years of marriage, and all we could now manage was a nervous hello/good-bye.

I didn't hear from him afterward. Nor did I track his comings and goings around town, any more than I asked after Alice. Though Portland was small, it was still possible to have a private life there, especially if, like me, you didn't show your face much around town.

So when I heard his voice on the other end of the line, I felt an instant tension . . . and sadness.

"Hannah, it's me," he said.

"Hi, there," I said.

"Is this a bad moment?"

"Did the detective call you?"

"He did."

"I think we need to prepare for the worst," I said.

"Are you going down to Boston tomorrow?" he asked.

"He wants me to identify her necklace . . . and maybe some clothes."

"Yeah, he wants me to look at them too."

"No need . . ."

"No, I want to go. In fact, I was going to suggest that we drive down together."

"No, thanks," I said.

"But it seems silly to take two cars. I could pick you up at eight, we'd be there easily by ten, and we could maybe have lunch afterward."

This threw me. I tried not to show it. "I don't think so, Dan. And I really don't think there's much need for you to be there. Still, if you are planning to be there, then I'll see you in Leary's office tomorrow at noon. Bye."

And I quickly hung up the phone.

I felt terrible afterward. Cursing myself for being so abrupt and dismissive. Still, in the months since he had left, I had hardened toward Dan. Whereas in the initial weeks after his shocked departure I might have been open to negotiation, now a sense of anger, mixed with desperate dejection, had colored my view of him. Especially as he didn't even pay me the simple courtesy of calling me after the revelations on *The Jose Julia Show*.

Not that there was a flash flood of calls in the immediate aftermath of the broadcast. But certain people did phone. Like my ex-boss Carl Andrews, who informed me that he was convening an immediate emergency meeting of the school board of governors and putting forward a motion that I be reinstated with back pay, and that I also be issued a formal apology on behalf of the school. "It's an apology I plan to make public in a press release to all state and regional papers," he said, then added, "I am not going to try to soft-pedal things and say I believed you all along, Hannah. Still, you know how uncomfortable I was about the prospect of losing you from the start—and, if you will come back, I will be hugely grateful. So too will your students . . . not that they'll ever show it."

The board resolution was passed nine–zero the next night. I received a nice check covering my back pay, was reinstated on full salary, and was sent a very eloquent letter of apology which, true to his word, Andrews got reprinted in *The Portland Press Herald*. The adjoining story—"School Reinstates Teacher Fired Over Book Allegations"—got play everywhere. So too did the news that, on the basis of the disclosures made on television, the U.S. Department of Justice had decided that I had no case to answer regarding the flight from justice by one Tobias Judson in 1973.

Mr. Judson, on the other hand, suddenly had many cases to answer everywhere. In the wake of the interview, he was attacked in many quarters for lying in print. Frank Carty—a columnist with *The New York Times*—used the case as an example of "a general Bush-era refusal to acknowledge that, in most human situations, there is no right or wrong person . . . there are just two competing versions of the truth. The fact, however, that so many conservative pundits and religious fellow travelers took Tobias Judson's story as the gospel truth—when, as it turns out, he wasn't simply embellishing the truth but also flat-out lying—shows a fundamental lack of critical discernment, and a belief that, so long as someone professes their Christian faith, they must be telling the truth. To all the Chuck Canns and Ross Wallaces of the world—who vilified a quiet, unassuming Maine schoolteacher, immediately presuming her guilt on the basis of the word of an ideological colleague—you owe Ms. Buchan, at the very least, an apology."

No such apologies were forthcoming, though I did drop Frank Carty a thank-you card. The American Association of Handicapped Persons, on the other hand, demanded an apology from Tobias Judson for the comments he made on Billy's disability during the interview. Judson issued one by press release around the same time as he returned to Chicago to discover that his show had been dropped from the local talk-radio station. "We may not approve of Mrs. Buchan's moral choices during the 1970s," the radio station said in their press release—which Rita scored for me—"but we also will not tolerate the maligning of an innocent party by one of our presenters, which is why Mr. Judson is no longer working for this station." Judson ate humble pie—and even went on NPR's *Morning Edition* to say that he got it all very wrong and was genuinely sorry for the pain he inflicted on me—and for his comments on "people with challenges," which he "profoundly regretted." But his publishers were still forced to withdraw his book from all shops after Greg Tolland threatened a $100 million defamation of character suit against them. I told Greg he was insane to be demanding such a sum. "Hey, let me scare those right-wing clowns," he said. But I just wanted it over. So when the publishers offered a one-off $300,000 payment to cover all damages—on the legal understanding that I would not pursue them for additional restitution—I accepted their offer on the spot. Tolland could have insisted on fifty percent of this fee—as we had agreed to this sort of split in the event any damages came my way. Instead, he just took ten percent, leaving me $270,000. I used it to set up the Elizabeth Buchan Travel Bursary, to be administered by the University of Maine and to provide a sum of money every year to a worthy undergraduate who wanted to study abroad but didn't have the financial wherewithal for the trip. Thanks to Rita, this gift to the state—and the fact that it was funded by the damages I received for being smeared—also received wide coverage, especially in New England, where *The Boston Globe* wrote an editorial praising me for my generosity and forgiveness, and saying that many people in Maine owed me an apology.

But I had received the apology I wanted from the school—and that was enough. Just as the retribution meted out to Judson seemed fair and reasonable. However, when asked by a journalist on the *Press Herald* whether I took pleasure in his downfall—and the fact that he was now considered unemployable as a broadcaster and a writer—I said that you'd have to be a deeply malicious person to enjoy the collapse of another person's career, even though that person had done you grievous personal injury.

Was I feeling that saintly? Not really, just worn down by everything that had hit me in the last few months and also cognizant of the fact that—as Rita, my great public relations brain, so wisely noted—the best strategy right now was to be magnanimous, forgiving, and determined to vanish from the public eye. This is why I refused all other interviews—bar that with the *Press Herald,* as they were my local paper—and I also told assorted publishers and movie-of-the-week types that I had no interest in seeing my story between hard covers or on the small screen. I didn't see what had happened to me as some great parable about sticking to your guns and telling the truth. Frankly, I saw it as a cataclysm that had ended my marriage, nearly terminated my career, and caused a disastrous ruction between myself and my son.

But around three weeks after all the fallout from *The Jose Julia Show* had ended, the phone rang one morning and Jeff said hello. He sounded cautious, a little circumspect, and formal. But still, he was on the other end of the line. And he had phoned me.

"I was just wondering how you were getting on," he asked.

"It's been a curious couple of weeks."

"With a good outcome, though. I watched the show."

I said nothing.

"I thought you did well, under the circumstances. And I was very touched when that Billy guy talked about how you only agreed to drive Judson to Canada out of fear of being turned in by him and being separated from me."

I chose my words carefully.

"As a parent, you know how you will do just about anything for your children."

A pause. Then Jeff said, "Yes, I do know that."

Another pause. Then Jeff said, "Our minister cited you in a sermon a couple of Sundays ago—talking about the way you used that settlement money to set up the travel thing in Lizzie's name, and how you also showed great courage in turning the other cheek. He glared at Shannon and me when he said that."

"I see."

"She's still really mad at you for what you said in that interview."

"That's her privilege. Are you still angry with me?"

"I'm feeling . . . well . . . a bit guilty, I guess."

"I see."

"Is that all you can say, Mom?"

"What else am I supposed to say?"

"I'm sorry, okay? I should have believed you when you told me he'd blackmailed you. I didn't. I was wrong. I'm sorry."

"Thank you for that."

Another pause.

"I've got to go now," he said. "I'm between meetings. I'll call again soon."

"That would be nice," I said.

He did phone around three weeks later—another tentative "Hello, how are you?" call, in which he made small talk and tried to act as if we had a normal relationship. At this point, it was early summer, and he asked what I'd be doing, and when I said that I'd agreed to teach summer school at Nathaniel Hawthorne High, he expressed surprise.

"What else would I do?" I said. "I like teaching. I'm glad to have my job back. And, quite frankly, it fills the time productively."

"But surely, after everything that happened, you need some time out, a summer off."

"No, after everything that happened, I need to be teaching. And you and the family? Where are you going this summer?"

"I've only got a week off—we're probably going to spend it with Shannon's family at Kennebunkport."

"That's nice," I said, refusing to fish for an invitation, even though it was less than an hour from Portland.

"I'd ask you down, Mom," he said, "but Shannon's still pretty adamant—"

"Fine," I said quietly.

"I've tried to talk her out of her position . . ."

"Fine."

"I'm sure, in time, she'll come around."

"Fine."

Another awkward pause.

"You ever get down to Hartford?" he asked.

"You know I don't. But let me say this: if you'd like to get together with me, I'd be very pleased to see you."

"That's good to know," he said. "Thanks."

Since then, he's been calling me once a week. Always from his office, always "between meetings," but gradually the chill has started to lift. We're not close, we don't make each other laugh, we're still terribly guarded, we've yet to sit down over a meal somewhere and talk. And though he keeps me up to date on the doings of my grandchildren, he still hasn't broached the idea of me visiting them as yet, though he has dropped many hints that he's still "in negotiation with Shannon" on this subject.

"Just give me a little more time, Mom."

"Fine."

"It's not fine. I don't like it. I want it to stop. The problem is . . ."

"I know what the problem is, Jeff."

I had, on one occasion, offered to apologize to her for the comments made—and, at Jeff's urging, wrote her a very short note, in which I said that what I'd said during that interview was taken out of context, but if I had hurt her feelings, I was genuinely sorry. A few days after she'd received the letter, Jeff called, sounding harassed, saying that Shannon felt "the apology hadn't gone far enough."

"What more could I have said?" I asked.

"She felt you should have been more, well, uh, humble."

"You can't be serious."

"I'm just reporting what she said . . ."

"The fact that I made the apology in the first place . . ."

"I know, I know. And you're right. Still . . ."

The subsequent silence said it all. On the home front, my son was a weak, browbeaten man.

"I *will* get her to agree to a visit," he said.

"I'm sure you will."

"Dad was here last week."

"I see."

"He came alone."

"I see."

"Are you at all in touch?"

"Surely you know the answer to that question, Jeff."

But now, contact had been made by Dan—and I had slammed the door on it, refusing his offer of a lift down to Boston. But why salve the man's conscience? I wasn't ready to be "just friends" with him.

Still, my residual anger toward Dan took second place to the realization that, at midday tomorrow, I finally might have to begin to accept that my daughter was truly dead.

I couldn't sleep. I got up at one point and walked down the corridor and stood in her room. It had long been stripped of its juvenilia. But I still could picture the big poster of the Ramones that dominated one wall when she was thirteen, to be replaced by Springsteen and R.E.M. And there was the old 1980s boom box that she traded in for a nice stereo system she bought with babysitting money, and on which she first played me Nick Cave ("He's my kind of depressive"). And then there were the stacks of books everywhere. She was always such a fanatical reader, with strong opinions about everything and might have been the only person I ever met who actually finished *Gravity's Rainbow.* She was always suggesting new writers to me. She talked about DeLillo long before *Underworld* came on the scene, and was reading tough-guy crime writers like Pelecanos when they were still obscure. I was always hopeful she might try her hand at fiction—she certainly talked about it enough. But the necessary discipline eluded her. Just like happiness eluded her.

Tears started cascading down my face.

My daughter is dead.

Four words I had refused to contemplate for all these long, terrible months.

I so wanted to speak to Margy now. But that was impossible. Margy had died seven weeks ago—and yet the idea that she too was no more was still hard to accept. Even though I'd been with her at the end. Another late-night call—from Rita, in this instance, around midnight in early September. She spoke in a near whisper, telling me that she was in a corridor at New York Hospital, where Margy had been rushed earlier that day.

"I've just spoken to her doctor. It's just a matter of days now. The cancer is everywhere. They're keeping her drugged up on morphine, because there's nothing more they can do. If you want to see her, I'd come tomorrow. They really don't know if she'll last another night."

I caught the first plane out the next morning and was at the hospital by nine. Margy was in a private room on the sixteenth floor. Her bed faced a window that was open to the midtown skyline. The back of the bed had been cranked up so she could look out. She was wizened, tiny, her skin the color of ash, her hair nothing but wisps. The cancer had triumphed—and had reduced her to this tiny denuded creature, dwarfed by the tubes and medical monitors that surrounded her. A plunger had been placed in her right hand. It was attached to a tube that fed her a self-administered dose of morphine whenever the pain became too unbearable. As I approached the bed, I expected her to be at least semi-comatose. But she was awake—and surprisingly lucid.

"Nice view, isn't it?" she said as I pulled up a chair by the bed.

"Great view."

"My town. But you know what the real irony of every New York life is? Everyone who's ever done time in this city thinks they have made some sort of impression on it. The truth is: nobody ever makes a lasting impression here. It's all . . . ephemeral."

"Isn't that the case with most lives everywhere?"

She shrugged. And said, "I'm not going to do a summing up—or any of that 'final curtain' shit. It's too depressing to think how little I've accomplished."

"Hey, that's stupid talk—and you know it."

"I do stupid talk well. Just as I'm now very aware of the fact that life always leaves you feeling gypped. And now . . ."

"I thought you were going to avoid a summing-up."

"Allow me a little self-pity, please."

"Don't I always?"

She managed a small laugh, then suddenly clenched over in pain and pressed down the plunger. There were more spasms of pain. They racked her completely. I was about to run for the nurse, but the morphine kicked in, and she stopped convulsing, the drug deadening everything, including her ability to speak. She looked up at me, glassy-eyed, and said nothing.

I sat with her for the next half hour, her hand in mine, her eyes as frozen as a lake in winter, the bright morning light streaming through the window, bathing the room in a harsh, fluorescent glow. A nurse showed up. She checked the monitors, shone a little penlight in Margy's eyes, checked the level of morphine, and depressed the plunger again.

"Would you mind waiting outside for a few minutes? I need to change her diaper."

My friend is dying in a diaper. Life isn't just randomly cruel. It is also absurd.

I went downstairs and stepped outside the hospital and lit up a cigarette, and thought about the inanity of smoking while, sixteen floors above me, Margy was dying of lung cancer. But the cigarette tasted wonderful, the nicotine had its balming effect, and I vowed I wouldn't smoke another one until I got back to Maine late tonight. I walked across the road to a little coffee shop, sat down at the counter, ordered a mug of coffee, indulged in a Danish, read a copy of *The New York Times* that somebody had left on the stool next to mine, checked my watch, noticed that forty-five minutes had passed, and decided to go back upstairs to Margy's room—and the continuing deathwatch.

But when I reached it, I found it empty—a cleaner mopping up the floor while, nearby, a technician began to dismantle all the machinery that had surrounded the now-vanished bed.

"Where's my friend?" I asked.

The cleaner looked up from her mop.

"She passed," she said.

"What?"

"Passed. Died."

It didn't register at first.

"And they took her away just like that?" I asked.

"How it's done 'round here," she said, turning away from me to continue mopping. Without thinking, I hurried into the hall, almost running right into the nurse who'd come into Margy's room earlier.

"I've been looking for you everywhere. Your friend . . ."

"So fast?"

"Cardiac arrest happens in a flash. Especially in terminal cancer cases. She felt nothing. It was very quick, very clean."

No, it wasn't clean, I felt like shouting. *The cancer had pillaged and savaged her for months. There was nothing clean about it at all.*

But I said nothing. Because I was suddenly crying. For the next fifteen minutes I could do nothing but cry. The nurse led me to a little room with an institutional-looking sofa and an armchair. She sat me down in the armchair and said she'd be back in a few minutes. This was obviously "the grief room," as there was a box of tissues on the adjoining table and a pile of pamphlets with titles like "Letting Go" and "Coping with Loss." I took in all these details as the sobs intensified. Just as another thought crossed my mind. Not a thought, actually, more of a remembrance. A visit to New York over a decade ago—and Margy bringing me to hear *La Bohème* at the Met. She was teary-eyed at the end. I found the production strangely cold. On the way out she said, "You seemed totally unmoved."

"Oh, it was beautifully sung and all that. The problem for me is that I've never really bought into that high romantic idea of doomed love."

"I wasn't crying because of that," Margy said. "I was crying because Rodolfo and all the others are in another part of the room when Mimi dies. I was crying because Mimi dies alone . . . which is probably how I'll die."

"Oh, come on . . ." I said.

"Allow me a little self-pity, please . . ."

Her exact words at the time. Her final words to me. And she did die alone—because I went out for a cigarette.

"Or because the nurse kicked you out," Dad said when I called him later that morning and started weeping on the phone.

"If I had come back after five minutes . . ."

"She would still have been drugged up on morphine and oblivious to whether or not you were there. So please stop this now. You've been through enough recently."

Dad was the first person to call me all those months ago after *The Jose Julia Show* to congratulate me for "sticking it to him" and to say, "Thanks to your friend Billy, that man is finished and you're vindicated."

When I sounded subdued, he said, "I know: Lizzie's there in your head right now."

"That she is."

"And you have to accept that you'll never be happy until Lizzie's found. How could you be otherwise?"

How well he always read me. Every time we spoke now, I could always sense him gauging my mood, trying to figure out whether I was down or having a reasonable day, if I was feeling particularly vulnerable, if I needed advice or simply a sympathetic ear into which I could rant. He was the first person I called after Margy died. And tonight, once the news came from Boston about finding the body in the Charles, Dad was the first person I phoned as soon as the conversation with Dan ended.

"This is difficult news," I said before giving him the rundown on Leary's call to me. When I finished, he said, "I don't want to sound absurdly optimistic, but a relatively common necklace isn't prima facie evidence that—"

"Dad, what do you really think?"

Silence. Then, "It sounds bad."

"Yeah, that's what I think too."

"Maybe it's best if you go down there without much hope."

"That's what I'm planning to do."

"I could join you, if you could use some support."

"The detective also called Dan—and he's coming. He even offered to drive me down. I said no."

"That's understandable."

"But you don't think it's right?"

"Did I say that?" he asked mildly.

"No, I was just trying to read between the lines."

"You are perfectly right to still be angry at him. Just as you are perfectly right to doubt your decision to be angry at him."

"Now you are reading between the lines."

"True. Why don't you see how you feel when you see him tomorrow. If he offers lunch and you still feel angry, turn him down."

"He might not even offer lunch."

"That's true. And changing the subject: how are plans progressing for Paris?"

"The flight's booked for the night of the twenty-sixth—and I've arranged the little commuter flight from Burlington to Boston at four p.m. that day, so I'll be able to stay with you until then."

"Paris for six months. I am envious."

"I'm terrified. Going to live in a big city for the first time is a huge step for a country girl like me."

"Thank God that witch hunt against you is finally over. Because you're about to commit the worst sin known to an American: moving to France."

I laughed. And then we lapsed into silence again. Finally Dad said, "Hannah, I know this sounds grim, but you have to prepare for the worst tomorrow."

"I am prepared."

The truth was: I was hardly prepared, even though the thought of Lizzie's death had haunted my every move for months. How can you prepare for the loss of your child?

When it was clear to me that I wasn't going to sleep, I picked up the phone and called the Onyx Hotel in Boston. The desk clerk said that there was a room available and yes, he'd alert the night porter on duty to expect me sometime around two a.m. I threw a few overnight things in a bag and locked up the house. I backed the car out of the drive and headed south.

I played Maine Public Radio as I maneuvered the car toward I-295. A late-night news bulletin came on before the station switched over to all-night classical music. I couldn't help but think of the time in late summer when I dodged all news, for fear that the next item would be about me. Just as I remember the dread I had of leaving the house, out of worry that it would be defaced again by the time I came back.

YOU WIN . . . I'M GONE.

The day after *The Jose Julia Show* was aired, I returned to Maine and found that the graffiti I had asked Brendan Foreman to daub across my front door had been whitewashed over. In fact, the entire front door had been repainted in a perfect high-gloss white. There was a Post-it left on the door:

Told you the next job would be on the house . . . Brendan.

That same afternoon there was a knock on the door. Outside stood

Mr. Ames from the Falmouth General Store. He had a big basket with him, wrapped in colored cellophane paper. He smiled a sheepish smile.

"Mrs. Buchan, ma'am, this is a small way of saying sorry to you for my rudeness in the shop some time back. I hope you'll accept this, just as I also want you to know that we'd greatly like you back as a very valued and honored customer."

With that, he handed me the basket—filled with gourmet crackers, and a tin of oysters, and jars of exotic chutneys and marmalades. Then with a nervous nod, he headed back to his car.

It still took me three months to start shopping again at his store, but when I finally crossed his threshold, he greeted me as if I had been in yesterday . . . as if nothing had happened.

And that, in general, was how people decided to play my return to the community. Courteous nods in the street. The occasional smile in the supermarket. Little else. When I returned to work for summer school, my colleagues largely said nothing more than "Nice to have you back," though two of them did pull me aside and tell me how shameful my treatment had been. And when the fall term began and I greeted my class, there was no great moment of Hollywood catharsis where my kids leapt to their feet and cheered as their vindicated teacher entered the room. On the contrary, they kept on talking among themselves as I opened the door. I walked to the desk, opened my briefcase, spread out my papers, and finally got their attention by saying—in a voice loud enough to transcend their ongoing din—"All right. Hope you had a good summer. Let's start . . ."

Among my students, routine apathy still ruled. Business as usual . . . and there was something reassuringly prosaic about that.

But whenever someone said a nervous hello to me in downtown Portland, or a woman at my gym came up and whispered, "I want you to know that many people thought you were so terribly wronged," it only seemed to accentuate the hurt and anger I still felt toward Dan. Surely, after Judson's revelations were exposed as lies, he could have called or sent a note, saying . . .

What? *Sorry I left you . . . especially as I now know you were telling the truth . . .* Or *I know running off with one of your friends was tacky . . .* ? What was there to say between us now?

I edged the car onto the interstate and tried to shove Dan out of my head by blasting the car radio. In the past year, I had driven the route from Portland to Boston so often that I seemed to know every minor turn, every small gradation of road surface, every damn billboard that decorated the way south. I was at the hotel by one-thirty a.m. The night guy checked me in, and relieved me of the car keys, and said he'd bring the car down to the adjoining garage. Once upstairs in the room, I tried to sleep. I failed. I channel-surfed, I read, I listened to the all-night jazz station, I attempted to keep my mind preoccupied with things other than Lizzie. I failed.

But around seven that morning, exhaustion finally overcame everything and I did drift off for a few hours. Then there was the jolting sound of the phone. "Good morning—this is your wake-up call . . ." It was ten-thirty a.m.—and after a few seconds of befuddlement, the realization hit me: this is the day when I find out that Lizzie is dead.

I was showered and dressed and in my car by eleven-fifteen. The traffic out to Brookline was diabolical—and I reached the precinct ten minutes late. Leary wasn't perturbed, as I had called him while stuck in a jam on Commonwealth Avenue and warned him I would be late. When I got there, I found Dan in one of the chairs facing Leary's desk. He stood up as I entered and extended his hand. I took it briefly, watching Leary watching us—wondering what he made of this stiff formal handshake, and how it spoke volumes about how everything in a thirty-year marriage can come so quickly asunder.

I took the other chair. Leary offered coffee. We both declined.

"All right, then," he said. "The medical examiner is backed up on the autopsy front this week, on account of that terrible fire in Framingham you probably read about. But he did say that, owing to the body being in the water for over seven months, they would probably only be able to identify it through DNA samples, taken from bones . . ."

I glanced over at Dan. He was sitting there with his head bowed, staring at the floor.

"Under the circumstances," Leary said, "I would strongly recommend that you do *not* see the body . . . even though it is your right to do so. I have seen what is left of it. If I was a family member—her parents—I'd find it far too traumatic. But again, I am legally bound to inform you that, should you insist on seeing the body, a viewing will be arranged."

I glanced again over at Dan. This time he did meet my eyes and quickly shook his head before turning away again.

"We won't be wanting a viewing," I said to Leary.

"I think that's wise," he said. "Okay, then . . ."

He reached over to a large envelope on the desk and picked up two plastic Ziploc bags. He opened the larger of the two and pulled out a large, faded piece of denim.

"This is the only bit of clothing they found on the body. I know it's probably ridiculous to be showing you a piece of old denim, but . . ."

"She did wear jeans," Dan said.

"Everybody wears jeans," I said.

"So there's nothing in this item of clothing that absolutely jars the memory?" Leary asked. We both shook our heads. He now reached for the smaller envelope. Then, laying a piece of plain white paper on his desk, he opened the other Ziploc and tipped its contents out onto the paper.

"This is the cross they found on the body," he said, holding up a small, elegant diamond cross attached to a silver chain. I felt a kick to the stomach. It was exactly the same cross that Lizzie had bought herself a year or so ago.

"The cross has a Tiffany hallmark," Leary said. "We contacted the Tiffany shop here at Copley Plaza. They sell them there."

"Lizzie bought hers there," I said quietly.

"Are you sure?" Dan asked.

"She told me afterward that she'd gone over to Copley Plaza to buy it."

What I didn't mention was that Lizzie informed me that she'd bought the cross because she was feeling "a little down, a little blue—so hey, there's nothing like treating yourself to a $2,600 piece of jewelry to chase away the Black Dog."

"I'm sure it's a beautiful cross," I had said.

"Isn't there something really sad about buying a piece of jewelry for yourself?"

"Hardly, Lizzie."

"When have you ever done that, Mom?"

I didn't know what to say—and she interpreted my silence as my answer.

"See, my point entirely," Lizzie had said.

"Well," Detective Leary said, "Tiffany's checked their records for us, and they turned up Lizzie's credit card payment for a necklace like this. Still, it could have been that she bought it as a gift for someone, which is why we didn't want to immediately jump to the conclusion . . ."

"She wore the necklace all the time," I said. "She loved the necklace."

Long silence.

"Well, that's very helpful," Leary said. "As of now, there's nothing more to say until the DNA tests come through. The trail has, otherwise, gone cold. I'm sorry to have dragged you both all the way down here for this, but we did need to know if the necklace was hers."

He stood up, letting us know that the interview was over.

"We'll be in touch as soon as we have conclusive data."

Dan and I walked outside together. The day was cold, gray, cheerless.

We said nothing until we were clear of the precinct. I looked up at Dan and saw that his face was awash with tears.

"She's dead, isn't she?" he whispered.

"I think so, yes."

His face tightened and I could see him doing everything possible to avoid breaking down. I took his hand and held it as he fought to regain his composure. When he felt he could talk again, he said, "Thank you."

"For what?"

"For holding my hand."

A beat. He looked up at the gray sky, then glanced at his watch.

"I've got to get back to Portland now," he said.

"I see."

"I had to reschedule a hip replacement for late this afternoon, so I could come down here."

"It's good that you came."

Another beat.

"Hannah . . ."

He tried to look at me, but couldn't.

"I miss you," he said.

I said nothing.

"I miss you and . . ."

"Aren't you happy in your new life?" I asked.

Another beat.

"No. Not at all."

"I'm sorry."

"Does that mean . . . ?"

"What?"

"I miss you."

"So you said."

"Could we maybe talk this over?" he asked.

"Talk what over?"

"The possibility that . . ."

"There is no possibility of . . ."

"I was wrong. So damn wrong."

"I see."

"And I now see that . . ."

He reached for my hand, but I put it out of his range.

"You terminated me, as if I was an employee," I said, my voice calm. "You wouldn't believe my side of the story, even though I begged you to. You left me for one of my friends. And after I was publicly vindicated, you didn't once call to—"

"I meant to call . . ."

"*Meant* means nothing."

"I was feeling shame and—"

"You still couldn't bring yourself to call me."

"I should have called you. I know that now."

Another beat. He said, "Please . . . let's try to meet up and just talk."

"I don't think so, Dan."

"I'm not asking for anything . . ."

"You know, in the first couple of weeks after you left, if you had called me and said, 'I've made a terrible mistake, I want to come home,' I would have been stupid enough to have taken you back. Because you just don't throw away thirty-four years like that. But you did throw them away—and you abandoned me when I needed you most. And now . . ."

I shrugged. And said, "Now I'm going to Paris."

"You're what?"

"Right after Christmas. I've negotiated a six-month sabbatical with the school. And I'm going to Paris."

"To do what?"

"To be in Paris."

Another beat. I could see he was trying to take this all in.

"And what made you decide to . . . ?"

I could have given him a detailed answer to that question—how, one morning, around five weeks ago, I walked into my classroom, looked out at that sea of bored faces, and thought: *I want out for a while.* Two hours later, I was in Carl Andrews's office, telling him, without embellishment, that I needed a break from teaching and wanted the forthcoming winter and spring terms off. A year earlier, Andrews would have told me this request was completely out of the question. But his residual guilt, coupled with the fact that, as he intimated to me on one occasion, the school board was very relieved when I didn't sue them for damages due to wrongful dismissal, garnered a different response.

"Given what you've been through recently, I think it's a very sensible idea. When the school board meets next week, I'll raise it with them. I can assure you they'll not only approve it, but insist that it is a sabbatical on full pay."

The following week, Andrews made good on that promise. And I started working the Internet, finding a short-term sublet in a central Parisian arrondissement. Eventually, the good old *New York Review of Books* came through for me—and after several phone calls and looking at some photographs of the place that the owner (a professor of French at Columbia) emailed to me, I agreed to a six-month lease on a small but well-furnished studio right near the Sorbonne. I would take possession of it on December 27.

"What made me decide to go to Paris?" I said, filling in the rest of Dan's question. "It's simple, really. I've always wanted to live there. Now I will for a while."

"There are a few weeks before Christmas," he said. "We could meet for a meal . . ."

"Dan . . . no."

He bowed his head and said nothing. Then, "I have to get going," he said.

"Okay."

"As soon as Leary has the DNA report . . ."

"We'll deal with that when it happens."

A small nod from Dan. Then he squeezed my hand briefly and said two words, "Good luck," before walking off toward his car.

Leary called me four days later with some news. Strange news. He said, "I've just learned that the DNA sample taken from the body's bones does *not* match the DNA taken from the hairs found on Lizzie's brush in her apartment. Which means the case is still open."

"So she's still alive?"

"Theoretically, yes. The medical examiner did point out that months in salt water can break down much of the DNA in the body—so it's difficult to conclusively say that the body we found wasn't Lizzie's. And, face facts, over two hundred thousand people go missing in this country every year. And though none of the local women missing were the types who had the wherewithal to buy a Tiffany diamond cross, who's to say that it couldn't be someone from out of state who came to the Boston area without anyone's knowledge and threw herself in the river? When it comes to working out human motivation, I've come to learn one thing: anything is possible. Just as I also know that you can never really put yourself into the mind of another person. It's always too damn murky."

"So she's alive and dead at the same time?"

"As I said: everything is possible; everything is murky."

I expected to hear from Dan after this, especially as Leary told me he was going to call him after me and tell him the news. But no call came from my ex-husband. Nor did he make any attempts at contacting me before the holidays, except by way of his official Christmas card—*Dr. Daniel Buchan wishes you and your family a peaceful Christmas and a wondrous New Year*—below which was scribbled, *"I hope you have a great sabbatical in Paris . . . Best . . ."*

Just before I closed up the house and packed my one suitcase and left for Burlington and then Paris, I did receive one more communiqué from Dan: *As of January 1, 2004, Dr. Daniel Buchan will be living at . . .*

It gave the address of a condominium apartment on the waterfront in Portland. Jeff called on the twenty-third to say that his father would be spending the Christmas holidays with them.

"And I guess you know that he's broken up with Alice?"

"I hadn't heard the news, but his change-of-address card did seem to imply that."

"I've kept trying to get him to call you, but he says that he knows what your response will be. So . . ."

"If he wants to call me, he can call me," I said.

"Really?" Jeff said, suddenly interested.

"I'm just saying he can call. Nothing more."

"And if he wants to call you in Paris?"

"I will take his call."

"That's great, Mom. When you're back in the States, we will have you over. I promise . . ."

I said nothing.

"And I really would keep telling yourself that Lizzie is alive. Because where there's hope . . ."

"There's always ambiguity," I said. "Everything is possible, everything is murky."

And ambiguity does rule most things, doesn't it? Dan tells Jeff he wants to speak with me. I offer to take his call, and in the days that follow, there is silence. An opportunity opens, an opportunity closes. I wonder what the hell is going on in Dan's mind. Does he want me back? Is he too scared to call? Does he fear rejection? Is he still feeling so damn guilty that he can't bring himself to face me? Has he decided he wants to try living on his own for a while? Or maybe he wonders what I'm thinking.

And the truth is: I can't figure out what my actual viewpoint is here, because it's such a jumble. Love, hate, anguish, betrayal, despair, fury, self-righteousness, self-doubt, self-loathing, self-appeasement, ego, arrogance, optimism, gloom, doubt, doubt, doubt . . . and then, more doubt.

But what's wrong with doubt? How can anyone hold a black-and-white view of things when, in the end, most human interaction is so profoundly gray? Those closest to us do things that are baffling. We, in turn, do things we don't totally comprehend. Because we never really understand others, let alone ourselves.

"My strength is made perfect in weakness."

Dad repeated the quote and simultaneously refilled my glass. It was Christmas night, the remnants of the lavish meal that Edith had made were still on the table. Earlier that day, Dad and I had spent a half hour with Mom. I held her hand in mine and told her I was going to Paris tomorrow, and surely she had great memories of Paris from when she was an art student there after the war, and I promised her I'd find that little café she always talked about on the Rue Monge, and . . .

She kept on staring blankly at me. I stopped my inane monologue. I stood up and kissed her gently on the head, then turned to Dad and said, "She'll die while I'm away."

"And would that be a bad thing?"

I knew the answer to that question, and didn't want to articulate it.

We went back to the house. We opened our presents. We drank champagne, then claret as we ate Edith's wonderful food. After that, we moved our chairs by the fireplace and drank brandy while indulging in a game that Dad always won—a game called Quotations, in which each player tried to stump the other by, well, you don't need to hear the arcane and complex rules that my arcane and complex father had dreamed up for this arcane and complex game.

My strength is made perfect in weakness.

"Come on," Dad said, "give it a shot."

"It sounds Shakespearean," I said.

"No, it's biblical," Edith said.

"Ten points," Dad said. "And another ten if you can name the book from which it came."

"Corinthians," she said.

"Correct," he said.

"You're frightening," I said to Edith.

"I will take that as a compliment."

"Your turn, Edith."

She smiled a small tipsy smile and started reciting:

"Oft fühl ich jetzt . . . und je tiefer ich einsehe, dass Schicksal und Gemüt Namen eines Begriffes sind."

I laughed loudly and said, "Isn't there a rule against quotes in the original German?"

"I was naturally going to provide a translation," she said, her voice martini-dry. "And here it is: *I often feel, and ever more deeply realize, that fate and character are the same conception.*"

"Novalis," I said. "Also known as the German poet Friedrich von Hardenberg."

"Bravo," Edith said.

"Twenty points for you," Dad said, "and an additional ten points if you can give us the shortened, Americanized version of the quote."

"That's easy," I said. *"Character is destiny."*

The phone rang. As I was closest to it, I reached for it.

"Hello and Merry Christmas," I said.

"Can I speak with Professor Latham, please?"

My pulse jumped. The receiver shook in my hand.

"Lizzie?" I whispered.

Silence. My father stood up, looking stunned.

"Lizzie?" I repeated.

Silence again. Then, "Mom?"

"Oh my God, Lizzie. It's you."

"Yeah, it's me."

"Where . . . where . . . ?"

The words weren't forming properly.

"Mom . . . ?"

"Where are you, Lizzie?"

"Up in Canada."

"Where in Canada?"

"Out west. Vancouver. Been here for, well, months, I guess."

"And you're okay?"

"Yeah, kind of okay. Got a job here. A waitressing job, nothing much, but it pays the rent. Got a little place. Got a friend or two now. It's . . . really okay, I guess."

She didn't sound really okay, but she also didn't sound really terrible either. And as much as I wanted to burst into tears now—and scream, *"Do you know how often I thought you were dead?"*—some small voice within me counseled prudence, and weighing each sentence with care before uttering it.

"So you went to Canada after leaving Boston?" I asked.

"Not exactly. Drifted around out West for a bit, then came up here. 'Course, I shouldn't be working here—I'm totally illegal—but I managed to land myself some false Canadian ID. And I'm using the name on the ID, so everyone here knows me as Candace Bennett. Been using that name so much now that I even think of myself now as Candace Bennett."

"It's a nice name."

"It's all right. But hey, the reason I called Granddad's is because I did phone home and got the message that you were now going to be in Paris . . ."

"That's right. I'm leaving tomorrow. For around six months."

"That's cool. Dad going too?"

"No, your father's staying behind."

"Oh, yeah? Why's that?"

"It's all a little complicated to explain. But . . . I don't suppose you were aware of the fact that a lot of people have been trying to find you over the last couple of months?"

"You mean like you and Dad and . . ."

"The police. When you went missing, everybody thought . . . some harm might have come to you. It was in all the papers."

"I don't read the papers. Don't own a TV. Or a computer. Don't even turn on the radio much. But I've got a little stereo in my room now, and I've found this place near me where you can buy old CDs for a couple of bucks, so I listen to a lot of music . . . and read. Great used-book shops in Vancouver. Lots of them."

"It's so wonderful to hear your voice, Lizzie. It's so . . ."

I started to sob.

"Hey, no need for the tears, Mom . . ."

"It's just . . . I am so happy to hear you, Lizzie. And if you like, I could come out to Vancouver tomorrow and . . ."

"No, I don't want that," she said, the tone now sharp. "I'm not ready for . . . I don't—"

She broke off, sounding distressed.

"Lizzie, that's all right. Really all right. I just thought . . ."

"You thought wrong. I'm still . . . *ashamed*. And if you tell me there's no need to be ashamed, I'm going to put down the phone . . ."

"I'm not going to say anything."

"Good, that's good," she said, still sounding agitated. "But when you get back from Paris, well, it all kind of depends on how I am then. My doctor here . . . When they found me sleeping on the streets a few months ago in East Vancouver—that's where I bought the fake ID, you can get anything in East Vancouver—anyway, when they got me to this halfway house for the homeless, one of the social workers convinced me to see this psychiatrist, who kind of diagnosed me as having this bipolar thing. And he's got me on these meds. And as long as I take the meds, I get through the day. And since I have been pretty good about keeping the pills popped, things are a lot more stable now. Like I can do the waitressing job, and I'm no longer thinking about throwing myself under the next subway train . . . even though Vancouver doesn't have a subway. But I *am* getting through the day."

"That's wonderful," I said, terrified of saying something that might make her end the call.

"It's *not* wonderful, Mom. It's shit. I hate being this way. I hate that I disappeared like that. I hate . . . myself. But . . . I do keep getting through the day. So . . ."

"Is there a phone number I might be able to call you on in the future?"

"I don't want you to have my number, understand?"

"Whatever you say, Lizzie."

Her tone downshifted a bit.

"But give me your number in Paris, if you've got one. I don't promise anything, but . . ."

"If you ever feel like calling, anytime, I'll ring you right back."

"But that would mean giving you my number. No one gets this number. *No one.* Not even my friends. They've got my cell phone number, but not *this* number. That's 'cause my number is *my number*. Got that? Got—"

She suddenly broke off. And said, "Oh shit, will you listen to me? I'm so fucked up, I'm so . . ."

"You are not fucked up, Lizzie. And you have a lot of people who still love you."

"Yeah, well, look, I've got to go now. Say hi to everyone, okay?"

"Will you take my Paris number?"

"Guess so."

I gave it to her. Then asked, "What are you going to do now?"

"Going to work."

"On Christmas Day?"

"We're open. And I've got to split. So . . . Merry Christmas, Mom. And try not to worry too much."

Click. The line went dead. I stood motionless for a few minutes, then put down the phone, then looked up at my father. We said nothing for a few moments, the shock setting in. Edith stood up and relieved me of the phone. Then, picking up the receiver, she dialed three numbers, grabbed a pencil and a pad off the side table, and then started taking down a number.

"What are you doing?" I asked.

"Via the wonders of digital technology," Edith said, "I have just dialed star-six-nine, which plays back the number of the last person who called here. So here is your daughter's number."

She held up the pad.

"It's a six-oh-four area code, which is definitely Vancouver. And if you'd like me to verify that it is her place . . ."

"She might freak if we ring her right back," I said.

"If I dial star-six-seven before the number," Edith said, "it hides the number of the person calling her. And if she answers, she won't recognize me, because I will put on a very German accent. So . . ."

She dialed the number. I could hear it ringing. And ringing. And . . .

"It's her voice mail," Edith said, thrusting the phone in my hand. I listened: *"Hi there, you've reached Candace Bennett. Leave your name and number, and I'll get back to you."*

I hung up before the telltale beep. I looked at my dad. I nodded affirmation that it was Lizzie's voice. My father put his face in his hands and started to cry.

We drank most of the bottle of brandy that evening. Before I was too intoxicated to talk, I called Dan and told him the news.

"You are absolutely certain?" he asked.

"Absolutely."

No response as Dan choked back a sob.

"Thank you," he finally said. "Thank you so much."

"'Everything is possible, everything is murky.'"

"What's that?"

"Just a quote I've gotten fond of."

"I'll call you in Paris, okay?"

"All right," I said.

Late that night, after Dad and Edith had gone to bed, I stood on the front porch, watching the snow fall, oblivious to the cold. I was drunk, elated, wrung out, trying not to imagine Lizzie's months of sleeping in the streets, and full of serious maternal dread about her current state of mind.

I can't leave, I told myself.

But what good will you accomplish by staying?

That's not the issue. I just can't leave.

Leave.

But it's selfish.

Leave.

I tried to toss up multiple arguments; tried to rationalize myself into staying. But that voice in my head was obstinate, defiant, and unwilling to let me talk myself out of this again.

Leave.

The next morning, I called Detective Leary. He reacted calmly to the news, saying, "It's nice to have a case that ends well, because they so rarely do."

He said that he'd have to involve the Vancouver police to get an actual "make" on Lizzie's identity. But as he was now aware of her fragile mental state, he would make certain they didn't come near her, that it was all done surreptitiously.

"You know," he said, "once word leaks out that she's been found safely, Lizzie could find journalists on her doorstep . . ."

"Is there any way around that?"

"Let me talk to my boss. The fact that she might disappear again if subjected to media intrusion might make him sympathetic to doing something diversionary about informing the press where she's living right now."

"Has it been done before?"

"No, but that doesn't mean it can't be done now."

On the drive over to the airport, I told Dad about my conversation with Leary and how I feared that Lizzie might fall into another vortex if she woke up one morning to find television cameras outside her place.

"The detective told you he'd handle it," Dad said. "He'll handle it."

"But . . ."

"No *buts*. I know what you're trying to do—and you won't be allowed to do it. Not this time."

"But—"

"Lizzie is alive. End of sentence. End of story. The narrative has been out of your control from the start . . . and it will continue to be. You can't fix other people, Hannah. You can only be there when they need you. And if she needs you, she will find you—as she did last night. So you are going to Paris."

When we reached the airport, my bags were checked straight through to Charles de Gaulle Airport. The clerk handed me two boarding passes and told me that, once at Logan Airport, the Air France flight would be leaving from . . .

The gate number didn't register. Nothing did right now.

Dad walked me over to the security barrier. I suddenly felt like I was thirteen years old, about to be sent off somewhere new.

"I'm scared," I said.

He hugged me. And said, "My strength is made perfect in weakness. Now go get on that damn plane. And call me tomorrow when you're there."

Twenty minutes later, I was airborne over Vermont. A quick change in Boston, and I was up in the clouds again.

The flight was empty. I had a row of seats to myself. I stretched out and slept all the way across the Atlantic.

And then, suddenly, it was morning. And the plane was banking steeply. And the hostess shook me gently and asked me to sit up. We were about to land.

I shut my eyes as we touched down. I opened them when the aircraft came to a complete halt. I stood up, removed my carry-on bag and coat from the overhead compartment, and followed the stream of passengers leaving the aircraft.

The customs officer was around my age, and didn't exactly seem pleased to be sitting in a booth at seven-thirty on a late-December morning.

"Passport," he said, holding out his hand. I pushed it through to him. "You will stay how long?" he asked in heavily accented English. I spoke without thinking, using the French I had been brushing up on for the past few months.

"Je ne sais pas," I said. I don't know.

He stared at me, surprised at the reply in French. He continued in French.

"Quoi, vous n'avez aucune idée de combien de temps vous allez rester en France?" You have no idea how long you'll be staying in France?

"On verra," I said. We'll see.

I could see him looking me over, wondering if it was worth demanding my return ticket home, or to see my traveler's checks or credit cards or other proof of liquidity. Or maybe he thought I was playing a stupid game with him. Or perhaps he saw me as I saw myself—a middle-aged woman who, at this hour of the morning, was looking groggy and just a little lost. Had he asked, *"Why are you really here?"* I would have truthfully replied, *"You know, that question has been plaguing me for the past fifty-three years. Do you have any answers?"*

But he didn't pose that question. He just said, *"Généralement, nous préférons les réponses précises."* Generally, we prefer definitive answers.

I replied, *"N'est-ce pas notre cas à tous?"* Doesn't everyone?

He flashed me the smallest of smiles, then reached for his stamp and brought it down on my passport.

"D'accord," he said, handing it back to me. Agreed.

And picking up my passport, I turned and walked into France.

ACKNOWLEDGMENTS

THERE ARE THOSE writers who never show anything to anyone while they are working on a novel, and there are those who drive those closest to them to an advanced state of exasperation by reading out loud every paragraph as it appears on the page. Though I hope that I don't fall into the latter obsessive-compulsive category, I do know that I couldn't get through the long solitary haul of novel writing without some input from the world beyond my desk. And in the instance of *State of the Union,* it was James Macdonald Lockhart who went beyond and above the call of agent-hood and read the first and second drafts of this book, chapter by chapter, as they arrived hot off the proverbial press. His intelligent counsel and support kept me buoyed when I suffered the usual doubts and despairs that are such a predictable by-product of my trade. I am greatly in his debt.

James works with Antony Harwood, who has been my agent and friend for the past twelve years. He remains the best professional ally this novelist could have, not to mention a mensch par excellence. And I am enormously lucky in my tough-as-nails editor, Sue Freestone—who, as I have said on several occasions, is often fierce to my face and fantastic behind my back (which, let's face it, is the better way around). More tellingly, she possesses the most important weapon in an editor's artillery: a first-class bullshit detector. My novels have been immeasurably improved under her tough, take-no-prisoners tutelage.

Noeleen Dowling in Dublin and Christy McIntosh in Banff remain my great constant readers—and I am hugely grateful to them for taking the time to peruse earlier versions of this novel. For the past three decades, that *dude extraordinaire* Fred Haines has remained one of the great constants in an ever-fluctuating world. He also proofed the second draft of this book—and gave me copious useful notes (no surprise there).

Finally, I would like to say a very large thank-you to my partner in domestic crime for the past twenty-two years—the ever-amazing (really!) Grace Carley—and our two equally ever-amazing children, Max and Amelia. On the afternoon some months ago when the first draft of this novel was finished, Max banged on the door of my office at the top of our house and asked, "Is it done yet?"

It is now.

D.K.

London, June 2005

STATE OF THE UNION

Douglas Kennedy

A Readers Club Guide

INTRODUCTION

While many American college students in the 1960s are marching in protests, using hallucinogenic drugs, and practicing free love, Hannah Latham, the daughter of a famous radical father and a painter mother, wants nothing more than to marry her doctor boyfriend and raise a family in a small town. Hannah gets her wish and settles in rural Maine with her husband, Dan, and their baby son, but she soon finds herself bored and isolated. One night an old acquaintance shows up at Hannah's door . . . and she makes a decision that will force her into breaking the law and will change her life forever.

Over the next three decades, Hannah's transgression remains a deeply buried secret, until a frightening incident involving her daughter, Lizzie, suddenly brings the past to light. As Hannah's life spins out of control, she is faced with the possibility of losing everything—and everyone—she has ever loved.

QUESTIONS AND TOPICS FOR DISCUSSION

1. How does Kennedy build suspense during the first part of the novel? Were you drawn into the story quickly?

2. How did Hannah's forced apology to her mother after their argument at Thanksgiving foreshadow future events in the novel?

3. When Hannah is campaigning for McGovern, she runs into a postman who tells her that "everyone's a crook." When she shares the story with Margy, Hannah says, "What else do we have except our integrity?" (p. 64). Discuss the theme of integrity in the novel. Is Hannah right? What is the relationship between integrity and truth?

4. When Hannah and Dan fight shortly before they conceive Jeff, Hannah tells Dan to give himself "an A-plus for having the most monumental ego" (p. 57). Years later, Hannah tells Margy, "[Dan's] a surgeon—of course he has an ego. The thing is, he always kept it under wraps. Until now—when I finally gave him the excuse to use it against me" (p. 444). Did Hannah's perception of Dan change, or did she just not allow herself to see him as he was? Do you think she was ever truly happy with Dan or did she make herself believe that she was?

5. When Hannah is with Toby, she has a fleeting thought: "*Why isn't this man my husband?* With that thought came a split-second reverie of a life with Toby . . . the fantastic conversations, the fantastic sex, the mutual respect, the sense of shared destiny . . . " (p. 149). Do you think Toby was completely tricking Hannah from the beginning or was he at all sincere? Why do you think she falls for him so easily?

6. When Toby's book is published, why do people seem to be more accepting of his crime than they are of Hannah's alleged crime? What does this say about the way men and women are perceived by society?

7. Discuss the relationship between Hannah and her father. While he is the catalyst for the event that nearly ruins Hannah's life, he is also

her biggest supporter and loves her unconditionally. Did you agree with her decision to mend her relationship with him? What did you think about him as a character?

8. Throughout the novel, people remind Hannah to stop beating herself up so much. Why is she so hard on herself? Why are people often harder on themselves than they are on others?

9. What does Hannah's experience after her secret is revealed to the public say about group-think mentality? Is it a comment on small-town life? What does the incident say about the nature of the media?

10. After Toby's appearance on *The Jose Julia Show,* a *New York Times* columnist writes: "The fact . . . that so many conservative pundits and religious fellow travelers took Tobias Judson's story as the gospel truth . . . shows a fundamental lack of critical discernment, and a belief that, so long as someone professes their Christian faith, they must be telling the truth" (p. 464). What do you think about this passage? Does it relate to any particular current events in the news?

11. What is ironic about the progression of Hannah's mother's health?

12. Did you sympathize at all with Dan? Could you see where he was coming from at all, even if you didn't sympathize with him?

13. Were you surprised by the outcome of Lizzie's disappearance? If the necklace found by the police was hers, how might it have ended up where it did?

14. What did you think about Hannah's decision at the end of the book? How do you think she evolved over the course of the novel? Did you like her as a narrator? Was there more that you wanted to learn about her?

15. If you've read other books by Douglas Kennedy, how did you think this one compared to his others? Are there other writers he is similar to? What do you think about his writing style?

16. Discuss any interesting quotes or passages you highlighted while reading the novel. What are some of the themes that resonated most strongly with you?

ENHANCE YOUR BOOK CLUB

1. In honor of Hannah and her father's reverence for Paris, host a potluck supper with French dishes. Take a look at http://allrecipes.com/Recipes/World-Cuisine/Europe/France/Main.aspx or www.ffcook.com, or browse your local bookstore for French cookbooks.

2. Listen to some classic sixties protest music by artists such as Bob Dylan, Phil Ochs, Pete Seeger, Woody Guthrie, and John Lennon. Make a mix CD of your favorites to listen to during your book club meeting.

3. Read a 2007 interview with Douglas Kennedy in which he discusses his background and his close ties with France: www.independent.co.uk/arts-entertainment/books/features/interview-american-writer-douglas-kennedy-on-the-kennedy-theory-of-human-behaviour-454073.html. Or learn more about the author at http://en.wikipedia.org/wiki/Douglas_Kennedy_(writer).

A CONVERSATION WITH DOUGLAS KENNEDY

What are some of the most important elements you hope that people take away from *State of the Union*? How has its relevance increased over the years since it was first published?

This might be the most American of my novels, as the subject is the United States during the radical ferment of the 1960s and the same country in the post-9/11 world. It's about left-wing extremism back then and the evangelical conservatism of the past decade and how the entire political debate has shifted in our country. But it is also a novel that examines the life of a woman who marries the wrong man as an act of rebellion against her parents—and finds herself trapped in a life she never wanted. The fact that this act of rebellion is an act of conservatism is one of the novel's many ironies. But then, frustrated by her marriage, she makes an error of judgment that comes back to haunt her decades later. In many ways this is a novel that looks at the frontier between the private and the public in life, the huge gulf that can exist between parents and children (even if the parent has tried to do everything right), and the way you can never really shake yourself free of the past. But it is also a morality tale for our times, and one that looks at the way, in the relentless world of the twenty-four-hour news cycle, political dialogue in this country has become so shrill, so Manichean, and so vindictive.

What did you most enjoy about writing this novel? Which parts were the most difficult?

It was fascinating for me to revisit the 1960s and to remember (I was thirteen in 1968) the immense, edgy complexity of that time and the way it was both a period of personal liberation and communal upheaval, in which all societal strictures and values were challenged. And I was able to examine the way that conservative thought in the postsixties world has largely been a profound backlash against that period of radical turmoil. At heart, it's also a novel about family and postulates a difficult idea: You can do everything right for your children, and they can still end up being strangers to you.

State of the Union was originally published in the UK and France in 2005. Along with several of your other novels it is now being published in the United States. You make your home in all three of these countries. Why do you think your work resonates so strongly in these different cultures?

The French, bless them, seem to adore the fact that I write big novels that have a nineteenth-century sweep to them but also aren't afraid to grapple with large, existential concerns. The British appear to like the fact that I am one of those novelists who is both literary and popular—and, as such, writes the sort of novels that keep you reading well into the night but also talk up to the reader. I hope my emerging American readership will also see that I am a most serious writer who happens to like making you turn the page and whose novels all engage with the question: What does it mean to be an American?

You're particularly popular in France and have been called "the most French and the most popular of American authors." What do you think makes you the "most French"? What do you love about France?

Well, I do speak French fluently! I think the French adopted me because my novels are so rooted in day-to-day life and ask all the big questions about how we entrap ourselves in lives we so often don't want. The modern French novel has always been a theater of ideas—short on plot, big on philosophic musings, and always screaming to the world, "This is art!" My view of the novel goes back to Balzac and the Flaubert of *Madame Bovary*—the social novel that speaks volumes about the way we live now and isn't afraid to engage with that huge concern: Why is happiness such a great, difficult pursuit?

What are you currently writing? Do you know what your next book will be about before you've finished the one you're working on?

I've just finished my new novel, *The Moment,* which is a love story set in Berlin during the mid-1980s, when the city was a divided one. The first draft was a two-year venture, and I must say I am very pleased with it. And, yes, I always begin to think about the next novel as I finish work on the previous one. How—and why—ideas arrive at this juncture of the creative process baffles me. But it's how it happens, and after ten novels I'm not going to question it.

Your books seem to cross many genres. How do you describe your work? Is it impossible to categorize?

I've never written the same novel. I've never tried to replicate any success from the past. I've always set a new challenge for me with every book. If there is a unifying idea behind all ten of my novels, it's the belief in the primacy of narrative and creating stories that are a reflection of the modern anxieties with which we all grapple.

Who are some of your all-time favorite writers? Do you admire the work of any of your contemporaries?

Besides Balzac and Flaubert, I bend the knee in the direction of Dickens, Trollope, Graham Greene, Richard Yates—writers who were so engaged with their moments in time. As for my contemporaries, I greatly admire Ian McEwan and Richard Russo and Richard Ford and Lorrie Moore and Colum McCann—writers who also engage so brilliantly with the way we live now.

What are you currently reading?

Intriguingly—given the subject of this novel—I'm reading *Nixonland*, by Rick Perlstein, which is a brilliant analysis of the creation of the culture wars that so dominate our national life now. It is the best sort of historical text—brilliantly written, brilliantly argued, and so eye-opening.

How do you enjoy spending your time when you're not working?

I live between London, Paris, Berlin, and Maine, so I travel a great deal. I am also a culture vulture and am constantly at the theater, the concert hall, the cinema. Curiosity is an underrated virtue—and an essential component of an interesting life.

Your novels *The Big Picture* and *The Woman in the Fifth* have recently been made into films. How involved were you with these projects?

I wrote the screenplay for *The Woman in the Fifth*—and then stayed out of the entire filmmaking process. I read the screenplay to the French film version of *The Big Picture*—and then stayed out of the entire filmmaking process. I have yet to see the film of *The Woman in the Fifth*, but the film version of *The Big Picture* is just superb. The cinema is like the casino—the house odds are against you, but occasionally you get lucky and a talented director does something wonderful with one of your novels. But if the film is a dog, there are two compensations: (1) you cashed the check; and (2) you will always have your novel.

Do you have a favorite of your own novels? Do you ever go back and reread your own work?

I don't have a favorite child, so I also don't have a favorite novel. And the only time I reread my books is if I am adapting one of them for the cinema. Otherwise I am always preoccupied with the next novel—which is the only way to live as a writer.